Nine Months

SARAH BALL

PIATKUS

Visit the Piatkus website!

Piatkus publishes a wide range of bestselling fiction and non-fiction, including books on health, mind, body & spirit, sex, self-help, cookery, biography and the paranormal.

If you want to:
- read descriptions of our popular titles
- buy our books over the internet
- take advantage of our special offers
- enter our monthly competition
- learn more about your favourite Piatkus authors

VISIT OUR WEBSITE AT: www.piatkus.co.uk

Copyright © 2002 by Sarah Ball

First published in Great Britain in 2002 by
Judy Piatkus (Publishers) Ltd of
5 Windmill Street, London W1P 1HF
email: info@piatkus.co.uk

Reprinted 2002

The moral right of the author has been asserted

A catalogue record for this book is available from the British Library

ISBN 0 7499 3287 2

Typeset in Palatino by Palimpsest Book Production Limited,
Polmont, Stirlingshire

Printed and bound in Great Britain by
Mackays of Chatham Ltd, Chatham, Kent

This book is dedicated to my sister, Mary, as it would never have been written without her optimism, encouragement and unshakeable belief in me. I can't thank her enough.

I would like to use up a page to thank: Dad, for being the most knowledgeable person I know and a fantastic resource tool. My brother, Simon, for launching me into an electronic world and introducing me to my favourite pastime – word-count!

To the rest of the family, in particular; Mum, Nan and Grandad, Mez and Mike, Jane and John (the best Bid's!) and Liz for all your words of encouragement and support. Mel, for squealing down the phone, every step of the way, and sharing my excitement (we'll go out more soon I promise!).

Heartfelt thanks to Lynn Curtis for thinking I was worth 'passing on' and Gillian Green at Piatkus for giving me the best job ever.

Many additional thank you's to: Rob and Gill Clayborough and Co., Big Lee, Debbie and Mike, Dave and Lucy, Dave and Sabine, Paul (Bel) Miller and family, Sue, Andy and Stuart, Katrina, Sonia (Mong!), the Bonifaces and everyone else who at some point has cheered me on, it really kept me going.

To Richard Shepherd, for giving me my first and only 'A' and making me think it was possible after all and James Keen for helping me realise I would be better off writing about one than owning one – thanks for all the recipes!

And lastly, but most importantly, hugs and kisses to Ellie and Sam, the cutest of all distractions. And to David, my best friend, thank you for your infectious enthusiasm, putting up with me when I was 'distracted', sorting out my disastrous computing style and making it look as though I knew what I was doing, for endless cups of your lovely tea and for making it possible for me to pursue my dream.

CHAPTER ONE

My hair whipped out behind me in one long silken stream, tossing this way and that as I cruised through deep space. My sparkling red dress clung tightly against my svelte figure, plunging to a dramatic cleavage that made Melinda Messenger's bosoms look like a couple of ping-pong balls on a bowling green. Silver bells tinkled from a place I couldn't detect. I changed my direction, seeking the source of the hypnotic notes, when suddenly an axe descended from a nearby planet, splitting my head into two evenly sized pieces.

'Shit!' I sat bolt upright, trying to hold my skull together and nosedived off the bed and on to the cold wooden floor. My elbow and the bedside table met and introduced themselves as I lashed out at the trilling alarm clock. I knocked it spinning on to the floor beside me and we both lay silent for a moment, casualties of the daily grind.

'Oh God. Why do I have to get up when it's still dark outside? It's not normal.' I scooped up the clock. 'Five-thirty. I bet even Lorraine Kelly's tucked up at this time of day.'

Normally I'm a morning person, up with the milkman so to speak. But over the last couple of days I've found it rather reminiscent of being born, wrenched from the warm cocoon of 14-tog into the unforgiving December air. If my customers had walked in and slapped my bottom until I cried, I wouldn't have been at all surprised. I could sense Christmas looming nearer, and with twenty-two days left to go the seeds of mania are finally sprouting. Bath is suddenly swamped with plagues of gift hunters and tourists. Owning a café in the heart of the city at Christmas is usually exciting and energising, yet this year the excitement has so far eluded me.

I stood up slowly and gingerly rubbed my temple. 'Shit!' I cursed again and made a bumbling attempt at a sprint towards the bathroom. In the nick of time I skidded to a halt by the toilet and proceeded to be violently ill.

After half-heartedly cleaning myself up I crawled back into bed and called Maggie.

'Mags, it's me.'

'What's up, mate? You sound rough.'

'I feel worse than rough. I've just brought up last night's curry.'

'Thanks, Holly, I was about to have a bagel.'

'I'm serious, I feel like death!'

She made a vaguely pitying noise. 'I thought you looked a bit pissed last night.' She laughed, then said, 'Hang on, you only had a couple of wines, were you sneaking them in when I wasn't looking?'

I drew my feet up, hugging my knees to my chest and nursed my tummy as it churned like a washing machine. 'No honestly, it's not a hangover, I hardly drank anything. I think I must be coming down with something.'

'Are you sure it wasn't the curry?'

'Well, how do you feel?'

'Great. Okay, so it wasn't that. Must be a bug then.'

'It's the first Saturday in December. I can't afford to be ill,' I whined. 'I've got to check the stock and write the Christmas roster. I was going to put up the decorations this morning and that's before I've thought about cooking for a few hundred shoppers.' My head felt as though Michael Flatley had called in to dance on my brain.

'Look, don't stress. I'm not the assistant manager for nothing, you know. I'll come in and start cooking. I can call the Saturday staff and get them to come in early. The roster and stock can keep a few more days. I might even dangle a few baubles from the counter if you're lucky. I'll pop up in a few hours to see how you feel.' She said this with a brisk efficiency that only emphasised my own helplessness.

'You're a real pal, are you sure you can cope?' I sighed gratefully.

'Of course. Now back to bed and I'll see you soon.' She hung up the phone before I could reply. I exhaled deeply and closed my eyes, thanking God that Maggie was dynamic enough for both of us.

Maggie May has been one of my closest friends since junior school. We've had more fights than

3

Kermit and Miss Piggy, yet I have more respect for her than anyone else I know.

When Maggie was ten her father ran off with a distant relative, never to be seen again. Maggie often says she wishes her mother would be inspired to follow his lead and I have to say I don't blame her sometimes.

A Rod Stewart fan down to her Cuban heels (hence calling her daughter Maggie May), Irene has been a constant source of painful embarrassment for her daughter. She struts about like Tina Turner at a vicars' and tarts' party, with a huge chest bursting from a black leather boob tube like a builders bum without the hair, and not content with resembling a large ocean mammal, she drinks like one too. Many of our girls' nights out had been tainted an embarrassing red from chance meetings with her in bars and clubs.

Last night was no exception. I'd been out for a curry with Maggie and Alice. Afterwards we had met Alice's boyfriend Oliver and his mate Noah (a real life African Adonis) at The Temple, a trendy new club in the centre of the city. We had only been there half an hour when Maggie's mother had arrived with a gaggle of middle-aged tarts. Too pissed to dance around their handbags they surrounded us with their lofty hairdos and proceeded to flirt unashamedly with Oliver and Noah. Irene overstepped the mark when she tried to slip her hand down Noah's combat trousers and got a torrent of abuse from Maggie. This resulted in the lads sloping off into the crowds not to be seen again and Alice fighting back tears, convinced that Oliver was going to break up with her.

The way I felt this morning I was wishing I had stayed at home last night, with a gin and tonic and a facepack.

Fifteen minutes later I heard Maggie arriving downstairs and made a mental note to take the customer bell off the front door. I dozed a little more, my head swimming in a soup of kitchen sounds. Wooden spoons banged against pans, pottery clattered together like percussion instruments and doors opened and shut, announcing the arrival of the kitchen staff. They were all comfortably familiar, the soundtrack of my life for the past four years.

I had invested in the café when I was just twenty-three, with a large percentage of a generous inheritance from my late grandfather. My parents were delighted with my surprising head for business and astounded that I hadn't used the money to go on the most major clothes shop of all time, followed by a holiday in the Canaries with all my friends. I have to be honest and say that that had been my second choice and it was a tricky decision. Fortunately, I thought about it seriously. I knew that if I wanted to follow my dream and set up in business I wouldn't get a better opportunity than that. My chances of another windfall were minimal and the prices of property were beginning to creep up. Instinct told me to put aside any fears about my age and lack of experience. I knew if I didn't take the plunge there and then the money would end up frittered

5

away on rubbish quicker than you could say, 'end of season sale', and I would end up always wondering what might have been. It was the best decision I had ever made, and despite an underlying fear of failure and a morbid need to trawl the papers for articles on percentages of folding businesses (with catering always being used as an example!), the Owl and Pussycat Café was still the longest and most passionate love affair I had ever enjoyed.

I was jolted awake once again by Maggie trying to sneak a tray of food and a pot of tea next to the bed.

'What time is it?' I croaked. My tongue felt as furry as a bearskin rug on a shagpile carpet.

'It's only eleven o'clock, I thought you might like a bite to eat. Are you feeling any better?' She parked herself on the bed by my feet as I sat up and stretched.

'Mmm, don't worry I don't think I'll be sick again. I'm just worn out. How's it going downstairs?'

She rolled her eyes skyward then pulled an expression of wide-eyed innocence. 'Don't you trust me with your baby?'

'I guess I can trust you in business, just not as far as men are concerned.'

'Lucky you have an all female staff then, isn't it? Mind you, as for that organic veg delivery man, let's just say I'd nibble his natural produce anytime!' She licked her lips Hannibal Lecter style and I couldn't help but laugh.

'You're gross.'

'No, YOU'RE gross! Have you checked the mirror

6

lately? Your hair looks like a tumble weed!' She ruffled my hair affectionately then clapped her hands together business style. 'Anyway as for the café, we opened at ten as usual. All the food's done. Today's specials are . . .' she pointed to a large crimson stain on her white apron, 'Ratatouille,' then to a yellow mark on her sleeve, 'this one's a spinach, mushroom and cashew nut gratin, and this here is the soup of the day: vichyssoise flavoured with nutmeg and thyme. The chocolate muffins are selling like hot cakes, funny that, them being hot cakes and all. Your boozy mince pies have had three compliments to the chef already, and Shelley called in sick this morning, so Alice has come in to help, which will save you a few bob in wages. All in all things could not be better, touch wood,' she concluded by reaching over to touch a photograph of my current boyfriend, Tom.

I slapped her hand hard.

'Youch!' she cried, snapping it back.

'I was just about to tell you how brilliant you've been until you did that,' I sulked.

'Well, there's no need for violence Mrs passive vegetarian earth mother,' she said sarcastically.

I poured out the Earl Grey she had brought up and bit into the warm cheese toastie.

'Ooh yes!' I mopped the juice from my chin. 'Now I definitely feel better. By the way, has Alice cheered up since last night?'

Maggie tutted distastefully. 'She's mooching about like a Jane Austin heroine. It's painful to watch. She hasn't heard from Oliver and I've told her that the

7

prat's not worth a second thought, but you know what she's like; I swear she enjoys being a martyr.'

I sipped my tea frowning at her. 'You've got to be a bit sympathetic. She's really in love with him and Oliver's good at manipulating her. And you don't see what they're like when they're alone.'

She clutched her stomach. 'Please, make room for me in the sick bed.'

I pretended not to hear her. 'Maybe I'll get up now and join you downstairs.'

'No way! You should have the whole day off just in case. We can all cope.'

'But I feel guilty, I mean I'm fine now.'

She got up and brushed the wrinkles from her short black skirt, then waggled a finger at me. 'Your trouble is you have too much conscience. How about Alice and I come up with tea when we're finished. Maybe with two people talking sense to her she'll come round.'

I smiled and fell back against the pillows. 'I'll give it my best shot.'

After Maggie had left I leaned over to retrieve my photograph of Tom and polished it gently with the corner of my duvet. I stroked the shaggy mop of hair that framed his face like moss around a tree, and admired the even tan he had developed from countless backpacking holidays. Tom made Michael Palin look like an agoraphobic couch potato and at this moment he could be anywhere in the world as far as I knew. The only postcard I had received was from New York where his journey had begun; it had been dated for the day after he had arrived, just over

8

a month ago. Every morning I bounded at the postman like a mad spaniel starved of breakfast. Maggie teased me that she was going to hang a sign on the door warning 'Beware of the chef.'

I sifted eagerly through the mail, but received nothing other than invoices and letters from charities beginning 'Dear Friend'. It appeared everyone wanted a piece of me except the one I cared about the most. A year of waiting for him was going to be harder than I had first anticipated. I threw off the covers and padded over to the bathroom. I needed a deep soak in the tub to soothe the ache I had for him.

On Thursday morning I woke up and tentatively opened one eye to peer around the bedroom. Fortunately it stayed still long enough to enable me to focus on the Andy Warhol print hanging opposite me. I opened the other eye, blinking hard. Still nothing. The furniture was surprisingly stationary. I got up to make myself a pot of tea and a round of toast and when it was ready I carried it over to the phone.

'Hey Mags, it's me.'

'Please don't tell me, whatever colour it was I don't want to know,' she groaned.

I chuckled at her and bit hungrily into the toast. 'It's okay, I wasn't sick this morning. I think it's finally gone.'

She made a 'hmmm I'm not convinced' noise. 'Are you sure? It has been coming and going rather a lot. You could just be having a good morning.'

9

'No, I'm sure, this is the most human I've felt all week. I'm going down to make a start.'

'Do you want me in early again?'

'Um, no thanks. It'll probably be slow to pick up today. If you come in just before ten, that'll be fine.'

'Okay then, mate, if you insist. See you later.'

I hung up and began to get dressed, excited at the prospect of getting back to work. It had been maddeningly frustrating to hear the café below running so efficiently without me. I had half hoped that I would be called upon to assist in some minor crisis they had unwittingly caused. But no, I was left respectfully alone to vomit in the bathroom as tasty cooking smells and the happy clatter and chatter of customers rose up to my apartment. Evidence that my presence was not required. I was as disposable as the toilet roll I had used to mop my face.

I hurried downstairs and unlocked the heavy door that led into the dining area. It was eerily cold and quiet inside so I flicked on the heating and the lights. I sat on one of the limed oak tables and drank in the atmosphere.

Tom's father, Marcus Delanci, was a talented interior designer. I had found him in the Yellow Pages and had invited him to come and see the place I had bought and to give me a free quote, naively unaware of the cost of personal interior design. We had hit it off instantly. I'm not quite sure why he had warmed to me. Perhaps I had reminded him of himself, as we shared a similar belief that the only way to be truly happy in our working life was to be brave, avoid the standard office career and get people to pay you for what you are most passionate about. In my case that was cooking, in his, decorating. My combination of stubborn determination, passion and the blind terror of taking such a risk must have been evident in my voice as we spent the morning chatting. We had finally agreed on a significantly reduced price for the work he would carry out in exchange for allowing him to use the café as an advert for his work. The drawings I had made of how I wanted the café to look had convinced him that we could get the local press interested in running a feature on the place when I was ready to open, benefiting us both with free advertisements. To be honest I didn't think he was motivated by money, more a fatherly instinct to help me out.

I had admired the outline of his body as he measured the dimensions of the dining area. He was gorgeous, in a George Clooney kind of way. I began to look forward to seeing him on a daily basis in loose-fitting overalls, paint spattered on his crease-lined face and bending over at regular intervals. It was at that point that he had turned and invited me back to his house that evening to draw up the final plans and meet his wife and kids. I mentally kicked my own backside for getting so carried away.

As it turned out, his 'kids' were both in their mid-twenties and could beat their father in the looks department quite nicely thank you very much. That was when I had first met Thomas Delanci and our relationship began.

11

I used to see Tom when I was out drinking with Alice and Maggie. We would stand at the bar and chat for a while until one of our friends dragged us away, but after a few months we got to the stage where we were familiar enough with each other to grab a table and chat until the pub shut. My friends slowly got to know his friends, and before too long we were all going on to clubs together or calling each other up. I saw Tom essentially as a good friend. He wasn't like a lot of men I spoke to in pubs, he wasn't into flirting and getting women into bed, he just wanted to have a good time, without complications.

I wasn't surprised to discover that Tom was into rock climbing and surfing, it fitted his style well. He had the body of a surfer: tall and lean, and his muscles had a hint of definition, although not enough to suggest he was seriously athletic. He often brought his friends into the café for lunch on Saturdays. Sometimes I would join them and laugh at their funny stories and other times I would be too busy so would work around them, occasionally catching his eye and grinning. Every now and again I would go over to his house for the evening. We would sit up in his room drinking bottled lager and watching videos. If I wasn't working too early the next day I would stay over. After sex, instead of saying he loved me, he would ruffle my hair or we would play fight. We never got too romantic and always referred to each other as 'mates'.

Our friends used to tease us if we went home together after the pub, winking at us and laughing

12

together. Sometimes they would make a comment about us 'being good together' or 'don't they make a great couple', and we'd just laugh along with them. I'd tease Tom, saying he was 'too scruffy, and like the brother I never had' or he would joke that I was a 'scary business woman that didn't have enough free hours in the day to indulge him in his favourite hobbies'.

One time Tom talked me into going rock climbing with him at a converted church in Bristol. I was amazed at how graceful he was, negotiating the wall like a spider. When it was my turn I felt so self-conscious in the harness, designed to draw maximum attention to my backside, that I only managed the first half-a-dozen moves. Tom had put his hands on my bum, trying to stop me from falling, but I had slipped away from him and crash-landed on the mat. I was convinced everyone was checking out my bottom, all trussed up in the harness, and laughing at it. When I went to the changing room later on I realised that Tom had left two perfect hand prints, one on each bum cheek, from the chalk he had used on his hands to give him more grip on the rock. I was so embarrassed I never went back again, despite his best efforts to convert me.

Tom and I fell into an easy pattern. We were good friends first and foremost. I don't think either of us wanted to jeopardise that by getting too serious.

I sighed out loud, trying to block thoughts of Tom from my mind.

Sitting back on the table I admired Marcus's

handiwork. He had made a fantastic job of turning my sketchy drawings into a tangible reality. The ceiling and walls had been painted with a *trompe-l'oeil* summer sky. A warm blue with fluffy white clouds dotted randomly amongst small silver stars. In the corner of the café was a cosy alcove with fretwork panelling for customers who enjoyed their privacy. Here the sky turned to dusk and the clouds reflected gold amongst harmonious shades of sunset red and blushing pinks. 'Lovers' corner,' Alice dreamily called it; 'horny corner' was Maggie's preferred description.

Where the ceiling met the walls Marcus had written the words to the 'Owl and The Pussycat' poem. They ran the circumference of the room like an ornate border in beautifully scripted silver italics, and standing proud like sentries on either side of the counter were two large wooden carvings. One was a wide-eyed spectacled owl, the other a sensuous black cat with a tail curled around its padded feet. The owl's hooked beak and the cat's nose had been slightly worn down by customers who had stroked them whilst waiting to be served. It wasn't something I had encouraged; instead the customers had taken to doing it almost as a superstitious gesture to bring good luck. In every available corner were lush green palm trees. The rest of the café was simple, in the Scandinavian sense of the word. The furniture and floorboards were stripped bare and lime waxed, and white muslin drapes dressed the huge floor to ceiling windows. It was fresh, modern and tasteful, and I still had to pinch

14

myself sometimes, as it was so hard to believe it all belonged to me.

I had deliberately shied away from the more stereotypical ideas of what a veggie restaurant would look like and serve. There were no pine tables, no panpipes or Enya playing in the background, no brown plates and above all else no brown food! As far as I was concerned no meat didn't mean no fat, no flavour, and no fun. I didn't subscribe to the wholefood approach, although I'm sure it was great for keeping you regular or whatever it was it professed to do. I just wanted to serve food that was exciting and indulgent. Dishes I could serve to meat eaters that they could enjoy without feeling like there was something missing. And so far I seemed to have succeeded. I was surprised how many customers told me they were actually meat eaters, and the majority of messages in the comments box were kind and praiseworthy. I always felt a jolt of panic when I saw a customer put something in the comments box. I was paranoid that I would lose favour, and people would decide I was 'old hat' rather than 'old favourite'. I analysed every remark for hints of a sway in customer opinion.

About once a week I'd get some smart Alec asking me if I did beefburgers, or 'didn't I feel sorry for the poor carrots?' as if they were the first person to think that one up. I usually just stifled a yawn and gave them a blank look. It was the same when I got chatting to blokes in the pub or at parties. When they found out what I did for a living they would always look surprised or intrigued and quiz

15

me about why I chose to abstain from meat, like I had to explain myself. Years ago I used to relish this. I enjoyed getting their attention, and used to argue fervently, thinking I could change the world, but after a while I tired of being a novelty to them and hearing the same arguments over and over again. Nowadays I took the stand that I am what I am; it was no more interesting than that. This attitude seemed to sit well with the customers as they knew I wasn't trying to change people's opinion or going to make them feel guilty; the café was for everyone to enjoy.

The rising sun was just beginning to nudge into view through the drapes. It hit the floor and bounced off the chrome appliances behind the counter. I figured it was time for action and began turning on the machinery, starting most importantly with the coffee machine.

Maggie arrived an hour later when things were in full swing. She flicked the sign to open as she came through the front door.

'Mmm, that smells good,' she said, heading straight to the cups and saucers to pour herself a large expresso.

I popped my head around the kitchen door. 'Go easy on the produce, you greedy moo.'

She sipped it with such enthusiasm you'd think it had been served in a Chippendale's belly button. 'One of the perks of the job,' she replied, challenging me with a grin and adding, 'Or should I say percolations?'

I groaned. 'That's awful.'

Looking me up and down she said, 'Blimey, you look so much more normal.'

'You mean I'm not crawling around on all fours, begging you to end my life.'

'If you had done that today I was going to insist on ringing the doctor,' she said seriously as she tied her long curly black hair back into a scrunchy.

'Well, I saved you the bother. I'm fitter than ever today. Raring to go,' I said, jogging on the spot and punching the air like a boxer to emphasise my point.

Maggie joined me in the kitchen, donned an apron and began washing vegetables for a soup. 'So, do you think you'd be up to a party on Saturday night?'

'Count me in. Where is it?'

She pulled an Elvis sneer. 'Well, that's the worst bit. It's at the lovely Oliver's house. But Alice really wants us to be there. Probably so the three of us can keep an eye on him. But the upside is my mother definitely won't be there and everyone else will; including Simon and Charlie, who I'm convinced both fancy you, so you're bound to pull.'

'Oi!' I chucked a mangetout at her, 'Simon is Tom's brother and Charlie's his best friend. Don't you think it would be a bit underhand of me to sleep with one of them, even if they were up for it? Which I doubt,' I stressed.

'And you expect him to be faithful, do you?' She raised her eyebrows as she spoke.

'Well, even if he isn't I don't think he'd manage to find any of my close friends or relatives to do

17

it with in Kathmandu or wherever the hell he is,'
I snapped. I couldn't help but feel mad at her for
her insensitivity. Maggie hadn't made an emotional
attachment to a man in her whole life. She seemed to
think it was a sign of weakness. I hadn't let on how
I felt about Tom and I swallowed hard, not wanting
her to see that I was hurt.

The metallic trill of the customer bell saved me
from any further discussion as she disappeared to
take their order.

CHAPTER TWO

I stood in my underwear, staring at my bed and fighting the urge to drop on it with exhausted abandon. It had been a tough week. The café had been packed for the past few days and I had been too busy to even sit down. That had probably been a good thing because if I had, I never would have got back up.

I surveyed my reflection in the mirror above the dressing table. My blue eyes had lost their usual sparkle. They were bloodshot and bordered by dark circles. My usually wild brown hair had lost its will to rebel against gravity and instead hung limply to my shoulders. I had dried my hair upside down to try and give it volume, but all I had achieved was to make my thick wiry grey hairs stand on end like antennae. I plucked them out, making my eyes water. When I waved my hands near my nose I got a distinct oniony whiff. Despite having a bath and washing my hands umpteen times I just couldn't rid myself of the smell today. It was impossible to achieve glamour in my line of work. Pathetic, I thought. Take away the possibility of a shag in the near future and I go completely to seed.

It was at times like this that I envied the people with nine to five office jobs. Many of my customers were young professionals, enjoying a day of shopping and relaxation before a big night out. Today I had longed to swap places with one, and then I might have felt more like a party.

It was strange that the reason I had decided to be my own boss was to avoid the usual office scenario; it had never appealed to me. Yet now I was succeeding as my own boss I had a nagging feeling every other woman had a better and more fulfilling job than I did. If you go by what you read in magazines, the average woman, like a number of my old school friends, was climbing a corporate ladder, holding her own in a man's world, yet managing to maintain her femininity. She would usually work in London and live in a Notting Hill-trendy yet fashionably shabby-type suburb. She'd wear Pied à Terre shoes, eat Prêt à Manger sandwiches, shop in Tesco Metro and be forever on the Net or mobile in an office with a padded swivel chair. She'd have holiday pay, a pension and lovely Christmas bonuses and office parties. She wouldn't be forced to wear practical casuals that are well washed from continual food spattering and sensible flat shoes so her feet aren't aching after a whole day with barely any time to sit down. She wouldn't spend hours washing bugs off organic calabrese, wiping tables and be constantly negotiating (begging) with a rather frightening bank manager.

I inwardly chastised myself for being so negative and made a brave attempt to pull myself together. Sorting through the garments slung haphazardly on the bed, I picked out my favourite cropped black trousers and a blue vest top and cardigan. I slipped the trousers on over my nicest whitest knickers and tugged up the zip. It jammed solid halfway up. I looked down, searching for a stray thread or piece of fabric that could be in the way. Nothing.

'I can't have put on weight, I've been throwing up for half the week!' I spun around and viewed myself in the full-length mirror. I didn't look any bigger. Dropping to the floor, I squirmed like a caught trout, wrestling with the zip. When it did concede to close it was about as comfortable as an all-in-one iron maiden. I set my belly free and picked out a satin skirt with a generous amount of lycra, vowing to steer clear of any nibbles at the party.

A car pulled up in the street below and clattered to a stop. That could only be Shelley. She worked part time at the café to finance her art degree. Driving a Hillman Imp seemed to give her kudos with her arty friends, and she was always quick to point out that Jarvis Cocker also drove one despite his rise to fame and fortune. I waved to her at the window, then grabbed a bottle of wine out of the fridge and headed out the door.

'Hiya boss, I picked up Alice and Maggie on the way, thought it would give you time to get ready.' She eyed me putting on my lipstick in the sun visor's mirror, adding, 'Not enough by the looks of it.'

21

'Sorry, I nodded off during the Brookie omnibus. It was half seven when I woke up, I couldn't believe it.'

'It's a sign of the ageing process, you know,' piped up Maggie from the back seat.

I turned to acknowledge them. 'Don't you ever say anything compassionate?'

She pursed her lips together in a Marilyn Monroe pout and whispered huskily, 'I love you!'

'I said compassionate not passionate, there's a difference you know.'

She snorted with laughter as Shelley jerked the car into the main road.

We pulled up outside Oliver's house. A three-storey stone terrace in Camden, not far from the city centre. Shelley's car had only just made it up the steep streets and we piled out the instant she ground to a halt, trying to hide the fact that we were grateful to arrive with our lives intact.

We could hear the music as soon as the car doors opened. Alice sighed, 'Something tells me old Mrs Jenkins will be around to complain in the morning. I wouldn't mind if Ol dealt with her but he always hides in the bedroom.'

'Typical!' I heard Maggie mutter.

I gave her a warning look and emptied the car of the drinks we had bought.

'You don't think you went a little overboard?' I asked, struggling with a twenty-four pack of cider, half a dozen bottles of Chardonnay and a large bottle of Martini.

Alice helped me carry them to the gate, laughing.

22

'You're kidding. You know what Ol's mates are like. They buy 800 cans of lager and a token couple of bottles of cheap sparkling wine for the laydeez,' she said waggling her fingers like inverted commas. 'Besides, since beer tastes like the water vegetables have boiled in, I'm not taking any chances!'

'She's convinced me,' said Maggie, leading the way to the front door with the remaining bounty.

Noah answered the door, looking astonishingly wide and shapely.

'Girls, let me take those,' he greeted, bending down to retrieve the stack of booze. A muscular version of a Mexican wave pulsated across his body and I noticed Maggie's eyes glaze over. She turned to follow him inside and walked straight into the stone wall. Fortunately for her, Noah had missed the incident and was on his way to the kitchen.

Alice went to her aid, steering her into the hall by her elbow. 'Something tells me Noah's going to end up warmed through, garnished and served on a bed of something other than filo sheets by the end of the night.'

'He might if he's lucky,' Mags agreed, checking out her cleavage in the full-length mirror.

I followed the noise that bubbled and spilled through the open kitchen doors. Walking into the crowded room, I immediately saw Oliver. He was leaning against the far wall, talking to a petite and shapely girl, with long curly red hair. She expelled a dirty chuckle that made Barbara Windsor sound virginal and slapped him hard on the arm saying, 'Cheeky!' The girl was obviously a walking *Carry*

23

On cliché and I wouldn't have been surprised if her skimpy white bra top flew off and hit him in the face. Oliver spotted me then and I noticed he quickly checked to see who was with me. The action of a guilty man, I couldn't help thinking. He whispered something to the girl he was entertaining and she teetered off on her quivering heels. Probably to be chased around the garden by a Benny Hill wannabe. At that point the girls joined me and Oliver sauntered over.

He passed us all a glass of Lambrusco from a nearby table. 'Hi babe,' he said to Alice, kissing her cheek. We all watched as she visibly melted into a pool by his feet. The girls gave me an exasperated 'Let's leave them to it' look and we sloped off into the crowd.

I weaved my way through the people in the room, looking for someone I might know. They seemed to be mostly men from the insurance company where Oliver was the area manager. Men outnumbered the women in the room by roughly five to one. This had obviously brought out the male's primitive competitive nature. Most were smartly dressed in expensive label shirts and were standing in various masculine poses, arms crossed, pushing out their biceps, chest out, or the casual one hand in the pocket and the other holding a bottle of lager.

The group of blokes closest to me erupted into hysterical drunken laughter after one of them had made a gesture with his hands as if to say, 'I swear it was this big.' All of them looked like they were having fascinating conversations about things

24

I knew nothing about and were too preoccupied to notice me pushing past. I felt completely left out, and it reminded me of a time in infants' school when my two best friends had been off sick. I had walked into the playground and seen the other children all having a hilarious time playing games together without me. I had been so embarrassed about being seen alone and friendless that I ran behind some trees. I had peered around them laughing, pretending to be engrossed in a game of hide and seek with lots of friends that nobody else could see. Unfortunately, I didn't think I could pull that off in here. I turned to see if I could locate Maggie and saw that she was in deep flirtation with Noah by the canapés. Shelley was nowhere to be seen. I walked out into the hall, feeling like a complete Billy-no-mates.

The music was even louder in the corridor. It was coming from the living room straight ahead, and I could see shadows on the wall of people dancing maniacally. I stood outside for a while, trying to decide whether to walk into the room and risk not knowing anyone in there either and having to walk straight out again feeling like a prat. Fortunately I was saved by a familiar voice coming from the stairs.

'Holly. Excellent, I'm so glad you came.' I looked up and saw Simon, Tom's brother, coming down the stairs. He looked unnervingly handsome in smart dark trousers and a loose-fitting pale blue shirt. My cheeks warmed up a little when I remembered what Mags had said in the kitchen on Thursday.

'I didn't realise you'd be here,' I lied blatantly. God, he really did look like Tom. If you had cut Tom's hair and kept him out of the sun for a few months they could be twins. Unfortunately, any sane woman would find it easier to fall for Simon. Of the two brothers he was the more stable and successful (he had shot up the corporate ladder and was now a manager in a major pharmaceuticals company). Tom on the other hand was planning on joining the family business, if he ever exhausted the travel bug. Simon was also the more romantic and open of the two; women found they could talk to Simon about anything. He knew what he wanted. Tom was as close to knowing that as a sweet-toothed four-year-old, dropped into the middle of a chocolate factory and told he was only allowed one thing.

'Have you heard from your brother lately?' I ventured, tossing my hair and trying to look blasé.

'Actually, yes. I got a postcard from him a few days ago. The lucky sod's in Hawaii, taking a scuba diving course. He'll be spending Christmas in Australia. Didn't say much else though, you know what he's like.' I racked my brain for something witty to say that would make me sound indifferent.

'Oh,' I said finally.

'Are you okay, Holly? You look like you're gonna cry,' he said frowning with concern.

'No, no, I'm fine.' *Smile, smile, look happy.*

He put a comforting hand on my shoulder, 'Do you miss him?'

'No, honestly, it's not that, I'm just tired. Bad

26

week and all that.' I managed a weak smile. The thudding bass from the living room was making my head pulsate sickeningly.

'Come on, you need some fresh air.' He took me by the hand and led me through the kitchen and out into the garden. The patio door clicked shut behind us, dulling the noise of the party, and we sat on a plump swinging chair overlooking the garden. The December air bit hard into my skin, making me pull my cardigan tight against me. We sat silently for a while, and then I became aware that Simon was looking at me intensely.

'I can't understand my brother sometimes,' he started abruptly. 'He's supposed to be intelligent, but how can he be when he can bear to be on the other side of the world from you?' He looked away in embarrassment, swirling the ice cubes in his drink around until they clattered together. He drained his glass and stared at me again. 'You look gorgeous tonight,' he whispered, reaching to tuck a loose strand of hair behind my ear.

Oh my God, I thought, Mags was right, he's going to kiss me. His face was perilously close and I could faintly smell a mixture of a spicy aftershave and the whisky on his breath. I figured he must be drunk and moved my head further back, trying to distance myself from temptation. 'Simon, I think you've had too much to drink. You don't really know what you're saying.'

'No, Hol, it's not like that. I mean I've had a bit to drink, that's true. But that's because I knew you'd be here. I've been trying to work up the courage to tell

27

you how I feel, I really do care about you.' He took my hand in his. 'I want to tell you, I need to . . .' He was leaning closer and closer.

Shit, he's sexy. His lips were just a hair's breadth from my own; I guess it wouldn't be too wrong, it's not like Tom and I are serious. He tilted his head the way you do before a deep kissing situation and I could feel his misty breath against my cheek, yes yes yes . . .

Suddenly a shrill scream exploded through the intense still of the night, making me bolt out of the seat, my heart punching at my chest. I felt like a burglar caught in the beam of a security light.

A raucous laugh erupted from behind the enormous willow tree at the bottom of the garden, then out ran the redhead I had seen Oliver talking to earlier. She was followed eagerly by a man probably twice her age. He picked her up and positioned her over his shoulder fireman style, admonished her by gently slapping her bottom and carried her back behind the tree. The girl kicked her legs, squealing with delight.

I turned back to Simon, feeling embarrassed and blurted, 'I'm sorry, I've got to go.' Then I fled back into the kitchen, leaving him alone on the patio staring after me.

The kitchen was now heaving with people all in a highly flirtatious state. I scanned the room searching for Alice, needing a sympathetic ear to bash but I couldn't see her anywhere. I was pushing my way through the room when suddenly I heard a nasal cry.

28

'Oh shit, that hurt!'

To my horror I realised I had walked straight into Caroline. She was bending down to rub her ankle and wiggling her foot, checking for permanent damage. Unfortunately, I hadn't even chipped the nail polish on her exquisitely manicured toes. She rose back to her full complement of six foot one. Taller than the average male, she was staggering to look at. Her hair was as long and shiny as a show horse's mane and her legs? Ugh! I didn't even want to go there for fear of developing a Ronnie Corbett complex. We had nicknamed her Mother Superior at school, not entirely due to jealousy on our part but mainly because of her relentless need to make us feel like pond scum. I tried to slope off before she recognised me but her eyes pinned me to the spot. I wondered if there was a laser dot on my forehead marking me as her prime target.

'Oh Holly, I should have known it was you,' she simpered. 'You never were any good at co-ordination, were you.' She laughed and patted me on the shoulder as if I was a reckless little puppy.

This was typical of Caroline. She was one of those people I would call a smiley bitch. She was able to get away with being patronising and unpleasant by saying everything with a seemingly sincere wide smile. She'd treat you as though you were her best friend and yet she would know exactly how to undermine your confidence with a little comment weaved into a conversation. Unfortunately men seemed to fall for it every time. She was never without some doting male in tow. What made it

29

worse was that if you complained to any of them about her they would always say something like, 'Caroline? No, that can't be right, she's lovely,' then just assume you were jealous.

She peered over my head (without even rising on to her tiptoes, I might add!). 'Where's that hippie boyfriend of yours tonight?'

'Tom? He's travelling abroad at the moment. Won't be back 'til next year,' I replied, fighting to keep my tone light and carefree.

Caroline raised an eyebrow in a gesture that said, 'Ah, she's trying to sound carefree, she obviously cares deeply' then she stared off into the distance, looking wistful. 'I wish I could just up and go like that. That's the trouble with my job, so many people rely on me, important meetings, endless paperwork. I swear if I didn't schedule in my trips to take a piss the place would collapse around me!'

I was never entirely sure what Caroline did for a living, but I wasn't about to give her an extra opportunity for self-congratulation by asking. Instead I nodded dumbly, taking a long gulp of my sickly wine and kicked myself for not downing a few gin and tonics before I had come out.

My drink had gone warm and clammy in my hand and the cloying smell filled my nostrils, making my head spin with sudden nausea. I tried to focus on Caroline's face as she jabbered on about her new company car. Her features appeared to be mysteriously vanishing, the way the Starship Enterprise crew did when Scotty beamed them up. Unfortunately, this was not a viable explanation for the vision before me. I decided I must be feeling a little dizzy.

'I think I'll have a little lie down now,' I mumbled to Caroline as I pitched forward and head butted her kneecaps.

CHAPTER THREE

'Holly, are you awake?'

I slowly opened my eyes and saw Simon sitting beside the bed. 'How do you feel?' Memories of Oliver's party intruded into my conscience and I felt my cheeks heat up with shame.

I groaned and attempted to smother myself with the duvet. 'Just kill me now, I don't deserve to live!'

Simon gave me a sympathetic smile. 'I wouldn't worry too much. Everyone was too pissed to remember your exit last night. In fact Cindy, the new recruit in Oliver's office, threw up in the chest freezer. It'll be murder chipping that out today.'

'Today!' I sat bolt upright and looked around the sunlit bedroom. 'I've been here all night?'

'I thought you needed to sleep. It's okay; everyone knows where you are. Shelley left at about three, Alice is in Oliver's room and Maggie hooked up with Noah, they're sleeping in the attic room.'

'Wow! Mags and Noah. That's excellent. I hope she's gentle with him, she can be a bit ruthless with men.'

32

'We had noticed this,' he said.

I wondered if by 'we' he meant men in general.

He looked at the floor, then shuffling uncomfortably in his chair, said, 'Listen, Holly, it's actually me who should be embarrassed about last night. I really am sorry.'

I started to tell him it was okay but he butted in before I had the chance.

'I spoke to Alice after we put you to bed. She told me what happened with you and Tom. I had just assumed that you had split up. You know what Tom's like, he never tells me anything. I didn't realise you'd seen him after the Halloween party and made up. I've made a complete prat out of myself.' He looked at me with his big sad eyes. 'Can we still be friends?'

I couldn't resist a mini flirtatious smile. I was enjoying having him make me feel all womanly and attractive.

'Come here, you silly sod,' I said, arms outstretched and wallowed in the big bear hug I got in return.

The party Simon had mentioned was Tom's leaving do. It had been held at the flat that they shared with Tom's best friend Charlie on Halloween night, despite the fact that his flight was due to depart from Heathrow at two o'clock the following afternoon.

Anyone who had seen us at that party would never have had us pegged as a couple, but that was indicative of our entire relationship. It was as

33

though we were holding an unspoken competition for who could act the least bothered about the other in public. We'd never discussed the depth of our relationship, which I guess was proof alone that it couldn't have been too deep. We messed around together, met up when he was in town, went out for a drink or a movie and had great sex. We never quizzed the other about previous lovers, never demanded or got jealous, and certainly never picked the names of our future children or went shopping together in Ikea. It wasn't that we weren't close. I knew him as well as I knew any of my other friends; we were affectionate and his parents treated me like one of the family. No one could really work us out. But how could they when not even I fully understood our relationship? Maybe it was his travelling bug that stopped us crossing the line between friends who shag and an official couple. We both knew he had planned this world trip for years. It seemed futile to develop the relationship further, then expect each other to sit and pine for a year. More worryingly I had also wondered if I was simply too mediocre to make him melt with devotion. Maybe if I was a stunning Gwyneth Paltrow type he wouldn't be able to resist falling in love and wanting me all to himself. Being a traditional woman in this area, I couldn't possibly bring myself to tell him how I really felt. He would have to start the ball rolling. I wouldn't allow myself to become one of those scary commitment obsessives that blokes tell horror stories about late at night, huddled around their pints like scouts around a campfire. So I waited

34

patiently for him to tell me he loved me, and waited, then I waited a bit more. Then the night of the leaving party came around and I didn't need to wait any longer.

I had felt sick to my stomach all day at the thought of him leaving. In my mind I had these desperately romantic pictures playing out. I would be driving blindly after him to the airport, crying into tissues then tossing them out of the window whilst weaving through a dense traffic jam the way they do in car adverts. I'd pull up at the airport, abandoning the car with the doors wide open at the front of the building, push past security, calling his name into a crowd of strangers. Then I'd catch sight of his floppy brown hair as he turned to the departure gate to leave. For some inexplicable reason he'd look back and see me pushing my way toward him. He'd give me a wide smile, then fight through the crowd, arms outstretched, ready to hold me. I'd sob heavily into his cuddly jumper, saying 'Please don't go, Tom. I love you. I always have.' And then he would smile, stroking my hair and with an emotionally hoarse voice reply, 'I love you too, Holly. I just didn't believe you felt the same. I'll never leave you again. That's a promise.' It would be Mills and Boon with knobs on. But unfortunately life had never perfectly imitated art.

What had really transpired was a miserable party where I moped about getting more and more drunk. I could hear Tom laughing with his friends about women he'd get to meet on his trip, gyrating hula girls in grass skirts, Singaporean air stewardesses,

35

you know the sort, typical male fantasies. It was churning me up inside. Alice insisted that he was constantly looking over at me for a reaction, but I couldn't see it. Simon, who was standing with us at the time, told me to go over and tell him how I felt, which pissed me off even more. Was I really that transparent? I told Simon that as it happened I felt nothing for Tom, I was bored by his travelling stories and was glad he was going so I could finally be free of him. I told him to say 'bye from me and not to pester me when he got back. Then I staggered out into the main road and hailed a cab home.

I couldn't have been back at the flat for long when I was woken by the clatter of stones against a windowpane. When I peered through the curtains I saw Tom. He was weaving drunkenly in the road, holding a bottle of wine and a small fir tree. When he caught sight of me standing at the window he broke into a chorus of Simple Minds, 'Don't you forget about me.' I hurried down to let him in, before someone called the Environmental Health.

'It was all I could find,' he explained, handing me the plant complete with large sods of topsoil.

I ushered him inside and up the stairs, dumping the tree in the kitchen sink.

'I thought it would *spruce* up your apartment,' he slurred, chuckling childishly to himself.

'I'll make us a coffee,' I said, avoiding eye contact and wishing I were sober enough to think straight.

'Holly,' he said in a completely serious and commanding voice, an achievement for someone that couldn't even balance. I spun around and there he

36

was, standing motionless, just staring at me with his mouth open. For a minute I thought he was going to be sick on the kitchen floor and nearly went to fetch a washing-up bowl. Then he said it,

'I love you.'

I was stunned.

'Oh,' was all my voice box could rustle up with such short notice.

He winced, as though I had slapped his face, making me realise how insensitive that must have sounded.

'I mean oh, as in "oh wow," as in "oh my God I wasn't expecting that," as in . . .' I looked into his translucent green eyes. I felt weak-kneed with the flood of affection I felt for him. I had never seen him look so vulnerable . . . so sexy . . . The look that passed between us was so meaningful it seemed to sober me up instantly.

'Oh shit, why did you have to tell me this now? Your timing couldn't be worse,' I said, then became literally tongue-tied as Tom stopped my meandering banter with a deep warm kiss. We sank down on the wooden floor, and for the first time since we had first begun seeing each other we didn't have fantastic sex, nor did we shag like insatiable rabbits. This time it was different, lingering and tender. The way he looked at me made me flush with embarrassment at the intimacy we were sharing. It was also quite miraculous considering he'd drunk at least a gallon of beer. I could hardly keep from giving him a standing ovation. Afterwards we cuddled up in bed with my head lying on his

37

chest, and I kissed his firm flesh whispering, 'I love you too.'

In the morning I woke up with a smug smile on my face and turned over; 'Ouch,' my bum was sore. I reached down to rub it better and felt the indentations left by the kitchen floorboards; my smile deepened. I looked across the ruffled sheets to the empty space where Tom should have been lying with a similar happy and gratified expression. He wasn't there. I checked the time, Eleven o'clock. He must have left to pack his bags. I hit the Tom-shaped imprint that remained on the bed, shouting, 'Why didn't you wake me, you sod?'

A note was my next thought; maybe he'd written one before he left.

Ten minutes later I abandoned my search, chucked on the only clothes I had that weren't in the laundry basket and bolted out of the door.

I hammered on the front door of Tom's flat. Charlie opened the door, dressed only in a pair of boxers, his hair spiked up on one side, as though he'd been buffeted by a strong crosswind. He stood blinking at the bright sunlight, only partially able to focus on me.

'Hey babe, good party last night. What happened to you?' He rubbed the sleep out of his eyes and yawned.

'Where's Tom?' I urged, ignoring the small talk.

'I dunno,' he shrugged. 'He didn't come home last night, y'know.' He raised his eyebrows and chuckled in a 'he obviously got lucky' blokish manner. Then he realised he may have just dropped his

38

friend in it, adding quickly, 'He left the party alone, probably just crashed in the garden.'

'He stayed at mine, you dozy prat.' My patience was dwindling rapidly. I barged past him and ran up to Tom's room. He had definitely gone. His room still looked like the aftermath of an explosion in a junk shop but there were vital pieces missing. His giant rucksack and the camera he had just bought were gone.

'Didn't he say goodbye?' I shouted at Charlie, who had followed me up the stairs. He was scratching his head, still looking half-asleep.

'Yeah, last night. I didn't think I'd get up in time to say 'bye this morning. I did hear a car a while ago though. Simon said he'd drop him off at the airport this morning.'

We both went to the window and looked down at the driveway below. Sure enough, Simon's shiny red beetle had gone.

'Shit!'

'I thought you finished with him last night?'

'I did, kind of. How long does it take to drive to Heathrow from here?'

CHAPTER FOUR

Physically, my journey east along the M4 had been an easy ride. The traffic was sparse and fortunately the Sabbath day had extended itself to traffic cones, which appeared to have taken a day of rest, probably gathered together in a warehouse somewhere giving thanks to the Minister of Transport. But despite the peace and quiet on the carriageway in front of me, there was an inner battle waging in my head. Half of my brain was yelling 'What the hell are you doing chasing after him like this? Have you no pride at all? You have a better than average shag and all of a sudden you're playing the last scene of *Gone with the Wind* as Scarlett O'Hara. Even if you do find him you can't change the fact that he's going. Even if he meant what he had said it wouldn't help him to know you feel the same. You'll just have more reasons to mooch around for twelve months.' Then I imagined him meeting up with other women on his travels. Maybe if he knew I would wait for him he could override his sexual urges. That did it, I squeezed the accelerator pedal further towards the floor.

At the same time as I was battling with my pride and new-found emotional state, the other half of my brain was arguing for an altogether different cause, yelling, 'What the bloody hell do you think you're doing on the motorway? Do you want to die horribly?' I had passed my driving test when I was eighteen, yet as far as motorways were concerned cowardice had always prevailed. A car sped past me in the middle lane, making me sigh, defeated, why is it whenever I get overtaken I take it so personally? They may as well flick their V's up when they whizz by, shouting 'stick that, you shit driver, eat my dust!' I had been overtaken by everything except for a heavy goods vehicle that looked as if it was carrying a NASA space rocket and a clapped-out camper van the colour of a nicotine stain. I had even considered overtaking that myself until its bonnet caught fire and it rattled to a stop on the hard shoulder.

By the time I had pulled into the terminal three, short stay car park I felt as though rigor mortis had taken over my body. I had sat bolt upright for the whole journey, my back rigid, arms tense, eyes staring. I had adopted that wide-eyed unblinking expression you only see in the severely deranged. But there wasn't time to calm myself down and freshen up. With only half an hour before Tom's flight was due to leave, I raced across the first-floor bridge and down the stairs into the enormous airport terminal. I barged past several people, banging my knee hard against the corner of a hard plastic suitcase, I bit my lip and tried to ignore the hot pain that spread down my leg. The airline desks

41

and baggage check-ins stretched as far as I could see and beyond. There were lots of queues of people checking in for flights, collecting their boarding passes and handing over luggage. I felt a momentary sense of defeat as I realised just how huge the airport was and how many people and flights they accommodated. All I knew about Tom's flight was the terminal and the time. I had an inkling it was a Virgin flight but I couldn't be sure. I spotted a woman in a Virgin uniform at an information point that didn't have a queue at it and ran over to her, trying to catch my breath.

'Can you tell me if Thomas Delanci has checked in yet? He should be on the two o'clock flight to New York,' I panted.

The woman smiled at me and checked her computer screen, typing and clicking. She seemed to be operating in slow motion and I hopped impatiently from one foot to the other, as though I needed the toilet.

'Yes Madam, Mr Delanci has checked in,' she said eventually.

'Can you tell me where I might find him now?' I said, willing her to say something useful like, 'Yes Madam, just over there.' Instead she blew out a sharp breath of air and said, 'Madam, his flight is on time and is about to start boarding. He may already have gone through to the departure lounge.'

I thanked her as I ran, catapulting up another flight of stairs. When I reached the top I stopped to get my bearings. I was in what looked like a giant and incredibly plush shopping centre. I hesitated, unsure where to go. A monitor hanging from the ceiling caught my eye and I saw Tom's flight on the list it displayed. The word 'BOARDING' was flashing urgently, snapping me out of my indecision and I ran decisively towards a newsagents. I ran past the magazines, knocking into people, pausing only briefly to make sure no one was injured by my carelessness. There was nobody there that caught my eye so I ran out and tried two more shops before I spotted a bar, deciding that it was likely that Tom would leave it until the last minute to board his plane. He and Simon would probably have a farewell drink before he left. I ran in and hunted through the tables. Several customers were staring at me curiously and I knew I must look a state, but it was too late to care about that.

Finally I realised that Tom must have gone through to the departure lounge. I left the bar and sprinted that way. Pushing past a group of people with cameras, I strained to see if Tom was already on the walkway. As I got closer I recognised a flash of an intricate design on the back of a man's sweatshirt and I knew instantly that it was Tom's favourite Stone Monkey climbing top. My heart leapt and I quickened my pace. I could feel my blood pulsing in my legs and a film of sweat now covered my face. I wiped it away with the sleeve of my top and, as I did so, I tripped over a partly opened sports bag that had been left on the floor.

Time seemed to stand still for a fraction of a second as I dived in the air; arms stretched in front of me like Wonder Woman, waiting to catch my fall.

43

I slid along, grazing and burning my palms on the abrasive nylon carpet, banging my elbows and chin on impact. I could see Tom moving further away and I tried to scramble up. There was still time. My feet had knocked some of the contents of the bag onto the floor so I made a fumbling attempt to stuff the flask and plastic box back where they had been. I rose up again and panic struck as I saw that Tom was disappearing from view. With my face screwed up with tension I managed to yell out a strangled, 'Tom . . .' The little old lady who had been standing near me as I fell, suddenly stopped adjusting her hearing aid and threw her hands up in the air shouting, 'BOMB! That lady said there's a bomb in that bag. Help, please, someone, there's a bomb in that bag!'

Tom was now out of sight at the bottom of the ramp. I tried to run after him but my legs had turned to jelly and were refusing to cooperate; I kept stumbling to the floor. I became aware that all around me pandemonium was breaking out. Suddenly, in a place that had been previously teeming with people, there was no one. Just me and the carrier bag. Armed Security staff had appeared out of nowhere and had started the process of evacuating the area and talking into walkie-talkies. Metal shutters rattled down over the shop windows and a tannoy announcement was advising people to make their way to the nearest stairwell and proceed in a calm and orderly manner to the lower concourse area. One of the security officers who was standing several feet away asked me to 'carefully step away

44

from the package' and when I did, I was approached by two burly-looking uniformed men who linked arms with me. I gave a pathetic struggle, trying to make a break down the empty slope, yelling 'Tom' in the direction I had seen him leave, but I was abruptly frog-marched out and away down some stairs.

I sat for two hours in a room not unlike a prison cell, intermittently being interviewed by one person and then left on my own before being interviewed by someone else. Finally I was finally allowed to leave the building with no charge against me. They had apparently abandoned the bomb alert when a Russian tourist had returned from the toilet wondering why his sausage sandwich and flask of borscht was being held captive by men with guns. I was given an extremely stern lecture on conduct in buildings with a high security risk, and how, if I had approached my problem in a calmer and controlled manner and asked for assistance, they would have been able to locate Tom for me. I could have requested a call to be put through to him, asking him to return to the departure area to talk to me if it was important. It was like an embellished, adult version of the headmaster's walk, don't run in the corridor lecture I received in junior school, only far scarier. I had bitten my lip hard and fought the urge to snivel into a hanky and whine, 'It wasn't my fault.'

They had offered to relay a message to Tom if it was urgent, but I just shook my head. I couldn't face him after that. What had in my mind been a romantic, impulsive gesture had been exposed as the silly and futile efforts of a foolish imbecile.

By the time I left the room I was crushed with embarrassment and had to make a pointed effort to walk with dignity out of the airport terminal to my car, where I locked myself in and burst into tears.

CHAPTER FIVE

Simon went downstairs to make us a cup of coffee. As soon as he left the room I checked under the duvet. Yes, I was still in the clothes I had worn last night, thank God. The thought of Simon and Alice struggling to undress me was too unpleasant to contemplate. It was difficult enough for me to take this tight skirt down without whipping off my underwear as well. I shuddered at the thought and got out of bed. I walked to the window and stared dismally at the view of the city. It was frosty this morning and the trees and stone buildings twinkled in the winter sun. If Tom had been here I'd have cajoled him into a walk in the park or along the river Avon, followed by a pub with a log fire, a proper Sunday couple type of activity. Instead I'd probably just go home to watch the *EastEnders* omnibus and drink the dregs of the wine in the fridge.

Simon came back then with a tray of coffee and biscuits.

'I figured you might be hungry,' he said, handing me a steaming mug with a Playboy bunny motif on it. He noticed my expression, explaining, 'I thought

47

you'd prefer that to the naked woman mug, with "drink me" written underneath.'

I tutted, 'I don't know why Alice gives that prat the time of day. He's a born womaniser.' I went to take a sip of coffee but the smell made me reel. 'Ugh, what did you put in this toilet water?'

Simon took it off me and had a taste. 'There's nothing wrong with it. Honestly, Hol, you're seriously weird at the moment.'

'What's that supposed to mean?' I snapped, offended.

He raised his eyebrows in a see-what-I-mean gesture, saying, 'Well, now let's see.' He counted off on his fingers as he spoke. 'You're moody, uncharacteristically lack-lustre at parties, you are on and off sick all week, you have a non-alcohol induced fainting spell, and you think your perfectly adequate coffee smells like a urinal. Need I go on?' When he put it like that he did make me sound a bit odd.

'Well, what are you trying to say, Simon?' I demanded defensively, aware that I was overreacting.

'I don't think you want to know what I'm trying to say.'

Now that got me. 'What? Go on, spit it out. Stop playing games, you think I'm on drugs or something, WHAT?'

'Well, it's just a thought, Holly, don't get mad at me . . .'

'WHAT? WHAT?'

'Do you think you could possibly be pregnant?'

I stared at him as if he had suddenly taken leave of

his senses, and was hopping about with a chopstick in his ear, singing 'I'm a llama,' or something equally ludicrous.

'Don't be so silly,' I snorted. 'I'm twenty-seven.' Then it was my turn to be stared at as though I was mental. I added sheepishly, 'and I'm on the pill.'

'It's not impossible,' he replied and asked, 'Combined or mini?'

I drew a breath; God, Simon must be the only man I know who would ask this. 'Mini, if you must know,' I snapped, feeling violated.

'Well, that's only about ninety-seven per cent effective, isn't it? Plus you have to be really careful to take it at the same time every day and not forget it.'

I rolled my eyes. 'Well, of course I knew that. What is this family planning counselling? I don't need it. Women my age know these things!'

'Okay, okay.' He held up his hands as if he was saying 'Whoa!' to a bolting horse, and explained calmly, 'It happened to a mate's girlfriend at Uni, that's all. She had a hangover one morning, must have thrown up the pill and got pregnant. Her symptoms were similar to yours; I guess you reminded me of her. I only mentioned it in case you'd forgotten to take it at some point. I didn't mean to offend you.'

I felt completely foolish then and looked away.

'You have, haven't you?'

'No!' I said meekly. 'No, of course not. Okay yes, maybe once or twice. Every now and again. Well, it's difficult to remember, isn't it? And it's not like I'm living with someone and we're at it every night.

49

I mean, there's always a day or two in a month that you miss, you just take them all in one go next time. That's how it's always been. I mean, I've been taking them since I was seventeen and it hasn't failed me yet. Will you stop shaking your head like that!' I yelled, slapping him hard on his leg. Then it hit me like a thunder bolt: I couldn't for the life of me remember when my last period was. I knew it had been a while. I sank down on to the bed. 'Oh God, I couldn't be. It just doesn't happen to people like me. I've got a business to run, no steady man in my life, I like going out and enjoying myself. I've only just learnt to take care of myself!'

Simon sat down beside me and put his arm around my waist. 'Holly, I didn't mean to scare you. I just think it's a possibility that should be eliminated. Maybe you should go get a test, just to be sure. There's a chemist open on the main road into town. I bet Alice would go with you. Do you want me to go fetch her?'

I nodded, staring blankly at the window, whilst thoughts chased around my head like cars in a Grand Prix.

Alice and I walked across the grassy bank of the river and sat on a bench facing Pulteney Bridge. There was a small package burning a hole in my coat pocket like a lit fuse on a stick of ACME dynamite.

Alice sighed heavily and tried again. 'Please, Hol, just come back to the flat and put me out of my misery. I can't bear the suspense any longer.' She

50

had been begging me for the past half an hour to no avail.

'I can't do it. I'm not ready yet. I don't know how to look after a baby. My life is catering for people. It's the only thing I've ever been any good at.'

Alice looked at me dryly. 'You could always look at it as just having another mouth to feed,' she joked.

'This isn't a laughing matter, it's serious.' She continued to smile at me. 'I think you actually want me to be pregnant, don't you? You've always been a sucker for Baby Gap, and you're always eyeballing the mums in the café like a womb possessed. I bet you're having an Auntie Alice fantasy right now, at my expense!'

She smiled guiltily. 'Would it really be so awful? Lots of women our age have a baby; times have changed. You wouldn't have to be housebound in a baggy tracksuit with Richard and Judy. I mean, look at Madonna and Posh Spice. Being a mother doesn't necessarily stop you having a life. You could still run the café, Mags could work more hours and your mum could look after the baby. God, she'll be ecstatic, you know how she's always wished she could have had more kids herself.'

I stared at her gobsmacked. 'I can't believe this! You've actually planned it all out. You probably hatched a plan together to break into my flat, stick pins in my condoms, and swap my pills for placebos. I haven't even done the test yet; I could easily have just had some mystery bug and a late

51

period. I'm sure that's all it is. I don't know what I've been worried about.' I turned away from her and stared fixedly at the water that crashed down the weir.

'Right then,' Alice said, jumping to her feet and grabbing my hand. 'If you're sure that's all it is, you won't mind coming back to the flat. There's an insignificant little stick I want you to pee on if it's not too much trouble.'

We sat together on the side of the bath. Alice was holding the stick that I had just performed over and the picture in the leaflet showing an example of a pregnant and a non-pregnant result. I was sitting holding large chunks of hair in my hands with my head between my knees. I heard her take a deep breath. Then she said, 'Blimey,' in a soft, surprised voice.

That could mean anything, I thought, after all she seemed convinced that it would be positive.

'Okay,' I said gripping my hair tighter, 'I'm ready.'

She cleared her throat, obviously enjoying playing such an important role in my current crisis.

'Well, the picture in the leaflet shows two thin pale blue lines for the positive result.'

'Yes, yes,' I urged. 'Is that me?'

'Not exactly,' she said slowly. 'Yours shows two of the thickest, darkest lines you've ever seen. You're not pregnant, you're VERY bloody pregnant!'

That night I called Mags to give her the news. She just repeated the words 'Oh my God, oh my God!'

52

until she had freaked me out so successfully that I burst into frantic tears.

After I had finished talking to her, Simon called to find out how I had got on. He was significantly more composed and told me matter-of-factly that modern pregnancy tester kits were so accurate that it probably wasn't even worth buying another one for a second opinion. This also caused me to burst into frantic tears.

He turned up an hour later with a bottle of Lucozade, offering moral support. I made him promise not to tell anyone, including his family and most importantly Tom. He agreed, with a pained expression.

The following morning I plucked up the courage to go to my local doctor's. I was still hoping that the pregnancy theories would be dismissed for something more palatable, such as a serious internal organ problem.

I sat in the waiting room, sweating profusely and wringing my hands. Sitting opposite me was a woman struggling to control a curious toddler. I picked up a copy of *Hello*, and peered at her surreptitiously over a picture of Posh Spice. I wondered if women with children were privy to some inside information, allowing them to spot a pregnant woman by some small sign I wasn't aware of. She didn't seem to have noticed my micro-bump. I shuffled about in my seat, making sure I stuck my belly out as far as possible. Another lady walked in then. She looked as though she could give birth to quintuplets at any given moment. The first woman, who was now extracting her son's hand from a vending machine, turned to greet her.

'Hello, love,' she said, patting a seat as a gesture for her friend to join her. The pregnant woman reached her hands behind her to hold the seat, slowly inching her bulging body downwards. 'How much longer is it now?' asked the woman.

'Three days,' she replied with an exhausted wheeze.

'Just a routine check, is it?'

The pregnant woman nodded, then looked around the waiting room and leaned in further. 'I've got terrible piles,' she whispered. 'I can hardly sit down. I'm terrified of going into labour, I swear if I have to push I'll turn inside out!'

Her friend stifled a laugh and gave her a sympathetic look. 'I suppose you've tried the high fibre diet,' she said knowingly. I tried to act as though I was oblivious to them, yet my eyebrows shot involuntarily skywards. Bloody hell! Do all pregnant women get piles? The buzzer sounded for my doctor and I trudged into his office with my buttocks tightly clenched, feeling ever more like a condemned woman.

The doctor sat at his desk, scribbling into his notes.

'What can I do for you, Miss Piper?' he asked without looking up.

'I think I'm pregnant,' I said with a faint voice. I waited for him to look up, astonished, exclaiming 'Good God, you're kidding me!' But he just carried on writing.

54

'I see,' he said in a deadpan tone. 'And what has made you think that?'

'Well, as far as I can work out I haven't had a period since mid-October, I'm being sick and my tester kit was positive.'

He looked up for the first time then. 'Sounds like congratulations are in order, then,' he said smiling sagely. 'Was it a planned pregnancy?'

'No,' I whispered, hanging my head in shame and feeling like the town strumpet.

'Are you planning to keep the child?' he asked, again showing a surprising lack of emotion. I stared at him, shocked.

'Of course!' I snapped, placing my hands defensively on my tummy. 'Look, don't you need to confirm it with a blood test or something? I mean nothing's definite yet, is it?'

'I don't think it's necessary to carry out any further tests. It's all quite evident that you are pregnant. If you would prefer some extra confirmation you could give me a small urine sample, which you can do now, if you like. I can let you know in seconds. But as I said, I don't see that it's necessary.' He fumbled around in his drawer and produced a sample pot, the size of a pinhead. 'The toilet's straight across the corridor if you wish me to test your urine.'

How on earth would I be able to aim into that piddling little thing? I thought, trying to focus on the thimble between his fingers. I declined the offer and he set to work. He asked a lot about family medical history, periods and about any symptoms.

55

I answered them all in a dull monotone, my brain working on autopilot. 'This is it, it's really happening,' I kept thinking. I had a surreal feeling that I was a character in a soap opera and that the situation was really involving some *alter ego* rather than me directly. The doctor asked me to lie on the couch so he could examine my abdomen. When he had finished he sat me down for a final talk. He explained that nothing would happen for the first trimester, then I would be seen regularly by the local midwife team. He would book me in for my first scan, which would be some time in early February. As an afterthought he added, 'You do already have a slight swelling in your abdomen, and your sickness has begun earlier than normal. If you are right in remembering your last menstrual period and date of conception, then there is even a slight possibility you're carrying twins. Are there twins in your family?'

'Did you say the toilets are across the corridor?' I asked and bolted for the door.

CHAPTER SIX

A large gathering of the Salvation Army, loud brass-instrument playing society, were murdering 'Come All Ye Faithful' to an eager crowd on the pavement below my flat. It was Christmas Eve and I had been celebrating by eating a packet of six Mr Kipling mince pies and picking the chocolate off a mini Yule log.

I had closed the café a day early. Normally I would have taken advantage of the final shopping day before Christmas. There would have been an endless stream of harassed shoppers, looking for a safe haven from the mayhem on the streets, and the tortuous screech of Noddy Holder in every shop doorway. But the past two weeks had been so wholly knackering, with late night shopping and office parties booked into the café. I hadn't had time to floss, let alone come to terms with my shocking discovery.

The phone rang and I answered it nervously, wondering if pregnancy was detectable by the tone of your voice. I tried to sound as young and fun-loving as physically possible.

'Hiya, Mum,' I squeaked.

'Hello, love. Are you all right? You sound a little stressed.'

Good grief, she's a genius, I thought, clearing my throat.

'No, I'm fine, just eating a mince pie and watching *It's A Wonderful Life*.'

'Ooh, wallowing in sentimentality and pigging out. Excellently festive of you, darling. I won't keep you, just checking you're still on for lunch tomorrow.'

I don't think I had ever spent Christmas anywhere other than the family home. It wouldn't be the same without her roast potatoes and onion gravy. I had a mental vision of me telling them my news, whilst we all sit wearing those silly paper hats around a spread-eagled turkey. My stomach lurched. It wasn't that I was scared of their reaction. Mum was modern and non-judgemental. My girlfriends at school had been hugely jealous, and all my boyfriends fancied her. I knew she wouldn't stress about me being a single mum. She's also one of these embarrassing women that peers into complete strangers' prams, cooing and smiling, with that doey, watery expression only the deeply maternal can achieve. I was sure that once my parents knew, Mum would spring into action, planning the route to the labour ward and signing up for a Mothercare World store card. She'd want me to be delighted, but I wasn't sure I could summon up the facial expressions to convince her I was.

'Of course I'm coming, Mum,' I singsonged.

'Do you want me to pick up one of those nut roasts from M&S? I'm just about to go.'

A hopelessly stereotypical veggie meal but I didn't care. Mum had bought me one of these every year since I became a vegetarian. It was almost as traditional as the turkey.

'Actually, would you mind if you got me a cauliflower cheese? Just for a change.'

She went silent for a second then said suspiciously, 'But you hate cauliflower cheese, love.'

'Well, I don't know, I just fancy it.'

'If you say so,' she said, not sounding convinced.

Like I said, she's a bloody genius.

By the time we had said our goodbyes I had a paranoid feeling that she had seen straight through me. One change of main course and that's me rumbled. I couldn't understand it.

The phone rang almost the instant I had replaced it on the cradle. This time it was Maggie.

'Can I come round?' she said in a wobbly voice.

'Of course you can, I'm not up to much.'

'I'll be straight over,' she said, hanging up before I had a chance to say any more.

Five minutes later she burst into the flat, out of breath and flung herself on the sofa.

'You won't believe what my mother's gone and done now . . .' she ranted in between deep breaths.

I fetched her a cold can of coke from the fridge and put it in her sweaty hand. 'Go on.'

'She's just announced she's getting married!'

'Married? She hasn't even been seeing anyone, has she?' I plonked down next to her, confused.

'She swears it was love at first sight. One of the cronies from her amateur dramatics society apparently. Don something or other. God, it's disgusting, isn't it?' She spat venomously.

'Maybe this will calm her down,' I offered, trying to be helpful. 'She might not feel the need to prove that she's young and attractive if she's got a man. She might stay at home more and stop flirting with your friends.'

'Shit! You could be right,' she cried, sitting up and looking instantly more perky. 'I hadn't thought of it like that. You're so clever.' She patted me affectionately on the knee.

I smiled back at her. 'So, when's the happy occasion?'

'First Saturday in April. It's going to be a big do unfortunately, white dress, the whole bit. She even wants me to be a bridesmaid, can you believe it? It'll be horrendous! Then they're going straight off to Las Vegas for the honeymoon.' She stuck her fingers down her throat, 'How tacky can you get! Rod Stewart's playing a gig there during their stay. Don's bought them tickets. He's a big fan too, apparently. Ugh! Probably looks just like him, knowing Mum. By the way, you're invited to the evening function, they're having a big buffet party at the Royal Hotel and she wants you to make the wedding cake, if you're interested.'

'Really? Oh wow, I've never done one of those before, I'd love to!' I bounced on the sofa in delight.

I'd always wanted to have a go at wedding cakes.

60

Not the traditional Dame Edna's ball gown style, but the more up to date, personal type. My mind flashed instant images of me all glammed up standing next to some fabulous culinary creation, surrounded by admirers.

Plus weddings were excellent opportunities for casual drunken snogging. I smiled dreamily at the thought.

Mags caught the expression on my face and tutted, 'Well at least someone's excited about the whole thing! Anyway, Holly, I'm sorry to go on, it's just a bit much to take in, that's all. How've you been, have you been sick this morning?'

Reality brought me back down on the sofa with a bump (literally!). For one brief moment there I'd forgotten I was pregnant. A second mental image of me rudely barged into my chain of thought. I was standing by a wedding cake, in an outfit resembling a marquee whilst balancing an orange juice on my bump. Everyone around me would be that lovely happy drunk where you can still dance without falling over, and still kiss without dribbling. I'd get the occasional pitying look, as if to say, 'poor thing, another statistic, a symptom of our crumbling society and diminishing family values. She'll never get a snog looking like that!'

'I felt fine until you said that,' I muttered. Mags looked at me with pity in her eyes (Oh God, it's started already!).

'What you need is to get outside, hit the shops with your good friend and treat yourself.'

'What, to some folic acid and a nursing bra?' I

sniped. Self-pity washed over me like a suffocating wave.

She hauled me up out of the sofa and fetched my bag, 'Come on, I know just the thing for you.'

Maggie weaved through the crowded narrow streets like a heat-seeking missile. She marched straight past Oasis and Jigsaw without even a sidelong glance, and guided me away by the elbow when I faltered outside Warehouse.

'Where are we going?' I whined like an impetuous child. She hushed me into silence before I could add, 'Are we nearly there yet?' Before I had time to suss out what was happening, she bustled me through a shop doorway. I looked around, disorientated. In front of me stood a large fake tree with round blinking eyes, laughing to itself. A three-foot owl sitting on a branch hooted then sang 'Twinkle Twinkle Little Star'. It reminded me of one of the Enid Blyton books, where a group of children would suddenly find themselves transported into a mysterious world of magic and make-believe. Then I looked down and saw a stack of potties and realised it was only Mothercare. I turned to shout at Maggie but she was disappearing towards a shelf laden with fluffy cows.

'Awww, look, Holly, aren't they cute?' She picked one from the display and held it up to my face, making a loud 'moo, moo' noise. I pushed it away, embarrassed by her, and then I spied a cuddly Miffy toy and squealed with joy.

'Oh wow, do you remember these?' I picked one up and gave it a squeeze. 'I used to have all the books, and a Miffy lunch box.' Maggie laughed at me and carried on exploring the store. I followed close by, still clutching my Miffy. She stopped next to a row of outfits and picked one from the rail. It was the dinkiest dress I'd ever seen. I stroked the fleecy fabric. It was so cute, a deep pink with little daisies on it. Mags rummaged around then passed me an even dinkier outfit. It was a cream romper suit, with floppy velvet ears attached to the hood. We both made a high pitch 'Ahhhhh' noise, making two young mums look up at us, laughing.

Maggie noticed them and said, 'Hi.' Then gestured at me explaining, 'It's all new to her at the moment. She only found out a couple of weeks ago.'

I could feel myself going crimson and tried to subtly kick her. Unfortunately my foot struck a little boy instead. He yelped in surprise and ran to grab his mother's legs.

Luckily she didn't notice and smiled at me, saying, 'Congratulations! Gosh, I didn't go in a baby shop for months after I found out. I think I was in denial.'

Her friend laughed and joined in. 'Oh, I was worse. Cried for four months solid and panicked right up until the birth.' She peered down at the few strands of spiky hair poking out from about forty layers of blankets and smiled proudly. 'I wouldn't change him for the world though.'

'Me neither,' said the first woman, cuddling her now crying child. 'Anyway, good luck.' They sauntered off happily, leaving me to gaze after the pram and the terrified little boy.

63

'I think I need some air,' I whispered and walked to the nearest exit.

I leaned against a wall, breathing deeply. Trying to gain composure. Maggie came out moments later.

'There you are. I got you something,' she said, smiling, and handed me a bag. Inside was the cuddly Miffy I had been holding. 'Come on, let's go buy a drink.'

We sat in a bar by the window, drinking cappuccinos. People passed by on the street outside, laden with last-minute presents and jumbo rolls of wrapping paper.

'Thanks, Maggie,' I said after a long pause.

'What for?'

'For trying to help.'

She tutted, shaking her head. 'My plan didn't exactly work though, did it? I think I succeeded in giving you a panic attack and a fear that you may have a deep-seated child abuse tendency.'

'That was an accident, I was aiming at you! Anyway, you did me a favour. I can see what you were trying to do and you've got a point. It's not all about me and my relationship with Tom, there's a baby involved too. And it's not all awful. I mean, so it's not how I wanted to have kids.' I sighed, stirring my coffee and watching as the bubbles popped and disappeared. 'It's not even close. But it's a baby all the same, and I need to get my head around it pretty sharpish because it won't just go away. It'll just take a little while, that's all, it's a lot to take in.

I've been imagining all kinds of horror scenarios,' I confessed with a hollow laugh. 'Like what if Tom gets frightened off and stays abroad? Or even worse thinks I engineered the situation to trap him. What if he leaves me to cope alone? I'll be a single mum. Having a baby is as much a turn-on as a boil on your bottom lip. No man would go near me. I'd never have sex again! But you're right. It shouldn't just be about that, and I can't keep denying what's happening.' I smiled and stared out of the window at a couple with a pushchair trying to cross the road. 'I was kind of hoping that it was a big mix-up. That I had inadvertently swallowed a pumpkin seed whilst I was cooking soup in the restaurant over Halloween. Somehow it had got trapped in my lower intestine and was sprouting and giving off some kind of plant-like gas that made me swell up and throw up. It could have caused a chemical imbalance that had even fooled the tester kit. I was holding some false hope that I'd have my first scan and the nurse would say, "Sorry, love, you don't seem to be having a baby after all. This looks more like a pumpkin plant to me."'

Maggie choked on her coffee and let out a deep belly laugh. 'Oh Holly. It's true what they say about pregnancy shrinking your brain and making you weird. I think we'd better go and buy you a book. Fill your head with useful facts, instead of this odd vegetable nonsense.'

We grabbed our coats and headed to the big bookstore on the corner of the street.

65

CHAPTER SEVEN

I woke up on Christmas morning feeling like someone had sneaked up on me in the night, poured quickset concrete into my ears then Sellotaped my head to the pillow. I just couldn't muster up the strength to lift myself up.

I had gone to bed at some ungodly hour the night before. Alice, Mags and Shelley had come over for a pre-Christmas drink. I had allowed myself one glass of mulled red wine, but had been haunted with images of a drunken hiccuping foetus and reverted to fruit juice. We had sat up late into the night, talking predominantly about babies. We had scoured my new Dr Miriam Stoppard pregnancy bible and the booklets I had been given at the surgery and we wallowed in weird and wonderful facts.

I was flabbergasted that they had all seemed jealous of me. Even Maggie had run off to find a ruler so that they could see exactly how big one inch was (length of a foetus up to eight weeks old, according to Dr Miriam). They had held it up to my abdomen in wonderment, exclaiming, 'Ooh, it's like a little tadpole!' You could practically hear the collective tick of their biological clocks, present in the air like background music. Shelley had read out the symptoms that I could be suffering, asking which of them I had experienced so far.

'Ooh, this is weird,' she said, reading out the last one. 'Some expectant mothers experience a heightened and more accurate sense of smell. It has been suggested that this is a throwback from our primitive ancestors where smell played a key role in sensing danger or spoiled food, enabling the mother to better protect her unborn child.'

'Yes, that's me,' I'd cried, excited that there was an explanation for all the smells I had been plagued with. 'That explains why my hands always smell of onions!' The girls had all wrinkled up their noses in disgust, but I liked the thought of having an almost animal-like sense of smell. It was like going back to nature, being at one with mother earth. I wondered if I'd also develop night vision, or an ability to predict weather according to the orientation of the hairs on the back of my hand.

Lying awake after they had gone, I realised that instead of feeling ashamed of my predicament, I felt proud. After all, I told myself, pregnancy is the ultimate feminine act. A symbol of womanhood and that all my parts are in fine working order.

I managed to get myself out of bed by rolling on to the floor and using the bedside table to steady myself. I shuffled over to my little plastic Christmas tree and sat on the floor next to the presents that my friends had left the night before. It seemed strange to open presents alone. I wouldn't have to fix a smile on my face and open them delicately, trying not to crumple the paper. I could just steam-roller through them if I wanted, ripping the paper off mercilessly, then go straight on to the next one. I could even pull a face if I wanted, or say 'ugh!' out loud, how liberating! Maybe I ought to take them with me to Mum's and open them there.

The thought of Mum's made me think of Christmas dinner. Cauliflower cheese, oh God, I've got to have you! My mouth watered in anticipation. Then I imagined something even more exciting; I could follow it up with a juicy summer fruit pudding. Oh yes, now we were talking! My eyes started watering then. I could actually have cried with yearning. Shit. Where the hell was I going to find a summer fruit pudding in the middle of winter, let alone on Christmas Day? There was an Indian mini-mart a few doors down that never closed for Christian holidays. I fetched my purse and coat and shot out of the flat.

I could see lights on in the shop and burst through the door like a marathon runner charging through the ribbon at the finish line. I waved my hands in the air, mouthing 'YES!'

The shop manager poked his head around the store room door.

'Summer pudding?' I ventured desperately.

He laughed to himself. 'You mean Christmas pudding, Miss Piper. Next to raisins on far shelf,' he said, gesturing behind me.

'No. Summer pudding. Have you got any in

the freezer?' I urged. He laughed again, shaking his head.

'It's Christmas Day, Miss Piper. You want Christmas pudding,' he insisted, trying to guide me to the right shelf. This was getting beyond annoying. I shook him off and dashed to the freezer section. I tossed aside the French bread pizzas and frozen peas. There wasn't even an apple pie. Mr Mistry stood watching, finding me a great source of entertainment. I pushed past him, grabbing a loaf of white sliced bread and a packet of fruit pastilles, dumping them on the counter and muttering, 'This'll have to do.'

Mr Mistry took my money, still laughing to himself. As I left the shop I could hear him say, 'You English eccentrics. It was never this much fun in Delhi.'

I went straight back to the flat and rustled up a fruit pastille sandwich. Then I realised I was still wearing my pyjamas.

By the time I arrived at my parents' house my stomach was as knotted as a string bag. Mum answered the door and gave me a big hug. As usual she looked amazing, in a willowy bohemian, no make-up kind of way. I was undeniably jealous. Weren't mothers supposed to look at their daughters' fresh youth and unblemished complexions and feel a small stab of jealousy? My mother probably wondered where on earth she'd gone wrong.

'Hello, babes, merry Christmas!' she said, ushering me in as Floyd, the family cat, rubbed around my legs, almost tripping me over. I followed Mum into

69

the living room and Floyd, bored after discovering I wasn't about to feed him, trotted off towards the kitchen, nose raised to the smell of the roasting turkey.

'I'm in the kitchen cooking the dinner. Come and say hello to Dad and Nanna,' Mum said.

My dad was sitting in an armchair with a large glass of whisky and a cigar. I gave him a quick peck on the cheek, trying to subtly squeeze my nostrils shut as I did it before the smell hit the back of my throat and made me queasy.

My only surviving grandparent was sitting by the log fire, all hunched up like Yoda.

'Hiya, Nanna,' I greeted, and kissed her forehead. She made a throaty grunt noise and joined dad by lighting a cigar. Ever since my grandpa had died she had taken up smoking them, she said the smell reminded her of 'the old bugger'. Nanna had always been quite foul-tempered. She was never out and out rude, more critical and prone to quoting outdated pearls of wisdom. It drove my mum spare and I decided it would be best to hold out with my bombshell until dad had taken her back to her flat.

I parked myself on the floor and toasted my hands in front of the fire.

'You'll get piles sitting on the floor, little missy,' Nanna piped up, 'and where are your slippers? You can't be comfy in those workmen's boots.'

'She's fine, Doris,' my mum interjected, sounding strained already. She handed me a generous glass of wine, saying, 'Have one of these, love, you know I hate drinking alone.'

I couldn't argue with her as she'd already poured it out, so I guiltily took a sip, vowing to pour the rest in a pot plant when she wasn't looking.

'Is she old enough to drink yet?' asked Nanna, sipping sherry and frowning.

No one answered her.

Mum stood at the living room door and said to me, 'You couldn't help me set the table, could you, love?' Winking as though she was in a pantomime.

I excused myself from the room and we ran to the kitchen, giggling like naughty St Trinians in a dormitory.

'I thought I'd better rescue you before she started moaning about "kids these days",' Mum said, taking off Nanna's wobbly West Country accent perfectly. She poured me out another glass of wine and basted the turkey. I had a sneaking suspicion that Mum was drunk.

It seemed that once her children were past that age of enchantment, getting blotto whilst cooking Christmas dinner was the highlight of festivities for the hard-working matriarch. She tried to top and tail a brussel sprout but it catapulted off the table and hit Floyd on the head. She doubled over at the kitchen table, laughing until she had to wipe tears away with the corner of a tea towel.

I took the chopping knife out of her hand, saying, 'Maybe I should take over now.'

'No, no, don't be silly. There's only a couple of the bleeders left. Now where are they?' She peered under the table and fell off her chair. 'Whoopsieee,'

71

she singsonged, picking herself up again. 'Don't know what's wrong with me today.' She gave up on the sprout hunt and put the ones she had already peeled in the steamer. The homely smells from the oven were making me ravenous, I didn't think I could wait much longer. I chewed nervously on a vegetable peeling and Mum plonked herself down opposite me.

'So,' she said, draining her wine glass, and topping it back up again. 'Any news?'

'What? I mean, why do you ask?' I stammered, taken aback.

'Just being motherly, sweetheart. Can't I take an interest in your busy life? I guess you do seem a little edgy though, and I noticed you shut the café yesterday. It's not like you to have a day off.' She furrowed her brow and looked me straight in the eye, making me fidget nervously. 'Is it Tom?' she asked gently. 'You must miss him a lot.'

I sighed heavily; I must have 'pining miserably' written on my forehead.

'No, it's not Tom. Well, maybe it is indirectly. Actually, there is something you should know.'

She nodded encouragingly. 'You can tell me anything, love,' she said, then hiccuped and giggled.

'Maybe I should leave it 'til tomorrow.'

'No, go on,' she insisted.

The kitchen door swung open and Nanna shuffled in.

I sat back in my seat; the suspense of the moment had vanished.

Nanna was very frail and slow. She could only

72

just manage to walk across the kitchen floor without falling over. It was difficult to resist the urge to take her arm and guide her. Anybody foolish enough to attempt that would soon wish they'd never bothered. She insisted that she was as physically capable as she always had been.

'Do you need any help, Louise?' she asked my mum.

'No thanks. It's all done,' Mum said and fetched her a chair. Nanna headed straight past the chair and started to wash up.

'Really, Doris, it's fine. We've got a dishwasher for that.' Mum's voice was blunt. She never did have much patience with Gran. Especially in the kitchen.

'Oh, you don't want to be running up your meter with one of those things. You want to do the job properly,' she insisted, dunking a plate in the grimy water. 'Got any soda crystals?'

Mum was halfway through speeding her head towards the kitchen table when the oven timer bleeped, saving her a great deal of pain.

'Is that the phone?' Nanna asked. 'You sit there girls, I'll get it,' and shuffled off out of the room.

I leapt up, spurred on by the thought of my cauliflower cheese, and began dishing the vegetables into serving bowls.

We all sat around the table, greedily eyeing the festive food and waiting politely for Nanna to get comfy. Dad opened another bottle of wine, much to my dismay and my mother's encouragement.

I fiddled nervously with a napkin that Mum had

73

folded into the shape of a water lily. I never could see the point of napkins. We used them once a year and I never missed them during any other hundreds of meals. I wasted a couple of minutes trying to decide where to put it. If I left it on my lap it would only fall annoyingly on the floor half a dozen times. I started to tuck it into my trousers, but stopped abruptly when I realised it would draw attention to my mini-bump. I wondered if it would be impolite to blow my nose on it. Nanna tucked hers into the collar of her blouse in the manner of a baby's bib and with a shaking hand, picked up a carving knife the size of a machete saying, 'Shall I be mother?'

'NO!' Mum and Dad shouted in unison, leaping out of their seats to disarm her.

'I'll do it,' said Dad, gesturing for us all to be seated. Carving meat and manning the barbecue were as close to cooking as Dad had ever got. It didn't seem fair to rob him of the privilege. We all sat down obligingly, and I began dishing out my vegetarian meal.

'What on earth's that?' asked Dad.

'Cauli' cheese,' I answered, trying not to dribble on the roast potatoes.

'Good God, you're not pregnant are you?' he joked, winking at Mum.

I sat gobsmacked, looking from one parent to the other, my mouth working like a landed trout.

'How did you, how could you possibly . . .'

Dad's face changed from flippant joviality, to a Jeremy Paxman type of quizzical.

74

Mum drew in such an enormous breath I thought that she would soon float away, then she said, 'Oh my God. That's what you were going to tell me in the kitchen.' She slapped her hand over her mouth. 'Is it Thomas's? Oh you poor thing.'

The emotion in her voice was all it took to start me blubbing uncontrollably.

Dad said, 'She can't be,' in a tone that suggested it hadn't occurred to him that I'd started having sex.

'Bloody hell fire!' croaked Nanna. 'You're still at school!'

'I'm twenty-seven!' I sobbed, wiping my face on the napkin. Mum came to me, hugging me tightly, whilst Dad and Nanna stared awkwardly at us.

'So, who wants stuffing?' asked Dad, trying to break the ice. Mum, never one to miss a well-timed innuendo, burst into hysterical laughter and asked Dad to pour her another glass of wine.

The meal became a confused occasion. Dad said even less than normal, Nanna kept looking at me, her nose wrinkled with disdain, and Mum had to bite her lip for fear of bursting into an excited grin. She struggled to be concerned and sensitive about my situation, yet had to practically sit on her hands to restrain from leaping in the air shouting, 'Yes, a little baby! A sweet little bundle of joy. Yipee-yi-yay!'

It had transpired that Mum had craved cauliflower cheese throughout her pregnancy. She had even made Dad drive to a local restaurant, where the owners were clearing up after a late night, and persuade them to open up and sell him some. A bizarre coincidence that was my undoing. It also served to convince Mum that I must also be having a girl.

After dinner we swapped presents around the tree. Nanna had bought me a nightie, not unlike the one Florence Nightingale must have worn.

'Won't fit you for long now,' she said, looking disappointed.

She opened her presents from Mum, Dad and myself, nodding and grunting at the lavender bath salts, hankies and electric footwarmer. The atmosphere was awkward and I sensed Mum and Dad had a lot of questions they were withholding whilst Nanna was still around. I busied myself by making a fuss of Floyd and avoiding Mum's worried gaze.

Eventually Dad got up and offered Nanna a lift home.

As soon as they had driven away, Mum collared me for a woman-to-woman chat. We sat opposite each other over mugs of tea, like Smith and Jones.

'Have you managed to get hold of Tom?' she probed, looking at me with sad and sympathetic eyes.

'Mum, I don't even know which country he's in.'

'Don't his parents know?'

I shrugged my shoulders. 'I haven't asked them.'

'Don't you think he should know, love?' she said softly.

'I can't tell him. I don't even know how he feels about me, let alone fatherhood. I've only had one postcard since he left, and that may as well have

76

been written to his bank manager for all the emotion he put in it.' I dabbed at a rogue tear that gathered in the corner of my eye. 'I don't want him to feel duty bound to support me. He could end up resenting me.'

'If you at least let him have all the facts, he could make up his own mind.'

I shook my head. 'I can't do it, Mum. I'm going to deal with this on my own. Besides, I've got seven months left. I can tell him anytime. He saved up for years for this trip. I'm not going to ruin it for him when he's only just set off.'

Mum took my hands in hers and squeezed them. 'It's your decision, honey. I'll support you any way I can.'

I thanked her for being so understanding, and then she finally let herself burst.

'Oh darling, a little baby. It's so exciting. You're going to be a wonderful mum. I can't wait.' She then leapt up and went to the kitchen drawer, retrieving a pad and two pencils. 'Now,' she said scribbling furiously. 'Let's see what you'll need for your layette. We'll have to hit the January sales with your father's credit cards.'

I relaxed a little then, the weight on my shoulders had lightened considerably and I let Mum's infectious excitement take over.

When I got home from Mum's there were two messages for me on the answering machine. The first was from Alice.

'Happy Christmas, Holly!' she had cheered at the

77

phone. I could faintly detect carol singing in the background. 'I forgot to tell you last night, Oliver's having a New Year's Eve bash at his place. Hope you can come. I'll call you tomorrow. By the way, thanks for the pressie, 'bye.' That reminded me, I still hadn't unwrapped the gifts under my tree. I went to fetch them then I curled up on the sofa, listening to the second message.

'Hello love, it's Fiona, Tom's mum.' My hands froze on the wrapping paper. 'Just called to wish you a merry Christmas. Don't want you thinking we've forgotten you, just because Tom's out of town. Marcus and I are having a little get together on New Years Day, we'd love to see you, if you're free. Bring a friend, darling, it starts at twelve,' she added and rang off.

Shit! Shit! Shit! I panicked, what shall I do? I had to tell them some time. Fiona was always popping in the restaurant. It would soon become obvious I was expecting their grandchild. Then again the counter is quite high, maybe if I just stood behind a large gâteau . . . No, it wouldn't work. What if they insisted on contacting Tom? Or Tom phoned them and they couldn't help blurting it out. It was too awful to contemplate. I shook these intrusive thoughts from my head, and opened my presents. The first one was from Alice. It was a thick encyclopaedic book on pregnancy and childcare. I opened the pages randomly and read the first paragraph.

New mothers often feel they need to prove their

78

capability, turning down offers of help as a matter of pride. You must learn to accept help when it is offered. As the weeks go on, your energy will dwindle and you will become grateful for willing volunteers. Grandparents in most cases can offer you valuable support. It will help you both physically and mentally to share your experiences with them. Not only will you benefit from the time out they can offer you, but you will also be giving them the joyful opportunity to develop a strong bond with their grandchild.

I snapped the book shut and opened Maggie's present instead. Inside the wrapping was a basket of hand-picked goodies, all with a stress-busting theme. There was a small bottle of Bachs rescue remedy, a jojoba massage oil, some aromatherapy bath oil, a herbal drink with added ginseng, a Toblerone and *The Little Book Of Calm*.

Half an hour later I sank into my aromatic bath, washed the Toblerone stains off my face, opened my *Little Book of Calm*, downed the herbal drink in one and fell asleep in the suddy water.

CHAPTER EIGHT

It was New Year's Eve and I was sitting on a stool in Oliver's kitchen, surrounded by so many colourful balloons I felt like I was sitting in one of those children's ball pits. I rubbed my feet, cursing my choice of four-inch heels. It had taken me hours to get ready, trying new and ingenious ideas to hide my little bump. Unfortunately it was that awkward bicycle tyre size, where it just looked like a sign of Christmas over-indulgence. I had resigned myself to wearing the dress I had bought for my Great Auntie June's funeral last year. It was knee-length and loose-fitting, and about as flattering as a bin-bag. I had piled my hair up, and added the heels to try and create a longer, leaner silhouette, but nothing could salvage my self-esteem tonight.

I squirmed around in my seat, trying to surreptitiously rearrange my bra, pondering on whether Wonderbras were in fact bad for the swelling maternal bosom. Being a mere 34B, when I had joyously discovered what a Wonderbra could do for an uninspiring chest, I bought half a dozen, and never looked back again (and my boobs never looked down again, either!). Unfortunately, now they felt like boulders and were as tender as a fresh bruise. I couldn't help wondering if I should opt for something more matronly. A bra with straps like seat belts, fashioned from breathable canvas, would probably be a midwife's recommendation. Still, what was the point in fighting it when my chances of ever feeling sexy again were minimal?

I sighed a hefty sigh and sipped my Coke. I had spent most of the party perched on this stool, sulking and watching the high-spirited guests breeze by, all rosy-cheeked from alcohol and sexual promise.

Mind you, despite the fact that I would far rather be as carefree and drunken as most of the other guests, being sober and sitting on the sidelines did have distinct advantages. I enjoyed that smug feeling of being in complete control, as everyone around me was losing theirs. I adopted a superior expression that I hoped was saying, 'I don't need to get drunk to have a good time. I am a sophisticated, mysterious woman, and am beyond such triviality.' Who was I trying to kid!

Mags hurried up to me, beaming with excitement.

'Come on, babe, it's New Year's Eve! Gish a smile.'

I eyed her jealously. She looked absolutely gorgeous. Her tight Miss Sixties dress hugged her neat little waist and accentuated her hour-glass curves. Her dark curls hung loosely down her back, a complete sex goddess if ever there was one. She

81

leaned on my shoulder, the way friends always do when they're pissed, 'Hot male totty at three o'clock,' she whispered, gesturing at a man helping himself to a beer from the fridge. 'Apparently he works in computing, but with a bum like a ripe peach I could overlook a minor detail.'

'I thought you were having a thing with Noah?' I said grumpily.

She rolled her eyes, looking bored. 'That was a one-night thing. I think I'm ready for a change of scenery.'

'I heard that, you floozy,' said Alice, who'd just joined us. She reached over to the table I was sitting next to and helped herself to a filo parcel. 'Actually, when I was helping Ol decorate the house for tonight, I had a bit of a chat with Noah.' She raised her eyebrows, waiting for some encouragement to continue. Maggie yawned, and didn't take her eyes off the computer guy. Alice gave up waiting and continued. 'He really likes you. He told me if you weren't so scary he'd ask you out to dinner, but he had a feeling you didn't "do" dinner.'

'He's got that right,' Maggie said, then noticed my disapproving face and went on, 'I don't see why it's so bad that I want to be single. I'm still young. I'm enjoying myself too much to want the whole burden of a relationship. I'm not looking for the love of my life. I don't want the whole dull marriage and babies stuff. No offence, Hol,' she said quickly. 'To be honest, I wish I did want all those things. But I don't think it's for me.'

'You could at least set Noah straight,' I said,

still reeling about the fact that she said having babies was dull. How dare she! I was having a great time.

She smirked. 'Look. Men have treated women like shit for centuries. They've been shagging around, making crappy excuses about genetics and that hunter-gatherer bollocks. I don't see why I can't strike a blow for womankind and give them a taste of what they've been dishing up for us for so long. Can I help it if I'm a child of the sexual revolution, a woman of the new millennium?'

'You're not a woman of the millennium, you're a man of the sodding fifties with that kind of talk. There's nothing modern about you; women have been saying the same thing for years. I can't see why treating people like crap, no matter what sex you are, can be disguised as some kind of post-modernist statement. It's a poor excuse for being a spineless tart. Male or female. You'll end up just like your mum, trying to prove to yourself that you're attractive by hooking up with as many men as you can, and never really knowing any of them. ' As soon as I had started ranting I knew it was a bad idea, but the words followed one another like cascading dominoes.

When I rattled to a stop, Alice and Maggie were both gawping at me like adolescents who'd stumbled on a strip show. Then Mags said the worst thing possible – nothing. She stared at me for a couple of seconds, long enough for me to see the hurt in her eyes, then picked up her drink and stalked off.

83

Alice voiced my private thoughts. 'Oh shit, you've really done it now!'

After half an hour of searching for Mags I could only assume she had gone home. No one had seen her since my verbal attack.

I pushed past a group of rowdy women who were playing some kind of drinking game. Two of them were standing, one was sitting and they were taking it in turns to bellow out something incoherent and down their drinks, slamming their glasses on the table. You couldn't look at them without getting an eyeful of tits and bums, but their faces were alive with various animated expressions. I felt like a prude in comparison; I was too sober and conservatively dressed. Even though in my clear-headed state they looked loud and daft, I couldn't help wishing I was like that tonight. All girls together, not giving a shit about the whole, I-need-a-man-to-feel-truly-fulfilled crap. I saw Alice waving at me from the other end of the room and went to join her.

'Still no sign,' I said to her. 'How about you?'

'Nothing. She must have got a taxi back to her flat. I tried calling her but there was no answer.' She checked her watch: 'There's only ten minutes to go until midnight. I can't find Oliver either.'

Noah came to join us, nursing a bottled lager and looking unusually miserable.

'Have either of you seen Maggie?'

Alice and I both rolled our eyes skyward. 'It's like the bloody missing persons bureau here,' I

84

said. Noah looked puzzled. 'Have you seen Oliver?' I asked him.

'No, not for hours, thinking about it. Let's go check outside, they might have gone for a breather.'

The three of us pushed through the gathering crowd and walked out into the street. A couple sat under a streetlight kissing passionately, but under close scrutiny they didn't look familiar. We looked up and down the steep slope of the street but nothing stirred. The party noises grew louder as midnight loomed. There was something about the strike of midnight that made you feel you had to be looking deeply into the eyes of someone you loved, or be single and huddled in a throng of similarly single friends. It was symbolic of what the coming year would hold for you. There was something tragically lonely about watching the telly alone, sitting on the toilet, or standing out in a deserted street when Big Ben was bonging. I couldn't bear the thought of starting the year so badly, pregnant and deserted, with the guilt of my argument with Mags hanging over me. I had to make up with her before the year was over. There was too much self-inflicted pressure to be happy at this moment. I knew Alice wanted to be in Oliver's arms in approximately three minutes' time. It was obvious that Noah had similar romantic plans about Maggie. There was an air of desperation hanging between us as time ticked on.

'Oh fuck it!' said Noah kicking the front wheel of Shelley's decaying Hillman Imp. 'I really wanted to be with her.' Alice and I went to him, giving him a pat on the arm and a small squeeze, in a shared moment of mutual understanding.

Suddenly there was the unexpected sound of metal groaning, as if under a great strain. We looked around and saw Shelley's car trundling backwards down the hill, gathering momentum as it went.

'Oh bollocks!' shouted Noah, who sprinted after the runaway car. I stood watching in horror as it made a beeline for Oliver's recently acquired and rather lovely Alfa Romeo.

'TEN . . . NINE . . . EIGHT . . . SEVEN,' chanted several hundred people in the various house parties and pubs nearby as the two cars impacted. Oliver's car crumpled in at the front, filled itself with activated twin air bags and drowned out the countdown as its security alarm screamed in protest.

We ran down the street to where the cars were knitted together.

'Shit,' said Alice, covering her mouth with her hands and staring at the damage. 'Oliver is gonna go spare. Poor babe loves this car!'

'La la la la la bum bum, la la la la la la bum bum . . .' sang a large snake of drunken people who were conga-ing out of Oliver's front door and up the short garden path. 'Ooh, look at that!' one of the men near the front exclaimed and wove the conga towards us.

It was at that point that the back door of the Alfa Romeo was thrown open and out fell the little giggly redhead that I had seen Oliver flirting with at his last party. Only this time she wasn't giggling, and it wasn't just her hair that was red. She tugged her

86

mini dress back to a decent length and whispered sheepishly, 'Can somebody call an ambulance.'

'What the hell's going on?' cried Alice, barging over to the open car door. I followed behind her, and the crowd conga-ed closer, blowing the occasional party hooter. There, sitting in the back of the car, with his trousers around his ankles and his hands covering his tackle, was Oliver. He groaned in pain, and a small trickle of blood worked its way down his forehead.

CHAPTER NINE

The first day of the rest of the year had started badly and was plummeting steadily downhill from there. I was in my car, heading for Marcus and Fiona Delanci's New Year's Day buffet. I had considered making my excuses and hiding at the flat, but there was a remote chance that Alice would turn up and I couldn't bear to miss her.

Last night, before it all went horribly pear-shaped, I had convinced Alice to be my 'friend' for the buffet. Alice was so sweet and reliable it would be unheard of for her to let me down without so much as a phone call. After she had unfortunately been brutally confronted with the truth about Oliver's infidelity, she had surprised us all.

Standing at the door of Oliver's car, a crowd had gathered. The conga line had disassembled, realising that the mood was a little too sober for mad drunken dancing. All eyes were on Alice, waiting for a reaction. I badly wanted to steer her away from the awful sight and lavish her with comfort, but this was her call, her time to give him hell, the piece of shit!

Alice opened her mouth to speak and the crowd held their breath.

'Are you okay?' she asked, with genuine concern.

ARE YOU OKAY?!! Had she taken leave of her senses? I mean Alice had always been too nice for her own good, but this was beyond nice, it was positively masochistic!

Oliver had tried to shake his head in response to her question, and had winced in pain.

'I think I'll call you an ambulance,' she said, and had walked back into the house. I followed close behind, begging her to slow down and talk to me, but she charged ahead like a robot. 'I need the loo,' she whispered, ducking into the downstairs toilet and locking the door behind her.

After ten minutes outside the door, willing her to let me in and pacing up and down, I was getting really worried. Outside I saw that an ambulance had arrived and Oliver was being carried on board, sporting an enormous neck brace and a pink cellular blanket. The redhead climbed in with him, holding his hand.

'Come on, Al, please, I'm worried about you.' Still only silence answered me back.

Simon hurried over to me. He hunted around in his trouser pockets and pulled out a fifty-pence piece, saying 'It's alright, Holly, I'll get her out with this.'

I stared daggers at him, shocked at his insensitivity. 'I don't think she's in the mood for bribery, Simon,' I spat.

He laughed and shook his head. 'Durr! It's a safety

89

lock, you berk! You can open it from the outside.' He fitted the coin into a slot in the door handle, turning it around. I stared at the door, feeling foolish when it swung open effortlessly. No need for a battering ram and the Bath rugby team after all.

We peered into the room but she wasn't there. I walked in, looking around the door. No tear stained Alice curled in a foetal position on the floor, just a toilet, a sink and an open window. A wide-open window. Alice had done a runner.

Simon and I had walked the streets looking for both Alice and Maggie, exhausting all possibilities, until he decided I needed to rest and took me back to my flat.

We had tried Maggie's flat but there was no answer, and had walked past Alice's house, but saw no sign of life.

The problem with Alice's house is she lives with her elderly mother. Her father had died a few years earlier and as Alice is their only child that hadn't moved abroad, she felt a responsibility to live at home and look after her mother. Although I had a sneaking suspicion that her mum was quite capable of looking after herself, despite her best efforts to convince Alice otherwise.

She was a puritanical woman, who was under the false impression that Alice was a teetotal, church-going virgin who happened to sleep over at my place a lot. The shock could have finished her off for good.

Fortunately she liked me. Owning a vegetarian

café was passable in her eyes, abstinence for morality's sake being something she could identify with. Unfortunately, Alice was banned from having anything to do with Maggie, who had made the mistake of wearing fishnets and singing 'Like A Virgin' on their porch when she was thirteen years old.

What I found sad, was that if she really knew Alice, she'd see that she was just the kind of daughter a parent should be proud of, a sensitive, caring type who always considered other people. But she couldn't see past her own rigid beliefs and judgements.

Due to these circumstances we knew we couldn't call at the door of Alice's house. Nor could we call the police, as even if they had taken us seriously, the first place they would try would be the family home. So, I spent the rest of the night sitting in the flat, chewing my nails down to my wrists.

Since then there had still been no sign of them. I had no idea where my two best friends could be. For that matter I didn't know where the man I loved was, either. Maybe I am just a physically repulsive person, I thought. Maybe they were all living together in a flat in town, drinking champagne and laughing at their brilliantly executed plan to ditch the boring pregnant one and start a new gang.

I pulled into the Delancis' driveway, fighting the need to turn the car around and drive to Mum's, for one of those special, all-encompassing hugs that made me feel five again. I chanted a 'be strong' mantra and parked the car next to Simon's Beetle.

91

I climbed out of my car, thanking God it was so freezing cold as it gave me an excuse to wear a big baggy jumper and a pair of loose trousers (good mini-bump disguise), and I knocked on the imposing double doors.

I loved the Delancis' house. It was a huge, seventeenth-century farmhouse in the country, backing on to woodland and a stream. They were the kind of rich people that didn't need to shove it in your face with designer snobbery and executive cars. Instead they were ordinary people that just happened to have pots and pots of cash.

You'd think that with Marcus working in the interiors industry he'd have a stunning interior. But on the contrary, they appeared to live like pigs! Clutter and mess littered the house, making it permanently look as though it had been ransacked and was being left untouched until the police forensics team arrived. Don't get me wrong, they weren't dirty people, just untidy.

Fiona opened the door and gave me one of those lovely European double kisses that I could never get away with without looking pretentious.

'Happy New Year! It's so lovely to see you, darling, I'm really glad you came. Did you come on your own?' she asked, looking out onto the driveway.

'Well, I was going to come with Alice, but she's been held up. I'm hoping she'll turn up later.'

She put her hands on my cheeks and looked at me properly. 'You do look well, really healthy. But you have tired eyes. I hope you're not working too hard like my Marcus does. That's the trouble with being your own boss, nobody to throw you out when it's time to go home.'

She led me into the house, continuing to talk as she went. 'Tom must be really missing you.'

I made a 'humph' noise. 'I don't think so. He'll have so much to see and do I doubt he's remembered me at all.'

Fiona stopped and took my hands. 'Darling, of course he misses you. He even considered cancelling his trip because of you. Didn't he call you on Christmas Day?' I shook my head, reeling at this revelation. She tutted, 'Shame. He called us in the morning. He was asking if we had seen you, and said he'd call you straight after talking to me. He made me promise to invite you today, not that we needed any encouragement. You're always welcome here. My son's in love alright. He's never been like this about anyone else.'

My heart grew feathery angel's wings and soared and fluttered all around my insides. I couldn't believe what she was saying. Maybe I hadn't screwed up after all. I didn't know whether to laugh gaily and dance around the room like Ginger Rogers, or cry at the missed opportunity of being together and the fear of our impending child extinguishing any feelings he had, like a soaked nappy on a barbecue.

'Holly!' shouted Simon, jumping down the stairs to welcome me. 'Thanks for coming.'

'Well, I'll leave you young people to it, drinks and nibbles are in the sitting room when you're ready,' Fiona said, walking off into the kitchen.

'Any word?' asked Simon.

'Nothing. You?'

He shook his head frowning. 'What do you think we should do?'

'For now I say we hold tight. See if Alice turns up here. Maggie doesn't worry me so much; she often disappears and turns up after a couple of days. She's got plenty of friends who would give her a bed. I just hate her being mad at me for this long. It doesn't feel right.'

Simon gave me a sympathetic smile. 'They'll soon turn up. Just don't worry so much. It's not good for either of you,' he said, eyeing my bump. 'Come on, I guess we'd better mingle.'

We entered the sitting room where most of the guests were chatting away in small, intimate groups. I noticed Marcus immediately. He had a large admiring crowd giving him their fullest attention whilst he recounted some story about a job he'd done recently. He saw me enter the room and excused himself from his mostly female audience.

'Holly my petal, give me a hug,' he greeted, wrapping his arms around me and squeezing me tightly. I tried to make sure it was a side-on hug, in case he detected my larger waistline.

'How's life at the Owl and Pussycat? Are you ready to start a franchise yet? Here's me thinking you'd become as widespread as McDonalds! You'll have to start branching out soon if you want to monopolise the industry.'

I smiled modestly. 'Running one is enough for me to deal with at the moment. I've been so busy lately, I'm finding it hard to keep on top of things. If it stays this busy after Christmas I'll have to take on another cook.'

'That's brilliant,' he congratulated. 'Fi's always on at me to take on extra help. It's difficult to trust someone else with your baby, though, isn't it?'

'That's why I'm so lucky to have Maggie,' I agreed. 'I'd be lost without her.'

'Oh I don't know about that, Holly, you're a natural business woman. You should give yourself some credit. Besides, with a chocolate gâteau recipe like yours, you'll never be without customers.'

His flattery was making me colour up so much I had to look down at the floor to gain composure. Marcus took my hand and led me across the room. 'There's someone I would really love you to meet,' he said, pointing at the back of a woman's head. She had short, spiked blond hair and was standing on her own, looking through the French windows to the garden beyond. He tapped her shoulder. 'Tamsin, I want you to meet Holly Piper, the girl I told you about.'

She turned and looked at me, smiling serenely.

'Holly, this is my little sister Tamsin. She's come down from Edinburgh for a few months. And these beauties,' he said, referring to the two sleeping babies she cradled so easily, 'are her twins, my two nephews Callum and Samuel.'

TWINS! screamed my throbbing brain, remembering what the doctor had said. TWINS! screamed my aching nether regions. No way are you squeezing one of those things through me twice!

95

'Twins!' I said shakily. 'Gosh, how lovely.'

One of the tiny boys smacked his lips contentedly, then lazily opened his eyes and looked at me. He emitted a soft gurgle, then a little whimper, followed by a sad cry, and closely followed by a scream that made my blood feel like liquid nitrogen. I had only ever heard anything remotely similar in Hammer House productions. All this noise not surprisingly woke up his sleeping twin and suddenly the two of them were going at it like a couple of girls at a Boyzone concert. Tamsin rocked them gently, cooing and hushing them with her soft, faintly Scottish accent, but I doubt they could hear their mother over their own din. Nor could they see her with their eyes jammed shut like that.

Tamsin looked at me, obviously embarrassed, and said, 'I'm so sorry about this. They're usually really good. I've only just fed them so it must be wind. Would you mind?' She held one of the bawling boys out for me to take so she could try and wind the other.

'Oh, I don't know, I'm not sure how to. I've never done anything like . . .' It reminded me of the time when I was offered a cigarette at the final year, junior school disco. I looked nervously around me; Marcus had been dragged away by a chatty old lady and everyone else was engrossed in conversation. 'Okay then,' I agreed reluctantly, and after more failed attempts than a jumbo landing in a thunderstorm, and a few anxious instructions on head support from Tamsin, I had successfully manoeuvred the baby into my arms.

I held him upright, stroking his back automatically with his head lolling against my shoulder. It actually wasn't that bad. My body relaxed, loosing its previous tension and reassuring me that the shock hadn't in fact turned me to stone. Little Callum, or was it Samuel, I had forgotten already, ceased his tormented cry and with an intake of breath almost looked as though he would smile. The baby that Tamsin was now sitting supported on her lap had also stopped his wailing and was nearly asleep again as he was rocked back and forth. He parted his lips and burped so loudly a couple of guests turned around and looked at me with disgust.

'That's better,' sighed Tamsin. 'Thanks so much, you're a natural,' she said, gesturing at her drunken-looking son. His head was resting on my chest and his eyes blinked slowly. 'I really need two pairs of hands. I had no idea how complicated it can be having two at once.' She laughed to herself. 'What's funny is when I found out I was having twins I was really excited. I'd only ever wanted two children and I was terrified of giving birth. I figured twins would be the perfect solution. Get two children, yet only endure one labour. What I hadn't expected was an emergency Caesarean. Now I can barely lift up one baby, let alone a pair. The first week back from the hospital I literally crawled about on my hands and knees.'

Don't listen to her; just block it all out, LA LA LA LA, my head was crying as it nodded thoughtfully, encouraging her to continue.

'Unfortunately, I'm on my own now. Their father

97

Oscar, my ex-fiancé freaked out at the thought of being a dad. He left when I was five months gone. Still,' she said, talking to her two boys now, 'who needs him? Not us. We're doing fine on our own, aren't we?' She looked as though she was trying hard to convince herself.

Callum or Samuel stirred, made a wet noise at the back of his throat, then vomited down my chest.

'Oh no, I'm so sorry. Here, have a baby wipe,' Tamsin said, searching her bag to find something for me to clean myself up with.

'It's fine, really,' I forced myself to say through gritted teeth as I felt the warm thick goo trickle further down my cleavage.

'They're hardly ever sick,' she said, taking far too long to find a cloth. 'That's another great advantage of breast-feeding, it's so natural their body hardly ever rejects it.' Great, she's telling me this rancid-smelling stuff that's trickling between my boobs is actually another woman's regurgitated breast milk. UGH!

'Don't worry about the baby wipe, I'll clean off in the bathroom, I need the loo anyway,' I whispered, handing the now sleeping baby back to her. 'Nice to have met you, Tamsin,' I added. A subtle way of saying, 'I'm off now, end of conversation'. Then I hurried away to clean myself up.

I walked out of the bathroom, wondering if it was too early to leave. Everyone was having such a good time I doubt they would have noticed anyway, and it didn't look as though Alice was going to turn up.

98

When I reached the top of the stairs I spotted Tom's cousin Andrew sitting amongst the clutter on the landing and looking down at the people milling in the hallway.

'Andy,' I cried, thankful to see a familiar face, another person who looked as though they weren't fitting in and were skulking about in the background. He jumped in the air like a jack-in-a-box and hid his roll-up behind his back.

'Oh, thank God it's you, thought it was one of the olds for a minute,' he sighed, relieved his habit hadn't been rumbled. 'Want one?' he offered, sitting back down again and taking a deep drag from the spindly cigarette.

'At the moment I'd kill for a fag, but I'd better not, thanks,' I said, sitting down by a pile of fabric samples and swinging my legs through the gap in the banister. I was grinning with delight at the fact that he hadn't considered me one of the 'olds'.

Andy was only fifteen; last time I saw him he was thirteen. There had been an enormous transformation. Our last meeting had been at Tom's grandma's funeral. He had still looked like a boy then, shorter than me and dressed in practical woollens by his mum. Now he towered over me in a gangly awkward pose. His voice was generally broken and low, with the occasional lapse into falsetto, followed by an exaggerated clearing of the throat to cover it up. At his granny's wake he had been full of fun (Granny's death hadn't come as a big surprise, the wake being more of a party than a sad occasion). He had played in the garden with Tom, having

99

header competitions and talking about computer games and technical Lego. Now just talking to me was making him blush a deep sweaty scarlet.

'So, how's Tom?' he asked. 'Haven't seen him since Granny Daisy croaked. Has he been round the world yet?' He exhaled his cigarette smoke and I leaned in, trying to inhale. Surely a pregnant woman couldn't help passive smoking occasionally? After all, I could have been a teacher, then I would have been exposed to a heady toxic environment in the staff room every tea break. Hang on, I thought, experiencing an unusual giddy headrush. That's not tobacco. I had only had one joint in my teenage years, having skilfully avoided peer pressure. But the strange sponge-brained feeling it gave me couldn't be mistaken for anything else. I sat back guiltily, worried that my tiny baby was being affected, and pretended I hadn't noticed.

'Tom went on his trip in November. Having a brilliant time no doubt. And if you ask me if I'm missing him I'll brain you. I'm so fed up with people asking me that.'

Andy took another long drag of his wacky backy. 'Oh man, that's so cool. I'm gonna do that when I'm older. He's a lucky bloke, Tom. He's got the lot, a loaded family, cool flat and a career he can get into whenever he likes. Bet Uncle Marcus takes early retirement soon and gives Tom the business. He'll be minted. He's even got the sexy girlfriend,' he said gesturing at me, then went a deep plum colour when he realised he was getting carried away. 'Man, all he needs is a sports car and he'd have everything

100

a bloke could ever want. Bet you he gets an Elise, when he gets back,' he said knowingly. I hadn't got a clue what he was talking about, but it sounded good so I muttered, 'probably'. My heart was swelling with pride at his appraisal of Tom and being considered sexy by a blossoming fifteen-year-old. I had figured that lads his age would consider anyone the wrong side of twenty-five as over the hill.

I smiled flirtily and he sighed, 'Yep, he's a top bloke, your boyfriend. Anyway, promise you'll stay here, I've gotta just take a piss. Look after this for me,' he said, handing me his joint. 'Finish it off if you like,' he added with a wink, then loped off to the bathroom. I took it gingerly and tried to hold it so that the smoke drifted away from me.

'Holly, what the hell do you think you're doing!' Simon shouted as he walked down the corridor. He snatched the joint out of my hand and threw it out of an open window. 'I can't believe you sometimes,' he barked, looking really disappointed.

'It's not mine,' I whimpered, looking around for Andy to back me up. There was nobody there. He ignored me, his face serious.

'I've been looking for you everywhere. Alice has turned up. She's in the garden.'

101

CHAPTER TEN

She looked terrible. Alice had always had fair skin, but today she looked ghostly white. She sat limply on a garden bench, her straight blond hair almost obscuring her face. Simon's overcoat was draped across her shoulders to protect her from the cold and she was still wearing the short blue dress she'd had on at Oliver's house the night before.

She looked up as I crossed the lawn to join her and I saw that her make-up had created an abstract art effect on her face. Black pools and streaks of mascara under her eyes were highlighted with pink stripes of lipstick that had been wiped off on to her cheeks. She looked like one of the extras you see in hospital dramas that had survived a horrific accident but had witnessed the death of a loved one. My heart broke for her.

'You poor thing,' I said, putting my arm protectively around her. 'I've been so worried about you, what happened?'

'I'm sorry,' she squeaked, sobbing into a man-sized hanky I presumed was Simon's. 'I'm sorry I ran off like that. The last thing you need is to worry about me. I just couldn't bear it. I couldn't bear all those people looking at me, pitying me. It was awful.' She sobbed harder. 'I bet they'd all known about Oliver and her. Everyone knew but were too scared to say anything. He made me look like such an idiot.'

'He didn't, Alice,' I interjected quickly.

'He did.'

'He didn't!'

'He did. He did, Holly. I bet everyone's laughing at me. I bet they think I'm so naive and stupid. The thing is I suspected he was seeing other people. I just didn't want to face up to it by asking him. Maggie was always hinting, but I just thought she was jealous. Can you believe that? Her jealous of me! As if.' Her sobs were coming so fast now I was afraid that she would hyperventilate and I'd have to fetch a paper bag. She looked at me with huge sorrowful eyes and whispered, 'I would have married him if he'd asked me. I probably still would. I love him so much. Am I a really stupid person?'

I cuddled her, kissing the top of her head. 'You're not stupid. You are the sweetest person I know. Oliver's the stupid one. And one day he'll realise it and he'll be kicking himself for ever more. And if he doesn't kick himself, Maggie will do the job for him, with pleasure.' She made a muffled snort noise, but I couldn't make out if it was out of amusement or an attempt to sigh and sob at the same time.

'I went to the hospital,' she whispered into my chest, too ashamed to look at me. 'She was with him, holding his hand. And the way he looked at her . . .

he never looked at me like that. I was so jealous I could have killed her. They had been having sex in the back of the car when Shelley's Imp crashed into it. He's got to wear a neck brace. His head was thrown back, so he got whiplash.'

'What about the blood on his head?' I asked, wondering as I said it if I should just keep my mouth shut.

'That was only superficial. Rachel, that's her name by the way. Rachel was apparently straddling him, facing the back of the car. When it got hit she was thrown towards him and bit his forehead.'

'She bit him?' I repeated, willing myself not to laugh at how ludicrous it sounded, but a chuckle escaped me before I could stop myself.

Alice's shoulders started shaking again. 'No, Alice, please don't cry. I'm not laughing at you, I swear.'

She sat back then wiping her eyes on the sodden hanky. 'I'm not crying any more,' she explained, her shoulders shaking with laughter. 'It is kind of funny, isn't it? Fancy biting his head. He had a huge bandage on it,' she could hardly talk for laughing now.

'It's just a shame she wasn't giving him a blow job,' I said and we exploded with laughter, periodically stopping, sighing, trying to be serious and then giggling again.

Marcus crossed the garden to where we were sitting. He was balancing a tray on his arm. Alice looked at me, panicked, and in a stage whisper asked if I could tell if she'd been crying. I shook my head, figuring it'd be too late to do anything about it now anyway.

'Hi girls, sorry to disturb. Simon told me what happened so I thought you might like this.' He crouched down in front of us and placed the tray by Alice's feet. On the tray were two steaming mugs of coffee, two large brandy chasers and two generous chunks of sticky chocolate cake. 'All the things Fiona asks for when she's having a crisis,' he explained, getting up again. 'I'll leave you to it. The party's in full swing if you want to join us, but don't feel you have to.' He gave us a wink and sauntered back to the house.

'Wow!' swooned Alice.

'He is lovely,' I agreed, watching him disappear. 'I'm hoping when Tom matures and settles down, he'll take after his dad.'

'Obviously I've been so blinkered by Oliver, I hadn't realised what a genuinely nice bloke was like,' Alice said. She leaned over and retrieved the glasses of brandy, downing one and handing the other to me.

'I think I'll pass,' I said, patting my bump.

'Oh God, sorry,' she said. 'I'd better have yours.' She downed the second one and smacked her lips together, shuddering. 'Wow, that's powerful stuff.' Then she helped herself to some chocolate cake. 'So, you haven't seen Maggie since last night?'

'I've looked everywhere. I feel so awful about it. I was so pissed off with my whole situation I guess I took it out on her. I went around to her flat but no one answered. I'm sure she was there but was avoiding me.'

'How about we go around together? I can ring the

bell and you can hide around the corner if you like. We'll soon talk her round.'

I helped myself to the remaining portion of chocolate cake, my appetite restored. If anyone could talk her round it would be Alice.

The curtains of Maggie's flat were pulled tight shut, just as they had been when Simon and I had gone there the night before. I parked around the corner even though there was a space right outside the house. I didn't want her to know I was there. We snuck down the driveway and I hid in the corner of the porch. Alice rang the bell and we waited. There wasn't a single sound from inside. She rang the bell again, then stood away from the front door to see if there was any curtain-twitching. She looked back at me and spoke in the manner of a ventriloquist, so Mags wouldn't know she was talking to someone,

'I think I just saw her look out the window.'

There were a few muffled noises, then the sound of someone walking across the tiled hall floor. The door creaked open and Maggie poked her head through the gap. She saw Alice and opened the door wider.

'Alice, Shelley told me what happened, I can't believe it. Come in.' She ushered Alice into the flat and looked around the street behind her. Before she had a chance to see me I flew at the door, pushed it open and barged in. Mags stood back in alarm as I whirled around, shutting the door behind me before she had a chance to throw me back out. It was like an SAS raid, executed flawlessly, mission accomplished.

'For God's sake, Holly, you scared me half to death!' she yelled catching her breath. 'Why didn't you just come in like Alice?'

'But you wouldn't have let me in! You've been ignoring me since the party. Simon and I called around half a dozen times last night but you wouldn't answer. You won't answer the phone. Then you did all that cloak and dagger stuff when we rang the doorbell just then.'

She was smiling annoyingly at me the whole time I was talking. 'I think you'd better come in, sit down and have a drink. You've got to stop stressing out, Hol. It's not good for you.' She showed us into her flat.

I sipped my tea and blew my nose noisily. 'I've been so worried about you both. I thought you'd never forgive me for what I said. I thought you'd all decided you'd finally seen my true colours and realised what a bitch I was. I'm so sorry, Maggie, I hate it when we fight.' She looked at me as though I was being completely silly and just laughed.

'Honestly, I couldn't be mad at you for long if I tried. I understand why you said those things. You've been on an emotional roller-coaster ever since Tom left and you have a good medical reason to excuse you.' She raised her mug in the air as a toast. 'To us! A man will never come between us again. Unless either of you are into threesomes, that is,' she joked, and we all shuddered at a vile mental

107

image and laughed, clinking our mugs together in the middle of the room.

We were just sipping the hot liquid to seal our pledge when the doorbell rang. Maggie dived on to the floor and gestured at us to do the same. We met in the middle of the living room. Maggie was frozen, her head cocked in the direction of the window. I started to ask her what was going on but she put her finger to her lips, silencing me. The doorbell sounded again and I could hear heavy footsteps by the bay window. Maggie's flat being on the ground floor made it easy for visitors to check if she was in. Fortunately she hadn't drawn back the heavy curtains all day, so whoever the caller was, they couldn't see us. Maggie crawled towards the window, made a minuscule gap in the curtains and pressed her eye to it.

'It's okay, he's gone,' she whispered.

'Who?' urged Alice.

Maggie snuck me a guilty look and muttered 'Noah.'

After what felt like hours of Alice and I extolling Noah's virtues she finally cracked.

'Look, you can stop now, I get the picture! I know he's gorgeous, and I know he's a genuine, decent bloke. He just scares me, okay?'

Alice looked bothered by this and sat forward, adopting a confidential, 'you can tell me' pose she'd seen the agony aunt on *This Morning* do. 'What do you mean, scared you? Has he been getting heavy with you, pressuring you or anything?' she asked softly.

'Don't be ridiculous!' Maggie scoffed. 'I don't mean that kind of scared. I mean I'm not used to getting so much attention. The only types that usually proposition me haven't even got a clean criminal record, let alone driving licence. Either that or they were my mum's suspect boyfriends, taking advantage whenever she'd left us alone.'

'That's not quite true,' I said.

Maggie shrugged. 'Maybe, but I don't know how to handle Noah. I can't decide if it's what I want or not. And he's not helping me by constantly pressing me for answers.'

'Well, do you like him?' Alice asked.

'I can't help but like him. You said it yourself, the guy's gorgeous! I just don't know if I can do the whole "couples" thing.'

Alice sighed, staring at her floor. 'Funny, I don't feel comfortable being anything other than a couple. I wish I was being chased by a desperate hunk.'

Maggie chucked a Kit Kat at her head. 'Oi! Not so much of the desperate, please! Besides, if you hadn't been so permanently gooey-eyed about Oliver, you would have been fighting off other suitors. They'll all come out of the woodwork now that pig's out of the picture.' Alice didn't look so sure.

'Come on, you pair,' I interjected. 'Let's stop moaning about blokes, let's enjoy ourselves. We don't need men to make us happy do we? Do we!'

They muttered agreements.

'How about I nip to the video shop round the

109

corner and get us some empowering films to spur us on?' I suggested.

They both nodded, looking perkier.

'Go on then, I'll order in some pizzas,' Alice said, going to fetch a menu.

'Yeah, and I'll make some mulled wine with that low alcohol stuff in the kitchen,' Maggie suggested, looking much brighter. 'Yeah, a proper girlie night, just what we need. Sod blokes.'

'Yeah! Sod 'em!' We all cheered.

Late into the evening I decided it was time to go. I had called Alice's mum to tell her she would be staying over at mine (in reality she had crashed out exhausted on Maggie's couch a couple of hours ago, as the previous night's drama had taken its toll).

We had all had a classic girlie time. We watched *Thelma and Louise*, then rewatched all the Brad Pitt bits. Then we watched Maggie's *Friends* collection and argued over whether Chandler or Joey was the most attractive, and whether anybody in their right mind fancied Ross when in his annoying whine and rampant hairdo phase. We had stalled the pizza delivery man, pretending we 'had the right change here somewhere . . .' whilst flirting like mad and promising to meet up with him sometime in The Oyster Catcher, one of our favourite pubs in the city.

Yep, it was a successful girlie night, just the tonic. Who needs men to have a good time?

I kissed Maggie goodnight and stepped out into the darkness. A freezing fog had enveloped the

110

street, giving it an eerie feel. I hurried around the corner to my car, the keys gripped tightly in my hand, ready to defend myself if necessary. As I rounded the corner I noticed a figure, cloaked in mist, fumbling in his pocket. My heart sank, oh God this is it, I thought. I'm going to star in a *Crimewatch UK* reconstruction. That would be my fifteen minutes of fame, forget the *Stars In Their Eyes* fantasy. I paused briefly, wondering whether to make a dash for the car or head back to Maggie's house. The figure looked up and saw me; I whirled around and slipped on the ice. Scrambling to get up I felt his hands on the back of my arms, lifting me up off the ground. Just like in my worst nightmares my voice was lost in my throat, I couldn't scream.

'Holly, it's Noah. For goodness' sake stop struggling or I'll drop you.'

I ceased thrashing about and squinted in the mist. I positively identified the man as Noah and placed my hands on my pounding heart.

'Thank God, I thought my number was really up then.'

He placed me down on the pavement, apologising profusely.

My guard was still slightly up, though. 'Why are you hanging around here anyway? You're not stalking Maggie, are you?' I asked suspiciously.

He laughed at me. 'Of course not. I'm on my way back from The Red Bar. I stopped off to drop a note through Maggie's letterbox.' He retrieved the letter from his trouser pocket and waggled it under my nose. 'I think she's been avoiding me. This is the only way I can communicate with her at the moment.'

'Do you want a lift back? My car's only over there. I don't feel like driving back on my own. It's a bit spooky out tonight.'

'Go on then, you've twisted my arm,' he said, walking over to the passenger door. 'But do us a favour and let me nip this in to Maggie's on the way.'

'I can think of a much better way of winning her round, if that's your intention,' I told him, unlocking the car to let us in.

His eyes shone wickedly, 'Excellent, insider information. I could use a bit of that!'

'What do you mean, ignore her?' he said, looking disappointed as we drove back to his house. 'Isn't she interested in me, then?'

'Well, that's just it,' I explained. 'I think she is. She just needs time to figure it out for herself. If you cooled off a bit and looked like you could do without her, I reckon that would be enough to make her realise she prefers you being around to not being around. Don't you see?'

He looked as if he may as well be reading quantum physics.

'I'm not sure. What if I ignore her and she thinks I must be a bastard, or worse, forgets me altogether?'

'Look, I've known Maggie a long time, I've met every bloke she ever dated. I know her complicated family history and I've just spent a significant

112

portion of this evening talking to her about you. Trust me. Ignore her, give her a month or two, throw her some bait and she'll be putty in your hands.'

'Okay,' he agreed, sounding amused. 'I trust you.'

CHAPTER ELEVEN

'I wish I could come with you,' Maggie said, stacking the dishwasher with the last of the lunchtime rush crockery. 'I don't think you should be going alone.'

'Yeah,' I agreed. 'Shame your boss is such a taskmaster, isn't it?'

She set the machine buzzing and churning into life, and dried her hands on a tea towel.

'It's gone all quiet in the café now. Couldn't we just lock up early?'

'Last time I did that a coachload of Americans turned up an hour later, looking for a quaint English diner. You never know. Besides, I'm expecting a delivery.'

'That's exactly my point. You are expecting a delivery! And it's very important that you have lots of support at a time like this.'

'Not that delivery! I meant I've got two sacks of organic flour arriving in half an hour. Somebody's got to let them in and sign the forms. I'll be fine on my own.'

In truth I had arranged to have the flour arrive this afternoon on purpose. It was the day of my

114

twelve-week scan and my heart had been in my mouth all morning. I had no idea what to expect. I had decided that I'd rather be on my own. If I was given any bad news, I wanted to have a chance to digest it before I shared it with anyone else. Besides, I was still clutching at the remote possibility that it was all a gross misunderstanding, brought about by plant seed ingestion. Humiliation would be easier to swallow without an audience to witness it. I checked my watch, 'Half past two, I'd better get going.'

'Hold on,' Maggie said. 'I think you're forgetting something.' She gestured to a freshly poured pint of water. 'Get that down you, and keep 'em crossed,' she laughed, pointing at my legs.

The letter I had received informing me of my appointment had advised me to drink a pint of liquid, half an hour before the scan was due. I should also avoid going to the toilet, that way my bladder would be full, making it possible for them to get a good picture of the baby. Although quite how that worked I wasn't sure. I had an image in my mind of the scan showing my baby rising up on the screen, waving, then dropping back down again as it trampolined on my swollen bladder.

I downed the drink in one, fetched my coat and was nearly at the door when the phone rang. Maggie answered it, waving at me to go. I was just disappearing out of the door when she called me back.

'Holly, I think you'd better take this.' She placed her hand over the mouthpiece and whispered, 'it's Tom.'

I took the phone off her, my hands shaking from

115

the adrenalin rush that was coursing through my veins.

'Tom,' I croaked, 'is that you?'

'Holly, at last,' his familiar voice replied. 'Sorry I haven't called before. I tried on Christmas Day but you weren't around. Thing is, I move around so much, I hardly ever get time. How've you been?' He sounded great; so clear I could imagine he was only a mile up the road, sitting in his flat. His voice was full of excitement and seemed energised. He must be having the time of his life, I thought sadly and tried to swallow back the painful lump in my throat.

'Are you having a good time?' I asked, ignoring his question.

'Hol, it's amazing, I've made loads of friends out here. I've seen some awesome things, I can't wait to tell you all about them. I'm in Bali now, I'm getting a flight to Kuala Lumpur in the morning.' In the background I could hear people talking nearby, one was definitely female. 'Listen, Hol, I'm sorry this is only a short call, Jimmy and Chris have just come in, and I've got to go. We're going out to the beach for a beer. I wish I could talk to you longer, there's some things I need to say.'

I heard someone in the background say, 'Come on, Tom.'

'I'll call you soon,' he said, then paused and added quietly, 'I just wanted to say, I miss you.' Then he was gone.

I held the phone in my hand, not wanting to put it down. My mouth was hanging open, wanting to speak, but he hadn't given me the chance. His voice was still echoing inside my head and I enjoyed its sound for a while, then a devilish thought taunted me, souring the moment. Is that Chris short for Christopher, or Chris short for Christine?

I slammed the phone back on its cradle as if it had stung me.

'Is everything okay?' Maggie asked. She had been standing watching me ever since she had passed over the phone.

'Why is it whenever I get nervous I need the toilet? I'd better go before I *go*!' I said and waved her goodbye.

By the time I arrived at the X-ray unit I was walking like a penguin and my bladder was threatening to explode under the strain.

'We won't keep you long, Miss Piper, if you would just like to take a seat over there,' informed a friendly young receptionist, gesturing to a tatty brown leather couch. I stared at the door of the consulting room, willing it to open. I rocked back and forth praying I wouldn't puddle on the floor, and finally the door swung open. A woman of similar age and bump size burst out of the room and shot straight into the ladies' toilets, which were conveniently situated adjacent to the X-ray room.

The receptionist smiled at me. 'You can go in now,' she singsonged.

Lying down on the couch, it dawned on me why I was here. I had been distracted by Tom's phone call and the need to think of things that wouldn't make

117

me want to pee. Now, with my tummy greased up like a stranded whale on a beach and my pubic hair wafting in a clinical breeze (scans were always more discreet on the telly!), I realised that I was about to see my baby, babies, or vegetable plant for the first time.

The radiologist turned her probe around, digging harder into my abdomen and clicking away on the computer with her other hand.

'Okay, I have it, would you like to take a look?' she moved the monitor so it was facing in my direction. I craned my neck to see the screen. It was difficult to make out at first. All I could see were fuzzy dots and shapes, then it moved. A leg kicked out, stretched, then shot back in again. Slowly I made out arms, chest, spine and a head, an enormous head, resting its chin on its chest.

'Oh my God, it looks like an alien!' I cried before I could stop myself.

The radiologist smiled. 'It's okay, they all look like this at first. They appear a little out of proportion at this stage. I've been measuring its growth and it's completely consistent with a twelve-week-old foetus. In the position it's lying in I'm not able to tell you what sex it is, you might have more luck at the twenty-week scan. You have a very normal baby, Miss Piper, and according to my chart,' she looked up the dates on a circular calendar. 'It is due on or near the 24th of July. Would you like a picture to take home?'

I nodded. 'Are you sure there's only one? There couldn't be another one hiding behind it?'

'Oh no, the scan would pick that up. There's definitely just the one,' she said, handing me a printout of a still from the computer and a wad of paper towels to mop up the grease.

'And it definitely is a baby, isn't it?'

She peered at me over her half-moon glasses. 'As opposed to a . . . ?'

'Never mind,' I said and went to relieve myself across the corridor.

When I arrived back I noticed Maggie and Alice were waiting for me in the café. They were huddled up together in lovers' corner, polishing off a bottle of elderflower wine. When I walked in they burst into life, firing questions at me like journalists at a press conference.

'Hold up, you pair, let me take my jacket off first!' I slung it on the counter and grabbed a can of coke from the fridge.

'Well?' they cried in unison.

'Well what?' I asked innocently.

'Is everything okay? Is it healthy?' Alice urged.

'Yep.'

'Do you know what sex it is?' Maggie said.

'Nope.'

'Are you only having one?'

'Yep.' They both looked disappointed. 'What? What did you want to hear, that I was having an all-male football team?'

'Have you got a picture of it?' Alice asked hopefully. I waved the computer still at them, placing it on the table. They pounced on it.

'What's this supposed to be?' Maggie moaned.

'Is that its head?' Alice asked, pointing at its bottom.

'Ooh, is that a willy?' cried Maggie, pointing at the umbilical cord.

'You two, what are you like? There's its head, that's its hand, see, it's sucking its thumb. And these are its legs, they're bent up to its chest.'

They squinted and leaned in for a closer look. They made a few 'ooh' and 'ah I see' type noises then looked at each other and burst out laughing.

I snatched it back, annoyed at them. 'You can't tell at all, can you?'

They both shook their heads, apologising. Then Maggie took the picture back off me.

'Hang on a minute.' She studied it once again. 'Yes, I can see now. That's its face, it's a side-on view isn't it? Oh wow!'

I beamed with pride, then she said, 'Blimey, isn't its head big?'

That night we went out for a quiet meal and drink at The Boatman by the river Avon. We braved the chilly night air and sat outside next to a small waterfall and threw the leftovers of our meal over the fence to the ducks. We had all picked half-heartedly at our dinner.

A couple of men who looked like students sat on the bench next to ours and looked over at us, grinning. Alice leaned in and whispered, 'I think the one in the rugby top fancies Maggie, he's been eyeing her up since we got here.'

120

Maggie flicked her hair back, enjoying the attention, but avoided looking at them.

'That's not like you, Mags,' I teased. 'Aren't you going to start a conversation with them and try and palm one of us on his friend?'

She grimaced. 'I'm not always out on the pull, you know. Besides, I'm not really in the mood tonight.'

'What's up?' I asked. She shrugged, tearing at a beer mat.

'She's upset because she hasn't heard from Noah in weeks, aren't you, Maggie?' Alice explained.

'I am not!' she cried, kicking Alice under the table.

Alice raised her eyebrows at me and mouthed, 'She is.'

'I just think it's strange, that's all, one minute he's all over me, telling me how special I am. Then the next thing I know he's suddenly too busy to talk to me. It makes me wonder if everything he said meant nothing to him.'

'I thought you weren't interested in him anyway?' Alice teased.

'I never said I was. I just like to know when I'm being lied to.'

'I don't think Noah ever lied to you; I think he got fed up of getting the brush-off all the time and tried to keep the last of his pride intact,' I said, nibbling on a cold chip.

'But it wasn't just a case of him chasing and me running. We also got on well as friends. Just because I didn't want to have a heavy relationship with him doesn't mean I didn't want to be friends. I miss him being around.'

121

I felt a stab of guilt and wondered if I should have kept my nose out of it.

A loud dirty laugh sent the ducks squawking fearfully away from our table and we all swivelled around in our seats.

'Oh my God!' cried Alice. 'It's Rachel.'

'Who's Rachel?' asked Maggie.

'Jaws!' Alice and I chorused, giggling wickedly.

She was leaving the pub with the middle-aged man I had seen her with in the garden at Oliver's party. They were all over each other. The man was just about to slide his hand up Rachel's top when she saw us watching and batted him away.

'Oh shit, she's coming over,' Alice cringed, sliding down in her seat.

'Hi, Alice,' Rachel said sheepishly, avoiding eye contact with Maggie and me. 'I just wanted to say no hard feelings, hey?'

Maggie snorted, giving her a look that could make plants shrivel up and drop their leaves in terror.

'I finished it with Oliver last week. Rupert's asked me to marry him.' She flashed a sparkler the size of a showerhead under our noses. 'To be truthful, I don't think Oliver will ever grow up. You're best off without him, Alice, honestly.'

'Bloody hell!' Maggie yelled. 'You'll be asking her to thank you for shagging her boyfriend next!'

Rachel backed off, glowing dark red with shame. 'I didn't mean that, I just meant . . .'

Maggie stood up, standing over Alice protectively. I half expected her to roll her sleeves up menacingly and put up her fists. Rachel whispered an apology and scurried off like a scared rabbit. She linked arms with her fiancé and dragged him towards the safety of the car park.

'You'd better watch her,' Maggie yelled loudly to Rupert, 'she bites!'

CHAPTER TWELVE

I stood naked in front of the mirror, viewing myself critically. My bump was still small and hardly noticeable. Before I had become pregnant I had imagined that from the moment you conceived the results were instant and dramatic. Even at only three and a half months pregnant I'd imagined I'd be waddling about with my hands laid comfortably on my bump, huffing and puffing like a wrestler and wearing gargantuan amounts of fabric. I was surprised to find myself a bit disappointed that I'd been wrong. I could still fit into my jeans, although now I had to wear them with the top button undone, and unless you saw me in one of my figure-hugging dresses you'd never guess. In fact even then you probably wouldn't guess. You'd just assume I was eating more than usual. The only thing that made my bump different from a roll of flab was the way it felt. Unlike fat, my pregnant bump felt harder. If you prodded it, it didn't undulate like a jelly, instead it was firm, like a tense muscle. When I breathed in it didn't shrink back like before; instead I sucked in as much as possible, but my belly stayed put.

I looked at myself from every angle and a silvery streak caught my eye on my left breast. I looked closer. I licked my finger and rubbed at it but it wouldn't come off. It was a stretch mark. I couldn't believe it! Under close scrutiny I noticed three more. They were bloody spreading! I had noticed that my Wonderbras were getting tighter and more uncomfortable but I thought that they were just shrinking in the wash; but now I could see, my breasts really had grown. They were rounder and fuller in a way I'd always wished for. I smiled proudly in the mirror, posing like a page three model, but the silver streaks and rounded paunch spoiled the effect. I sat down glumly, not wanting to get dressed.

I remembered all the late night Ricki Lake and Oprah programmes I had seen where some overweight woman would blame her children for her loss of figure. She would cry bitterly and talk about her failed marriage and suicide attempts, all brought on since she had given birth to Brad/Joshua. And Ricki/Oprah would nod in agreement saying, 'Honey, I felt just the same until my personal trainer changed my life.' Was I doomed to a similar fate? Okay, I had never been Kate Moss, but that was what worried me. I had always fluctuated from nicely slim to stocky and ample. I was easily affected by external conditions. If I went out for a curry my tummy would hang over my knickers the next day. I always spent two months after Christmas fighting the pudding's revenge, and if I missed an evening meal I'd wake up in the morning feeling like a sex goddess.

I had tried dieting but in my case it was always a stout failure. The decision to diet was always prompted by a massive binge where I had become so full, I had convinced myself that I could never feel hungry again and could manage quite nicely on the occasional slice of toast. The following morning, shamefully remembering my night's debauchery, I would abstain from breakfast. A couple of hours later I would be feeling slim and lovely again, proud of my strength of will. About half an hour after that the smells of the café would be cruelly taunting me. I'd be flagging from a plummeting blood sugar level and my body would be screaming for an instant energy boost before it packed up altogether. Due to the slow release mechanism of energy in healthy foods, they simply wouldn't do. It would have to be something with a high fat and sugar content to get me up and running. Then I would devour three caramel slices and be on a chocolate high until dinnertime. Therefore whenever I feel the urge to start another diet, I vow to take up a more healthy and productive pastime, such as smoking.

Due to all of these circumstances I was convinced that if anybody was going to find their weight affected by pregnancy, it would be me.

I heard the thud of the morning post hitting the mat and sprang back up to get dressed. It was Valentine's Day after all. There was still the freak possibility that Tom had managed to work out the foreign post timing to accurately predict when a Valentine's card should be posted to arrive on the day in question. It wasn't impossible. And besides,

I might have a secret admirer, a hopefully charitable admirer that adored illegitimate children.

I skidded on the mat and sifted through the collection of envelopes. There were two bills, one invoice, one sales pitch from a paper napkin supplier, a new chequebook, a letter from the local high school inviting me to place a student for a week's work experience (free labour, an exciting prospect, not to be sniffed at), and what was this? It looked like a card, it felt like a card, bloody hell, it was a card! I checked out the handwriting, there was no mistaking the spidery scrawl, it was a card from Tom! YES! I danced a jig and hugged the card to my chest. I was so happy; I just enjoyed the moment for a while. I sashayed over to lovers' corner and made myself comfortable, then I hungrily tore open the envelope. The picture on the front was of a beautiful seascape, with two lovers kissing in the waves, like the scene in *From Here To Eternity*. There was a pint of beer in front of them and a barbecue sizzling on the beach. The writing underneath the picture said SEASONAL GREETINGS FROM OZ! It was a sodding Christmas card! I opened it up, swallowing back my disappointed tears, and read the message,

Gooday Holly!

I hope this gets to you in time for Christmas, I only arrived yesterday so it might not. I'm having an unbelievable time here already. Tomorrow we're off to see Ayers Rock, we're having a BBQ there to watch the sunset, apparently it changes colour, I can't wait. It's so hot I'm

127

forever in the shower, I wish you were in there with me! That's the hardest part about travelling alone, you want to share it with someone special.

Anyway I'll write again, or call you as soon as I can, say 'hi' to everyone for me,
Love Tom. xxx

My heart was racing when I had finished reading. Okay, so it may not have been a Valentine's card, but the sentiment was the same. It was affectionate, and he obviously missed me. He had signed it 'love' and had basically said that I was someone special. I fanned my face with the card, smiling from ear to ear, then I read it all over again.

A short while later Maggie arrived for work. She was smiling smugly.

'Did you get one?' I asked, and she knew instantly what I was talking about. She whipped a card from her back pocket like a gun from a holster.

'What about you?' she asked. I retrieved mine, also conveniently situated in my back pocket for easy access. We traded cards and read each other's.

'This is a Christmas card,' she said, confused.

I rolled my eyes at her.

'I know, I know, but it came today so it still counts. Just read it!' I took Maggie's card out of the envelope and studied it scrupulously. 'Tasteful, no chintzy hearts and flowers, no smutty nudes, no sign of being bought from a petrol station. So far so good.' I read the inscription inside.

Maggie May,

I'm always thinking of you. I'm not far away, and one day, you will be mine, oh yes, you will be mine!

Love?

'Okay,' I said stuffing the card back in the envelope. 'Sounds like a bit of a weirdo if you don't mind me saying. Could possibly be a social outcast with an unhealthy fixation, maybe a serial killer, at best a stalker that lives with his mum and works at an army surplus shop.'

'Or he could be someone that happens to know me quite well and knows that *Wayne's World* is one of my favourite films,' she snapped defensively.

I remembered the scene where Wayne stands in front of a Fender Stratocaster and says a similar thing to what was written in the card. 'On the other hand, I'd go with that theory, you might sleep better. Any idea who?'

She paused, pretending to think about it – like she hadn't been doing that all morning, I'm sure! 'Well, I suppose it could be Noah. Although he hasn't looked that keen lately. Or it could be Ajay, the student who keeps coming in and spending his grant money on coffees and telling me to get one for myself, like I work in a pub! But I'd rather it was Noah.'

I grinned at her. It's working, I thought. She's really starting to want him!

The delivery man from the grocer's knocked on

the window, interrupting my chain of thought, and I went to let him in.

Alice came in during her lunch break and ordered a quiche and salad.

'Did you get any?' she whispered to us both. We nodded happily.

'She didn't, she got a Christmas card,' Maggie teased, pointing at me as though I was a liar.

I ignored her. 'What about you?' I urged.

She produced a card from her coat pocket and put it down on the counter. 'He wants me back,' she said weakly.

'Oh my God,' Maggie cried, looking disgusted, 'here we go again.' She waltzed off into the kitchen with her hands in the air.

'You can't stay in on Valentine's Day,' Alice had protested. 'You'll just end up mooching about, all melancholy and watching some crappy telly programme.'

I had rather liked the sound of that, and stuck to my guns, insisting I was too exhausted to have a good time. They had offered to stay in with me, but I had thanked them kindly and declined, explaining that I just wanted to sleep. If I hadn't been pregnant I think they would have argued some more. Instead they let it go, on the condition that I call Shelley's mobile if I changed my mind.

Back in the flat, though, I couldn't settle. I had turned the telly off, being unable to concentrate on it anyway. All I could think about was Tom's parents.

I knew I had to tell them. Ever since I had gone for the scan, I knew I couldn't put it off much longer. Everything was progressing normally and I was beginning to show. Soon it would be blatantly obvious. I owed it to Marcus and Fiona to be up front with them. Besides, if they heard it from me, I might be able to convince them to keep it to themselves. If they found out some other way, they might not be so willing to hear me out. They might tell Tom before I could stop them. I had to do it soon.

For the third time this evening I picked up the phone, but it happened again. An all-over body tremor spread throughout my body, making my hand go so limp I couldn't grip the receiver properly. I knew that if I tried to talk my voice would come out sounding like a nervous yodeller. I replaced it back on to its cradle and paced the room trying to figure out what to say.

Once I'd rehearsed it a couple of times in my head I lunged at the phone and dialled quickly, before I lost my nerve.

Simon answered. My voice dried up and my speech was forgotten.

'Holly, is that you?' he asked.

'Simon, what are you doing there?'

'I'm just visiting, why what's up?'

'Nothing, nothing. It's just, I was going to speak to your parents. I think it's about time they knew the situation. I had a speech all worked out, and now you've ruined it by answering the phone.'

131

'Ahh, I see,' his voice had dropped conspiratorially. 'I think you're right. But I don't think you should tell them over the phone.'

'I know, I wasn't going to. I was going to invite them for a meal on Saturday. Ply them with good food and wine, and then tell them.'

'Food and wine, hey. Can I come? You'll need moral support of course. Best if you don't do it alone, besides, it'll look better if you invite the whole family. It'll look less formal, less suspicious.'

I considered it for a moment. 'I think you're right.'

'Do you want me to ask Mum for you?'

I breathed a sigh of relief. 'Would you?'

'Hang on.'

I knew this was cowardly, but I was so relieved to get away without having to talk to them that I didn't care. I could hear some rustling in the background, then Simon saying, 'Mum, Holly wants to invite us for dinner on Saturday, can you make it?'

There was a soft surprised 'Oh', which must have been Fiona, then a 'Hang on a minute,' followed by some more rustling and mumbling.

After what felt like years Simon picked the phone up again. 'She says that they're sorry they can't make it this Saturday, but can the Saturday after.'

'That's fine by me.'

'Excellent. She says thanks for the invite, they can't wait.'

After I had said my goodbyes to Simon, I flopped down on the sofa. Tom's family were so nice, I wondered what I had been so worried about. I

132

picked up the sketches I had been drawing for Irene's wedding cake and a fresh pad of paper. Now that I had made the phone call my mind was clear, and I could work on the designs properly. Besides, with the meal nearly two weeks away there was no point in worrying about it yet.

CHAPTER THIRTEEN

'What's up, face ache?' chided Maggie, after she'd finished serving caffè lattes to a couple of middle-aged business men. I had two days to go until the dinner party with Tom's family, and I had been fretting all week. I had hardly said two words all morning. Instead, I just let Maggie pour out a moaning monologue about the preparations for her mother's wedding. 'Hello! Earth calling Holly. I was asking if you thought I should go to the hen night. What do you think?'

'Oh, sorry, I was miles away. What do I think about what?'

She tutted loudly and rolled her eyes. 'Roll on next week. I might get a conversation out of you when this Saturday is over and done with.'

'That might just be the start of it if they insist on tracking Tom down.' I sighed, rearranging the chocolate brownies absent-mindedly. The customer bell pinged and a woman struggled in, laden with shopping bags and soaked from the rain. She dumped her bags by the coat stand and pulled the hood of her jacket down.

'Phew, somewhere warm and dry at last. I'm soaked to the skin. Hi darling, you'll have to excuse the state I'm in,' she said, laughing and gesturing to her hair, which hung like wet rope. She still looked immaculate. Like Andie MacDowell in the final scene of *Four Weddings*.

'Hi Fiona,' I greeted, cringing at the thought that she had heard my last comment. I adjusted my apron, allowing it to hang more loosely over mini-bump, and stood behind the safety of the cash register. Maggie slunk off with a cloth and spray to clean the tables.

'How are you?' I asked, smiling and trying to act normal.

'Starving! I've been shopping all day. Having Tamsin and the twins stay is such a tonic. But I can't help spoiling them rotten. It's costing me a fortune! You should see the jumpers I've got them. They're going to look adorable. Oh, I am going to miss them when they go back.' Her eyes glistened with emotion at the thought, but she laughed it off. 'Anyway, sweetheart. I really am looking forward to Saturday. Simon keeps saying that he hopes you make that beautiful meringue roulade like you did for that Christmas do, a few years ago. We all love your cooking.' She hung up her coat and brushed the damp creases from her tight trousers. 'I have to ask, Holly, and don't get me wrong, it's lovely to be invited over, but is there a particular reason for the meal?'

'Oh no, no reason. I just thought it would be nice. We don't see so much of each other now Tom's away

135

and I hardly saw you at your New Year's buffet. You know me; I love an excuse to cook for people. You'd think I'd be bored with it by now.' I wondered if my rambling was giving the game away.

'Excellent, so it's just an informal get together?'

I nodded, forcing a smile.

'In that case. I hate to be a nuisance, and please say if it's a problem, but would you mind if Tamsin and the twins came along as well? I hate leaving her in the house alone, and the poor thing hardly ever gets out now with the babies being so young. I'll provide anything you like, drinks, desserts, after-dinner mints.' She looked pleadingly at me.

'Of course she can come,' I assured. 'It's no bother. It's not as though we're short of room,' I laughed, gesturing to the spacious café that spread out before me.

'Oh that's great, thanks so much, Holly. I really am grateful. And Tamsin was only saying the other day how well you got on at the party. She said you were a natural with Callum, stopped him crying in no time. Dear me, we could have done with you at three o'clock this morning. Poor love woke up the whole house, cried for hours. She took him to the doctor this morning, turns out he has a virus. Still, they get over these things so quickly at that age, I'm sure he'll be fine by Saturday. Anyway, listen to me nattering away, and I'm so hungry I think I could faint!' She squinted at the day's specials, written on the board behind me. 'You'll have to let me have a bowl of your cream of asparagus soup, and do you have any of those yummy onion and herb rolls?'

* * *

Saturday had been relatively quiet. Driving rain and gales had kept the sightseers and shoppers at bay. All day rain lashed relentlessly against the windows. Every customer who burst in through the doors made some comment about it.

That was one problem with working somewhere where there was a steady stream of different people: you ended up repeating yourself over and over again. There were days when I felt if one more person walked through the doors and said 'Ooh, it's awful out there isn't it? or, Isn't it lovely weather today?' I would have to round them all up and lock them in the walk-in fridge. Then I could let them all out an hour later and say to each and every one, 'Bit nippy in the fridge today, don't you think?'

Due to the lack of customers, I was able to prepare the evening meal during the day and close up early. Maggie stayed behind to help me clear up, and I still had time for a bath before they arrived. I couldn't help wishing that the day hadn't been quite so relaxed. If I had been rushed off my feet, like a usual Saturday, I would have had a hard time trying to fit it all in. Then maybe I wouldn't have had to spend the last half an hour going to the toilet, then leaving the toilet only to decide that I needed the toilet again.

I surveyed the café. It looked so different at night, with soft lighting casting a warm glow. In the day it was bright and busy, now it looked dreamlike and romantic.

I only opened the café in the evening for the

odd pre-booked, well-paying party. I didn't advertise the service, but I was occasionally bribed with offers too tempting from regulars, mostly around the Christmas period. I always loved the atmosphere in the café at night; it reminded me of when my parents had dinner parties in the evening. I'd be tucked up in bed early, but the exciting sounds of clinking glasses and the smells of special food always lured me to the top of the stairs. I had pushed the two biggest tables together to make a medieval-sized banqueting area and decorated it with a vase of freshly cut flowers and half a dozen small candles. The flames twitched nervously, casting flickering shadows on the wall.

I glanced at my watch, eight o'clock exactly; they'd be here any moment. I leaned against the counter and stroked the black nose of the pussy cat carving. 'Wish me luck, puss,' I whispered, then I reached over the counter and helped myself to a bread stick from a packet I'd forgotten to put away. I walked back and forth, nibbling the breadstick, until I realised that I had created a Hansel and Gretel type trail of crumbs on the floor and had to fetch a dustpan and brush from the cleaning cupboard.

There was a knock on the door just as I was crouching on the floor, bum waving in the air like a flag.

'Damn,' Simon said as I let him in. 'I shouldn't have knocked. I had a great view from there.'

I gave him a hard stare and adjusted my newly acquired ankle length, A-line dress. 'Can you tell?' I whispered, before the rest of his family followed him in. He looked me up and down and grinned appreciatively.

'You're looking good, babe. Don't panic.' He winked and handed me a bottle of wine.

I was engulfed in kisses as his parents and Tamsin walked in, carrying a box of goodies and pushing a pram. The babies were fast asleep together and looked so peaceful. Tamsin parked them next to the speakers, which were emitting the sultry tunes of Nina Simone.

'Won't that wake them up? I can turn the music off if you like.'

'Oh no, they love music, it helps them sleep. I actually think it's better not to creep about quietly. If they're used to noise, they're less likely to be bothered by it.'

'They get enough of it at our house, don't they?' Fiona said, taking out another bottle of wine and some Aqua Libra from the box. I wondered if they would notice if I hid a notepad and pen behind the counter. Then whenever Tamsin offered another wise nugget of knowledge on how to look after children, I could jot it all down for future use. Marcus gave me a big bear hug and produced a pretty pot of peonies from behind his back.

'Ah, they're lovely, thank you.' The oven timer bleeped. 'That means the bruschetta are ready, why don't you all get comfy? Simon, you can open the wine and I'll bring the food through.'

The table was laden with different things to eat, the plan being to put it all on the table at once, then everyone could just help themselves to however much they liked. That way hopefully no one would notice that I had the appetite of a small bird, and I wouldn't have to keep fetching things from the kitchen and risk them catching sight of mini-bump.

It smells fantastic,' Marcus said, as he helped himself to a generous portion of tagliatelle.

'Mmm,' Tamsin agreed. 'I haven't eaten this well for ages.' She slapped her hand over her mouth and looked mortified, stuttering, 'Not that your cooking isn't lovely, Fi.'

Fiona just laughed and shrugged her shoulders. 'I'm the first to admit my cooking leaves a lot to be desired. Ever since I discovered Marks and Spencers don't just do good knickers, I put the saucepans away and I don't think I've seen them since!' She picked a sprig of watercress out of the green salad and looked coyly at Marcus. 'It's a good job I'm good at accounts, otherwise I'd be a hopeless housewife.'

I noticed a twinkle in Marcus's eyes as he sipped his wine and admired his wife. They had such a perfect marriage. I felt a jealous pang in the pit of my stomach. If only Tom would settle down, we could be like that, I thought dreamily.

'Have you heard from Thomas lately?' Fiona asked, as if reading my thoughts.

'Well, a couple of weeks ago I got a Christmas card from Australia,' I said, moving the food around my plate with my fork, to give the impression I was about to eat it.

'Blimey, you're lucky,' Simon laughed. 'I didn't get one, neither did Mum or Dad.'

140

'He's not even in Australia any more, is he?' Fiona said. 'Isn't he in Bali now? Surfing probably. He called us when he arrived. He sounded as though he was having the time of his life.' I swallowed hard; trying to look pleased for him.

'Well, he had better make the most of it,' Marcus grinned wickedly. 'He's got a lot of work to take on when he gets back. He's got to prove that he can really knuckle down if he wants to go into business with me.'

'Oh, you're too hard on him. You can't expect him to have the same drive as you. I don't know if I want my son to be a workaholic like his dad.'

'His education cost us a fortune, it'd just be nice to see it put into action, that's all. Then maybe he could treat his old dad to the occasional drink for a change. Speaking of hard work,' said Marcus, changing the subject at last. 'How's it going at the café?' he asked me. 'Last time we spoke you were thinking of taking on extra staff. Did you have any more thoughts on that?'

'Actually I did. I've got a lad from Avon Valley Comprehensive starting on Monday. It's not a permanent solution. He's just a placement from the school for work experience. Doing "A" level food technology, apparently. He'll only be here for a week, but it'll be nice to have an extra pair of hands about the place. Then if it works out I'll take on another permanent cook after he's gone.'

'Brilliant plan. Get in some free help whilst you can, I like it,' he chuckled.

We carried on talking shop and about the twins

whilst we all ate. I kept an eye on how much everyone was drinking, happily noting that the third bottle of wine had nearly been drained. The merrier they all were the better. Simon kept catching my eye, giving me meaningful looks and kicking me under the table. I tried my best not to look at him.

Eventually Fiona and Tamsin cleared away the empty bowls of food and the used plates, and I brought out the dessert. I knew it was the ideal opportunity to make my announcement. My heart was pounding in my ears and I cleared my throat to speak.

'Actually, if I could have everybody's attention for a moment, there is an announcement I'd like to make,' said Tamsin, beating me to it by seconds. I couldn't believe it! Everybody looked at her and she played nervously with her spoon.

'Well, firstly I would like to thank you all for being so kind and hospitable to me since the twins were born. I think I would have gone spare up in Edinburgh all on my own. It has been hard since Oscar left me. You are really the only family I have now, and I hate the thought of being so far away from you again. What I mean to say is that if none of you have any objections, I'd like to move down here permanently. I've spoken to head office and they're allowing me to work part time from home. They also have a branch in Bristol that I can report to monthly. I've even found a flat in the centre. So if no one minds . . .'

She was answered with hugs and kisses from everyone. Fiona was clapping her hands with joy.

'That's wonderful news. I'm so thrilled,' she said, dabbing at her eyes.

All the sudden noise caused the two sleeping babies to start stirring. One of them gave a soft moan and shuffled about in the pram. Realising that we were making too much noise, we shushed each other and crept over to where they were sleeping. Fiona, Tamsin and I peeped into the pram and saw them curled up together, having fallen back to sleep. They were so peaceful. Fiona tucked their crumpled blanket back around them and stood back.

'It's going to be so lovely having you live nearby,' she whispered. 'I don't think my boys will be ready to have children for years yet. By the time I become a grandma I'll be too old to enjoy it.' She leaned over and stroked one of the babies' rounded cheeks and said tenderly, 'We're going to have lots of fun together.'

I turned and saw Simon looking at me across the dining table, silently urging me to say something. All I could think about was what Fiona had said. By not ready to have children did she mean due to circumstances, or did she mean that they were not emotionally ready for the responsibility? The more I thought about it, the more convinced I became that I had better sit on my bombshell a little longer.

CHAPTER FOURTEEN

I wiped the sleep from my eyes and opened the morning's post. In the pile was a letter from the hospital, it was an appointment for my twenty-week scan. I checked the date on the calendar; it was in just over four weeks from now. Time seemed to be whizzing by. Maybe Simon was right. Maybe I should just bite the bullet and try to contact Tom. After all, if he did love me and wanted it to work out, he could come back and we could go through this together. It would be so nice to have someone special holding my hand at the scan. Soon I would be starting antenatal classes. I could just imagine all the other women having a loving, supportive partner with them, and then there would be me in a corner all alone. I was so confused.

At nine o'clock, as I put the sandwich board out on to the cobbled street, I noticed a gangly teenage lad, milling around outside. He was clutching a school bag and fiddling with some papers.

'Can I help you?' I asked.

He looked nervously all around; he was either working out an escape route, or confirming that I was talking to him. The little street was empty. 'Are you Mrs Piper?' he enquired awkwardly.

'Actually no, I'm Miss Piper. But I prefer to be called Holly,' I said lightly, trying to relax him.

'Oh,' he muttered, looking desperately uncomfortable. 'Sorry Miss Piper, erm, Holly. I'm from Avon Valley.' He thrust the papers he was holding in front of my face.

'Ahh, I see, you're the work experience placement.' I skimmed over the introductory letter from his form tutor. 'So you're Alexander. Pleased to meet you.' I held out my hand and he shook it limply.

'Alex,' he corrected, pushing his long fringe back off his face, 'Call me Alex.'

'I'm sorry, Alex, I completely forgot you were coming. Come on in, I'll show you around.'

After I had served my first regular of the morning (Mrs Brannigan, a cream-loving octogenarian with a penchant for gossip), I sat Alex down for a more in-depth chat.

'So,' I started, pouring him a cup of tea from the pot. 'What can you cook?'

He added three sugars to his cup and stirred noisily. 'Well, erm,' he looked upwards, as though he was trying to roll his eyes back into his brain and look for inspiration. So far I wasn't convinced he'd find much. 'I've done fruit scones, eccles cakes and teacakes. Last year I made a Christmas cake for my final project.'

'Rrrright!' I said slowly, 'So, you're basically good at bready cake-type desserts with raisins in them.'

'I sometimes put cherries in the scones,' he piped up proudly.

'Do you ever cook anything savoury?' I asked, ever hopeful.

'Oh yes, sorry. I can make a mean spaghetti bolognese, I wasn't sure whether to mention that, you being veggie an'all.'

'I see,' I said, smiling through clenched teeth at him and sipping my tea.

Why was it every male I had encountered was convinced they could make a 'mean spaghetti bolognese'? It must be the signature dish of all single men in the western hemisphere. Spag-bol'-makers were particularly rife in universities, each convinced it was the perfect way to win over women, impressing them into bed with their 'new man' domesticity. It usually consisted of half a pound of fried minced meat, and a jar of cook-in sauce. This culminated in using all the different sized saucepans available in the culinary world and creating enough washing-up to make even Nanette Newman's hands shrivel up like dried prunes.

'Would you mind if I kept you on washing-up duty and keeping the eating area clean just for now? Maybe when you've got the feel of the place you can try out some serving and cooking. I think we should break into it gently.'

He agreed but looked disappointed and noisily slurped his tea.

By lunchtime Alex had relaxed into his new role and was beginning to surprise me with his enthusiasm.

146

It did appear to outstrip his ability, but he was so keen to learn I figured it would only be a matter of time before he got a grip of things. He was one of those rare male breeds who really enjoyed cooking and cleaning and had so far made himself solely responsible for clearing the tables and washing up. He had rearranged the crockery cupboards to make everything more easily accessible and had even learnt how to use the coffee machine. By the time Maggie had turned up for work the café was gleaming and as organised as a Sergeant Major's underwear drawer. Alex was taking real pride in his work. I could overlook the fact that he'd broken one plate, two glass tumblers and a teapot lid. I put it down to first-day jitters.

'Blimey, you're a bloody miracle worker,' Maggie said as she put on her apron. 'I've been telling her to put the saucers there for ages. How did you manage that?'

Alex looked flustered and jammed his hands into his pockets, shrugging his shoulders. I got the distinct impression he was staring at her chest. Admittedly it was hard not to when it was fighting to get out of her tight T-shirt.

Maggie, always aware of her ability to capture a male's attention, bent down slowly, looking at the storage area under the counter. She stood up, smiling wickedly. 'I love what you did to the cubby holes,' she said, one eyebrow raised. Then she breezed past into the kitchen whispering, 'cute,' at me and winking. The poor lad looked as though he'd need a stretcher to take him home tonight.

147

Half an hour later, the lunchtime rush was in full swing. A queue stretched to the door and Maggie and I were jostling each other behind the counter, taking orders and dishing out food. Alex was doing an impressively efficient job keeping the tables clear for the next occupants. Glancing at the door to check on the state of the queue, I noticed Simon standing at the back. A few seconds later Alice also turned up and waved at me, mouthing that she would come back later, then she noticed Simon and stopped to talk to him. By the time we had worked our way through the queue Alice and Simon were engrossed in conversation.

'Oi, had you two come to see me?' I said to them, leaning on the counter in exhaustion.

Alice realised that the queue of people had vanished and sauntered over looking sheepish. All the tables in the café were full and the room buzzed with sounds of people eating and talking. Maggie was icing another chocolate gâteau and Alex was stacking the dishwasher. I loved seeing the café full of people enjoying themselves and I surveyed them with pride.

'You're busy for a Monday,' Alice said. 'I thought I'd be able to have a coffee with you before I go back to work.' She checked her watch, pulling a face. 'I've got to be back in ten minutes. How about a drink tonight instead? The Oyster's got some promotion on, a pound a drink all night. We can sit out in the garden and have a natter.' She batted her eyes at me and gave me a winning smile.

'Sounds good, can I come?' Maggie interrupted, making a space for her cake on the counter.

'What about me?' Simon asked, looking put out.

'You can only come if you don't bring Noah,' Maggie said.

'I wouldn't worry too much, he went skiing with Charlie last week, they haven't got back yet. What about you, Holly, will you come?' All three of them looked at me with doey-eyed pleading faces.

'Go on then,' I agreed, 'but I must leave early. I can't have a late night, I'm knackered.'

Alice and I arrived at The Oyster Catcher at eight o'clock and the place was absolutely packed. We had arranged to meet Maggie and Simon in the garden. The nights were still too cold for many people to want to sit outside, despite the outside heaters, so we knew we could get a good table. Alice led the way, trying to shield me from getting too crushed in the heaving crowd.

'Why don't you go and bag us a table and I'll get the drinks in and find you in a minute,' she yelled. I gave her a thumbs up and pushed my way towards the back exit.

Sitting at a table in the corner nearest the door I caught sight of Noah and Tom's best friend Charlie. I attempted to duck behind a couple of girls that were standing nearby, but I had already been spotted. Noah shouted at me to come and join them and patted a small space on the little sofa next to him.

I reluctantly obeyed. 'Hiya,' I greeted, sitting

149

down in a hunched forward position to make sure neither of them would spot my bump.

'Holly,' Charlie grinned, kissing me on the cheek. 'God, it's been ages since I saw you. When was the last time, before Christmas wasn't it?' He clicked his fingers, trying to remember.

'Probably. Simon told me you and Noah have been away skiing, is that right?' I asked, in a vain attempt to change the subject.

He nodded absent-mindedly, still thinking.

'Yep, just got back this afternoon, dumped our bags off and came here straight from the airport, actually. I remember when I last saw you now,' he said slapping the table. 'It was the day after our Halloween party. Did you catch Tom before he flew off?'

'Oh, um no, I didn't bother going in the end. There wasn't any point,' I lied.

'I got a postcard from him when he was in Australia, lucky bastard.' He had thankfully accepted my lie, no questions asked.

'Who are you here with?' Noah asked, looking around.

'Alice is at the bar, she's just getting the drinks in. Then we're meeting up with Simon and Maggie in the garden.'

I watched Noah's eyebrows shoot upwards, in the manner of a dog's ears when it hears a fridge door open.

'How is she?' He was suddenly fascinated by the head on his beer.

'Oh, you know Maggie, always upbeat. Her mum's

150

getting married in a month, so that's stressing her out a bit. She's been keeping an eye out for you in the pubs when she goes out at night, though. She's been wondering where you've been hiding.'

He smiled at that, his gleaming white teeth a striking contrast to his dark skin. 'Good. I haven't been here much, actually. I went skiing with Charlie, and I've been over in Dublin a lot, sorting out a contact for work. It's been pretty hectic lately.'

I saw Alice balancing a tray of drinks and yelling, 'Excuse me!' at a group of blokes standing in her way. I caught her attention, waving her over, then leaned in and whispered to Noah.

'Look, if Maggie turns up now and catches us all sitting together she'll think we've set her up. We'd better go and wait for them outside. Why don't you come and find us in a little while?'

'We might,' he said, obviously enjoying his new playing-it-cool role. I said goodbye and gestured to Alice to follow me into the garden.

'What were you talking to Noah about?' Alice asked, catching me up.

'Oh, we were just talking about his holiday.' I pushed the back doors open, feeling the cool air chill the back of my throat and work its way downwards. Scanning the few people dotted randomly on the old wooden picnic tables I noticed that Maggie and Simon had already arrived. They were sitting under an oak tree at a table already littered with empty pint glasses and crisp packets.

There were speakers in the garden set above the door; when we passed underneath them we

151

were blasted with the sound of Robbie Williams. Simon looked up and saw us, then joined in with Robbie, belting out 'Angels', and holding his arms out to us. Why is it lads always want to be Robbie Williams?

A couple of people on a table nearby turned to see who Simon was singing to.

Alice and I exchanged a look that said 'God, how embarrassing!' Then we sashayed over to them with grins on our faces, feeling important.

'At last,' Maggie yelled at us, budging up on the bench to give us more room.

'We're not that late,' Alice said, checking her watch.

'I know, but Simon and I were early. We started without you.'

'I can see that,' I said, gesturing to the empty glasses. 'It's a good job we got a round in.' We sat down and the wooden bench creaked rudely in protest. Alice dished out the drinks.

'Did you see anyone we know in the bar?' Maggie asked. I shook my head, taking a sip of my coke, and shot Alice a warning look.

'Brrr, it's a bit cold.' I rubbed my hands together and sat closer to Simon.

'Well, you're not sitting inside, Holly, it's far too smokey in there for you. Do you want to wear my coat?' He started shrugging his fleece off his shoulders. 'I'm not cold at all.'

I thanked him but declined. This is how it should be, I thought. Having somebody protecting me, caring. God, feminists would have me burned on

152

a bra bonfire! I've got to start being an independent woman. A role model for my future child.

'So, girls,' Maggie announced, banging the table with a glass to get our attention. 'You are both coming to this wedding, aren't you? I'm going to need all my friends at hand to help dilute the concentration of horrendous family members. I'm only accepting terminal illness in its advanced stages and premature labour as a valid excuse.'

Alice and I both nodded our heads dutifully.

'You can both bring a friend, by the way.'

'Excellent,' Simon said. 'Can I be a friend?'

'You can be mine, if you like,' Alice invited, patting his arm. 'There's no one else I can ask that knows Mags and Holly. And Shelley's going to be away that weekend.'

'Thanks Alice, I'd be delighted,' he said with mock formality and they clinked their glasses together, laughing.

I watched them jealously. I had been planning to invite Simon myself; now I had no one.

'Who are you going to bring?' Maggie asked me.

I shrugged my shoulders sulkily.

'Come on, you've got to bring someone, the more normal people there the better,' she insisted. I told her I'd think about it and sipped my drink, watching Alice and Simon as they chatted animatedly between themselves.

By half past ten I was getting more and more restless. Alice was the happiest I had seen her in ages and I was glad for her, but ultimately it only served to make me more fed up. They were all

153

getting pretty drunk and I began to think about heading back home. I fumbled about under the bench for my bag and half stood up, ready to say goodbye, when Maggie suddenly tugged hard on the bottom of my cardigan, sitting me back down with a thud.

'You can't go yet,' she urged.

'Why? I'm really tired.' I made an exaggerated show of stifling a yawn.

'Please, not yet.' Then she gestured to the back door of the pub. I turned and saw Charlie wandering towards us with Noah in tow balancing a tray of drinks, a bag of scampi fries clamped between his teeth.

'Hey look, it's Charlie and Noah, budge up everyone, make some room,' Simon said, shuffling further up the bench.

'All right, mate?' Charlie said, slapping Simon on the back. 'We saw you all through the window. I got in a round for everyone seeing as it was so cheap.' He handed Simon a beer and gave Alice, Maggie and myself a glass of wine each. I took mine guiltily, deciding that just one wouldn't hurt. I didn't want to arouse Charlie's suspicion by not drinking.

'Cheers, mate, thanks a lot,' Simon said, patting the space on the bench between us for Charlie to sit down.

Noah sat opposite him, between Alice and Maggie. He sat angled to face Alice and began chatting to her, asking if she'd seen anything of Oliver since New Year's Eve.

154

Maggie gulped down half her wine in a matter of seconds.

'He sent me a Valentine's card, but I haven't seen him since then, fortunately,' explained Alice, looking instantly more glum. 'I know he's split up with Rachel.'

'Well, don't let him talk you into taking him back. You're far too good for him,' Noah said flirtatiously. He was blatantly trying to make Maggie jealous and I glanced over to see if she had noticed. I was pleased to see her looking at Noah with a thunderous expression.

'Alice, where did you say you worked?' Simon asked, butting into their conversation.

'I'm a receptionist at Hill View Surgery. You know, the big old building next to the theatre.'

'Hey, that's where I'm registered,' he said, his face brightening.

'Oh wow, really? But I've worked there for five years now. I've never seen you in there.'

He snorted, puffing his chest out. 'You think a healthy specimen like this ever needs to see the doctor? Besides, I've been on an advanced first-aid course, I could examine myself.'

'I wondered why you always spend so long in the shower,' Charlie teased.

'Bastard!' Simon grunted and leaned in to carry on chatting to Alice.

Noah turned to start talking to me so I excused myself and headed for the bathroom, leaving Maggie looking forlornly after me, with only Noah to talk to.

155

I took ages in the loo, hoping that Mags and Noah would be forced to strike up a conversation in my absence. By the time I walked back out into the garden they were laughing and joking together like old friends.

I scooped up my bag. 'I think I'm going to push off now,' I said to them all. 'I can't stay awake much longer.'

'Are you sure?' Alice asked, looking guilty at not having paid me more attention. 'Do you want us to walk you back?'

'No, don't worry, you stay here. It's only around the corner.'

'I'll take you back,' Charlie offered, hopping up and fetching his coat before I had time to protest.

'Are you sure?'

'No problem.'

We stepped out of the noisy pub and into the still night. The old stone buildings lined the little street where we walked and our footsteps echoed on their crumbling walls. Charlie set the pace by ambling along, his hands in the pockets of his combat trousers. He was doing that kind of walk you do when you're feeling all happy and content. He took slow, lazy strides, as though he was in no hurry to get anywhere.

'So, not drinking tonight?' he asked eventually.

'Oh, er no. I'm pretty tired. I think alcohol would have finished me off.'

We walked on in silence for a few minutes.

'Do you think when Tom gets back, he'll settle down?' he asked suddenly, catching me by surprise.

It was the million-dollar question. What my whole life seemed to be currently revolving around.

'I don't know, I've not really thought about it,' I blagged, nearly convincing myself. 'Why do you ask?'

'I dunno,' he said, shrugging. 'Don't you ever wonder when you're going to meet that special someone, or if you already have? I mean, we're all coming up to thirty, my parents were already married with two kids at my age. Don't you ever feel like time's running out?'

I burst into shocked laughter, unable to believe my ears. 'Since when were you looking for a serious relationship? You are the loosest bloke I've ever known. You'd shag anything that sat still long enough!'

Charlie was a club DJ, and his job was very much about lifestyle. He stayed out all night, almost every night, spent most of his days in bed and wasn't shy of taking the odd class A.

Women followed him around like groupies. He scored highly in the looks stakes, he was tall, lean and had a street style that flattered his physique. I wasn't surprised that whenever I had stayed over at the house he shared with Tom and Simon, there was usually a new gorgeous but bleary-eyed woman in the kitchen, padding about in one of Charlie's T-shirts making coffee and moaning about him snoring like something out of a zoo. He was the kind of mate I was wary about Tom having. How could Tom consider settling for a lasting relationship when Charlie was flaunting

157

his laddish lifestyle under his nose? What bloke in their right mind wouldn't want a piece of the action?

'But can't you see, that's exactly why I do sleep with lots of women,' he insisted. 'I'm on a hunt for the perfect one. I haven't got time to hang around doing the whole Hugh Grant dithery thing. I've got to get in there, suss them out and move on, until one day, BANG, I'll find a woman I can actually enjoy having breakfast with.'

'There are more productive ways of sussing a woman out than getting her into bed, you know. Don't you think it takes time for things to develop? I mean, what if you had known someone for years and slowly, gradually they got under your skin. Then they go off somewhere for one reason or another and it dawns on you that you can't be without them.'

'Nah, that's bollocks,' he said, taking a cigarette from his pocket and lighting it, flicking the match into the gutter. 'If they were that special you would have noticed straight away.'

I gave up quickly; it was pointless trying to convince him. His laddish attitudes were ingrained and impossible to change. He was just the kind of bloke that women countrywide would write into magazines complaining about.

'Dear Marge, My boyfriend's always looking at page three girls, does that mean he thinks my tits are too small?' Or, 'Dear Marge, I met this gorgeous bloke at a club last week, we ended up back at his house and had sex. He promised he'd call me, but

158

since then not a dickybird. Do you think something awful's happened to him?'

Still, despite his faults there was something lovable about Charlie and I enjoyed our walk back. At the pub I was beginning to feel like I was invisible. Mags and Noah had been engrossed in reciting quotes from *Blackadder* and roaring with laughter, whilst Alice and Simon had talked quietly, huddled over their drinks. It was nice to have somebody's undivided attention.

Standing outside the café, I toyed with the idea of inviting him in for a coffee but decided in Charlie's book that was tantamount to flashing my tits at him and twanging a condom under his nose. I wished him goodnight and pecked him lightly on the cheek, then made my way up the dark stairwell. Before I turned on the kitchen light I walked across to the window and looked down on the dimly lit street. Charlie was sitting on the curb below the flat, his hands on his knees, and looking deep in thought. After a few minutes he got up, gave a backward glance at my front door and walked away, kicking at some stones on the path.

CHAPTER FIFTEEN

When Maggie arrived for work the next morning it was immediately obvious that she was nursing a hangover. Rather than homing straight in on the coffee machine, she poured herself a glass of tap water and leaned against the sink, moaning softly.

'Are you listening to the radio?' she asked in a tiny voice, flicking off the hyperactive DJ's monologue before I could reply. 'That's better.'

'Poor love. It's a hard life, drinking to excess with the bloke you fancy and generally having a brilliant time. You realise I haven't had a hangover for months!'

'Don't pretend you envy me, you vision of health,' she moaned, sizing me up. 'You with the complexion of a rosy apple polished on a young farmer's thigh. Ugh, and your hair is doing that annoying bouncy thing, put it away before I faint with inferiority!'

I laughed at her absently, feeling the ends of my hair. She was right; I had more vitality than a butcher's dog this morning. With the bouts of morning sickness forgotten and the tiredness being replaced with a new-found energy I was beginning to enjoy being pregnant. I was even growing my hair longer in an effort to look more like a feminine earth mother type (basically copying off Madonna!). I grabbed a scrunchy and pulled it back into a low ponytail.

'Can you make a creamy mushroom and fennel soup and I'll do the bread?' I asked, washing my hands in the sink next to her.

She took her hands away from her face and looked at me in disgust. 'Do you want me to vomit? Do you actually want to bring me to my knees with nausea?'

'Oh yes, sorry. I remember cooking that when I had morning sickness. The smell was like . . .'

'Please stop. I'll do the bread.' She fetched a big mixing bowl from the bottom cupboard.

'So, you have a good time last night?'

'Er . . .' She looked as though she was trying hard to remember what happened last night. 'I think so.'

'You looked like you got on well with Noah.'

'Yeah, he's a good laugh.'

'Did you ask him about the Valentine's card?'

'No, didn't want to bring the subject up. But we were talking about *Wayne's World*, "Bohemian Rhapsody" came on and he started doing this,' she started head-banging then groaned, clamping her floury hand on her head. 'Oh God, that hurt. Yeah, so he was doing what they did in the car, in the film, y'know. It was obviously him that sent it. Oh shit, oh shit!' She froze, her mouth open and her hands limp over the bowl of dough.

161

'What? Are you going to be sick? Maggie, don't be sick in the kitchen, run to the loo, quick!'

'No, it's not that. I just remembered something I did. Oh God, Hol, I invited him to the wedding. What am I going to do?'

'Well you could try erm . . . going to the wedding with him perhaps. What's the problem?'

'Oh come on!' She slapped the dough on the floured surface and began kneading hard. 'He's going to know, I mean, think, I fancy him now. It's not like saying, "come to the cinema, I fancy seeing this film and no one will go with me", or, "hey, I've got a spare ticket to some evening thing". I mean that would be forward enough, but a wedding, a wedding is the ultimate in coupley dates. He's going to think I've got plans for his future, BIG plans!'

'Maggie, how could anybody ever think that of you! If he knows you at all he'll take it with a pinch of salt, a chance to have a laugh. Don't stress.'

'Hmm, I'm not sure,' she said, pulling a face. 'Have you got any Nurofen in the medicine cabinet?'

Half an hour later, Alex, the work experience student arrived.

'Hey Al, how's it hanging?' Maggie greeted, as he took his coat off, making him blush. She chucked a tea towel at him. 'I've made a lovely lot of washing-up for you. Warn me before you switch on the dishwasher, though. My head might explode.'

'Hangover,' I explained to him. 'Hi Alex, sorry about the boring washing-up. I thought when you've

162

got through that lot I'd show you how to work the till, it's only a simple one. Then so long as we don't get a sudden surge I'll let you have a try at serving if you fancy it. See how it goes, okay?'

Alex got the hang of the till really quickly, laughing at how basic it was, which caused me mild offence. Kids at school nowadays have so much knowledge and experience with all things electronic they leave me feeling prehistoric. I find that whenever I have the misfortune to be stuck in the middle of a conversation about computers I become bad-tempered, defensive and stubborn. I am ashamed of my own ignorance.

'You should get a computer in the café,' he said with youthful enthusiasm, obviously in his element. 'You wouldn't need anything too flash. An early generation Pentium would suit you; you'd get one second-hand pretty cheap. Then you could log all your recipes and menus into a database. It's so easy. You could do all your accounts, rosters and stock on spread sheets, even design adverts and menus for the tables if you had Corel Draw, and maybe advertise on the Net.'

I nodded blankly, trying to make like I had a grasp of what he was on about, but basically all I had heard was *'blah, blah, blah'*.

'Well, I don't really have the time for all that; maybe in the future. Besides, I'm quite happy with the way I do things at the moment, actually.'

I could hear Maggie chuckling to herself in the kitchen. 'You mean three Black n'Red jotters and a packet of Post-it notes?'

163

'Yeah, well I don't really need anything else,' I snapped defensively, convinced I could see Alex hiding a smirk.

Shelley saved me from resorting to a Victor Meldrew-style grumpy outburst. She breezed in wearing a tiny tight vest top and mini skirt with huge knee-high boots. Her red hair was wild and curly, she had piled it on top of her head, letting a few tendrils hang loosely, softening her face. Alex looked completely captivated.

'Holly, I have got to eat something soon I'm starving. Have you got any homity pie ready yet?'

'I just took one out of the oven.' I checked my watch. 'Shelley, it's only half past nine. Are you sure you wouldn't rather have something more breakfasty?'

'I had breakfast four hours ago, I've been up since the crack of dawn working on a piece for my exhibition.'

She spotted Alex standing dumbstruck next to me. 'Oh hello, you must be the work experience student. I'm Shelley, I work here part time.' She leaned across the counter to shake his hand and whispered, 'Friendly advice. Maggie isn't as scary as she first appears. Loves puppy dogs and doesn't even kill spiders. Just don't go into the store room alone with her, she's a sucker for a man in uniform.' She pointed at Alex's regulation white apron. He let out a high-pitched nervous laugh and shifted from one foot to another, not knowing where to look.

'Alex, how would you like to serve Shelley? You were watching yesterday, so you've got the general

164

idea and it'd give you a bit of practice before the real customers start arriving. Shelley can show you what to do.'

He agreed, not taking his eyes off Shelley for a moment.

'Excellent, can I have a homity pie and salad and a pot of tea?' she said. Alex looked nervously at me.

'Right, you do the salad, I'll fetch the pie from the kitchen,' I suggested, disappearing before Alex could chicken out. I decided he might be less nervous if I wasn't watching over him.

In the kitchen Maggie and I listened round the corner to see how he was doing. We could hear the clatter of him dishing the salad out on to a plate.

'Would you like undressing?' he squeaked, then corrected quickly. 'I mean dressing. Would you like some dressing?' Maggie and I clamped our hands over our mouths, trying to fight back the giggles.

Just then the phone rang, making us both jump. Alex turned and saw us crouching by the door and looked mortified.

'I'll get it,' I said, pretending I had been reaching for the phone all along. 'Mags, can you get Shelley's pie for her and help Alex to serve?' I gave Alex a thumbs up sign. 'You're doing fine,' I mouthed and picked up the phone.

'The Owl and Pussycat, Holly speaking.'

'Hello darling, it's Mum. Are you okay?'

'Oh fine, feeling much less tired now.'

'Great, so you fancy coming shopping tomorrow? You do still close early on a Wednesday, don't you?'

165

'Yes, that sounds great. I guess I've got to start getting some things. Spread the cost.' I picked at a chocolate cookie Maggie had left on the side to cool and popped it into my mouth. 'Ow, ow, ouch, ahhh . . .'

'Oh my God, what? Are you okay, Holly speak to me!' Mum panicked.

'It's okay, I just ate something too hot.' I fanned my mouth by the window.

There was a long, worried pause before she said, 'I don't know if I like you working there up until the baby's born. You're going to be tempted to overdo it.'

'Mum, the only thing I'm in danger of doing here is overeating! You mustn't worry about me, I'm not ill.'

'I know, I'm sorry, I just want you to look after yourself.'

'I will.'

'Okay then, how about I pick you up at the café at two? We can hit the shops straight away. But make a list of what you need. There's a lot to think about.'

I said goodbye, sighing to myself. I couldn't believe Mum sometimes. She worries I've over exerted myself by eating a cookie, then arranges to drag me all over Bath on a major shopping expedition. The physical demands incurred on a shopping trip with her were comparable to competing in a decathlon. She was born to shop and would dart about like Anneka Rice, leaving me trailing behind carrying the bags, with a view of her backside weaving between terrified pedestrians

166

as she shouted, 'ten minutes to go, keep up, keep up!' Even with my flourishing energy supplies I wasn't sure I was ready for that.

'That'll be forty-eight pounds fifty, please,' I heard Alex announce to Shelley in a voice that sounded wobbly and unsure. So much for my basic technology, I thought and went to help him out before he died of shame.

'Come on, sweetheart, don't dawdle. There's only a quarter of an hour before the shops shut. Chop! Chop!' Mum nagged from several paces ahead of me. She executed a perfectly dangerous right turn, cutting up a little old lady pushing one of those tartan bags on wheels. I muttered a brief apology but she shot me a look that would sour gold top and I've scurried after Mum into the Technicolour baby shop.

We were both loaded up with bags of baby essentials already, most of which my mum had insisted on picking up the bill for. It felt odd letting her pay for everything. It was as though I was still a dependant, not quite able to take care of my own affairs. A small indignant part of me wanted to insist that she put her plastic away, but I knew it wasn't worth hurting her feelings to save my pride. Besides, the café may be doing all right for itself but I was no Branson. The wage I paid myself was only equivalent to that of the average fresh graduate that had taken any old temp job just to tide themselves over. The rest of my profits went straight back into the business.

'Steriliser,' Mum said, clicking her fingers and pointing at me.

167

'What? Look, Mum, there's no need for that; I won't be having any more children for a long time yet. Let's face it, no man will come near me for a long time yet.'

'Duh, not for you, silly. For bottles and feeding bowls, everything needs to be sterile.' Mum laughed to herself and began sorting through the boxes on the shelves in front of her. She picked one out and handed it to me. 'I read an article in *Baby World* that recommended this one. You put it in the microwave, see?' She held a diagram of an immaculate woman holding a microwave door open and smiling at its steaming plastic contents. 'I thought it would suit you, what with you using them so much anyway.'

I took the box and jammed it under my arm, still looking at her.

'What?'

'You read an article in *Baby World*?' I repeated incredulously.

'Oh, that old thing, it was in the doctor's waiting room, I just happened to pick it up. Ooh, look at those, Holly, come and see,' she cooed, changing the subject and making for a rack of newborn dresses. I shuffled after her and dumped all my packages on the floor by her feet as my arms finally gave in. I shook my hands, trying to stimulate the circulation back into action.

Mum picked the first dress up and read the label hanging off the back.

'Newborn, six to seven pounds. Gosh, you were ten pounds six, this would never have fitted you.'

My jaw dropped open and my eyes instantly

168

began to water. 'Ten six! How come you never told me before? That's a fully-grown toddler, it must have been agony!'

She gave me a dismissive wave of her hand. 'Don't be silly, Holly, I didn't feel a thing. It was a beautiful experience. All that fuss they make on the telly is just for dramatic effect, all that screaming and swearing. Ha, I was singing Beatles songs and knitting a poncho when you came into the world. I've worked up more sweat plaiting my hair.'

Slowly my pulse ceased from banging in my ears and reverted back to its usual steady rhythm. 'Really?' I whispered.

'Holly, there's nothing to worry about. Trust me.'

I took the little dress off her and held it over my swollen tummy, stroking the fabric until it lay snugly against me. 'It's amazing, isn't it? That it's going to get this big. I mean how on earth does it all fit?'

Mum's eyes took on a dreamy expression. 'It's hard to believe that there's a living, breathing, perfect baby in there, isn't it?'

We looked at each other, smiling.

What's wrong with me? My emotions are up and down more often than a soap star's backside. I shook the sentimental moment from my mind and looked self-consciously around the shop. My eyes fell on a familiar-looking woman standing a few feet from us. She was leaning on a double buggy and staring at my bump.

I looked down at the two babies and it suddenly dawned on me where I had seen her before.

'Hello, Holly. What are you doing here?' she asked.

I tried to tuck my tummy back in and slouch, but with the intrusive shop lights beaming down on me, it was like trying to hide a basketball under a bed sheet.

'Mum, this is Tamsin, Tom's auntie. She's recently moved down from Edinburgh, remember I told you about her?'

Mum said hello, then noticed the twins lying patiently in the pram, staring unblinking at a washing line of toys that hung above them.

'Look at these two lovelies,' she cried, homing in like a bee to a jam sandwich.

'I was just, erm, just looking for a present for the twins actually,' I blurted in a clear moment of inspiration. 'Oops, caught red-handed!' I made a mock gesture of trying to hide the outfit behind my back.

Tamsin leaned forward and took it off me. 'Holly, it's a dress. You know the twins are both boys.'

'Are they? Is it? Gosh, I thought it was an, erm, a tunic.'

'Right, I can see how you would have thought that,' she said sarcastically, pointing at what was looking more and more like a miniature ball gown by the second. It had the words, 'what little girls are made of', stitched on the front panel under a bunch of appliquéd flowers. An awkward silence followed, broken only by my mum's efforts at entertaining the babies with farmyard animal noises and a finger puppet.

'You're pregnant, aren't you?' she asked, looking me directly in the eyes.

'What? Ha ha ha, no, ha ha, NO! Of course not. I mean I've put on a bit of weight over Christmas, you know how it is. Gosh, I must wear more flattering clothes.' I tugged nervously at my baggy trousers.

A shop assistant cleared her throat and made an exaggerated play at looking at her watch. Mum noticed and stood up, collecting the steriliser off the floor.

'Darling, I'll just go and pay for this, I think they want to close up soon.'

Tamsin looked at the box Mum was taking to the counter, then scanned her eyes over to the pile of shopping bags I had left on the floor nearby. They were sporting the names of various local baby shops and a Winnie The Pooh mobile was protruding out of one. She turned to me, her eyebrows raised.

'Did I tell you Mum's best friend is about to become a grandma? Yes, it's a shame actually. She's really quite ill. Mum offered to go shopping for her and get some things for the baby, they do need a lot of stuff, don't they? Babies I mean.' I tried not to visibly cringe at my lame excuse.

'Oh I see, well, I'd better let you get on. You're obviously quite busy,' Tamsin said, looking hurt. I told myself that was because she was disappointed about me not being pregnant after all, rather than upset that I had found it necessary to lie so blatantly to her.

'I'll see you soon then,' I called after her, feeling about two inches tall.

Mum had been standing nearby and had heard the whole thing. I turned back to her. 'Do you think she believed me?'

She just looked sympathetic and said nothing.

Sitting in my spare bedroom that same evening, surrounded by baby-related purchases, I found myself thinking the same thought over and over again: 'It's not meant to be like this.'

My fantasies of having children had always been preceded by a dream romance fantasy, a white wedding fantasy and a painting the nursery together with me heavily pregnant wearing dungarees and sporting a cute smudge of paint on my nose fantasy. That was obviously never going to happen now. I just had to accept it.

A gentle tapping at the door saved me from my self-pitying cloud of gloom.

'That'll be Alice,' I said to mini-bump, patting it happily, relieved to have some company.

I swung open the door saying, 'Thank God you're here,' but it wasn't Alice standing outside, it was Tamsin. I slammed the door shut and pressed my body against it before she got the chance to say anything.

She knocked on the door again. 'Come on, Holly, please let me in.'

'Sorry, it's not a good time. I've just come out of the bath,' I yelled.

'You have not!' She opened the letterbox and crouched down, peering through.

'Look, you don't have to see me if you don't

want to. I just thought you might like someone to talk to. Somebody who can understand what you're going through. I'm good at keeping secrets and I thought you might like this,' there was a rustling noise, followed by a thump as a giant Toblerone landed between my feet. My resolve dissolved and I opened the door, peering behind her into the street suspiciously before shutting the door behind us.

'So, are you going to admit you're pregnant now, or am I going to have to take a blood sample,' she joked, waving her hair grip at me dangerously.

I showed her through to the kitchen, switching the kettle on as I went.

'Look, I can understand you have a loyalty to Marcus and Fiona but I really don't want them to know just yet,' I said eventually.

'It's okay,' she smiled. 'No one will hear it from me, scouts' honour,' she added, crossing her heart, slapping her thigh, then giving me the peace sign.

'Something tells me you never even made it to the Brownies.'

'Well no,' she admitted laughing, 'but Dad was a Mason, and I did Morris dancing on Thursday nights.'

We were silent whilst I made the tea, and when I handed Tamsin her steaming cup she tapped the side of it with her fingers. 'Holly,' she started nervously.

'Yeeees.'

'Can I ask you a personal question?'

'I guess we have no secrets now,' I said, leading the way to the sitting room.

173

'Well, I was wondering, is the reason you're keeping it so secret that it's not Tom's baby?'

The tea I had just sipped decided playfully to avoid my throat, do a U-turn and travel up through my nose instead, making me cough and splutter.

'Is that what you think? Oh God, no, it's definitely Tom's.'

'Then why all the secrecy?'

I tried to explain to her the feelings I was having, and how worried I had been about making Tom feel forced into doing something his heart wasn't in.

When I had finished she said, 'I think you're right.'

'You do?' I said, taken aback.

'Yes, after all, it's your choice.'

'You don't think I'm being selfish or unfair to Tom?'

'Look,' she said resolutely, putting down her tea. 'It's a big shock you've had, it'll take time to adjust. Just be ready to face the music when it does come out; you can't keep it a secret for much longer so use this time to prepare yourself. To be honest Tom hasn't called since Christmas, he's useless at getting in touch, and he moves around so much even if you did want to tell him you'd have a job tracking him down.'

My heart lurched at the thought of him having so many amazing experiences that he had forgotten all about us. Suddenly I felt nauseous.

'It's all such a big mess,' I croaked.

Tamsin smiled kindly and placed her hand on my arm. 'Look, you do have one thing in your favour.

Marcus and Fi are going to spend ten weeks in the south of France; he's got a contract out there to do up a villa. They're leaving tomorrow night, so that'll buy you some time. You've got to stop worrying so much though. At least try to enjoy it. Having a baby is an amazing thing.'

As she said that I felt a small kick at the lower half of my bump. 'Oh my God, I think it just kicked!'

'AHHA HA HA!' we yelled in unison, pogoing up and down with our eyes fixed on my mini-bump.

'This is going to be so much fun,' Tamsin said breathlessly, beaming with excitement.

Two more cups of tea and half a jumbo Toblerone each later were had verbally dissecting every symptom of the early stages of pregnancy. I had a few rogue suspicions that the reason Tamsin was so excited about my situation was that it made her feel better about her own. A bit like when you discover that you've put on three pounds after a weekend of bingeing, phone a friend to moan about it and discover that they've put on four. Whatever her reasons were I didn't really mind. I was just happy to be able to talk to someone who completely understood.

'The stretch marks on my boobs faded really quickly,' she was saying. 'They were only tiny. It's the ones on my belly I think I'll always have, they look like scars. Do you have any there yet?'

'No, I don't seem to be getting any,' I said, trying not to be too smug about the elastic properties of my skin.

'That's good, then.' She smiled knowingly.

Why is it women that have had babies have 101 different facial expressions that hint to a wealth of knowledge only mothers are capable of knowing? Knowledge that would strike fear into the heart of any ovulating woman.

Tamsin had a faraway look in her eyes and was laughing to herself. 'Oh God, I had the worst cravings. I'm sure I read somewhere that you're only supposed to have that for the first couple of months, but I swear I had it for all nine. I've never experienced anything like it; I used to get so frustrated if I couldn't have sardines I'd end up crying! I mean, couldn't I have at least craved something that didn't smell like the insole of a shoe?'

I giggled, making myself more comfy on the sofa. 'Mine haven't exactly been unpleasant, more a case of poor timing. It was summer pudding on Christmas Day, and now that Christmas is well and truly over I've been obsessing over a piece of Christmas cake. I drove to the supermarket as if my arse was on fire and the best I could find was a bloody cherry Genoa, no marzipan or royal icing, nothing!'

Tamsin cracked up laughing. 'Oh you poor thing what did you do?'

I hung my head in shame, 'I made one last week, it took me hours!' I muttered.

Tamsin laughed even harder.

'I iced it and everything, there's still some left if you want a piece.'

'Oh, I couldn't possibly deprive you,' she said,

holding her hands up. 'Besides, I can't stand marzipan.' She smiled to herself whimsically. 'Oh, this is really nice, you're bringing it all back. I'm almost jealous of you, I'd love to be pregnant again.'

I looked up, surprised. 'Really? It sounds like you had a pretty hard time if you don't mind me saying, what with Oscar, and then having a Caesarean, you must be knackered with twins on your own.'

'Yeah, but it's not all dirty nappies and the broken nights you always hear about. I mean, okay, I'm not doing the textbook nuclear family bit, and it hasn't always been easy, but the thing is, I've got two little people in my life now and they are the best things I've ever done. It's like no matter what I do, I've got my own self-made family and it makes me feel stronger, and despite the fact that it ties me down more, I feel strangely liberated. No one can take that away from me. And the whole single parent thing doesn't seem to have the same stigma attached to it any more. People actually respect me for it. I mean, I meet people who ask what I do and I tell them I mostly look after my kids and they nearly always say, "ooh, that's the hardest job in the world!" People really see it as hard work, not just an easy way off the career ladder. You wouldn't believe how many women have actually said they envy me, how they wish they could be concentrating on a family, rather than being forced into jobs they don't care about because they can't find a man they like enough to have kids with.'

I looked at her sceptically, not convinced.

'Don't get me wrong, I'm not saying that's all

women want out of life. Of course there are tons of women happy to concentrate on their careers. What I'm saying is that a mother is no longer seen as a second-class person, we're as hard worked as anybody else, and bringing up children that are bright and happy is just about the biggest achievement there is.'

I stroked my bump absently. She was right.

Tamsin glanced at her watch then sat up, looking around for her jacket. 'I hadn't realised how late it was getting, Fiona's looking after the twins so I'll have to go. How about we go out for the day on Sunday, get away from it all? We could go for a walk and a picnic, or go shopping at that big mall in Bristol?'

'Shopping,' we both said in unison, laughing.

'I'll call you tomorrow,' she said, leaning over and planting a kiss on my cheek. 'And if you need to talk anytime, you know where I am.'

CHAPTER SIXTEEN

Friday was Alex's last day at the café and he was even quieter than usual. I got the feeling he wasn't looking forward to going back to college.

'Is Shelley working today?' he asked hopefully, almost as soon as he arrived. Shelley had worked most of the day before to stand in for Maggie, who was having an extended weekend to catch up with some old friends. Alex had found it difficult to get any work done with Shelley nearby and had spent most of the day staring at her with big doey eyes and slipping in and out of daydreams. I was almost relieved that Shelley had to go into college today, I wanted to make sure his last day was productive so I'd have enough achievements to write on his report form.

'I'm afraid it's just you and me today, Alex, sorry,' I said. It didn't seem that long ago that I had a crush on my Business Studies teacher. It took me about a year to get over the embarrassment of him snatching a note off me as I passed it to Maggie, and reading it aloud to the class. It said something along the lines of,

179

M, I can't bear it any longer, I LOVE him! Did you see how close he was when he leaned over to read my work, AHHHHH! He's such a dish, even better than Simon Lebon. Meet me at the gates after, we need to discuss, love H.

To be fair, I don't think he realised it was about him until after he read it, but after that my crush was miraculously cured and I turned my attention to the lad that worked at the cinema instead. Everything had felt so intense at that age.

I spent the morning cooking whilst Alex served and cleaned in near silence. I let him have a long lunch as he'd worked so hard, and when he sat down with his meal, Alice came in to see me.

'A word,' she whispered and gestured to the kitchen.

I showed her behind the counter and we huddled by the sink like a pair of old gossips. 'What's going on?' I urged, looking into her eyes. She looked excited but edgy, like someone who had seen a fifty-pound note on the floor but wasn't sure whether to pick it up in case it was actually part of a national experiment on honesty, where after you'd pocketed it a camera crew would pounce on you, grilling you on criminal tendencies.

'I saw Oliver today,' she whispered naughtily.

A sense of dread and foreboding gripped me. 'Yeeees,' I said cautiously.

'Don't look like that, it's okay, I was cool with him.'

'I can't believe you've even graced him with a conversation after what he did to you.'

She waved her hand dismissively; obviously not wanting to be reminded of what a cowardly shit he really was. I wanted to scream at her. She was only lucky Mags wasn't here.

'He came to see me at work. I couldn't believe it; he'd bought me the biggest bunch of flowers. He's never bought me flowers before. He gave them to me in front of everyone.'

A tut escaped me before I could stop myself. 'Alice, please be careful, I don't want to see you get hurt again.'

'You don't understand,' she said, leaning on the work surface and gazing out of the kitchen window. 'It's not like that. He just wanted to talk. He said he was ashamed of how badly he'd treated me. I swear, Holly, there were tears in his eyes when he said it.'

My mind cruelly pictured him standing outside the surgery where Alice worked, rubbing Vick under his eyes before he went in, to get the desired watery effect. I wouldn't put anything past him.

'He wants to meet me for a drink, just so we can clear the air. He said he totally expected me to hate him, and that if I blew him out he'd understand, but he'd keep trying because what we had really meant something to him and he couldn't just forget it.' She spoke as though she was reciting a letter. She had obviously been playing those words over and over in her mind since she had seen him.

'Alice,' I ventured cautiously, 'it has been two

months since New Year's Eve. I mean, don't you think he could have come to you earlier with this?'

'Exactly,' she said happily. Her cheeks were glowing a worrying rosy pink. 'But don't you see that that makes it seem all the more genuine.' She ignored my doubting expression. 'He's had lots of time to think about it and sort himself out. He could easily have just gone out and met someone else, but he hasn't.'

How do you know he hasn't? I wanted to say. Or maybe he couldn't find a woman and knew if all else failed, he could rely on Alice. I felt ashamed of having such unkind thoughts. It wasn't so much that I thought Alice was naive. Instead she just always seemed to want to think the best of people. She reserved judgement until she had rock solid evidence. This, I had decided years ago, was a quality and partly why I loved her so much, but it was infuriating when I saw her hurt and broken. I wondered how many more times it would take before she lost that ability to see good in everything and ended up cynical and bitter. Probably more times than I could bear to stand by and watch, but was it really my place to interfere?

I heard the sound of customers standing at the counter and excused myself so I could see to them. When I came back Alice was stirring the soup that I had left simmering on the hob.

'This smells gorgeous,' she said, wafting the steam that rose from the pan under her nose.

'Help yourself, it's your favourite, tomato and basil. I don't think there'll be many more people wanting soup this afternoon, and it won't keep.'

She shook her head, smiling at me. 'I don't think I could eat a thing, I'm still all adrenalin from seeing Oliver.'

'So,' I said, starting to stack the dishwasher, 'you told me what he said to you, what did you say to him?'

'He didn't really give me a chance, actually, just swept in, caught me by surprise and said his piece before I could argue. Then he asked me to meet him for a drink on Saturday. He's going to The Boatman in the evening. He said not to give him an answer then and there, but that he'd go and wait anyway, and if I didn't turn up he couldn't blame me. Then he went. Just like that,' she said clicking her fingers.

'What are you going to do?'

She rolled her eyes sighing. 'I know it's foolish and gullible and everything else but I really want to go. I think after everything that's happened I deserve an explanation. It might help me get over him.'

I slammed the heavy metal door of the dishwasher shut, locking the handle down firmly.

'Are you mad at me?'

'Al, it's your decision. I've got to respect it. I could beg you not to waste your time on him until I'm blue in the face, but if he's not out of your system yet then anything I say will be lost on you. If Mags can't persuade you, no one can. Just be kind to yourself.' I waved a wooden spoon, squinting my eyes at her. 'You deserve to be treated like a goddess, anything else is not good enough in my book.'

She gave me a brief hug and a kiss. 'Thanks, babe,' she said, then grabbed a piece of carrot that was

183

lying in a pile on the chopping board and popped it into her mouth. 'I'm gonna have to run, Jackie's filling for me at the surgery on the condition that I only took half an hour. So, you'll come with me on Saturday?' she asked, making her way back through the café.

I was about to try and argue when a customer caught my eye and asked me for another cup of coffee.

'You're a pal,' she whispered, 'see you tomorrow,' then was gone.

When Alex had finished his lunch I gave him a recipe for a baked cheesecake to make. He set about fetching all the ingredients whilst I did a stock take. Business was slow in the afternoon and I toyed with the idea of closing an hour early and crawling up the stairs for a sleep. I was exhausted. Then I suddenly remembered I had a check-up at the doctor's at a quarter to four. I checked the kitchen clock; I only had five minutes before I was due to be there.

'Oh hell, I'm sorry, Alex, I'm going to have to nip out to the doctor's. It had completely slipped my mind until now.'

Alex looked panic-stricken at the thought of being left entirely on his own.

'Don't worry, I'll close up on my way out. All you'll have to do is remember to take the cheesecake out of the oven in half an hour if I'm not back. I'll put the timer on to remind you.' I set the oven clock to start counting down, then grabbed my coat from the cupboard. 'There's not much to do now, so you can just start tidying up and packing things away.'

'Okay, I can manage,' he said looking a bit happier. I said goodbye, promised not to be long and raced off to the surgery.

At the doctor's everything seemed to be going well: blood pressure low, pulse normal, bump size swelling nicely (the midwife's words, not mine). There was nothing untoward in my urine sample and the baby's heartbeat was fast and strong (although it sounded more like a euphoric dance beat than a pulse in there). A textbook pregnancy, she told me, so far, so good. She talked a bit about the antenatal classes they ran at the surgery that I should be starting soon and gave me a photocopied list of the dates and times it ran on and what the subjects were. I took it warily, unsure about the idea of being in a group of happy couples and being the only one without a partner to wrap his arms around me and pant or whatever it was they did.

'It's probably not what you imagine,' Constance, the midwife, said, reading my mind. She leaned against the table and removed her glasses. 'There are a lot of single mums just like you; the classes we run are actually just for women only. There are special separate classes for Mum and partner and even then you'd be surprised how many women take their mum or sister, rather than a boyfriend or husband. I really think it'd be worth your while going along.'

I promised her I'd think it over and wandered out of the surgery; the words 'single mum' were still echoing painfully in my head.

As I walked out of the door I heard somebody call my name.

'Hey, Holly, hold up.' I glanced back over my shoulder and saw Charlie running towards me. I turned away from him and starting walking quickly back towards the café. 'Shit, shit,' I muttered under my breath, hoping he hadn't seen me look at him. I felt a hand on my shoulder as he caught up with me.

'Holly, are you ignoring me? I was shouting my head off back there and you looked right at me.'

'Me?' I questioned stupidly. 'Sorry, Charlie, I was miles away.' I kept walking and he fell into step alongside me.

'I saw you coming out of the doctor's, is everything okay?' he asked, looking concerned.

'Oh, fine yes, it was nothing y'know, just a routine thing.'

He nodded, satisfied. 'Have you shut the café?'

'Yes, closed up early and left Alex, my work experience lad, in charge so I'll have to get back,' I said, picking up pace and hoping he'd get the hint and go away.

'Mind if I come with you? I've got some news and I'm dying to talk it through with someone.'

'Sure,' I said through gritted teeth, wishing I'd worn something baggier today. I pulled my coat around me self-consciously.

We walked together down the little street that ran

186

behind the café and as I approached the back door I could sense that something wasn't right.

'Is that smoke?' Charlie asked, stopping to stare at the kitchen window.

I looked over and saw thin wisps of black smoke escaping through the partly opened window. 'Oh my God,' I cried, flying towards the back door and wrenching it open.

Inside the kitchen an acrid grey fog burned my throat and stung my eyes, forcing me to squeeze them almost shut. I felt Charlie brush past me as he raced inside.

Through the dark clouds I could see flames licking a couple of feet into the air. They appeared to be coming from the top of the oven. I put my hands out, feeling for the wall where I had hung the fire extinguisher but Charlie beat me to it; he aimed the hose at the oven and swamped the flames in foam. It was all over in an instant.

I opened all the windows to allow the smoke to disburse and went into the café looking for Alex.

He was just walking through the door of the store rooms. 'What's going on?' he asked when he was hit by the thick fuggy air.

'You tell me!' I snapped, waiting for an answer.

Alex looked nervously at the scene behind the counter then back at me. 'I don't know,' he squeaked. 'I didn't do anything. I washed up, took the cheese-cake out when the oven bleeped, then I went to tidy up the stock room. Somebody phoned for you when I was in there, so I haven't even been in the kitchen, honestly!' I could see tears filling up in his eyes and threatening to spill over and my anger dissolved.

'Don't worry, Alex, I'm sure it's not your fault,' I said gently.

'I think I can see what did it,' Charlie said, poking his head around the door behind me.

Alex and I followed him back into the kitchen.

The smoke had almost gone, leaving in its place a vile charred smell. Looking around, I could see there was no serious damage. The fire had started on the oven and had fortunately been contained there. The smoke had left a dark brown residue on the wall behind the cooker and the ceiling above. There was a small, white mountain of foam covering the oven's surface, which had splattered haphazardly on the nearby walls and floor.

'One of your burners was still on,' Charlie explained, his voice hoarse from coughing. 'I think what happened was when you took something out of the oven, you put it on the burner, not realising it was still lit.' He pulled a scorched baking tin out from underneath the foam with a tea towel. 'Exhibit A, ah ah, hot, ow shit,' he said flinging the tin into the sink. It sank down, making the water hiss and steam. 'And exhibit B,' he added, fishing out what was left of an oven glove and dumping it in the bin nearby.

Alex stood in the doorway, looking mortified.

'It's alright, Alex, please don't worry. I'm sure it was me that left the burner on when I moved the soup. It's only a minor problem. Won't take long to clean up.' I smiled, hoping to convince him that it was okay.

188

He smiled back, not quite so confidently. 'Do you want me to help sort it out?'

I shook my head. 'No, it's fine. Why don't you head off now? You can call in tomorrow and pick up the report, I've not finished filling it in yet.' Alex looked terrified at the thought of me adding, minor fire, to his list of achievements. 'Don't worry, it'll be a glowing report. You've been an asset to us. If I'm out when you come over I'll leave it with Shelley,' I added, knowing that'd cheer him up.

I fetched his coat and showed him out. When I returned to the kitchen Charlie was already cleaning up the foam.

'Thanks so much,' I said, leaning against the door and watching him. 'You don't have to do that though, it won't take me long.'

'Don't be silly, it's no trouble,' he assured me, smiling.

I grabbed another cloth and joined him.

'This wall might need a lick of paint though,' he said, gesturing to the wall at the back of the cooker. The heat of the fire had made a section of it bubble and blister.

I knew it was only a small problem, but it could have been a lot worse. My hands started to shake and a rogue tear plopped on to the cooker.

'Hey, don't worry,' Charlie said, putting an arm over my shoulder. 'I'll have it looking as good as new for you in an hour or so. No problem. Tom's not the only one who's handy with a paint brush, y'know.'

'I'm sorry, I feel really silly,' I sniffed.

189

'I remember when one of the tweeters in my speakers blew, I think I felt like crying. They were my pride and joy, just like this place is yours. I totally understand, and, hey, with a caffeine injection I work twice as fast,' he joked.

An hour later the kitchen was foam-free and cleaner than it had been in ages. Charlie had even washed down the walls. The smell still lingered but he convinced me that it would go in a day or so. All I needed to do was touch up the paintwork.

We sat at one of the tables by the window sharing a pot of tea and a plate of cookies.

'You look so tired,' Charlie said, studying me. 'I guess it must really take it out of you.'

'What must?'

'Y'know,' he said, nodding at my bump. 'I'm not blind, Hol, anyone could see you're pregnant.'

I stared at him open-mouthed. I had been so caught up in the café, I had forgotten to hide it, although admittedly that was getting near impossible these days anyway.

'Does Tom know? I'm presuming it is Tom's, right?'

I nodded gloomily. 'He doesn't know, and that's how I want to keep it,' I said, a warning note in my voice.

'Things didn't go so well with you two, then?'

'It's not that, I really like Tom, maybe too much. It's just complicated.' I sighed, not wanting to go into details.

'He'd be a brilliant dad,' Charlie said, pouring us out a second cup of tea.

190

'You reckon?'

'Definitely, he'd be great at playing with kids. He's enthusiastic, fun, loves toys, he still plays with technical Lego and he's got a wicked remote control car.'

I smiled wryly. 'This is exactly my point, he hasn't even grown up himself yet. And what about the responsibility? He couldn't hack it. No offence but I bet the thought of being a dad scares you half to death, doesn't it?'

'On the contrary, if the right woman came along there's nothing I'd like more,' he said seriously, heaping an enormous amount of sugar into his tea.

I snorted with laughter, 'How could you cope? You could never give up the party lifestyle for nights in with smelly nappies and burping sessions.'

'Ahha!' he cried, waggling his finger at me, 'that's where you're wrong, you see. The reason I was on my way over to see you, the news I had to tell you before your café nearly burned down, was that I've quit the clubbing job. I'm going to become a policeman.'

'You! A policeman! I can't believe it. This is a joke surely.'

He grinned proudly. 'I'm dead set actually, I've been accepted by the Avon and Somerset constabulary. Forget DJ Wide Boy, It'll be PC Bradley in future – not as catchy I admit, but it will look better on a CV and my mum will find it easier to talk about at coffee mornings. I've always wanted to do it, I just got sidetracked by the nightlife, but it got too samey in the end. I had to get out of that

191

scene before it drove me nuts. Anyway, I've already got through the tests, and I start my training at FHQ in Portishead in three months' time.'

'FHQ? Isn't that a men's magazine?' I asked, dumbfounded.

He let out a deep belly laugh. 'Force Head-quarters, Holly, that's where I'm going.'

I couldn't believe what I was hearing. It made me realise that I had never really known Charlie at all; I'd dismissed him as a shallow party animal and he was surprising me all the time. And if Charlie could surprise me, anyone could. It was an encouraging realisation.

We chatted about pregnancy and the police force for another hour or so and I found myself really warming to him. He was so relaxed and confident, it didn't occur to him to doubt himself. Whatever he was on, I needed some of it.

'I'm going to have to get back, I promised Simon a pint and a game of pool tonight,' he said, standing up to go. 'I really enjoyed our chat. We should do it more often.'

'That'd be nice.'

'Actually, what are you doing tomorrow night? We could go for a quiet drink somewhere.'

'Yeah, why not. Oh shit, sorry, I just remembered Alice has roped me into keeping her company at The Boatman tomorrow. She's meeting Oliver and wants moral support, although I think I'll just end up being a gooseberry.' I wasn't looking forward to the pros-pect.

'I could come with you if you like?' he offered.

192

'Okay,' I said quickly before he changed his mind. 'You can give me a lad's perspective on what you think Oliver's game is.'

'That guy is a twat!' Charlie hissed through gritted teeth, downing the dregs of his fourth pint.

We were sitting in The Boatman garden on a wobbly bench, inching further and further away from Alice and Oliver.

Oliver had spent the past half an hour boasting about a profitable risk he had just taken on the Stock Exchange, and he had Alice eating out of the palm of his hand. I hated just sitting back and watching. You could practically see hypnotic spirals swirling in her eyes.

'I'll get the next round, shall I?' Oliver said, reaching into his back pocket and retrieving a fat-looking wallet.

'No really, you got the last ones. It's my shout,' Charlie countered, fumbling in his jacket for his own wallet.

'No no, I insist. Same again, everyone? You sure you only want a Coke, Holly?'

I nodded, thankful that Oliver was too wrapped up in impressing Alice to notice the growing bump I was sporting.

'Just a half for me,' Charlie said, looking like he wasn't planning on staying much longer. Oliver collected up our empties and strode confidently into the pub.

'You don't mind if we head off after this drink, do you?' I asked Alice.

She smiled a watery drunken smile. 'Course not, you look tired. Thanks for keeping me company, though. It gave me the upper hand turning up with friends, stopped me looking too keen.'

'And are you keen?'

She smiled guiltily, 'No.'

'Nice try, Al. Please just promise me you'll make him sweat a bit. You are going home tonight, aren't you?'

'Holly,' she cried and attempted to slap my leg, only she missed and hit the table instead. 'What do you take me for? I promised Mum that I'd be back by midnight. Ugh, I sound about twelve, don't I?' she cringed, giggling. 'Look, we're just going to talk some more. You have nothing to fear.'

When Oliver returned, he struck up a quiet conversation with Alice, clearly not wanting to include us. Charlie and I exchanged a look, and then we swiftly gulped down our drinks. Charlie thumped his glass down on the table noisily and wiped his mouth with the back of his hand. Then we said our goodbyes and bid a hasty retreat.

'God what a wanker, he really loves himself doesn't he?' Charlie grumbled as we walked around the side of the pub and out of the front gate.

'He must have something going for him if Alice thinks he's so great,' I said, racking my brains to think what it could be. 'I hope she'll be okay with him.'

'I don't think she'll ever be okay with someone like that; she wants to find herself a decent bloke.'

I laughed at the irony of hearing him say that. I

wondered how many girls had said the same thing about him. If Charlie thought Oliver was bad, there were no two ways about it, he must be!

'Are there really any decent blokes out there?' I pondered.

'Hey, I don't mind admitting I'm a bit of a tart, but I'd defend Simon and Tom to the ends of the earth. Now they are model examples of what a decent bloke is. Alice could do a lot worse than getting it together with someone like Simon.'

'Has he said anything to you about Alice?' I quizzed curiously. 'I have noticed they've been getting on well lately.'

'Not in so many words, no. It's not long since he had a thing about you.'

I looked at the path, embarrassed, and said nothing.

'He did tell me that she had invited him to Mag's mum's wedding. He looked pretty chuffed about it too.'

'Maybe you shouldn't tell him about her meeting Oliver tonight then, it might scare him off,' I suggested.

Charlie pulled a face and looked guilty.

'You didn't! Oh Charlie!'

'Sorry, I thought he should know. There's no point him wasting his time if her ex is on the scene.'

I half agreed, knowing if the shoe had been on the other foot, I would have told Alice.

'So, Maggie is taking Noah, Alice is taking Simon, who are you taking?'

195

I grinned at him, realising that he was fishing for an invite. 'You?' I asked in a little girl's voice.

'Glad to hear it,' he said linking arms with me. 'I don't suppose they need a DJ for this do, by any chance?'

'I doubt you've got enough ageing rocker records to cope with the job. It'll be back to back Rod Stewart, I'm afraid, just being seen there could tarnish your hardcore reputation for good. As if becoming a copper hasn't done that already,' I teased.

Charlie laughed to himself, then he sat down on a bench in the deserted street and patted a space next to him. 'It's so peaceful here,' he whispered, leaning back to look at the moonlit sky.

I joined him on the bench, stretching my legs out and resting my hands on my bump. 'Oh, I think I can feel the baby kicking,' I said feeling around to be sure.

Charlie sat up excited. 'Really? Can I feel?'

'Course, it's only a tiny movement so you have to concentrate.' I smoothed out the fabric of my jumper and placed his hand where mine had been. We both sat silently for a few minutes holding our breath.

'Oh wow,' he said eventually as I felt the baby move. 'I felt it. That was really amazing.'

We stared at each other, grinning, his hand still on my stomach, and I suddenly became very aware how warm it felt against me. I could hear him breathing deep and fast, then he took his hand away and sat back again. 'That was really amazing,' he repeated softly to himself. My heart was pounding so loudly in my chest I was worried he could hear it too. He jumped off the bench and extended a hand to help me up. 'Come on,' he said, not looking at me. 'Let's get you out of the cold.'

CHAPTER SEVENTEEN

'How come the more artificial these places get, the more popular they are?' I grimaced, eyeing a plastic palm tree with disdain.

Tamsin laughed, testing the temperature of a bottle of milk by shaking some on her wrist. 'It's like those naff dance records that only have about two chords and some bouncy Swedish girl repeating the same thing over and over that get to number one. The more they sound like they've been made in a bedroom with one small keyboard and a guy with a backward baseball cap, the more they seem to sell. I tell you, I fear for the nation's sense of all that's tasteful and decent.' She held up a fry and laughed as it drooped limply in her hand. 'Reminds me of Oscar,' she joked, then shuddered at the memory.

'You don't miss him, then?'

'Not any more. Maybe when the boys were first born, but that was more because I needed an extra hand than anything else. We got carried away without really stopping to think about what we were doing. I don't think he was right for me. There was never any real spark. I just feel sad for the twins.' She looked down at Callum, who was noisily gulping down his drink whilst his brother slept in the double buggy. 'I think they're going to find it difficult when they realise his father isn't interested in them. It's such a shame; I think a child needs a father figure in his life,' amending quickly, 'Ooh sorry, Hol, I didn't mean anything by that.'

'It's okay, actually I've finally decided I'm going to tell Tom about the baby the first chance I get. I don't know how to contact him, and I don't think I want to, but if he calls I'll tell him. And I'll come clean to Marcus and Fiona as soon as they get back. I guess I was hoping the problem would go away.' I stared down at my swollen tummy. 'It's hard to ignore it now.'

'It'll all work out fine, you'll see.' Tamsin squeezed my hand, then she sat back cradling Callum, who had nodded off in her arms. 'Hey,' she said, her elfin face brightening. 'I think I will treat myself to that pair of shoes after all, I've decided I deserve a treat.'

I groaned. Tamsin had been debating about the price of a pair of sandals for the past hour. 'Couldn't you have decided that when we were at least vaguely near the shop? It's miles away from here!' I flexed my toes, unsure I could make it there and back without the aid of a motorised cart.

'Look, how about I nip back there and leave you with the twins? It'll be much quicker.' She pointed to Mothercare. 'You could have a browse in there if you like and I'll meet you back here as quickly as I can.'

'Oh, I don't know. I'm useless with babies; what if they wake up and see me instead of you? They'll scream the place down.'

Tamsin stood up, tucked the sleeping Callum in next to his brother and slung her handbag over her shoulder. 'If they cry just push the buggy around, they'll soon nod off again. You'll be fine. You need the practice,' she warned, and kissed me goodbye. 'Now stop panicking, I won't be long,' she called back to me as she jogged off in the direction of the shop.

Okay, stay calm. They are fast asleep, what could go wrong? I told myself, glancing around nervously.

Samuel shook his arms fitfully in his sleep and let out a strangled cry, screwing his eyes up crossly.

Typical, I thought. I swear babies just don't like me. 'It's alright, darling, Mummy won't be long,' I cooed sweetly to him.

Big mistake. At the sound of an alien voice whispering in his ear his little eyes flew open and stared at me, horrified.

Okay, so talking to him was a bad idea.

His body was twitching nervously as he drew breath for the mammoth wail that followed. I remembered what Tamsin had said about a moving pram sending them to sleep and sprang up collecting all our bags, and then I sped off like a getaway car towards Mothercare.

Just a few seconds of mobile pram was all it took to have Samuel back in a land of blissful slumber. I was amazed at the transformation, and I looked at his now relaxed cherubic face proudly. Maybe I had what it takes after all.

200

I pushed the twins up and down the aisles of Mothercare, beaming at the parents and children that were there. Occasionally a mum would catch my eye and give me a conspiratorial worn-out but vaguely amused look, as if I understood how she was feeling. I felt like I'd been given access to an exclusive club. I entertained an image of myself as an international ambassador for children the world over, so chosen because of my ability to bond with them on their own level. I imagined myself on the streets of Calcutta, arms outstretched as children crowded around me cheering. I could be a Princess Di or Geri Halliwell figure.

A woman of my age was wrestling with a boy next to a stack of Tweenies dolls.

'I want it, I want it, I want it,' he whined repeatedly.

'Jonathan, hush, will you. You'll wake that lady's babies up,' the mother begged, looking apologetically at me.

'It's okay,' I said smiling, 'they sleep through anything.'

'They're lovely,' she whispered looking into the pram. 'How old are they?'

'Oh, er, four months now. Gosh, time flies,' I said trying to cover up for having to think about it. 'It's expecting another one that does it, my brain keeps malfunctioning,' I joked, assuming she'd understand.

She eyeballed my bump and looked confused. 'Gosh, how far gone are you?'

'About four and a half months,' I answered proudly,

then doing the basic arithmetic realised what I'd said and felt myself turning a shade of red.

'Okaaay,' the woman said, grabbing her child's hand firmly. 'Well, good luck.' Then she whisked her son away, giving me a peculiar backward glance. I looked around to make sure nobody else had overheard but they were all shopping, oblivious to me.

I wandered over to the maternity section and spotted some booklets on giving birth. I hung all of the shopping bags I had been carting about on the handles of the pram, then leafed through the first two on the shelf. In the back of one were lists of all the things you might need to take to the hospital. They were huge! A pre-labour bag, a post-labour bag and a baby bag. I looked at the list in more detail, making a mental note of things I still needed to get. I wrinkled my nose up at the thought of wearing an oversized T-shirt to give birth in. Big T-shirts were so unflattering. I'd have to get something more fitted. Reading on, I noticed one of the items was disposable knickers. What the hell are they? I wondered, and why would I need those awful sanitary towels that look like sleeping bags? I don't think so; a girl's gotta preserve some dignity. Nope, it'd be a new pack of Marks and Spencer's best and a box of Tampax Super, I thought to myself, tutting. God, they expect you to become frumpy overnight, don't they?

An old lady walked by and shot me a filthy look, shaking her head. Then a couple of young girls burst out laughing and hurried out of the shop, glancing back at me then setting off giggling again. WHAT?

I felt a tap on my shoulder and turned to see a shop assistant. 'Erm, your babies,' she muttered pointing at the pram behind me.

I looked around for the pram but it had gone. I started to scan the shop frantically then realised that it had in fact been right in front of me all the time. The weight of my shopping hanging on the back of the pram had tipped it up. The two babies were at an obscure angle, fortunately not quite upside down. Thank goodness they were strapped in! They were both wide-awake now and appeared quite happy, gazing at the world from a new and fascinating perspective. Callum was kicking his legs in the air like he was Cindy Crawford on an exercise mat, and Samuel seemed intrigued by the fact that his dribble for once was sliding UP his face! These kids are going to love Alton Towers, I thought to myself, thanking the assistant and setting them back upright again.

I sloped out of the shop to meet Tamsin, feeling like I'd failed at the first post. So much for my Princess Diana fantasy, Prince Philip was more my calibre.

That night Alice and Maggie came over for a drink and a chat and I told them about my day with Tamsin and the babies.

'I just don't think I have that *thing*,' I moaned, not expressing myself too clearly.

'What thing?' they asked in unison.

I popped open another can of coke and took a small sip. 'It's just something all mums seem to have, it's a thing! It makes them competent and capable. I mean look at Tamsin, she always looks good, she's trendy and she's always in control. She never flaps about anything. She could feed the twins standing on her head, in the middle of a typhoon. It's a motherly instinct she's got that allows her to cope. She's a natural. I just haven't got that, that *thing*!'

'I bet if you told her how you felt, she'd tell you she felt the same when she was pregnant,' Maggie offered helpfully.

I raised my eyebrows sceptically.

'No, she's right,' Alice piped up. 'How do you know what kind of mum you'd be before you've even had it? Most women will have doubts; it probably makes you a better mum in the end to be worried. It shows that you care enough to want to be good.'

I thought about that for a minute and decided Alice was probably right.

'You really ought to go to these antenatal classes, then you'd see there were women who felt just the same as you,' she said.

'Ooh, yes, I got it, I got it!' Maggie cheered.

'That's not fair, I want to sit on your side, you always get it,' Alice complained sulkily.

They were sitting either side of me on the sofa, each with a hand on my bump, feeling for the slightest little movement. I slapped their hands away and pulled my top back over my belly.

'I've had enough now. Alice, your hands are bloody freezing!'

Alice waltzed off to the kitchen and brought back the biscuit barrel.

204

'So, last night,' I started, crossing my legs on the sofa as Alice doled out the custard creams.

'Last night?' Maggie joined in, sensing some gossip was about to unfold.

'She met up with Oliver. Charlie and I went along to keep her company,' I explained.

Maggie's eyes grew wide and for a minute I was worried that she was going to give Alice a mouthful. 'How could you do that?' she spat incredulously.

'I had to give him a chance to explain,' Alice said pathetically.

'What happened? You're not back together again, are you? The answer yes to that is not an option, by the way,' she warned.

'Don't be mean to her, Maggie,' I chipped in. 'It's Oliver you should be mad at, not Alice.'

'Okay, stop it the pair of you,' Alice said holding her hands up at us. 'No, I'm not back with him, although he did ask a number of times. I told him I wasn't interested and we just talked.'

'So nothing happened after me and Charlie left?'

'Not that I'm aware of, no.'

'What do you mean "aware of"?' I asked, getting worried.

'Well, I was pretty drunk. The details are sketchy. God, I had to go to church this morning with Mum. I thought I was going vomit in the pew, it was awful.' She peered over at us, hoping that she'd successfully steered the conversation away from Oliver but we just stared at her, waiting for more info. 'I remember him walking me home, because I fell in a bush. But past that it's all a blank,' she muttered.

205

'Great!' Maggie groaned. 'I can't believe you let him get you that drunk. God, he's manipulative!'

'I did have some say in the matter, you know, I didn't have to get drunk. I really wouldn't worry Mags, I know what I'm doing.'

'Really? I thought you said you couldn't REMEMBER what you were doing. Strewth Al, you're the limit!' They stared at each other hotly for a moment then Alice broke their gaze and I thought I saw tears threatening in her eyes.

'I'm sorry, hon,' Maggie said eventually and added in a ridiculous voice. 'It's only coz I love yer!'

They chinked their glasses as a seal of their truce and I breathed a sigh of relief that the tension had vanished as quickly as it had begun.

'So what were you doing out with Charlie then, Hol?' Maggie grinned suggestively at me.

I slumped in my chair as four beady little eyes focused on me. 'It's a long story.'

The nosy pair made a show of plumping up their cushions and making themselves comfy.

'What a hero,' Alice said, holding her hands to her heart like a swooning damsel after I told her about Charlie putting out the fire in the café.

'I can't believe that little pipsqueak nearly burned down the café. I would have throttled him!'

'Don't be so ruthless, Maggie, it was just as much my fault as his. You know how I'm always leaving the burners on.' She grudgingly had to agree with that. 'Anyway, one thing's for sure, it's put me off

206

hiring extra staff just yet. I just can't trust anyone with the place like I trust you and Shelley.'

'So, what happened after you left the pub?' Alice asked.

'Oh, you know, he walked me home, that's all. Nothing really.' I didn't want to tell anyone about what had happened on the bench. Not that there was anything to tell, it was only a look we shared, a strange moment that had passed between us. Maybe Charlie hadn't even noticed it. Maybe I was just so sex-starved I was looking for some excitement in the wrong place. Like some sad desperate that gets turned on when someone innocently pushes past them in a crowded train.

'Actually, I invited him to be my partner at the wedding, is that okay?' I tried to say this as casually as I could so they wouldn't read anything into it.

'OOOOOH,' they both teased laughing and nudging each other.

'It's not like that, you two,' I protested, but the fact that I took it so seriously made them laugh even more. I stared at them indignantly, snapping, 'If you hadn't noticed, I am pregnant with my boyfriend's child.'

Just then the phone rang. I froze to the spot.

'Go on, Holly, it might be him,' Maggie joked.

'Who, Charlie or Tom?' Alice said smiling.

I apprehensively picked up the trilling phone and took it into the other room, just in case it was Tom. I knew that now I'd made the decision to come clean, there was no backing out of it. I breathed out slowly; trying to calm myself down, then picked up the receiver.

'Hello?' I whispered.

'Hi, is that Holly?' a male voice asked.

'Yes.'

'Hello, Holly, it's Oliver here, how are you?'

I was half-relieved that it wasn't Tom, and half-disgusted that Oliver had the cheek to call me up and speak to me in a tone of voice that I personally would only use for my closest friends. 'Fine,' I snapped defensively.

Oliver ignored my cold manner, saying, 'Good, good, glad to hear it.' You could tell this guy was a salesman, I thought. He was slick. 'Actually, I'm having a little problem and I wonder if you could help me. Alice was supposed to come over for dinner tonight and she hasn't showed. She doesn't like me calling her at home – you know what her mum's like – so I was wondering if you had any idea how I might get hold of her?'

'Funny, she never mentioned it,' I sniped and carried the phone back into the living room. I handed it to Alice, mouthing 'Oliver' at her. Maggie pulled a face and frowned at Alice and we both sat in silence listening to her monologue.

'Really? Are you sure? Oh God, I'm really sorry, I think I had a bit too much wine last night and it went completely out of my head . . . Oh, okay that sounds lovely . . . No, no nothing important . . . Right, give me ten minutes or so and I'll be there . . . Me too, 'bye.' She put the phone down and cringed at us. 'Oops!'

'You're not actually going to go, are you?' Maggie said.

'I've got to. Apparently we arranged it last night, and it sounded like he's gone to a lot of trouble.'

'Do you want me to drive you over there?' I offered.

'It's okay, I'll take you,' Maggie said, getting up and fetching her handbag. 'I was going to head off and get some sleep anyway. I've had a heavy weekend.'

Alice fetched her bag as well, apologising for the short visit, then kissed me on the cheek. 'Can I just refresh my make-up?' she asked Maggie, who gave her a stony look and pushed her towards the door.

The next morning I woke up early; my back was aching from sleeping awkwardly so I got up and dressed straight away. I wandered down to the café, made myself a big pot of tea, then sat down at a table with the designs for Irene's wedding cake. It was more or less organised now, but I needed her to provide some photographs to help me with the decorations. She was coming over to go through them with me this afternoon.

I could feel the baby moving stronger than ever this morning and I stroked it as I was doodling. 'You and me, hey pumpkin,' I said affectionately. 'It's gonna be fun. I'm going to teach you all kinds of things, how to ride a bike and swim, the endless culinary possibilities for vegetables. You're gonna love sprouts – they're like sweets but better, trust me! Then there's the old rule of avoiding men until you're old enough to retire – quite normal, I promise you. We're going to have wonderful evenings together in pub beer gardens. I know an excellent one with climbing frames and all sorts. We'll be the best of friends.'

It occurred to me that as I spoke, I was picturing the baby as a little girl and I wondered if this was some psychic connection we had, a mother's instinct that I had tapped into subconsciously. A girl would be nice, I thought. I started trying to think of girls' names that would be funky and different, yet would have a low tease factor for when she got to school.

I was deep in my maternal fantasies when I thought I heard someone tapping at the door. I checked the time; it was only half past seven, too early for a social call. A chill spread down my spine. I crept across the room and pulled back the drapes covering the front door.

Alice was standing outside, holding a huge bag and looking as though she was in the middle of a crisis.

I unbolted the door and ushered her inside, planting her at the table where I'd been sitting.

'I'm sorry, Hol, I know it's early, but I didn't know where else to go.'

'Don't worry, what's happened?'

She slid forward on the table and cradled her head in her arms, making pitiful little sighing noises.

I stroked her back. 'It can't be that bad, whatever it is,' I encouraged.

'No, I guess not,' she agreed, sitting up and

rubbing at her puffy eyes. 'I mean it really is about time I left home anyway. It's gone on far too long.'

'You've left home? How come?'

She rolled her eyes to the ceiling. 'Last night I went to Oli's for a meal remember? It was so romantic, candles everywhere, yummy wine and food,' she smiled at the memory and fiddled with a napkin on the table. 'Anyway, we ended up in bed and I fell asleep. I woke up at four and realised the time. Mum was expecting me home last night because I thought I was just going to yours. So I got my stuff together and ran all the way home. I didn't bother waking Oli up; he was totally out for the count. When I got home she was sitting in the kitchen next to the phone apparently about to call the police. It was so awful; she went berserk and even called me a slut! She went on and on about how my father would turn in his grave if he knew what I'd been getting up to, and how I was going to send her the same way with all the worry and stress I caused her. After everything I've done, I couldn't believe it.' A tear escaped and sploshed on to my notepad and I noticed that her hands were still shaking with adrenalin. 'I mean I'm twenty-seven, and I have already sacrificed so much for her, and for Dad when he was sick and I gave up my degree. But she still talks to me as if I was fifteen. I just can't do it any more.'

I passed her a paper napkin so she could blow her nose. 'So what happened next?'

'Oh, I told her I couldn't live with her any longer and packed my stuff. She followed me around saying that I'd be back, and that I couldn't survive

211

in the real world, and when that tack didn't work she started complaining about having one of her funny turns and said she had a migraine coming on. Something inside me just snapped and I told her to shut up and then I left,' she said, wincing at the memory.

My eyebrows shot up in surprise. For as long as I had known Alice she had never said anything bad about her mother or had ever complained, no matter how bad it got. It was strange hearing her talk like this.

'I went straight back to Oli's house after that and told him what had happened.'

'And what did he say?'

'Well, it's what he didn't say that gets me. He's got that big house all to himself, he's even got a spare bedroom he never uses. I was kind of hoping that he'd offer to let me stay with him. But no, I should have expected as much. He just gave me a hug, told me it would all work out and went back to sleep. Then when he got up for work this morning he told me he was going to a conference in Glasgow all week and he'd call you to find out where I am when he got back.'

'He's such a git!' I spat, furious at him.

Alice's face softened. 'Well, I guess moving in together is a big thing. It was unfair of me to just turn up with a bag and expect him to completely change his way of life without any hard thinking.'

'Well, he could at least have offered for now, since you've got nowhere else to live.'

212

I looked at her sad blue eyes framed by a curtain of pale blond hair. She looked angelic.

'You poor thing,' I sympathised, giving her a hug then getting up to make her a drink. 'How come everyone treats you so badly? It's so unfair. You completely don't deserve it. From now on it stops, okay?' I said resolutely, hoping to inject a dose of 'girl power' into her life. 'You're staying with me for as long as you like, on the condition that you let me vet your phone calls. If Oliver thinks he can use you whenever he has a whim, he's about to realise that he'll have to get past me first, and with a body like mine that's a tall order!' I joked, sticking my bump out to show Alice how wide I was getting. 'I can even block doors!'

I strutted about trying to look butch but just managed to make myself resemble a space hopper with legs.

Alice laughed gratefully then burst into tears.

CHAPTER EIGHTEEN

The day of my twenty-week scan had arrived, and I found myself feeling excited at the prospect of seeing my baby on the screen. Maybe I'll even find out the sex, I thought as I pulled into the outpatients' car park.

'Are you nervous?' Alice asked. She had begged me to let her come and I was grateful for the company this time. I had left Maggie in charge of the café, but I could tell she had felt left out and wanted to be here too.

'No, I'm not nervous, everything should be fine. She's certainly growing normally, anyway,' I said, unravelling the yards of seat belt I needed to wrap around my now quite huge bump.

'So, you think it's a girl, do you?' Alice said.

'Oh, did I say "she"? I guess I just don't like calling it "it". I don't have any idea what sex it is really,' I said, not wanting to tell her my feelings about it being a girl in case I was wrong and ended up looking as though I had no maternal instincts at all.

We made our way down the wide corridors to

the X-ray ward and sat down in the busy waiting room.

'Hey, Maggie and I were talking about her mum's hen night this morning, she's having it on Saturday,' Alice said. 'She's been invited but doesn't want to go, so we've agreed to go out for a meal instead, that way we can avoid Irene and all her loud and scary cronies. It's probably best to steer clear of any pubs in town just in case, so we thought we could go to that Thai restaurant you like near the Royal Crescent.'

'Yum! That sounds lovely,' I agreed. 'Just me, you and Mags?'

'Yep, and Shelley. A girlie night out.'

The past three weeks had passed by in a haze of girlie nights in and out. Alice had been staying with me since she had left home and was currently looking for a flat to rent, without much success. I hadn't seen much of Charlie. The last time I had seen him I had promised to call and arrange to go out for a drink, but with Alice staying with me I simply hadn't found the time. That would be my excuse to him anyway, the truth being that every time I had an evening free I had talked myself out of calling him. I was scared of the way our relationship was getting so close so quickly. As Irene's wedding got nearer I found myself spending more time thinking about my impending date with Charlie than I did thinking about Tom. I was confused about what it could mean, and wondered sadly if it meant I was forgetting Tom, and how on earth was it possible since I was carrying his child.

'It's been ages since I've seen Simon,' Alice

remarked, flicking absently through a copy of *Hello* magazine. 'I hope he hasn't forgotten that he's agreed to be my "friend" for the wedding.'

'Why don't you give him a ring?'

'Well, I did try about a week ago, actually. I left a message with Charlie asking him to tell Simon to call me, but he hasn't done yet.'

I thought about the conversation I'd had with Charlie, when he admitted telling Simon that Alice had met Oliver for a drink. It might explain why Simon hadn't contacted her lately.

'Maybe Charlie forgot to give him the message. You should call him again tonight,' I suggested.

'You're right. Oh, I forgot, I said I'd meet Oliver tonight after work, for a drink at the Red Bar.'

'Again? That's the second time this week. Are you sure you're not back together?'

Alice shook her head and pulled a face. 'I think I made a big mistake sleeping with him that night when I left home. He's kind of acting like we're a couple again, as if he owns me or something. It's weird, I just don't think I feel anything for him any more. He's let me down so many times that I just look at him now and I feel numb. It took a while, and I think I had to see him again after what happened with Rachel, I just couldn't get it out of my head. But now, what with leaving home and everything, I don't know, I just feel different, like I need a change of scenery.' She looked at me grinning, her eyes twinkling. 'For the first time, I actually feel like I have the upper hand over Oliver and I just don't want it. The way he's been crawling around me has made me realise that he's actually pretty pathetic.'

'That's brilliant, Al, I'm so glad! So are you going to tell him tonight?'

She cringed, biting her lip, and said, 'Ahhh, well that's the hard bit. I think I'll just see how it goes.'

'Come on, you've got to set him straight sometime.'

'I know, I know, it's just difficult. I've never dumped anyone before and I'm just not the "dumping" type. I may not love him any more, but I still care about him and I feel bad about it.'

'It sounds like you don't have any option, do you? Not unless you get Mags to do it for you, but she won't be gentle, I warn you!'

'You're right. I'll do it tonight,' she said with new resolve.

'Miss Piper?' I heard the receptionist call impatiently, for the third or fourth time by the looks of it.

I stood up and signalled to her, apologising, then I picked my bag off the floor and made my way to the X-ray room with Alice following close behind.

Looking down at my bump, I was reminded of the last time I was here. Then I had found it so hard to believe I was pregnant. Now, lying on my back and looking down I was amazed how much it had grown since then. I certainly didn't need to worry about my pubic hair being exposed this time as whether it was or wasn't I wouldn't have known, I couldn't see past my belly.

The radiologist pressed the probe hard into my abdomen and I felt my baby kick back against it in protest, making it bob up and down on my tummy. 'That's my girl,' I thought, 'you show her who's boss.'

Alice held my hand tightly, but I wasn't sure whether it was for her benefit or mine.

On the monitor a vision started to appear. It was grainy at first, but soon it became clear that we were looking mainly at the baby's head. A hand twitched in a semi-wave, and I saw her face as she squirmed about. Her tiny turned-up nose and mouth were so well formed. She was a perfect baby. You could see all the bones in her ribs and arms as she moved.

'Wow,' Alice said quietly. 'It's so thin.'

'Well, it is an X-ray dear, you are just looking through its skin,' the radiologist explained, giving her a weary look.

Alice nodded relieved, saying, 'Ahh, I see.'

I smiled at the screen as if the baby could see me. The image kept changing as the radiologist checked her from all angles. Her spine, her feet crossed under her bottom, the top of her head. I kept looking for some indication of a presence or absence of a willy, but the images changed too quickly.

'Can you tell what sex it is?' I asked.

'Erm, I've had a look for you but to be honest it's difficult to tell. Your baby has its feet tucked up tight against its bottom. I don't think I could say one way or the other. But everything seems fine anyway, it's still growing as it should, no problems are being indicated, and July 24th still looks to be the due date. Would you like a picture to take back with you?'

I agreed and sat watching as she froze an image of the baby's face and printed out a copy, then I got up ready to go. Alice was still staring at the screen.

'Come on, Al,' I said, nudging her gently. She stood up and followed silently behind me as I went straight to the toilets.

'Are you alright?' I asked from a cubicle.

'What? Oh, yes, I'm fine,' she whispered.

I flushed the loo and came out, adjusting my skirt. 'I never know whether to have my skirt over the bump, or under it. What do you think?' I looked up and saw Alice crying softly to herself, looking at her image in the mirror.

'Oh, hon, what's up?'

'Nothing really, I'm just being silly,' she croaked, crying harder. 'It's just seeing the baby like that. It was so perfect. I really envy you. I know it's awful but I can't help it. I'd do anything to be able to have a baby.'

I hugged her hard, stroking her silky smooth hair. 'It'll happen one day, when everything's right. You wouldn't want one now surely, don't make my mistake. Find the perfect man first and enjoy it for a while.'

'I know you're right,' she said, snorting into my jumper. 'But what if it's too late? What if Oliver was my only hope?'

I shook my head furiously, 'Not a chance. If anything splitting up with Oliver was the best thing you could do if you want to have a happy family

219

in the future. Somehow Oliver doesn't strike me as the family type. So now you're free to find a decent man, who isn't a commitment phobic. Don't worry, one day soon you'll have a close relationship with your toilet, kiss goodbye to your waistline and develop the figure of a weeble. Then you'll wonder why on earth you were so eager in the first place.'

Alice laughed, rubbing her nose with the back of her hand. 'You're right again, Holly. Sorry I'm such a wreck,' she said pitifully.

'Think nothing of it,' I assured her. 'Now let's go see Maggie and plan our girlie weekend.'

Blossoms, the Thai restaurant, was just getting busy as we made our way to the table we had reserved by the large bay window. The impressive buildings of the Royal Crescent curved away from us, lit up by the setting sun. The stone walls were basking in warm light and the tiny windows were dazzling as they reflected the sun in turn. A mist was settling on the lawn in front of the arch adding to the dramatic effect. You could almost imagine Mr Darcy 'taking a turn' with Elizabeth on the dewy grass, or riding his horse across the cobbled street, silhouetted in the fading light.

'Why are you smiling?' Maggie asked as she sat herself down on the chair opposite me.

'Was I smiling?' I asked innocently.

'Isn't it gorgeous?' Alice said appreciatively, taking in the view. 'You can see why this place is so expensive, can't you?' She passed us all a menu.

'Phew, it's a good job we don't do this too often,' Shelley sighed, checking out the prices.

'Okay, I was going to spring it on you at the end, but if you're all just going to order plain rice I'd better warn you that it's my treat, so make the most of it!' I announced grinning at everyone. I was bombarded with a string of, 'oh you can'ts' and, 'no really Holly'. But I held up my hand to silence them. 'Please let me do this for you. I want the chance to thank you all for being so supportive. I'm feeling flush at the moment with the café doing so well, and I put some money aside for this, so you must let me.' They exchanged glances, grinning wickedly, then all agreed and barraged me with thanks until I began to get embarrassed. Then they gathered around the menu again with added gusto.

Maggie went and ordered drinks from the bar, as they wouldn't allow me to add them to the final bill, particularly as I only allowed myself one glass of wine and would be drinking Coke for the remainder of the night.

When she returned we clinked our glasses together in a joint toast, to the baby, to Maggie's mum (may she never chat up anyone under the age of thirty again!), to Shelley's successful art exhibition and to Alice's new found 'sanity' (Maggie's words); I preferred 'freedom'.

I watched them enviously as they quickly downed their first glass of wine and Shelley topped them all up again. Getting stupidly drunk with the girls was the one thing I missed more than anything now I was pregnant, although looking down and seeing my feet came a close second. I sipped my wine slowly, trying to make it last, and studied the menu.

'So, when do the antenatal classes start?' Shelley asked, settling back in her chair.

'Wednesday at two o'clock,' I grimaced.

'Are you sure you don't want me to come with you? I'm owed quite a few days of holiday at work,' Alice offered kindly.

'Honestly, I'll be fine. I think it's just for the mums, actually. They have special classes in the evenings for partners to go to, so I'll just avoid those.'

'Well, you know I'm always willing if you need me,' she insisted.

'You just want to befriend all the women, don't you? So you can be surrounded by a dozen little newborns after they all give birth,' Maggie teased.

'The thought had never crossed my mind!' Alice protested, but her guilty smile gave her away. 'I can't help it. I'm just a people person.'

'A baby fiend, more like,' Maggie countered. 'Honestly, Holly, you'll never get rid of her now. The attraction of living in such close proximity to a cute little tot will be too great for her!'

'Hey, it's not my fault I can't find a flat. Have you seen the prices they're asking? I don't understand how most people manage.'

'My rent's pretty reasonable,' Maggie said. 'Plus, Mickey from the flat upstairs, you know the guy that sounds like he dances with hobnailed boots and a pogo stick, told me he's leaving in a month or two. Do you want me to ask if the landlord's got anyone to take his place yet?'

'Are you mental?' Alice snapped, incredulous. 'Of course I do, your flat's gorgeous!'

'Okay, I'll have to check. Mickey might not have even handed in his notice yet. I'll have to give you a ring tomorrow. Gosh, it would be excellent having you live upstairs. Think of all the fun we'll have!'

They squealed excitedly together and Alice looked delighted at the thought. Another pang of jealousy bit me. My two best friends were going to be holed up together having a great time, whilst I was in my flat alone. Well, not quite alone I thought, stroking my bump guiltily. Besides, Tom could be home by then. We might be in family heaven, enjoying our beautiful child and stealing time when she was asleep to make love in the next room. A happy fantasy, but I wasn't convinced.

The waitress came and I ordered a selection of deep fried vegetables and dipping sauce for everybody to start with, then a red vegetable curry and fragrant rice for myself. The girls took turns in ordering and I sat back, staring emptily through the window as the sun dipped below the horizon and mist swirled dreamlike in the gloomy pools of streetlight.

'I really shouldn't have eaten all that,' I groaned, propping myself up on my elbows.

'Hey, you're supposed to eating for two these days. Doesn't that involve eating *twice* as much?' Shelley teased.

'I can't understand how that's physically possible, I mean when you think about it, the baby is taking

223

up most of the space in there. It's elbowed all my other organs out of the way, and now my stomach's sitting somewhere up here,' I indicated to where my heart should be. 'If I ate twice what I normally do, my lungs would have so little room I'd end up with one down each arm!'

All three of them burst into drunken laughter at the thought.

'Oh, you poor thing. It was so delicious as well,' Alice sympathised.

'Why don't you all have some dessert? I promise I don't mind at all. My treat, remember?' I offered.

They all shook their heads and promised they were full, although I suspected that they were being polite, as they knew I couldn't manage it.

Maggie clapped her hands together. 'Right, girls, what's next? The night is still young, and I for one don't fancy going home just yet.'

'Yeah, let's check out a club. The Cellar has been brilliant lately. Can we go there? Maggie should be safe, it's not really Irene's scene, there's no eighties nights for a start, and they've got loads of comfy sofas if you want to put your feet up,' Shelley added looking pleadingly at me.

'Oh, I don't know, I'm pretty beat,' I said wearily, embarrassed by my lack of staying power.

'Oh please, Hol, don't go yet. We hardly do anything like this any more. We'll look after you, I promise,' Maggie begged.

I reluctantly agreed and Alice offered to walk home with me if I got too tired.

I'd never been to The Cellar before, as it hadn't

been open long. It was hidden away below the pavement on the same street as Blossoms; I would have walked straight past it if Shelley hadn't pointed out the steep staircase leading down to a narrow door.

We walked in and were hit by a thumping bass that vibrated my whole body. Great, my baby is really going to thank me for this, I thought to myself, looking around sulkily.

It wasn't like the clubs I was used to, no gigantic halls full of dancers with podiums, balconies and sophisticated lasers. Instead it had the appearance of somebody's front room. There were simple angular sofas and armchairs dotted in every available space. The walls were brilliant white, and were broken up by the occasional lilac or turquoise geometric shapes painted at random. It was modern and clean in appearance and by the looks of it attracted a lot of local art students, going by the number of young Bohemians there were, having serious discussions and smoking roll-ups.

'This place is so cool,' Maggie shouted and led the way to an empty sofa. Shelley indicated that she was going to get the drinks in and I asked for just a glass of water.

I felt horribly out of place and looked around anxiously. I half expected people to be whispering to each other and pointing me out.

'God, I feel old,' Alice grimaced as we flopped down beside each other. 'Let's not stay long,' she whispered.

I smiled at her in relief, wishing I was curled up in

225

bed. The curry I had eaten had given me indigestion and I was beginning to feel queasy.

I turned around to locate Maggie and warn her that we were going after the first drink, but I couldn't see her anywhere.

Shelley came back a few minutes later with the drinks and said, 'I can't believe Maggie, she's chatting up some poor sucker already,' and she indicated through an arch into the next room. I peered over and recognised her dark red dress as she stood with her back to us, waving her hands enthusiastically. I rolled my eyes at Alice, disappointed that she was going for a new bloke only a week before her wedding date with Noah.

Shelley leaned in towards Alice. 'So, Al, how's your love life? Are you really seeing Oliver again?'

'Well, no, not exactly. We met up for a drink this week but there's nothing in it any more. It's history.'

Shelley looked puzzled. 'Oh, right. That's weird because I saw him in The Red Bar last night and he said things were going well for you.'

Alice looked nervous and bit down on her bottom lip.

'Al, how can he say that? You told me you ended it when you met him for a drink after work,' I asked, confused.

She started inspecting her nails, making a show of being engrossed in removing a speck of dirt. 'Well, I tried, but it was difficult to get it across.'

'You said you told him to, and I quote, "stay out of your life for good because he made you sick!" I

226

think that's getting your point across loud and clear, don't you? '

'Well, I, er, maybe I didn't quite say it out loud. But I thought it,' she said in a barely audible whisper.

'Alice, you lied to me,' I said, stunned. It was so unlike her.

'I'm sorry, I didn't mean to, I just didn't want to disappoint you. And I was going to tell him. I just can't, it's too mean.'

'I don't believe you,' I spat. 'After everything! When are you going to stop letting people tread all over you like this?' I got up and retrieved my jacket from the back of the sofa.

'Where are you going?' she asked in a wobbly, fearful voice.

'I've just had enough,' I snapped and stalked off, losing myself in the crowd of people that had now gathered in the middle of the room. My head was spinning with the noise all around me and I felt unstable on my feet. I was so tired.

'Holly,' I heard someone cry after me. I turned and saw Charlie. 'Hey,' he greeted. 'Maggie said you were over here. She's talking to Noah in the other room.'

I looked over his shoulder and saw that Maggie was indeed flirting enthusiastically with Noah and I smiled, happy for her.

'Are you going?' Charlie asked, disappointed.

'Well, yes, I'm so tired. And I don't feel too good.'

'Come here, just sit down a minute, you look

227

pale.' He steered me over to a sofa hidden out of the way behind the chrome bar and sat next to me holding my hands. 'Do you want me to take you home?'

'It's okay, there's a taxi rank right outside. I'll get a cab,' I muttered, unable to look him in the eyes.

'Holly, are you sure you're okay? I get the feeling you've been avoiding me.'

I didn't say anything, just concentrated on breathing slowly, trying to calm my heart rate down.

He stroked my hair tenderly and I felt myself relaxing. I leaned against his shoulder and breathed in the smell of his shirt. After a while he moved his hand to my back, stroking me in a gentle rhythmic motion that soothed away all the tension that had built up. He buried his face in my hair, kissing the top of my head and I felt so cared for, I just let myself enjoy it. It had been so long. Finally I looked up and our eyes locked together. He dipped down and kissed me softly on the lips. I felt them part and I kissed him back, enjoying the electric sensation it sent down my spine. With my eyes closed I could almost imagine I was kissing Tom. Lovely Tom, with his messy hair and lazy smile.

My eyes flew open and I sat back blinking. What the hell was I doing? Nausea wiped away any feelings I had felt in an instant, and I stood up trembling. I was so stupid. I was pregnant, for God's sake, I couldn't just go around snogging people when I needed affection, I had responsibilities. I felt shameful and cheap.

'Charlie, I'm really sorry.'

228

'No, I'm sorry, I shouldn't have. I was bang out of order,' he said running his fingers through his mouse-brown hair and looking stricken with guilt.

Indigestion burned at my chest as it pounded furiously. I knew I was going to throw up. I muttered something incoherent and went in search of the ladies' toilets.

Ten minutes later I emerged from a cubicle, having been sick until I felt weak and drained. I snuck out of the main entrance and fell into the first cab I saw.

CHAPTER NINETEEN

I sipped a cup of coffee, tapping my fingers absently on the side of the cup.

'Honestly, Hol, you're a nervous wreck! You should relax and enjoy it. If it's really awful no one's going to force you to go again.'

'I know, I know,' I agreed, staring blankly at the half-full café.

Ever since the weekend I had felt edgy.

I had made up with Alice almost immediately. One look at the expression on her face when she walked through the door, not long after me, and I had just melted and hugged her. I filled her in on what had happened with Charlie and we sat up well into the night dissecting the situation.

We made a pact that she would fend off Charlie for me if I returned the compliment with Oliver. I needed time to think about the situation and work out how I was feeling before I saw Charlie again, and Alice was hoping that by cowardly avoiding Oliver, he'd get the message and she would avoid a scene. I liked to think my reasons were more honourable.

I glanced at the clock in the kitchen. 'I guess I'd

better go. The last thing I want is to have to walk in after it's all started and have them all look at me.'

'Well, you just have fun. I'm sure you will,' she said kindly, giving me a friendly wink.

I waved goodbye to Maggie and some of my regular customers and headed out to the car.

By the time I'd crawled through the traffic and arrived at the clinic I was ten minutes late and feeling rattled.

Road works had been strategically placed on all the various main road junctions, to cause maximum disruption. The conspiracy theorist in me had come to the conclusion that this was actually a shrewd plan by the council to encourage more people to use their public transport. Make us all stew in our cars in single-lane traffic for a week or two, crank up our blood pressure to near boiling point, then launch the 'Let's all bus it to work campaign' and watch triumphantly as we abandon our cars in droves and buy a season ticket with the Badgerline.

Bastards, I thought to myself bitterly as I waddled into the surgery.

The receptionist took one look at my bump and pointed wordlessly to a closed door at the far end of the corridor. Sellotaped on the door was a piece of A4 paper that read ANTENATAL GROUP IN SESSION.

My heart flipped at the thought of walking in there on my own. My hand touched the door and I faltered for a moment, half-tempted to leg it back to my car. Only the thought of battling back through

231

the traffic stopped me. I needed a sit down and a drink.

I pushed the door slowly open and gingerly stepped in.

About fifteen pairs of expectant eyes looked up at me, then down at my bump and looked away again disappointed.

They were sitting on those uncomfortable school-type chairs, in a big semi-circle and facing into the middle. A couple of the chairs were empty and so was the floor space that the women were staring at with various expressions of boredom showing on their faces.

I picked an empty chair next to a girl with dyed red hair that had been fashioned into a spiky pony-tail. She was slouched really low down on the chair; her feet clad in huge studded biker boots were crossed casually.

A couple of seconds after I sat down she looked up, stared at me for what felt like a lifetime, then gave me a slow menacing smile. Great, I thought to myself, glancing around at all the other seemingly more normal women, I would end up sitting next to the scary one that nobody else likes.

I was immediately ashamed of myself for being so judgemental and plucked up the courage to speak to her.

'What's going on?' I asked.

'The physio's a no show,' she drawled, chewing her gum as she spoke. 'Five more minutes of this and I'm outta here.'

I nodded at her. 'I'm Holly.'

232

'I'm Harley,' she answered in return, not looking at me. Then sensing I was about to expand on that comment she added in a monotone, 'yes, as in the motorbike. And no my last name isn't Davidson. My parents weren't that perverse.'

I looked back at the floor, embarrassed that my mind to her was obviously an open book.

When the door finally swung open I was glad of the distraction.

A tiny middle-aged woman hurried in, carrying a large bag and balancing some paperwork and boxes on top. She negotiated her way into the centre of the circle, dumping her cargo on the floor.

'Ladies, do forgive my tardiness. The traffic was shocking,' she said, fumbling about with her papers. When she had finished she stood up, put on a pair of glasses that had been perched on her head and surveyed us all. 'Right, let's get started. I'm Maxine. You can call me Max. First of all what I'd like to do is get to know your names and get you all to know each other a little better. So here you are.' She handed out a biro and a sticker to each woman in the room. There were a few unenthusiastic groans and mutters as everyone realised that we would have to wear nametags.

I hated things like this.

Group sessions of this sort nearly always involved some cringeworthy exercises for the purpose of 'getting to know' one another. These usually consisted of taking it in turns to stand up, tell everyone your name, what you did for a living and what you liked to do in your spare time. I always found it

233

particularly embarrassing, as once I had announced I was a vegetarian chef, people intrigued by my unusual occupation would barrage me with numerous questions. And if there was one thing I really hated, it was being the centre of attention.

People inevitably made themselves sound as boring as possible when placed on the 'hotspot', thus avoiding any unwanted attention. Then there would always be one batty individual that had ambitions to become an actress. She would attempt to keep standing for as long as possible, telling anyone who would listen what a bubbly, people person she was, how all her friends thought she was 'mad' and how much she adored her dogs Fred and Ginger.

Harley looked up and rolled her eyes at me.

'Okay,' Maxine said in a perky, 'aren't we all having lots of jolly fun' tone. 'What I want you to do is spend a minute talking to the person sitting next to you, then when I call time, I want you to each take a turn standing up. Then, I want you to tell us the name of the neighbour you've been talking to, and a snippet or two of information about them.'

She produced a stopwatch from her pocket. 'Are you ready?'

Everyone shifted in their seats and looked at the person next to them nervously.

'Go!' she cried clicking down the button on her stopwatch in an exaggerated movement.

'Well, we've already got the name bit all wrapped up,' Harley said dryly. 'Ugh, doesn't it just make you squirm?'

'I know,' I agreed.

Harley looked with disdain at the women sitting around her, talking in hushed whispers.

'Er, shouldn't you be telling me something about yourself now?' I asked, feeling like a teacher's pet to be going along with Maxine's social exercise.

Harley snorted at me. 'Well, why don't you tell them I shag animals. It'll be hilarious,' she said, cackling wickedly.

I stared at her in shock.

This was a complete nightmare! I was stuck with the devil's henchwoman, who was at the moment sporting a sense of humour less sophisticated than Beavis and Butthead. All the normal nice women would forever associate me with her and think I was her friend. It was unspeakably awful.

'No come on, what job do you do?'

'No, really, I'm an animal shagger!' she whispered.

Okay, kill me now, this is officially the lowest point in my life and I've lost the will to breathe!

'Look, obviously I can't say that, so what do you really do?' I pleaded, trying not to look as panic-stricken as I felt.

'Oh, alright then.'

Yes! Thank you, God.

'I work in a sperm donation clinic,' she said, patting her bump and laughing to herself.

Shit, shit, where's the door, I'm out of here!

'Time's up everyone,' Max singsonged. 'Why don't we start at the far end, and work our way anti-clockwise,' she suggested.

235

No, no, please don't!

All the women in the room shifted their attention to me and I found myself blushing to the tips of my hair.

I stood up shakily. 'Well, er, this is Harley. And she, um, she . . .' I had no choice. 'She says she works in the sperm donor clinic.'

A few murmurs and titters rippled across the room, and I immediately sat down and began to scrutinise my feet.

'Oh yes,' Max said brightening. 'I thought I recognised you. I've seen you in the corridors when I've been up at the infirmary, visiting patients.'

I looked at Harley in surprise, who was nodding and smiling at Max. Maybe she had been telling the truth after all.

'Okay, Harley, why don't you stand up and tell us something about your partner here,' Max said, indicating me.

Harley gave me an impish grin and stood up. Worryingly, I realised that she didn't know anything about me.

'This is Holly,' she announced. Everyone looked at me again, nodding. 'She was saying how much she enjoys holding Ann Summers parties at the weekends, to make a bit of money,' she announced in a completely deadpan voice, then sat down.

'Actually, that's not true,' I jumped in quickly before she said anything else.

'Really? What do you do, Holly?' Max asked, looking confused.

Everybody was staring at me, quite probably

fascinated by my skin's ability to turn such a deep and almost alarming scarlet.

'I run a vegetarian café,' I whispered, then looked at the woman sitting next to Harley in the line, hoping the attention would now be diverted to her.

'Gosh, really? How fascinating,' Max exclaimed. 'So, how long have you been vegetarian?'

'Since I was fourteen,' I squirmed.

'Wow! That's brilliant. I couldn't do it myself, mind, I love my lasagne too much.'

A smattering of women laughed politely in agreement with Max.

'So will the baby be vegetarian?' she asked.

This was fast turning into 'the Holly Show' and it had to stop.

'No,' I said abruptly, but they all carried on looking expectantly at me. 'Well maybe. I'll let it have chicken and fish, then see how it goes. I think it should be the child's decision. I won't push it either way.'

There, now can we please start staring at someone else instead!

'Very wise,' Maxine said in approval. 'So the Ann Summers parties are just a sideline are they?'

I shifted uncomfortably in my seat. If I accused Harley of making it up I would just look petty and be subject to even more unwanted attention. 'I guess so,' I said defeated, giving Harley a dirty look. I felt like I'd been transported back to some awful classroom nightmare, and I'd been made to partner the class weirdo.

237

The attention finally shifted to the next woman along, who was introducing us all to Claire, a mobile hairdresser who liked going to the theatre.

I looked accusingly at Harley who was still sniggering into her jumper.

'The look on your face! Classic!' she said.

I looked away, not amused.

Everyone took their turn calling out various names and occupations. By the time they had finished I doubt I could have recalled a single one.

Most of the women appeared to be older than me, which I found really surprising. I mean, I had read somewhere that women were having children later in life, but I hadn't expected to feel like the odd one out. Okay, Harley seemed a few years younger than I did, but then I could have been biased by the fact that she had a mental age of a prepubescent schoolboy. There was one other woman that looked about my age, who seemed nice, but she was trying to avoid looking in our direction. I think Harley scared her.

'So, now we've all introduced ourselves, I'd like to start by congratulating you all on your impendings. It is an exciting time for you all, no doubt about it. Possibly even frightening or overwhelming for others. You've got a lot to think about, that's for sure. So, what my job as a physiotherapist involves is talking to you about several things. These include posture,' she started, looking around until her gaze stopped on Harley and her eyes opened wide. 'That for a start I don't want to see, unless you want to end

238

up in a corset and unable to get up the stairs. Now I want you to sit up straight, back against the chair, that's better,' she said as Harley sat up straight and looked outraged at being told how to sit. 'And there are far too many crossed legs in the room as well,' she continued.

Several of us uncrossed our legs hurriedly before we were also made an example of.

'Now, don't you all feel more comfortable for that?' she said smugly.

I nodded along with her, although quite honestly, sitting with my legs uncrossed was so alien to me that my centre of balance was now so out of kilter, I thought I was going to tip over.

'Other topics up for discussion will be relaxation, exercises and labour,' she continued. 'The midwife will be taking all your other classes. But first of all and most importantly I need to stress my speciality . . . Pelvic floor exercises.'

The room was suddenly split between magazine readers, who were nodding knowledgeably, having read about how these would improve your sex life, and non-magazine readers who were blinking blankly.

Maxine launched into great detail on the importance of pelvic floor exercises, how they would give you an easier labour, and reduce your chances of becoming incontinent after the birth. Which, she told us, was a lot more common than you might think, with a lot of women finding it impossible to do aerobics for years afterwards for fear of an embarrassing little incident.

239

Okay, so I was convinced.

She stood in the centre of the room, legs spread apart, knees bent, pelvis thrust forward. It wasn't a good look for any self-respecting woman.

'Now I want you all to do them with me. You have to imagine you're sitting on the toilet in mid-stream and you're trying to stop the flow. Those are the muscles that you need to be clenching. Hold it for as long as you can, then release and do it again. If you want to check how strong your muscles are, you simply insert two fingers into your vagina and squeeze hard. Not now, obviously!' she joked.

Okay, so this isn't particularly shocking language. Everyone in the room had one, after all, and she was hardly going to call it a front bottom, now was she? But it did sound peculiar having this strange woman discussing it so bluntly in front of us. I squirmed about in my seat again, feeling awkward about seeing her straddled in front of me, two fingers held under her crotch to demonstrate where you would insert them.

The last time I had had to sit through a discussion on anything this delicate was when we had our 'special assembly' that the boys were barred from attending. That involved an equally eccentric woman in a pink jump-suit, calling us all 'little flowers' and demonstrating the absorbency of a tampon by shoving it in a glass of water and showing how it puffed up like a little sheep.

I glanced around the room at the other women to see if any of them were sniggering, but they were all looking her straight in the eye and appeared not to be in the slightest bit shocked. I tried hard to adopt a similar pose, but felt silly and unworldly. I wished that Alice and Maggie were here.

At this particular moment a young man with his arm in a sling burst into the room and came face to face with Maxine's provocative two finger and pelvis stance. He looked a little shocked and stammered an apology, his eyes fixed to the spot.

'It's all right, lovey,' Maxine said to the man. 'I'm just showing these ladies my crotch. It's my job. You can stay if you like, I'm sure it's nothing you haven't seen before. I'll keep my knickers on.'

The terrified male left hastily, knocking his bandaged elbow on the door in his hurry to escape.

'That got rid of him,' she laughed and continued with her demonstration. 'Okay, everyone do it with me now, one, two, three, squeeze,' she said, and the room fell completely silent. You could have heard a pin drop in the corridor outside. Maxine looked around. 'Now remember it's important to keep breathing. There's no need to starve yourself of oxygen!'

Fifteen women blew out their stored up air and gasped for breath with relief.

'Another way of checking on the progress of your vaginal muscles is to try it on a willing partner, if you know what I mean,' she continued as we all sat about, clenching and unclenching. 'Just give him a squeeze and ask him how it feels. If he comes out looking like a gnawed chipolata, you know you need to cut down a bit, okay?'

241

Some of the women gave a nervous laugh at that point.

'Now, you mustn't be embarrassed, folks,' Maxine said, sensing that some of us had found her last remark a bit too personal to be comfortable with. 'It gets a lot more gruesome than this, I warn you. It's true what they say about leaving your dignity at the door when you give birth. And I wouldn't bother collecting it on the way out either. After I had my two children, I lost all sense of embarrassment. I could have dropped my knickers in the street and pooed in the town centre without so much as a batted eyelid!'

Somehow, I found this very easy to believe.

The next hour was taken up mainly with exercises and relaxation.

The relaxation part was a particular hit with the women in the group, and when our class came to an end, Maxine quietly gathered up her paperwork and tiptoed out of the room. We had all been lying with our eyes closed, on mats and cushions, all strategically placed to offer the maximum support and comfort. Maxine had instructed us to visualise a place that was special to us personally, a place where we're always happy. Normally I would have chosen a massive clothes shop, added an 'everything must go' sale and then created a heavy snowfall that blocked all the roads into the city, making it possible to browse in peace. Life didn't get a lot more blissful than that! Sadly, a fantasy like that didn't have quite the same effect when you're sporting a body like a weeble. Instead I picked the grassy slope looking on to Pultney Bridge, my favourite spot in the city, made it a warm summer morning, and added Tom lying lazily next to me, my head on his chest, maybe with an obligatory piece of grass lolling from his mouth in true summer fashion.

I could almost smell his skin, hear the rustling leaves and water coursing down the weir.

God, I needed the toilet.

I sat up to go and noticed that most of the women had now disappeared, Harley included. A couple were breathing rhythmically as though they had fallen asleep. I crept out in search of a toilet.

By the time I had fought my way back through the traffic I was exhausted.

Maggie had already closed up and gone home. I found a note on the counter saying she had to go for her bridesmaid's dress fitting, poor thing. She said that she would call me to find out how the class went later.

I checked over the takings, locked them away, then trudged up the narrow staircase.

I got into bed fully clothed, curled up under the duvet and continued my relaxation exercise where I had left off, lying on a grassy bank, warm and contented, with Tom deliciously close by.

CHAPTER TWENTY

Friday was Tom's birthday.

I thought about him all day whilst I rattled about in the kitchen, letting Maggie and Shelley handle most of the customers. I couldn't deal with making friendly conversation. I managed to be sympathetic to Maggie as she rattled on about her mother's wedding and how awful she looked in her bridesmaid's outfit, but my mind kept flitting back to Tom, wondering how he was celebrating and who he was with. Tamsin had heard from Marcus that he had started his three-month trek in India. I pictured him chilling out on a beach in Goa, drinking cheap lager, and found myself annoyed that he was having the most incredible time and experiences, whilst I was stuck living out the responsibilities that came with my occupation and current expectant state. I knew I had no right to be mad at him, it was my choice to keep him in the dark, but as the days went by I was getting impatient for a phone call. I had decided if he had any feelings about me, he ought to contact me soon. If he didn't call or write then there probably wasn't much future for us after all. My hope was beginning to wear thin.

It was so unlike the previous year.

I remembered how he had phoned up on his last birthday, completely out of the blue. He had arranged a big night out with a group of friends that weekend, so on the night of his birthday he hadn't got anything planned. He invited me over to the house as Simon and Charlie were out, and I went around straight away, touched that he had chosen to spend the evening with me. I had got him a card, but no present; our relationship was still so relaxed that it hadn't even occurred to me that I'd see him on the day. We had spent the evening holed up in his bedroom, trawling through Charlie's extensive CD collection, taking it in turns to pick a favourite song and explain why we liked it so much. There were candles dotted all over his bedroom and we were sprawled on the floor, teasing each other unmercifully about his love of the Moody Blues and my painful attempt at singing along to Kate Bush's 'Wuthering Heights'.

We revelled in nostalgia, and I learnt so much about him that night, not just his taste in music but things like what he was like at school, his first experiences of sneaking out to pubs and clubs, how he had hated all his lessons except art and preferred taking himself off into the countryside, exploring. He confided that when his grandad died, just before his fifteenth birthday, he had gone off on his bike to think and had discovered an old disused stone barn, perched at the top of a steep hill. He had climbed up into the loft, where you could see out of a glassless window to a view of the river Avon and the canal that ran parallel to each other in the valley below. He stayed there all night, despite being a bit spooked, and in the early morning he stayed to watch the sunrise before he cycled off home. When he eventually went back he found his dad had been so worried about him that he couldn't bring himself to talk to Tom for two days. Tom said that it'd made him feel far worse than if his dad had given him a complete rollocking. He never even told his friends about the barn as he was sure they would want to hang out there and have parties and he couldn't hack them ruining it for him, it was his special place, and he still went there sometimes when he needed to think. Tom had laughed then, embarrassed, and admitted that I was the first person he had ever told.

That night, exactly a year ago, was the first time I had seen Tom for what he really was, not just flighty, irresponsible and good for a laugh, but deep and thoughtful with an infectious curiosity and enthusiasm. It made a refreshing change from most of my previous boyfriends, who were all pretty much one-dimensional and didn't want much more out of life than an impressive pay cheque and a fast car. I began to want more out of our relationship than what we had, but a few days later he had flown out to Greece for a couple of months backpacking and I tried to dismiss my feelings as wasted energy.

'So, next time you see me I'll be looking like a

246

lampshade,' Maggie said, breaking my daydreams as I packed away the last of the dishes.

Her dress was apparently quite short and flared out at the bottom, the hem decorated with powder blue rose buds.

'I think it sounds nice.'

'Hmm, how I let her talk me into it I'll never understand. Most people go the whole hog first time round and opt for the registry office for their next marriage. Trust my mum to get it the wrong way round. It's so humiliating!' She wrung out a dishcloth and furiously wiped down the work surfaces.

'Well, it'll soon be over.'

'Maybe I shouldn't have insisted she let me bring all my friends, at least then nobody I care about would be witnessing my ultimate destruction in the fashion credibility stakes.'

'Don't worry, you could make anything look sexy,' I assured her.

She gave me a stern look and threw the dishcloth back in the sink. 'Well, there's no getting out of it now. I won't see you again before the service, so I shall have to see you at the hotel at half past five to set up the cake.'

Irene wasn't getting married until four o'clock and the evening do was starting at six. I had agreed to go early to meet Maggie whilst Irene and Don had their photos taken. Alice, Simon, Charlie and Noah were supposed to meet us at the hotel as none of us were going to the actual ceremony. Simon had finally called Alice to confirm that he

247

was still coming, but Alice was worried that he was unusually brief and formal on the phone. I wasn't sure whether Charlie would turn up on Saturday any more; I hadn't even spoken to him since what happened in The Cellar. He had phoned me twice on Sunday but Alice had told him I was out and he hadn't called back after that. I decided that Alice was such a bad liar he had sussed that I was standing in the background, shaking my head and mouthing 'I'm out!' I felt so awful about the situation; I toyed with the idea of going over to his house and apologising, but, well, I was very busy putting the finishing touches to the wedding cake, and, well, I basically just kept finding things to do.

I waved Maggie off, locking the door behind her, then sat down at one of the tables, kicking off my shoes. My feet were throbbing from standing up all day. I hadn't even managed to sit down at lunchtime.

There was a tap at the door only a few moments later.

'Alice, you and keys seem to repel each other like the poles on a magnet,' I grumbled half to myself as I got up to let her in. Only it wasn't Alice's face I saw peering at me through the door, it was Charlie's.

My heart skipped a beat, then started up again by thundering hard in my chest. I was part excited, part guilty to see him. My eyes were drawn to his mouth, remembering the sensation of his kiss and I shivered.

I drew a deep breath and unbolted the door,

248

fixing what I hoped was an easy, platonic smile on my face.

'Hi, this is a nice surprise,' I said, beckoning him inside.

He smiled back, looking grateful that I was acting as though everything was normal. 'I hope you don't mind me calling around like this,' he said and held up a pot of paint before me. 'Call it a peace offering if you like, I just felt as though I had some making up to do. The stunt I pulled on Saturday was a low act, and I figured what better penance than to offer my services to you as a handyman and fix your scorched kitchen wall.'

'Oh Charlie, you don't need to do this. I'm hardly blameless myself, am I?' I said, feeling my cheeks colour as the subject was brought up.

'It's different, though,' he said, his eyes darting nervously from me, to the window and back again. 'You're in a really vulnerable situation just now and I took advantage of it. And Tom's a decent guy; he doesn't deserve me stirring things up for you. I was a twat. Can you forgive me? I'd really like it if we could just put it all behind us.'

'Of course,' I said, unsure if I really meant it. It was a huge relief things could be so easily sorted out between us, and yet I felt a stab of disappointment that Charlie was able to just forget it.

'Thank God for that,' he said smiling at me. 'So are you going to let me make it up to you? I'm nifty with a paintbrush . . .'

'Only if you accept dinner. It's the least I can do.'

'Done! So we're friends then?'

'Friends,' I agreed, trailing after him as he led the way into the kitchen.

An hour later Charlie had finished preparing the wall and was making good progress on the coat of fresh white paint. I was working alongside him, whizzing up a simple pesto sauce for us to eat with some tagliatelle when he had finished.

As I roughly chopped the basil, Alice arrived back from work.

'Yum, smells like pesto,' she said, sniffing the air like a bloodhound and dumping her bag and coat on a nearby table. 'You really shouldn't, you know, it's about time I cooked, don't you think? Not that I'm in your league or anything, but I could always treat us to a take-out.'

At that point Charlie poked his head around the kitchen door and waved a paintbrush at Alice, making her jump.

'Oh, hi, Charlie, I wasn't expecting to see you there,' she effused then shot me a nervous glance. 'Well, I'll leave you to it, shall I? I've got lots of things to do.'

'Don't be silly, Al, *please* join us, I've made plenty,' I invited, raising my eyebrows in a pleading gesture.

'Oh, er, if you're sure,' she said, checking with more eyebrow movements and meaningful looks, eventually gathering that I really wanted her there.

Alice fetched Charlie a bottle of lager from the chiller and poured us both a Coke, whilst I finished off the sauce and tipped it in a serving bowl with the steaming ribbons of pasta.

'It's ready,' I called as Charlie was standing back to check that he hadn't missed coating any patches of the wall. 'It looks great,' I enthused. 'I'm so grateful.'

'Oh don't be daft, it was nothing,' he assured me, and I caught a serious expression in his eyes, but chose to ignore it.

'I have some brilliant news,' Alice announced as we sat tucking into our meal. 'I've arranged to take the flat above Maggie's. My contract starts on May 1st.'

'That's excellent. I'm so pleased for you.' I leaned over to kiss her on the cheek, but felt a stab of sadness at the thought of being alone again.

'Shame though, I was just getting used to being here, and I won't be able to top the in-house catering,' she joked, mopping up the last of the sauce with a piece of ciabatta.

'I wish you could stay.' I put my fork down with a clatter; my appetite had vanished.

'Don't be silly, you need all the spare room you've got for when little pumpkin down there comes along.'

'I know, but I'm really going to miss you. You'll have such a laugh with Maggie that I'll hardly see you when the baby comes,' I said sadly.

'Are you kidding? You are the closest I'll get to having a baby for years yet. You'll be sick of the sight of my broody face!'

'I hope so.'

'Right, I guess I'd better be going,' Charlie interrupted, pushing his chair back from the table. I couldn't help feeling relieved. There was still tension between us.

'Oh, okay, if you're sure,' I said, standing up with him. 'Well, am I seeing you tomorrow, for Irene's wedding?'

'Of course. I'm seeing you there at six, aren't I? Noah and Simon are meeting me in The Red Bar at five, so we'll all come together and see you there.'

Alice said goodbye to Charlie then subtly excused herself to wash the dishes, leaving us alone.

I walked him to the door. 'Thanks again for, you know.'

'No problem, don't mention it,' he said, and I got the impression we weren't talking about the painting anymore. He gave me a glancing peck on the cheek and wandered away down the street.

CHAPTER TWENTY-ONE

Saturday started off drizzly and grey. I started to worry that it was going to rain all day and be miserable for Irene's wedding, but around lunchtime the clouds kindly dispersed and the sun came out. By late afternoon the puddles on the road had dried and the birds were singing in the warm light. The trees I could see from the café were covered in pastel shades of blossom. It was a perfect day to get married.

I had shut the café early to allow myself enough time to have a bath and get ready. I was determined to make an effort. I didn't want people to think that just because I was pregnant I could only do the frumpy, shapeless look. I had bought myself a gorgeous outfit, after much deliberation and annoyance about spending money on something that I was hoping I would never fit into again after the baby was born, but Alice had convinced me it was worth it. Looking in the mirror at my reflection I was glad I had.

I was wearing a pair of cropped fitted black trousers and flat, chunky mules in black suede.

My top was a long floaty tunic. It was white, with capped sleeves and a cute little hood. Very trendy, I thought and admired the delicate embroidery on the hem. My bump was hard to ignore, but with me hardly eating anything lately due to constant indigestion, the rest of my body looked refreshingly slim. A number of my elderly, female customers had commented on how I had a very 'neat' bump, which was apparently 'all at the front'. This, they assured me, meant I was having a girl. They said this with a wise authority, the way ladies that sell 'lucky lavender' tell me that I'm going to have a very happy life, have half a dozen children and should avoid the colour red.

'Wow, you look stunning,' Alice whistled appreciatively as she wandered back into my bedroom. 'I hope I look that good when I'm pregnant.'

I had twisted my hair up and pinned it in place, letting a few tendrils hang softly against my face, and I passed Alice a large daisy, to pin into the twist of hair at the back.

'Well, there's still time for the thread veins, water retention and fat ankles, you know,' I said holding my head still for her.

'Yes, but I think I'll still be insanely jealous of you,' she said, smiling at me in the mirror.

I laughed at the thought of her wanting to be me. I couldn't bend down without a burning feeling in my throat, I had started being sick again despite the books saying that the sickness only lasted for the first twelve weeks, and it took me hours to get to sleep at night as I couldn't sleep on my front anymore and hated every other position. And there was Alice in the mirror looking so fashionably petite, in a gorgeous little dress that accentuated her tiny waist and made her look sexy and feminine. She had let her hair hang loose down her back and had weaved in two thin plaits on either side of her face, making her look dreamy and hippyish.

'I guess we should be heading off,' I said and spritzed myself with perfume.

'Right, you'd better carry the cake, if I dropped it I'd never forgive myself.'

We walked over to where it was waiting for us on the counter.

'It's brilliant, Holly, you've such a talent.' Alice bent down to look closely at the decoration.

Rather than having a tiered cake, it was mainly one huge rectangle. I had made this to look like a giant table; the white icing was draped over so it folded naturally in the corners, the way a tablecloth would. I had made little sugar flowers in blue and cream to line the table, the same colours that Irene had chosen for everything. Then for the main decoration I had made figures sitting at the table. With the help of the photos provided by Irene, I had made a miniature bride and groom, then sitting either side were models of the best man and bridesmaid (Irene's sister, Sylvia). At the end of the table was a miniature Maggie, and on the other side sat a little version of Don's brother. I had made the figures out of soft icing, which I had moulded like plasticine. I had exaggerated particular features the way cartoonists do with caricatures

255

so that everyone would know who they were. With Maggie I had accentuated her wild curly brown hair, and given her a bodice-ripping cleavage, I knew she would love that. For Don's brother I had exaggerated his bushy beard and half moon glasses, and with Irene's sister it was her round smiley face and ruddy cheeks. It was comical, which is how Irene had wanted it; she was always game for a laugh. The *pièce de résistance* was peering from under the tablecloth. I had made a model of Rod Stewart peeping out, giving the impression that he was hidden under the table. I made him look fed up, as though he was annoyed that Irene was now happily married and unavailable. It had taken me hours to get him looking right, and the blond streaks in his hair had been a nightmare! But looking at it now there was no mistaking who it was, and I was really pleased with the result.

I lifted it carefully into the box and replaced the lid, then Alice opened the door for me so I could carry it out to the car.

When we arrived at the hotel there was already a lot of commotion. Huge trays of food were being laid out on long banquet tables at the edge of the room by staff dressed in black and white penguin uniforms. At the end of the dining hall another room was attached, separated by an ornate archway. There were colourful lights tracking patterns on the floor as the DJ tried out the sound-system.

Some guests had already arrived and had got themselves a drink at the bar. Others were sitting on the lavish armchairs and dining chairs that filled the dining room. Scanning around, though, there was no one I recognised. Most looked over forty, with the occasional nine- or ten-year-old that were slouched at tables, looking bored beyond belief. One was even playing a Gameboy under a table until his mother noticed and clipped him across the head.

Irene had decided to have a large buffet and a disco rather than a formal sit-down affair. Maggie was so relieved about that, as for a while she thought she'd have to sit at the top table with the family, on show in her dress. At least this way the lights would be dimmer and she could avoid the relatives and hang out with us all.

A table had been specially set aside for my cake and I felt a glimmer of pride as I set it down on the pristine tablecloth. It would be the focal point of the buffet, and already a handful of catering staff had gathered to admire it. I caught one of them saying, 'that's just the kind of cake I'd like when I get married', and I had to restrain myself from kissing him. That reminded me, I thought, and I went to retrieve some cards I had printed with my details on and placed them in a silver dish at the end of the buffet table, just in case. It had been Irene's idea; I wasn't sure it would be worth it but she had insisted that I give it a try.

Alice came back from the car with the wedding presents we had bought the couple and stacked them on an allocated table near the entrance.

'Hi everyone,' Maggie called as she followed Alice through the door.

257

'Wow, you look lovely,' I gasped, taken aback by her appearance. I had never seen her look so feminine. She had little blue flowers pinned in her hair, which was hanging in loose Pre-Raphaelite curls. She did indeed have a fantastic cleavage on show in the sweetheart neckline of her blue silk dress, but she still managed to look girly. Her dress was a bit on the full and frilly side, but not nearly as bad as Mags had made out. It was probably the first dress I'd ever seen her wear that wasn't tight and slinky, so it was obviously quite alien to her. The girly effect was rather hampered by the fact that, rather than smiling prettily, she scowled like a cross child and squirmed, tugging at the front of her outfit as she crossed over to us.

'They'll be here in ten minutes,' she announced to the people gathering in the room. The caterers stepped up their scurrying movements; the way ants do when you stamp on the ground near their nest. She waved at some people she recognised and mouthed a few polite 'hellos'.

'God, I feel like a Christmas turkey,' she muttered to us under her breath.

'Well, I think you look amazing.'

'Me too, your hair looks awesome,' Alice agreed.

Maggie fiddled with one of her ringlets irritably. 'Mum forced me to let the hairdresser have a go at it. I was quite prepared just to dry it upside down, but they insisted. Are the lads here yet?' She glanced over to the entrance where people were now arriving in full force.

'I don't think so,' I said, making a play of looking

258

around, but I knew they weren't as I had searched the building when we got here and hadn't stopped eyeballing the door since.

Staff were now touring the room with silver trays laden with glasses of champagne, ready to toast the arrival of the newly weds. Maggie downed one immediately, put the empty glass back on the tray then took two more.

'They're here,' someone cried excitedly, running back into the room.

Everybody stood up expectantly, glasses raised, and when they walked in the guests cheered and tried to clap but found they couldn't with their drinks in hand, so just cheered louder instead.

Irene and Don walked in with their arms linked together, beaming at everyone.

I found myself getting a huge, hard lump in my throat. They were neither my friends, family, nor my peer group, but I was still so excited for them. I could see the joy in their faces and I felt a confusion of admiration and jealousy at their happiness. Weddings did this to me every time. Sometimes I would see a bride in a car, looking nervously out of a window as she sped to a church somewhere, or I would walk past a church as a couple were posing for photos with their families, and always a lump would ache in my throat and a rush of emotion would bring tears to my eyes. It was what I wanted for myself more than anything else I could imagine. I know it's cool to have the career and be independent now, but no matter how hard I tried to convince myself I was happy, there was always a nagging feeling that I wasn't fulfilled, that something was missing.

Alice and I shared a doe-eyed look. 'I wish that was me,' she whispered.

'Me too,' I agreed, adding, 'only with a different dress.'

'Oh yes, something a bit more . . . simple. And with a slightly younger man, obviously.'

'Would you have a marquee?' I asked her. 'Only, I've always thought they were really romantic.'

'Oh, me too,' Alice agreed smiling dreamily.

Maggie cut us off by tutting loudly. She rolled her eyes and muttered, 'Sad . . .' under her breath.

A man from the wedding party handed the couple a glass of champagne each and proposed a toast to them. Afterwards Don made a small speech then announced that the buffet was open, they would cut the cake in about an hour and that we should all relax and enjoy ourselves. Maggie needed no more encouragement than that and homed in on a vacant sofa. She flung herself down and kicked her high-heeled shoes off.

'I wonder where the guys are,' Alice said, looking anxiously at the door again.

'The bastards are probably having a brilliant time in the bar and have decided this place isn't really their scene. I wouldn't blame them, I suppose,' Maggie muttered and stared with disdain at her mother, who was shrieking with laughter and chatting flirtatiously with a pensioner on the other side of the room.

'Maggie,' cried a middle-aged man, peering at her

260

over thick rimmed glasses. 'You look ravishing.' I recognised him from the family photos as Irene's sister's husband.

'Hello, Uncle Vinnie,' Maggie greeted, looking desperately around and realising there was no escape.

'Would you like to introduce me to your little friends,' he said, smiling lecherously at Alice and me.

Maggie shot us an apologetic look and dutifully told him our names. Uncle Vinnie insisted on shaking our hands very slowly with a tight clammy grip. 'So you're the clever little thing that made the wedding cake,' he said to me, leaning in unsteadily close. I got the impression he had already had a few drinks and hoped it was a hip flask I could see bulging in his trousers. 'I must say you did a very flattering job of the missus. First time I've wanted to eat her in twenty years!' he drawled with a throaty laugh. I prayed he wouldn't fall in my lap.

'Er, Uncle Vinnie, I think Auntie Sylvia wants you,' Maggie butted in, coming to my aid. Sylvia was standing by the food, staring daggers at Vinnie, who gave her a sheepish wave.

'Hey up, I'm in trouble again. I'll catch up with you charming ladies later,' he said and wandered back to his wife.

'Don't count on it,' Maggie muttered under her breath. 'Sorry about that,' she said to us.

'Oh I thought he was quite sweet,' Alice said, convincing no one.

We met a whole selection of Maggie's family as we sat there, picking at the plates of buffet

261

food Maggie had fetched for us and waited for the lads to arrive. Some I recognised from family get-togethers and Christmases from years gone by. Most commented favourably on the wedding cake, all asked similar questions about my pregnancy. There were more speeches as the cake was cut, and I felt a pang of disappointment as the silver knife cut through the pale blue icing and the cake proceeded to be sectioned off and dished out to the eager guests. All that effort and it was hacked up in minutes. Still, I had managed to take a photograph of it at home, to put in a portfolio. I couldn't bring myself to eat it though, it didn't seem right somehow.

After the formalities were over the disco started up on cue, playing Rod Stewart's, 'You're In My Heart'. Irene and Don swayed together on the dance-floor, spotlit, as the guests looked on. Halfway through the song it stopped abruptly and Barry Manilow's, 'Copacabana' interrupted. The happy couple broke apart and started bopping wildly. The majority of Maggie's family stormed the dance-floor and joined in with them until you couldn't see Irene any more as she was surrounded by people flailing their arms in the air and gyrating their hips. Don's side of the family seemed to prefer milling around at the side of the room, drinks in hand, staring blankly at the dancers.

'It's so cheesy,' Maggie complained as we wondered back to our sofa.

'I'm going to have to go to the loo again,' I said.

'Again! Are you sure you're okay?' Maggie asked. 'You're not going to do a runner and abandon me with these people, are you?'

I assured her I'd be quick and waddled off.

When I returned I saw that Charlie, Simon and Noah had arrived and I felt a rush of relief and excitement. They all looked gorgeous. Simon was smart and suave in a well-cut grey suit, his collar was undone and his tie loosened. Noah was dressed all in black, with his collarless shirt hanging loose, and Charlie wore smart beige trousers and a loose short-sleeved shirt, silver sunglasses perched on his head.

Noah and Maggie were laughing by the bar, fetching more free wine, Alice and Simon were whispering intimately and Charlie stood awkwardly next to them, obviously feeling like a gooseberry. He saw me enter the room and gave me a wide easy grin.

I joined them, kissing Charlie's warm cheek. 'What took you so long?'

'Oh, I'm really sorry. We got drinking at The Red Bar and forgot the time. You look fabulous.' He held my hand and looked me up and down. 'In fact I hate to use a pregnant woman-type cliché, but you actually look radiant.'

'Thank you.' I beamed shyly. We found a couple of vacant sofas with a table and relaxed into the cushions. Alice and Simon sat opposite us.

'Simon, I've hardly seen you lately, how've you been?' I asked when Alice and Charlie went to fetch their drinks from Maggie, who seemed to have forgotten all about us as she larked about with Noah at the bar.

'Well, I thought it might be better if I kept my distance for a while. Y'know, with Alice seeing Oliver again. I wanted to give her some space,' he confided shyly.

'You like her then, I thought you might.' I gave him a knowing smile.

'What's not to like? She's so lovely.' He watched her as she leaned elegantly over the bar to fetch another glass. 'What do you think, Hol? Is it back on again with her and Oliver? Am I just wasting my time?' He looked worriedly at me, preparing himself for the worst.

'Of course not. She's finally over that git at last. It took a while, but she's definitely available now.'

Simon's face brightened and he thanked me with a confidential whisper as Alice and Charlie returned with drinks for everyone.

Charlie passed me a Coke. 'I bet you can't wait until you can start drinking properly again, can you?'

'Oh you know, I'm not too bothered actually. I don't miss it as much as I thought I would,' I said sipping my Coke. In truth the thought of being able to drink again scared me, as that would mean I would have had my baby, which would mean I would be a mother, a single mother, alone. I didn't relish the thought of doing it all without Tom. I tried to block out the inevitability of what was going to happen. I was excited about seeing my baby and the relationship I hoped we'd share,

264

but my predominant emotion was fear, fear of the unknown.

Charlie sensed my mood change and quickly diverted the subject to his police training, which was due to start the following week. 'Four weeks at the station, then I'm off to Portishead for fifteen weeks. It'll be like going back to Uni,' he said brightly.

This darkened my mood even further as I realised he wouldn't be around for the remainder of my pregnancy and wouldn't be back until after the baby was born. I felt deserted. Maybe Charlie's right about drinking, I thought, getting drunk might be my only solace at the moment.

The evening passed by quickly as we sat getting occasional visits from wedding guests and I met more and more complete strangers. The lads were fairly drunk thanks to their pre-wedding pints, and even Maggie and Alice were beginning to slur and giggle at everything. Noah and Simon talked the girls into dancing and they trooped on to the dance-floor, laughing, and attempted to dance to the disco music. They looked pretty daft as they were so used to more upbeat club music they couldn't remember how to dance to the slower seventies and eighties rhythms. Simon and Noah hammed it up like John Travolta, posing a lot, and Maggie and Alice giggled and whispered to each other like schoolgirls. When 'We Are Sailing' came on, they shamelessly joined in with everyone else as they waved their arms above their heads and sang along, too drunk to care any more. I wished I was uninhibited enough to join them, but I would have felt foolish and clumsy

265

with my bump. Instead I chatted easily to Charlie; any awkwardness had passed and as we talked I realised I couldn't help constantly comparing him to Tom. I came to the conclusion that Tom was more sensitive and genuine, whereas Charlie was more of a lad. I didn't think I would ever be able to fully trust Charlie. He had that sparkle in his eye that suggested he was a bit of a 'ladies' man', and I wondered how many other women he had made feel as though they were the only woman on the planet as far as he was concerned. I felt embarrassingly naive to have been swept away by him. I needed an ego boost and Charlie had helped me to feel desirable, despite my current physical state, but it hadn't been any more than that.

'Look at those two, it's gruesome, isn't it?' Charlie cringed, pointing out Maggie and Noah as they kissed passionately, oblivious to the people dancing around them. Dire Straits, 'Romeo and Juliet' was playing and the guests had paired off into smoochy couples. Alice had her head rested on Simon's chest and they were barely moving to the music.

'I think it's lovely,' I said, watching them. I was really pleased that they were all getting on so well. Alice in particular deserved to be happy.

The DJ broke the romantic ambience by fading the song down and announcing that the bar was to be closed in half an hour as Don and Irene were leaving to go to their hotel, in some secret country location. There were several groans as people realised the drinking and partying was nearly over, and some of the male members of Maggie's family were whistling and laughing suggestively at the thought of the couple in their hotel.

'Go on, my son!' Uncle Vinnie yelled, slapping Don on the back as they made their way outside.

Everyone gathered at the entrance to the hotel where a smart silver Jaguar was parked, waiting to take them away. Irene hugged and kissed people goodbye and when she got to me I was enveloped in a heavily perfumed bear hug.

''Bye darlin, and thanks again for the gorgeous cake, you did a brilliant job. And look after that bump, won't you. Make the most of when they're small and cute, coz they don't stay like that for long, just look at my Maggie May.' She pinched Maggie's cheeks.

'Yeah, thanks Mum, have a great time,' she squeaked as Irene hugged the breath out of her body.

'My little girl, everybody, isn't she gorgeous?' Irene yelled to the people crowded by the car. Maggie looked mortified. 'Right, it's bouquet time, ladies, and Maggie, you make an effort, you hear. It's about time, isn't it, love?' She turned her back on the jostling women as the men scrambled to one side. Irene's middle-aged friends were almost set for a punch-up as they pushed and shoved each other. Irene tossed the bouquet in the air and it sailed high above the heads of the women, who now resembled a rugby scrum. It turned once in the air, then fell straight down towards Alice, who caught it automatically. Irene's friends stopped fighting and groaned with disappointment, eyeing Alice jealously. Irene and Don slid on to the plush cream leather seats of the car and with a final wave, they silently pulled away. When they had disappeared into the distance I saw Alice turn back to catch Simon's eye and she smiled shyly.

The guests were already piling back into the hotel to make the most of last orders. I wandered around waiting for Alice, Simon, Charlie, Maggie and Noah to all meet up by the doors, as I wanted to say goodbye and head off.

I scanned the driveway, looking for Maggie, who I had last seen heading for a bush with Noah.

A figure suddenly stepped out of the shadows by the entrance. I looked hard as he staggered closer, trying to figure out why he looked familiar, then I realised with horror that it was Oliver.

He was clutching an almost empty bottle of whisky and could barely walk in a straight line.

'Hello, Holly, nice to see you again,' he drawled menacingly, and I looked nervously around for Alice. She was walking towards me, looking dreamily at the flowers she still held. She hadn't noticed I had company. Simon was also oblivious as he chatted to a guy they had all been dancing with earlier.

Alice joined me, smiling beatifically. 'Aren't they gorgeous?' she said, showing me the flowers, but I didn't answer. She looked up to see why I was so quiet.

'Oliver, what on earth are you doing here?' she exclaimed, taken aback.

'Well now, isn't this cosy. You and all your *happy* little friends. Haven't you been having lots of fun without me?' he said, pointing his bottle at her. 'Now, isn't it time you came home? Come on, let me escort you.' He offered her his arm. Alice just continued to stare at him with wide eyes.

'Look, I think you've had a bit too much to drink. Why don't I find Noah and he can take you back,' I reasoned, searching the drive desperately for one of the lads. Where were they!

'No, you keep out of this. Come on, Alice, come with me. Don't be silly now.' He started tugging at her elbow and she shrugged him off, making him stumble backwards slightly.

'You're making a complete fool of yourself, Alice. You've obviously had too much to drink. I saw you flirting with that guy, Simon, isn't it? I saw you through the window. Silly little Alice, you think he likes you, but he doesn't. I saw them all in The Red Bar tonight, they didn't spot me behind them but I could hear them talking about you. Simon was saying what a pushover you'd be, and well, it looks as though he was right, doesn't it?'

'That's not true!' Alice spat, tears welling in her eyes. Her pale skin was flushed and turning blotchy, the way it often appeared when she was nervous. 'He'd never have said that.'

Oliver just shrugged his shoulders and smiled. 'It's okay, honey, I forgive you. I can see you wanted to hurt me, you wanted me to see how it felt. Well, it worked,' he slurred and clutched his chest in a mock, wounded gesture. 'I'm hurt, okay. So let's

269

just call it quits now. You're obviously being led on by your cheap friends, but you don't want to end up like that.' He nodded in my direction.

I stared back at him, willing myself to retaliate but I was so shocked that any words I had were suspended in the back of my throat, unable to surface. Oliver started pulling her down the gravel path. I shouted to Simon, who looked over and waved, indicating that he'd only be a minute.

'Get off me!' Alice yelled, trying to twist her arm free, but Oliver was determined.

I yelled at Simon again, who must have sensed an element of panic in my voice this time as he broke straight into a run.

Charlie came out of the hotel entrance then and saw that something was wrong. He rushed forward and grabbed Oliver from behind, making him release Alice. She ran to me sobbing. Oliver swung at Charlie with the whisky bottle but missed and the bottle landed on the gravel, splitting into two jagged pieces. Simon reached us and went straight to where Charlie had Oliver in an armlock. Simon's face was tight with rage and he punched Oliver hard in the stomach, making him double over in pain. Charlie let go of him and he dropped to his knees on the drive, gasping for breath.

'If I catch you anywhere near Alice again, you scum, I won't spare your face next time, you hear me?' Simon warned through clenched teeth as he hovered over him, his fists still clenched.

'Come on, mate,' Charlie said, pulling Simon away from him.

Noah and Maggie ran across the lawn towards us; she was trying to do the zip up on her dress and the last few buttons of Noah's shirt were undone, making it flap as he ran.

'What the hell happened here?' he shouted, looking at the groaning heap that used to be Oliver curled up on the ground.

'He was hassling Alice, trying to drag her off. I think he's pretty drunk,' I explained.

'God, you scumbag,' Maggie spat, leaning right over him. 'You don't have a human bone in your body, do you? When are you going to learn how to treat people with respect? Alice is way too good for you, you prat, you're lucky she even breathed the same air as you . . .' She was laying into him so much Charlie eventually dragged her away and told her to get a grip.

'I'll take him home,' Noah offered, helping Oliver stagger to his feet. He put one arm around his waist to stop him falling over again and started to walk him down the drive. Oliver didn't say anything else, he just moaned as though he might be sick and his head was hung low against his chest.

We watched them limp away for a moment.

Alice just stood, crying softly to herself; she still had her hand still clamped over her mouth and looked shocked. Eventually Simon turned to us, his hands trembling with adrenalin.

'I'm really sorry,' he said to Alice. 'I've never hit anyone in my life before. I don't know what came over me.'

271

'It's okay,' she whispered, then looked at me. 'Can we go home?'

'Of course we can,' I said gently, but Alice had already started towards the car park in search of my car.

Simon chased after her. 'Alice, do you want to talk about it?' he asked her anxiously. She just brushed him off, shaking her head and kept on walking.

'I'd better take her home then,' I said to the others and glanced sympathetically at Simon. He whispered to me that he'd call around at the flat tomorrow and I nodded and waved goodbye to them all.

CHAPTER TWENTY-TWO

Alice traced a figure of eight into the now thick mush of cereal with her spoon.

'Would you rather have some toast?' I offered, putting some under the grill for myself.

She didn't answer.

'It's not so bad, you know. At least Oliver has got the message now. Why are you so worried?'

'Do you think Oliver was telling the truth, about overhearing Simon say I was "easy" in the pub?'

'Of course I don't!' I put my knife down on the counter and sat opposite her. 'Al, he's not like that. I mean he just doesn't talk like that, ever. Oliver probably heard Simon say you were lovely and then put his own sleazy spin on it. You can't trust anything Oliver says. He doesn't do anything unless it'll benefit himself.'

'I hope you're right,' Alice said. 'I just feel a bit funny about the whole thing. I mean I never would have believed Simon could hit anyone either. You know how I feel about violence. Maybe I don't know Simon that well after all.' She pushed her breakfast to one side and slumped down in the chair.

'Look, I was as surprised as you were about that, but I think you're being unfair. Simon looked pretty wretched after he hit Oliver, and you heard him, he said he'd never hit anyone before in his life. I think if it shows anything, it's how he feels about you.' I smiled at her. 'It was like a natural instinct to protect you. In a funny kind of way it was quite romantic, don't you think?'

An involuntary smile flickered on Alice's mouth. 'Well, I have to admit, I was glad he did it.' She grinned guiltily. 'Am I awful?'

'You're a bloodthirsty, homicidal maniac, what do you think?' I teased, getting up to check my toast.

Over the following three weeks Alice heard no more from Oliver. Noah and Maggie were getting on like a house on fire, and Alice and Simon were seeing so much of each other you could hardly tell she was supposed to be living in my flat. Charlie had started his training, so we didn't see very much of him and I no longer enjoyed the company of my stand-in platonic boyfriend. Whenever we all went out I felt like a spare part. This wasn't because of anything Alice or Maggie did. In fact they bent over backwards to include me in conversations and not be too lovey dovey with their new men. But that almost made it worse. I could tell they were trying hard for my benefit; there was a hormonal intensity that was hard to ignore, the air was thick with it whenever we went anywhere, so I began to turn down their invitations to pub outings and evening meals.

I persevered with the antenatal class and was

relieved to see that Harley had given it up as a bad job. With her not frightening people away it was easier to make friends with the others.

I was also keeping myself busy by making two new wedding cakes. I had received some phone calls after the wedding, enquiring about my availability and prices. I was thrilled at my new sideline. I knew that after the baby was born, Maggie would take over a lot of the running of the café. It was nice to know I had a new venture to put my energy into. If it worked out, it would be a brilliant way of working from home and making extra cash. And after four years of almost solid work building up the café, I was starting to look forward to having a change of scenery.

At the end of the month Alice was set to move into the flat upstairs from Maggie. She had banned me from helping, worried that I'd overdo it, and promised that she'd call that evening.

As she packed her bags and we talked about her new flat, I fought back tears, hating to make her feel guilty about a decision that was so obviously right for her. It was her first stab at living alone and she was understandably excited.

'I can't believe I didn't do this years ago. Now I understand how people feel when they leave home and go to Uni,' then seeing my hurt face she added, 'Oh, I'm sorry, Hol, I'm not excited about leaving you. It's more the thought of being independent from my mother. Staying with you wasn't a permanent thing. It was more like a lovely long sleepover,

275

like we used to have in the summer holidays at school. Please don't look so fed up, it's not as though I'll be far away. I'll be within walking distance from you, and it's even closer than where I used to live with my mum. You'll still see loads of me,' she assured me as she gathered up her last box and slung her coat over the top.

'I know, I know, I'm sorry. It's just . . . oh I don't know, I got used to having you around. You're good company.'

'Well, I can still stay over, can't I?' She coaxed me into a smile. 'You know how I love our late-night chats.'

'Deal!' I agreed, forcing myself to look happy and I followed her down the staircase.

Her car was loaded down with bags and boxes. I never realised how much stuff she had in my flat. We hugged goodbye as though we wouldn't see each other again for months and I stood on the pavement waving at the weighted-down rear of the car.

When she had gone I trudged back up the stairs and walked all around the flat, checking the rooms and cupboards. It seemed so empty. There was nothing left of her. Nothing, except for half a jar of lime marmalade in the fridge and a nearly finished packet of Garibaldi biscuits. I knew I wouldn't eat either of them, but I didn't have the heart to throw them out. I was acting like an over-sentimental mother with 'empty nest' syndrome and I knew I was being ridiculous but a part of me felt like this marked the end of an era. Alice and Maggie were happier with their current boyfriends than they had been with any of their ex's. They made the perfect double-date set-up, and soon I would be a mother with new priorities and interests. I wondered if we would drift apart. I shuddered, feeling anxious for the future.

I gave Alice half an hour to get to the flat and start unpacking her bags then I called her mobile.

'Hello?' she answered breathlessly.

'Al, it's me.'

'Hello, darlin', did I forget anything?'

'No, no, it's not that, I just wanted to invite you for a meal next week. A kind of late goodbye meal. You can bring Simon and I thought I'd invite Noah, Mags, Charlie and Tamsin.'

'That sounds wonderful!' she enthused. 'Count me in. You know how much I'm going to miss your cooking.'

'Excellent. How about next Saturday?'

'Perfect! Do you want me to invite Simon, Mags and Noah? They're all here helping out.'

'Okay,' I said, my voice breaking at the thought of them all being together without me. I heard Alice walking down some stairs and mumble to them.

'Yep, they're all free. Thanks for the invite, Hol, I shall have to go, I'm parked in someone's space . . .' The phone cut out. I stared at it for a little while, embarrassed at acting so clingy and insecure. I knew full well that I was planning to cook up a storm and be the perfect hostess, just to remind them that I was still here and I was still lots of

277

fun. I hoped they hadn't all seen through my plan and I fetched my address book to call Charlie and Tamsin.

Charlie and Tamsin, oh my God! It suddenly occurred to me that as they were both young, single and attractive, they might also hit it off. Charlie had already demonstrated that the presence of a baby was not going to dampen his interest. The last thing I needed would be to have those two pair off as well, then I really would be up couple creek without a partner. I'd just have to make sure they didn't sit next to each other, I decided, punching Charlie's number into the phone.

The following Saturday I prepared most of the food for the dinner party during the day. I cheated by using the leftover cherry tomato and basil salad, adding cucumber, red onion and feta cheese to make it a Greek salad, then whilst Maggie dealt with the late-afternoon surge, I prepared the ingredients for a three cheese and spinach filo pie. I made some fresh rolls as an extra and a strawberry tart with a sweet vanilla custard for pudding. The sun streamed in through the skylight window and it felt like the height of summer as we sweated in the narrow kitchen.

With the turn in the weather, the customers were happy to take their time and stayed longer into the afternoon. They didn't eat much, just sat lazily sipping cold drinks and chatting amiably with their friends. Maggie got annoyed with how long they were staying in relation to the small amount of money they were spending, but it didn't bother me. I was flattered that they were content to enjoy the afternoon in my café and argued with Maggie that if you wiped out all the customers that only had a cup of tea or coffee and a piece of cake, keeping only the big spenders, we would probably go bankrupt. Still, when we hadn't managed to shut the café forty minutes after we were supposed to, due to people lingering on, I couldn't help but finally share some of her frustration and wished they would go home.

After we did finally succeed in shutting the café Maggie stayed behind to make the eating area look as nice as possible for the dinner party. Then she disappeared to get ready and I went upstairs to put my feet up. 'We're going to be the perfect hostesses,' I muttered dreamily to myself, stroking my bump rhythmically. 'Just twenty winks to recharge the old batteries.' I plumped up the cushions on the sofa and sank into them, letting my eyelids droop heavily.

I was woken up by Maggie gently shaking my shoulder.

'Wah?' I muttered, rubbing my eyes.

Her face filled my vision. She was all curly hair and big, red lips. 'Holly, it's quarter past eight, we're all here, you daft thing! Have you been asleep all this time?'

'Oh piss,' I groaned, sitting up and swinging my legs off the sofa. I looked down at my outfit. I was still wearing the baggy tracksuit bottoms and T-shirt I had worn to cook in and I could smell old food in my hair. 'Oh, I've not even had a shower yet.'

Maggie looked at me with an amused sympathy. 'Don't worry, they're all downstairs. Tamsin and Charlie haven't arrived yet. I'll dish out the wine and put the pie in the oven. You get in the shower, freshen up and come find us downstairs.'

'You are an angel,' I whispered gratefully and hauled myself off the sofa.

'It's my pleasure,' she grinned. 'I'll be the perfect hostess for you.' Then she skipped off, back down the stairs. Humph.

Half an hour later I had finished my shower, donned a strappy A-line dress, as the warmth of the days sun was still lingering, and applied a small amount of make-up. I could hear my friends laughing downstairs and I eagerly went down to join them.

When I wandered into the café they cheered and clapped, raising their glasses. Charlie passed me a small glass of white wine and I took a large gulp. Tamsin gave me a kiss on the cheek and a pretty bunch of flowers.

'I'll put those in water,' Alice said, leaping to her feet to find a jug.

'You put your feet up,' Simon said, fetching me a chair and sitting me down next to him at the table.

'Now, everything's under control in the kitchen,' Maggie called from the kitchen doorway, a tea towel slung casually over one shoulder. 'The main course will be ready in quarter of an hour, so I've put Holly's bread rolls out on the table for everyone.'

They all hungrily swooped on the bread and the butter was passed around the table.

When Maggie joined us back at the table, I thanked her again for helping me out.

'Honestly, Hol, it's no trouble. We all decided whilst you were getting ready that you've been working too hard. You need a break. The last thing you need is to be running around after us. I swear you'd be getting up off your deathbed to cater for your own funeral, wouldn't you?' she teased.

'Yes,' Tamsin cut in, 'you're going to need all your energy after the baby's born so you've got to take it a bit easier.'

'But I like being a hostess,' I protested meekly, trying to get up and pour everyone another wine but Noah put a strong hand on my shoulder and took the bottle.

'You sit down, Holly, they're right. We're going to look after you tonight.' He went and fetched a corkscrew from behind the counter.

As we ate I noticed that Tamsin and Charlie were sitting together and chatting about her twins.

'So, what do you do?' she asked him.

When he had explained to her that he was a training police constable her face lit up, intrigued.

'Yes, you're going away soon, aren't you, Charlie?' I cut in.

'Well, yes,' he answered looking puzzled. 'But not for ever. It's only fifteen weeks at headquarters, then I'll be resuming my training at the station on Manvers Street.'

'Oh wow, so you're going to be my local bobby

then,' Tamsin grinned, leaning closer towards him. She fiddled with a short strand of her spiky blond hair and looked at him from under her eyelashes.

'Here to serve and protect you, ma'am,' he joked in a deep manly voice.

'Ooh, my hero,' she giggled, taking another sip of wine. I wondered if she was already slightly drunk.

Maggie brought my enormous Greek pie and salad through and presented them on the table.

'Wow, that looks delicious, Maggie,' Noah said and everyone agreed, eyeing it ravenously.

'Oh, it wasn't me that cooked it, it was Holly. She did all the food,' she corrected in an attempt to steer the credit back in my direction.

Everyone complimented me and got their plates ready as Maggie dished it out. I made several attempts to get up and help but eventually had to give in to the calls of 'sit down Holly,' and, 'you take it easy'.

As we sat eating and chatting I felt a slight twinge in my abdomen. I rearranged my dress, making it hang more loosely, but it didn't appear to help.

'Are you all right, Holly?' Alice asked, noticing I had gone quiet.

'Oh yes, I'm fine. Just the baby kicking,' I said, not wanting to worry everyone and ruin the happy atmosphere.

When the others were taking their plates into the kitchen Tamsin whispered to me, 'Did you know that Marcus and Fiona are due back next Friday?'

I felt my heart plummet and my head spin. This

was it. No more denial. I would have to tell them and confront the situation. They'd tell Tom and he would probably decide to stay abroad rather than be forced into new responsibilities and maintenance payments.

The pain in my abdomen was getting stronger and started to make me feel uncomfortable.

'I'm sorry, Holly, I thought you ought to know. Then at least you can prepare yourself,' she continued.

I tried massaging my bump to relieve the discomfort, but it was useless. The pain was getting more intense.

'Is everything okay? You look really pale,' she asked, starting to look concerned.

'Mmm.' I screwed my face up, trying to concentrate on controlling the pain. Tamsin looked around for Alice and waved her over.

'Alice, I really don't think Holly looks well,' she said. Alice put her hand on my shoulder and crouched down, scrutinising my face.

'Hol, what's up?'

'Nothing really, just a bit of pain, nothing too bad. You just keep enjoying yourself. There's a strawberry tart in the fridge for . . . Ahhh.' I doubled over in agony as a stabbing pain bit into me. I couldn't ignore it any longer.

'Shit!' Tamsin said. 'I think I'd better take you to the hospital.' The others had noticed that something was up and gathered around me. They all looked worried, which scared me even more.

'Honestly, I'll be fine in a minute. Maybe I should

just have a little lie down in the corner. You can all carry on eating. I'll be fine,' I assured them. I tried to smile but the pain was getting unbearable and I was beginning to panic. Something was wrong.

'Right, this is silly. I'm taking you to the Royal United,' Tamsin said and grabbed her coat off the rack, searching for the car keys in her pocket.

'Oh shit, I don't want to go to hospital, it'll probably be nothing and I'll just look silly. I'd much rather stay here and have a good time with you lot,' I moaned pathetically and gripped the table for support.

'I'd rather we took you in and it was nothing, than not take you in and it turn into something serious. Now get your coat, Hol, and don't worry.'

Maggie had already fetched my coat and she draped it over my shoulders, giving me a hug. 'I'm sure you'll be fine, Holly, but Tamsin's right. You really ought to check it out. And don't worry about us, I've got the keys so I'll lock up.'

'Oh no, please stay, I've made a tart and everything,' I whimpered, nearly in tears. 'I wanted you all to enjoy yourselves. You will stay, won't you?' They all nodded their heads dutifully and waved me off.

'Help yourselves to drinks everyone,' I cried from the door, stooped over in pain. 'Do you want me to fetch a few bottles of wine from the store cupboard before I go?' I asked them, grabbing on to the doorway as Tamsin tried to drag me away.

'Holly, just go!' Maggie said sternly. 'I can do that.'

284

I relented and wished them all a nice evening, apologised about fourteen times then walked gingerly over to Tamsin's car.

The roads to the hospital were quiet and we were there in minutes. We parked in the outpatients' car park and followed signs for the maternity ward. Tamsin raced down the labyrinth of corridors and I limped behind, begging her to slow down.

'Please, I really don't think it's an emergency or anything,' I pleaded with her, embarrassed as people were beginning to stare at us, wondering what the problem was.

We pushed through the swing doors of the maternity section and entered a busy ward. There were women everywhere, some in blue uniforms and others in dressing gowns cradling tiny newborns and others pacing corridors in nighties, nursing enormous bumps.

'Can I help you?' one of the midwives asked us as we looked around for assistance.

'Yes please, my friend Holly is six months pregnant and she's getting quite a bad pain,' Tamsin interjected before I had time to answer for myself.

'I see, let's get you in a ward and have you monitored,' she said and whisked me down another corridor and into a semi-dark ward, half-full with mums and new babies. She instructed me to lie down on the bed and drew the curtain around us. Tamsin sat down on a chair by the bed.

'Have you bought your notes with you?' she asked, referring to the booklet you get when you're pregnant that the midwives fill in every check up.

285

'Oh, no, I didn't think to,' I whispered quietly.

The midwife looked at me as though I was a half-wit and sighed. 'Right, where's the pain?'

I showed her exactly.

She felt my abdomen, firmly pressing her hands into my tummy like a pizza-maker manipulating dough. I winced. 'Is this pain constant or does it come and go?'

'It's constant.'

'It doesn't ease off at all?'

'No.'

'Any bleeding?'

'No.'

'Are you going to the toilet more frequently?'

'No, I always go a lot.'

'Pain passing urine?'

'No, but then I haven't been to the loo since this started.'

'When did it start?'

'About two hours ago, and got progressively worse.'

'Right,' she said, wheeling some monitors on trolleys over by the bed. She wrapped up my bump in thick Velcro straps and listened to the baby's heartbeat.

'Heartbeat's normal,' she said to herself. A machine started up, tracing a jerky black line across the paper.

'What's that?' I asked, scared by the clinical machinery.

'This graph shows me whether you are experiencing any contractions,' she said, observing the read-out.

286

'Oh God, I knew it,' Tamsin said, rubbing her face with her hands. 'You think she's in premature labour, don't you?' she asked, making my body tense in fear.

The midwife kept her eyes fixed to the chart.

'Well, that's too early to say. I'm going to monitor this for the next hour, but it's unlikely. If it was labour the pain would be more likely to be coming and going.'

I relaxed again. The midwife rolled my sleeve up and took my blood pressure.

'It's quite high. Is it usually high?'

'No, it's always been low.'

'I see. Now, I'm going to unstrap you just for a few moments, and I'd like you to go to the toilet across the corridor and have a wee in this.' She handed me an enormous jug from the cupboard by the bed.

I took the jar, almost delirious at the luxury of being able to pee in a specimen jar with a diameter I could actually aim in for a change and I limped off to the ladies. When I came out there was a nurse waiting for me by the door. She took the jug from me and instructed me back into bed. There I was strapped up again and left alone.

For a ward with about six newborns in, it was reassuringly quiet. Only the occasional sound of a baby crying, but it was soon lulled back to sleep or given a pacifying feed.

'What do you think it is, Tamsin?' I asked her, trying to disguise the fear I felt.

'I've no idea. I never had any problems with the twins. Not until the birth.' I scrutinised her face and decided she looked worried. 'Just relax, Hol, if you want to sleep don't mind me.'

'I couldn't sleep. It hurts too much,' I sighed and curled up on the hard bed, pulling the stiff, starched sheets over me.

Almost exactly an hour later the midwife returned. She checked the readings on the machinery and tore off the print out. 'Okay, I think we have the answer,' she said sitting at the foot of the bed.

I braced myself for serious news.

'You have a bladder infection. Very common in pregnancy.'

'Is that all?' I felt immediately ashamed at my inability to cope with the pain of something so small. How could I go back and tell everyone that was all it was?

'Don't look so embarrassed,' the midwife assured me. 'It can be a very painful condition and you were right to come in. Now, we had to monitor your baby as urinary tract infections can occasionally trigger premature labour, and your high blood pressure does worry me a little. I'm going to insist on *complete* bed rest for the next three days. I've got you a prescription for antibiotics and you must stick to it. I only want you to get up to go to the loo. I'll be contacting your local midwife to check on you on Monday. But you must call the ward if you're worried about anything or think the pain's getting worse.'

I nodded soberly and Tamsin took the tablets for me, helping me out of bed. 'Let's get you home and off your feet,' she said gently.

288

* * *

When we got back to the café I was taken aback by how immaculate it was. All the plates had been cleared away and washed up, the floor and tables had been polished and the counter gleamed brightly. On the table where we had eaten was the vase of flowers that Tamsin had bought me. Propped against that was a note. I recognised Maggie's writing on the front and I unfolded the paper and read it.

Dear Holly,

We didn't want to stay around in case you needed rest. Can Tamsin call and let us know how you are so we don't worry about you? Hope everything's okay. We saved your delicious-looking tart, as we wanted to eat it with you.

Love from, Mags, Alice etc. xxx

PS. I think Charlie might like Tamsin's phone number!

I smiled to myself as I read it, touched at how thoughtful they'd been. I was selfish not to want Tamsin and Charlie to get on.

'What does it say?' she asked, grabbing it out of my hands before I had a chance to hide it. Her eyebrows shot up when she read the postscript and I detected a colouring in her cheeks.

'He is nice, isn't he?' I goaded.

'Who, Charlie? He's gorgeous,' she said grinning at me.

CHAPTER TWENTY-THREE

The following week I achieved absolutely nothing, zero, zilch. Not a stroke of work was undertaken, my wedding cakes were in stasis, my flat was a tip and my hair was beginning to weave itself into dreadlocks. I had surprised myself by taking the midwife's recommendation for bed rest totally to heart.

On Monday my blood pressure was no better, and although the pain of my infection was easing off as the antibiotics kicked in, I was still advised to put my feet up in bed. Maggie took over the running of the café, something she always relished doing and I enjoyed a whole week off. On Friday the midwife visited again and was happy to see my blood pressure had dropped back to near normal, surprising as all week I had been stressing about the return of Tom's parents so much, I'd worked myself into a gibbering neurotic state.

The tolling bells of the Abbey roused me out of bed late on Sunday morning. The day of rest, I thought to myself. No such luck. Fiona and Marcus had arrived back from France late on Friday night, according to Tamsin. It was showdown time. I had to tell them today. They had invited Tamsin and the twins over for Sunday lunch, so I knew they would be around in the afternoon. I had planned it carefully with Tamsin, who had agreed to take over a couple of bottles of wine and was going to adopt the role of drinks monitor, hopefully getting them into a state of amiable generosity. But I wanted to sort myself out first. I had to blitz the flat, look at the week's takings, and most importantly, have a bath.

I washed up, vacuumed, tidied and organised throughout the flat, poured over the accounts, started on the compost heap of laundry and had a quick, vigorous bath. Anything to take my mind off the inevitability of my visit in the afternoon.

By half past two I had no more excuses to stay in the flat and was ready to go to Marcus's house. I drove slowly, racking my brain for a reason to turn around and go home. All the road signs were tempting me to take a detour; Bristol, London M4, Weston Super Mare; it was a lovely day to go to the seaside. I could just go and see my parents, I thought to myself. It had been a while since I'd seen them. But by the time I had convinced myself that my parents would be desperately hurt if they didn't see me right there and then, I was already on the lane that led to the Delancis' house. The only place to turn around now would be in their driveway and they were bound to see me. I pulled in behind Tamsin's car and took a deep breath.

The heavy brass knocker resounded loudly against the large oak door and I looked over to the windows

291

to see if anyone was looking out; there was no one in sight. I was about to knock again when Fiona opened the door; she was wiping her hands on a tea towel. When she saw me her face lit up with genuine pleasure.

'Holly, what a lovely surprise, do come in.' She opened the door wide then kissed my cheek. 'We were just in the kitchen washing up. It's only Marcus and Tamsin, though, Simon's gone for a pub lunch with your friend Alice.' She ushered me across the hall and into their large open kitchen. Marcus was drying dishes as Tamsin put them away. The twins were in identical bouncing chairs, contented just to watch their mum and were kicking their feet wildly.

Marcus turned around and saw me walk in. 'Hey, look who it is! Lovely to see you.' He put down the plate he was holding and kissed me lightly.

This was an awkward moment for me as I had hoped they would notice that I was sporting a decent sized bump and work it out for themselves, sparing me from any big announcements. Unfortunately, the penny was refusing to drop.

'So, how've you been?' Marcus asked me.

'Oh you know how it is, busy, busy,' I said, leaning back slightly to make my bump look even more prominent. Still nothing. Now I was stuck, I hadn't prepared myself for actually having to tell them and didn't have a clue how to start.

'So, how did you find the South of France?' I stalled.

'Oh, I'm afraid we didn't have time to do much

292

sightseeing. It was a huge project; I had to completely redesign this guy's house. It was a nightmare. Everything that could have gone wrong did. And we had a very tight schedule. It was touch and go for a while.'

'Sounds stressful,' I sympathised.

Fiona groaned, shaking her head. 'The most stressful job yet. We're so glad to be back,' she agreed. 'Would you like a coffee?'

'Love one.'

Fiona set about rooting through cupboards and fetching mugs and I caught Tamsin pulling a grimacing face at me. I looked at Marcus, who smiled jovially at me and continued to dry the dishes. He paused with his back to me for a moment, his hands in suspended animation, and then he whirled back, looking at me again. Finally he noticed. He looked me up and down quizzically then looked back to my face, puzzled.

Eventually he said, 'Holly . . . forgive me if I'm mistaken, but you're not pregnant by any chance, are you?'

A crash punctuated his question as Fiona dropped a mug on the quarry-tiled floor. She looked at me, her eyes wide. 'You are, oh my God, you're pregnant!' she exclaimed, clamping her hand over her mouth.

I nodded, smiling feebly. 'Six months,' I said, looking from Fiona to Marcus as they tried to do the arithmetic.

'Six months,' Fiona repeated. 'Six months and you didn't tell us. Why the hell not?'

293

'Fiona, please,' Marcus interrupted, 'let her talk.'

Fiona paused, visibly thinking quickly, then said, 'It is Tom's, isn't it? I'm assuming it's his. Am I right?'

I nodded again and burst into tears.

Suddenly I was bombarded with a barrage of questions. Marcus pulled out a chair and sat me down, offering a clean hanky from his pocket and placing a protective hand on my shoulders.

'When is it due?' Fiona asked.

'July 24th.'

'But I don't understand. Tom won't be back by then. Does he know?' She drew up a chair and sat opposite me.

I shook my head sniffing. 'I didn't find out until after he'd gone. It's so difficult. I'm scared of what he'll say. I can't just call him up and drop a bombshell like that. If he was here we could talk it through, but with him being so far away, it just complicates everything.'

'Darling, we've got to tell him,' she said resolutely. 'He'd want to know. He needs to.' She leaned forward in her chair and looked at me intently. Marcus joined us at the table and was agreeing with Fiona. I felt my hands begin to tremble at the suggestion and I gripped the mug hard, hoping the scalding china would numb them into staying still.

Fiona continued, 'I'm sorry, Holly, this is such a shock for us. I don't know what's best. I mean Tom's in India at the moment. We don't have any hotel numbers for where he's staying because he didn't

294

book them in advance. He wanted to just explore and book when he got there. He's not flying from India until June 25th, and you're going to want to tell him before then. He has phoned from India, but says it's near impossible to get a call out, he waited two and a half hours for an external line from the last hotel he visited, so he warned us he probably wouldn't get in touch, apart from letters, until he flew to Cairo. I don't know what to suggest.' She looked at Marcus to see if he had any ideas, but he was also shaking his head in defeat.

'Holly, you should have told us earlier, we could have helped you. We could have contacted Tom. It's going to be difficult to let him know what's going on now. I can call the British Consulate and see what they suggest, but they don't usually help in these kind of circumstances, I doubt they'd be much use to us. With so little to go on they certainly won't send people out looking for him. I know he's based in Bombay at the moment but that's an enormous city, we'd have no chance.'

'I'm really sorry,' I said quietly, avoiding looking at them. I felt so selfish. I should have thought more about their feelings, and Tom's rights as a father. I hadn't realised how much everyone else would be affected by the news. 'I'm such an idiot,' I squeaked, wiping my tears away with Marcus's hanky.

Fiona said nothing, she had fallen silent, still trying to take it all in. Her silence made me feel even worse.

Marcus put his arm around me once more and said, 'You mustn't worry now, that's all in the past.

295

The important thing is we know now and we can help you.'

Tamsin, who had been trying to make herself invisible in the background, took over making coffee for us all and swept up the broken pieces of the mug Fiona had dropped.

We shared a large cafetière between us and sat around the table sipping the hot liquid; all of us had only one thing on our minds. There was a lot Fiona wanted to know: was it progressing well? What did my family think? Had I been ill? Had I had a scan? Did I know what sex it was? What was going to happen to the café? The list went on and on, and I didn't have all the answers.

'The thing is,' I started, when Fiona appeared to have exhausted every avenue of questioning, 'I'll understand if Tom isn't interested in being a father. It's a lot to expect of him and he's still young for all that responsibility, I wouldn't pressurise him into anything.'

'But it *is* his responsibility,' Marcus said, confused. 'He'd want to pull his weight. I know my son, he'll do whatever he can.'

'And he loves you,' Fiona added. 'He won't let you down.'

I sighed, watching a drip of coffee track down the side of my mug. 'I don't know. You have to understand that our relationship was quite casual. He was often away, so we never had the chance to let it really develop. We mainly got on as good friends, and we never discussed the future.'

Fiona looked at me; I could see she was full of

sympathy, but there was also a hint of disappointment that I seemed to doubt Tom's integrity. 'Give him a chance,' she said. 'I think he might surprise you. He really does love children, more than most men his age, I'm sure of that.'

Tamsin agreed, saying, 'He was so excited when I told him I was expecting, he loved the thought of seeing them grow up,' then added limply, 'I mean I know he hasn't met them yet, but he couldn't wait to.'

Fiona squeezed my hand. 'Whatever happens we will support you in this. I know you seem to be coping well at the moment, but if you ever need anything, anything at all, you only need to ask.'

I smiled back, thanking her. I was so relieved that they had taken it well; they didn't seem too hurt or angry that I hadn't told them earlier and I was cheered by their certainty that Tom would do the right thing. Even if it didn't work out with us, I didn't want my child to be without a father that was interested in her. They were so sure that Tom wouldn't let me down. I hoped this wasn't just parents' need to believe the best of their children.

When I got up to leave I felt an enormous sense of relief that it was out in the open, no more sneaking around. They were such a kind family. I should have gone to them earlier. Fiona promised to come and visit me in the café and said that they would contact me as soon as they heard anything from Tom. Fiona was insistent on telling him as soon as possible. I asked them to try to get a contact number that I could call if Tom got in touch with them. I wanted to tell him myself and try to minimise any feelings of betrayal he might feel for not finding out earlier, but I agreed to let Fiona tell him if there was no other way. I insisted that they mustn't tell him he had to return. I wanted Tom to do what felt right for him, and I couldn't be responsible for the decision to abort the trip he had planned for so long. They reluctantly agreed to that, obviously not wanting to cause a scene and have me upset.

Marcus hugged me, ruffling my hair in an attempt to lighten the mood. 'A grandchild, hey? Not exactly the conventional method of going about it, but then you never were a conventional girl, were you?' he teased. 'Still, I can't think of anyone I'd rather have produce a grandchild with my son, than you.'

I hugged him back, promising to keep them in touch with all the developments and said goodbye.

Tamsin whispered that she would call me soon and I was grateful, knowing she'd fill me in on what was said after I had gone.

I pulled away down the drive and glanced back at them standing at the doorway waving me off. I thought I saw Fiona and Marcus share a worried look just before they turned back into the house, but I couldn't be sure. I drove home feeling exhausted and emotionally drained. All I wanted was for it all to be over, for the fear to pass and for things to get back to the way they were. But I knew they never would.

* * *

On Wednesday I had my antenatal class. Once again we had been grouped into a circle. I sat with a professional-looking woman called Veronica on one side, and a reassuringly more down to earth-looking woman called Wendy on my right. We all listened patiently as the midwife talked us through the birth process.

She held up a pair of plaster of Paris hips for us all to see, holding a plastic baby doll in the position it would be if it was travelling normally down the birth canal, demonstrating how its head would tip backwards. When it reached the end of its journey, she pushed it through the hole in the hips, saying in a dramatic, David Attenborough tone, 'And now, your baby is born.' As she attempted to push it through, the hinge on the plastic hips broke off, splitting them in two. The pieces fell away in her hands and clattered to the floor.

'Well, obviously your hips won't quite be able to do this, ha, ha,' she joked, trying to cover her embarrassment. 'But I can assure you, your bones and muscles will be able to stretch an awful lot more to accommodate the size of your baby.' She returned her props to her desk and cleaned her glasses on the front of her uniform. 'Now that we've been through the basics of what happens in childbirth, I would really like to spend some time talking through any fears you may be having about what's going to happen,' she said, leaning against the desk. Next to the now broken hips and the baby doll I noticed there was a TENS machine and a canister of what I guessed to be gas and air, attached to some breathing apparatus. I wondered keenly if we were going to get a demonstration of those today.

'I think it's much better to address your fears for the delivery now, rather than hope they go away and have a rude awakening on the day of the birth,' she continued. 'I want you all to be prepared for any eventuality, although I must stress the majority of you will have a completely normal, textbook labour. Now would anyone like to start the ball rolling with any fears they may have?' She looked around the group for a volunteer.

Claire, the mobile hairdresser, put her hand up.

'Yes, love?' The midwife smiled encouragement at her.

'Well, I guess my biggest fear would be having stitches,' Claire said.

This was obviously a fear that was shared with the other women, as there was a smatter of agreement. I was really surprised. I had hardly given any thought to the birth, other than obviously the end result. Mum had told me how easy it all was and Tamsin seemed to avoid discussing it so I guessed she didn't have much to say about it at all. Okay, I wasn't naive, I knew it could be horribly painful, but I certainly hadn't given any other possible complications a single thought. Surely stitches weren't that common?

'Yes, an episiotomy used to be performed almost as standard practice for first-time mothers,' the midwife was saying. 'It is becoming less popular these days. Midwives are keen to avoid it unless it is necessary to deliver the baby quickly, as we now believe small tears heal better . . .'

My stomach was churning at the appalling, graphic images my mind was conjuring up. I looked at the floor, trying not to listen. I thought instead of the women you hear about constantly, who push out their baby in a paddy field, attach them to their breast, then proceed to do a day's hard labour before walking the twenty miles back to their hut with a bucket of water balanced on their heads.

Wendy leaned in towards me and whispered, 'My biggest fear is trying to push the baby out and pooing on the bed!'

I recoiled away from her. 'Surely that doesn't happen?' I asked, shocked at the thought.

She nodded her head knowledgeably. 'My sister-in-law's a midwife. She says it happens all the time; the midwives are taught to whip it away quick as possible and deny it ever happened.'

I was beginning to worry about my blood pressure and breathed deeply, trying to relax myself. The midwife was describing a Ventouse delivery, where what sounded like a big, sucking, sink plunger, was used to help ease a baby out, resulting in the baby having a head shaped like a cone for a day or so. The midwife laughed at this, but I couldn't for the life of me think what was so funny. My head was swimming with fears I'd never considered until now. This talk was supposed to calm your anxieties, not give you nightmare fodder to dwell on.

After what felt like years of discussion on Caesareans, distressed babies, forceps, haemorrhaging and

301

other gory scenarios, the midwife called a break for tea and biscuits.

We milled around, chatting politely, whilst waiting for the kettle to boil.

'That sounds like a lovely idea,' Wendy was saying to a woman called Philippa, who then turned to me.

'And what about you, Holly? Would you like to join us for a little get together and a few drinks at my house? It'll be a week on Saturday. I'll have to make it early, say five o'clock as my boys will be around.' Philippa was an older mum, I would guess in her early forties; despite her glamorous image and expensive outfits she was clearly the oldest woman in the group. Although the antenatal class was primarily for first-time mothers, Philippa's children were now twelve and fourteen years old and she felt she wanted to be reminded of all the basics, as maternity practices had changed so much since her last child was born. Every now and again she would pass the odd comment like, 'Gosh, in my day you were bedridden for a fortnight.' or, 'My husband was having a brandy at the Rotary Club during that bit.'

'That sounds great,' I told her, touched to be included. I thought she had probably invited all the other women in the group as well, but that didn't spoil it for me, and I looked forward to the opportunity of getting to know everyone better.

When the class was over and we were all filing out the door Philippa pulled me to one side.

'Darling, you will refrain from bringing along any

Ann Summers . . . paraphernalia won't you? Don't want to give my boys ideas if I can help it!'

I nodded dumbly and muttered, 'okay', too embarrassed to contradict her.

On the day of Philippa's get together I was determined to make a good impression. I had bought an expensive new dress in a soft navy blue that reached down to my ankles, which I hoped made me appear elegant and feminine. The majority of the ladies in my group were immaculately dressed. They seemed mature and sensible and above all else, well composed. In comparison, they made me feel young and foolish. I really wanted to fit in, knowing that when the baby was born I would benefit from knowing some people in the same boat. I needed allies.

When I arrived at the house I was taken aback by its grandeur. It was situated on a leafy lane, high up on a hillside. It was an elegant Bath stone town house that must have had five storeys. There was no front garden and the steps to the front door rose from the pavement. As I stood waiting for the door to be answered I looked behind me, awestruck by the view. It was a scorching day and the air was clear, making everything look even more spectacular. You could see the whole of Bath stretched out before the house. The Abbey at the centre, the river Avon glittering in the afternoon sun and the golden curves of the Crescent buildings. A hot air balloon was suspended in the air above the river and I wished I could be there, drifting safely away from all my cares, instead of having to face all the people I could hear chatting gaily behind the closed doors.

The front door swung open and a young teenager acknowledged me with a grunt. He gestured for me to come in and when I followed him inside he disappeared back up the staircase, shouting, 'Mum, it's one of your lot.'

'Hello, darling,' Philippa welcomed, landing two air kisses in the general direction of my cheeks. 'You're just about the last one to arrive. We're all in the garden, it was such a beautiful day we thought we'd get the barbecue going. Nothing like eating alfresco with food cooked on an open air fire, hey?' She led me through the airy hallway and out through a pair of patio doors that opened on to a vast expanse of lawn.

Stepping into the garden, I realised that Philippa had only invited a select group of women from the antenatal class. They were gathered on the spacious wooden decking, some reclined in garden chairs, others huddled around a huge table that was laden with salads and nibbles. The row of women sitting at the table with their backs to me looked like a herbaceous border as their flowery sundresses mingled together. There were also half a dozen women I didn't recognise at all, friends of Philippa's, I presumed. She had obviously gone to a lot of trouble. The smell of chicken cooking hit me, and I noticed that Philippa's idea of an 'open-air fire' was a deluxe gas-powered barbecue the size of large sideboard. I doubted if the chicken would taste any different if it had been prepared in the confines of a hotel kitchen.

'Now, before you panic I remembered you were a vegetarian so we have a large selection of veggie food.' She pointed out a stack of boxes of soyaburgers and sausages and a sizzling line of large brown discs sitting next to the chicken thighs on the griddle.

'Oh, you didn't have to go to any trouble,' I said, embarrassed at the quantity. I hoped the others would help eat them.

'No trouble at all,' Philippa assured me. 'And there's no red meat in the house anyway, just chicken and fish. I could never stomach red meat in any of my pregnancies.'

I walked over to where the others were standing by the food and was greeted with several polite 'hello's'. One of the women, who I thought was called Ingrid, offered me a plate. The only man in the garden, who I assumed was Philippa's husband, wandered over to the barbecue, beer in hand.

'I think it's all ready, ladies,' he called and began serving the meat and burgers out on to several large serving platters. I helped myself to salad as Philippa told me a little story about each dish: 'The potato salad is a recipe I bought back from South America, it's got quite a kick to it', and, 'Now, the tomato sauce is my speciality. I don't allow ketchup in the house and make a batch of this up almost every week.'

She must have been slaving away for hours and was obviously keen to impress, so with her watching me as I filled my plate, I felt obliged to sample

305

everything. Another woman brought over the plate of vegeburgers, saying that the sausages would be ready soon. There must have been a dozen on the plate, all trussed up with buns and more salad. She placed them in front of me and I noticed the others were all helping themselves to chicken, so I reluctantly took two.

'Now, drinks everybody,' Philippa called, positioning herself by the patio doors and waving her arms like a flight attendant. 'I've put everything out on the table over there.' She gestured to a round table decorated with a white cloth and a ring of folded napkins. 'There is wine for those who don't mind partaking in a little tipple, and then there's a big selection of fruit juices and sparkling non-alcoholic wine. Do help yourself to anything you fancy.'

A throng of women gathered around the drinks table, pouring from the various jugs of colourful liquid. There were two open bottles of wine on the table and I would have enjoyed a big glass of red, but they were sitting untouched and I would have been embarrassed if I was the only one drinking. I heard one woman say, 'Yes, I haven't had a drop of alcohol since I got pregnant,' and her friend agreed earnestly, 'Rupert and I have been trying for a baby for two years and I didn't even touch a drop whilst we were trying.'

I was ashamed when I thought of the amount I drank, still well below the ten units a week the doctor had given me as a maximum, but I didn't have the willpower to give it up altogether and still saw

306

it as one of my favourite indulgences. I grudgingly poured myself a glass of the non-alcoholic wine and followed the others to the table where I plonked myself down next to Wendy.

Everyone was hungrily tucking into the food.

'Don't you just love having the excuse of eating for two,' Ingrid said, patting her bump, which must have been twice the size of mine. The others were agreeing and telling stories about the types of food they'd craved.

'I seem to have trouble eating anything at all,' I said to Wendy. 'I get indigestion if I eat more than a round of toast for breakfast!'

'Oh, right,' Wendy said miserably. 'I wish I had that problem. I never stop being hungry, and I've put on three stone already.' Then she looked at my overloaded plate, obviously wondering why I had helped myself to so much food if I had such a problem eating. I flushed with embarrassment and listened hard to the discussion the other women were having, hoping for a change of subject. They were all discussing going back to work and sharing tips on finding decent nannies.

'I had a fabulous girl from Singapore to look after my boys,' Philippa was saying. 'I tried to contact her again when I discovered I was pregnant and she was still living at the same address. She's had five of her own children since then. Five, imagine! My concern for the overpopulation problem would stop me having any more than three, and I feel pretty selfish having that many!' There were nods of agreement from around the table and the other

307

women all professed to only wanting one or two. I was reminded of my conversations with Alice where we had competed on who wanted the most children; Alice would swear she wouldn't stop until she had eight. It had never occurred to me that we were actually being politically incorrect.

Philippa's husband butted in, waving a dish of parcels wrapped in silver foil. 'Trout's ready, everybody,' he called, laying it in the centre of the table. The women 'ooed' and 'ahhed', congratulating him on the lovely food. 'And which of you is the veggie?' he added.

I waved my hand in the air.

'Your sausages are done, madam,' he said, placing another plate straight in front of me.

'You must tell me what you think,' Philippa said to me. 'Especially with you being an expert and everything. I'm always looking for alternatives for the boys that are high in protein. They do miss their red meat, poor loves.'

'Well, I won't be able to eat all these,' I said meekly, 'so you must all help me.' They all thanked me then helped themselves to the parcels of fish. I had to at least try and eat, I thought to myself; it would look awful if there was lots of veggie food left over and all the meat had gone. I'd look really ungrateful. So I tucked in, chewing slowly and deliberately, wishing I had bought my bottle of indigestion remedy with me. I was now getting it on prescription and had taken to swigging it straight from the bottle like some old wino with a litre of Thunderbird.

308

A lady dressed very similarly to Philippa and with the same shoulder-length honey blond hair wandered out into the garden smiling at us. She looked at Philippa, whispering, 'He's out for the count,' and plugged the monitor she was holding into the extension lead that was also running a small midi system.

'This is Yvonne, everybody,' Philippa introduced. 'She's my old school friend. She's just had a baby, haven't you, darling?'

Yvonne glowed with pride. 'A little boy called Ralf, he's only three weeks old.' She pulled up a chair at the far end of the table.

'She's been a mine of information and has helped to bring back all those happy memories from when my boys were born.'

'Can we see him?' Wendy asked keenly, dying to coo over a little newborn.

'I'm afraid he fell asleep in the car on the way here and will probably be out for another hour yet,' Yvonne said, fetching a plate and reaching over for a chicken wing.

The women all looked dismayed. 'I'll bring him down as soon as he wakes up, though,' she promised. This seemed to satisfy everyone.

'So, Yvonne, tell us what the labour was like,' Ingrid asked, who was sitting opposite her.

Philippa butted in. 'Oh, she had the easiest time, you won't believe it! She's an inspiration to us all.'

Yvonne beamed even harder and leaned in conspiratorially. 'I was in labour for an hour and a half,' she boasted. 'I only pushed three times! The doctor said he couldn't believe I hadn't done it before, I was so calm. No drugs either, not even gas. I wanted to experience everything naturally.' By the look of self-congratulation on Yvonne's face, she was obviously of the belief that this was all down to her being marvellous, having a massive pain tolerance, perfect childbearing hips and a push that could batter down doors. I had an inkling that her easy birth was more due to the lucky lottery of nature, and her numbers had just come up.

Wendy looked at me, rolling her eyes, and I was glad to see I wasn't the only one who wasn't in awe of this woman. Yvonne continued her banter, telling everyone how clever little Ralf was, and how breast-feeding had whittled her figure down to half a stone less than her pre-pregnancy weight.

'Thank God I didn't get pregnant earlier,' Wendy whispered to me. 'If she'd been in my mums' and tots' group I'd be a sure case for post-natal depression.'

I grinned at her in agreement, chewing on my second burger. I was beginning to feel the first twinges of indigestion and discomfort and tried to wash the stodgy food down with a large drink, but I felt as though I had a dense ball of dough, sitting heavily in my stomach. The pile of veggie food didn't look any smaller and I felt terrible about the expense Philippa had gone to. Still, she can obviously afford it, I told myself, glancing around the luxurious back garden. There were no other houses in sight, and the lawn appeared to merge into the dense green woodland that stretched away from the house as far as the eye could see. The sun had dipped slightly lower in the sky, and I was no longer under the shade of the parasol. I could feel the heat of the sun's rays, despite the time of day, as it shone on my arms and the top of my forehead.

'Holly, my love, don't be polite, you must help yourself to seconds. I got them especially for you,' Philippa pressed, interrupting my chain of thought. She continued to watch me so I smiled back at her, putting another couple of sausages on my plate. I was beginning to feel quite queasy but I made myself nibble the end of a sausage and scanned the veranda looking for somewhere I could stash my unwanted food. I wished there were pockets in my dress.

The chat had now become a discussion on men's role in the labour ward and several of the women were swapping stories on what their husbands would be like.

'Mine's such a terrible exaggerator,' one of them was saying. 'If he so much as grazes his hand in a rugby match he tells all his mates he's sprained his wrist and wears one of those stretchy arm support things. I could have the easiest labour in the world and he'd be bragging about the pints of blood everywhere and how he nursed me through near death!'

My stomach did an ominous flip.

Ingrid was laughing. 'What about you, Holly? Is your man going to be there?'

A deathly silence seemed to settle on the women as they waited for me to entertain them with an amusing anecdote.

311

'Well, er, I hope so. He may be abroad, I'm not sure yet,' I stuttered, an all too familiar feeling growing worse in my stomach. The others were looking at me incredulous and there were cries of 'abroad?' and, 'How on earth could you let him out of your sight at such an important time?'

'Philippa?' I whispered, trying to get her attention as the other women were swearing to weld their respective partners to the hip until their little ones arrived. She looked at me quizzically. 'Can you tell me where the toilet is? I shall have to be excused.' I tried to look casual and disguise my growing unease.

'Of course, darling, third floor up if you want the main one. First door on your right.'

I thanked her and walked calmly out of sight, breaking into a run as soon as I was safely inside. I bolted up the stairs two at a time, pushing past Philippa's eldest son, who was heading for the shower with a towel wrapped around his waist.

'Terribly sorry,' I said, getting to the door before him. 'Nature calls, won't be long.' Then I shut and locked the door behind me. I heard him retreat to his bedroom and slam his door in irritation as I knelt dejected on the floor by the toilet and retched into the bowl. I moaned, holding my stomach as I noisily brought up the barbecued treats Philippa had worked so hard on. I was hugely relieved that the bathroom was so far away from the garden, giving me some much needed privacy. My eyes smarted as I choked again, and my head swam. I was going to have to make my excuses and go

312

straight home, I decided, hoping they wouldn't think I was rude going before they had started on dessert. When there was nothing left to bring up I slumped against the toilet bowl, my throat hurting and feeling perilously close to tears. The other women were all so composed, I couldn't imagine them doing anything like this, even in the privacy of their own homes. I wondered how on earth they managed it.

When I finally felt the room wasn't spinning any more I got up gingerly, holding on to the loo for support. For one horrible moment I thought I was going to be sick again and I positioned myself ready. I retched and burped loudly, but my stomach was purged.

I took a look at myself in the mirror. My make-up was still intact, and despite a slightly pale hue in my face there were no tell-tale signs. I swilled some water around my mouth and gargled, then stepped nervously out of the bathroom door; there was no one in sight. Philippa's son came back out of his bedroom, still in his towel.

'It's all yours,' I croaked and made my way down the stairs on wobbly legs.

I fixed a radiant smile on my face before I walked out on to the veranda and prepared to make my excuses.

When I walked out all the women there turned to face me, as though they had been waiting for me to return. A silence had descended on the group and their faces were aghast with various expressions of horror and disgust. Philippa had pushed her food away and was looking as though she might be ill, and several other women were looking away in embarrassment, or glancing at each other with their eyebrows raised. I looked around at them, confused; there wasn't a single noise, not a murmur, except for the sound of water spraying somewhere; it sounded like a shower. Then I heard a boy singing to himself and looked around to where the sound was coming from. I spotted the monitor plugged in next to the midi system. The classical CD was no longer playing. I realised that the baby monitor was picking up the noises from the bathroom. They had heard everything. My knees went weak as I stood there, mortified.

'I guess I shall have to go, I'm really not feeling too good,' I stammered and turned on my heel, racing to the safety and solace of my car.

CHAPTER TWENTY-FOUR

'There's no way I'm ever going there again,' I protested to Alice and finished off the dregs of lager in my glass. We had taken advantage of the fact that the café was closed on a Wednesday afternoon and had enjoyed a leisurely walk down the canal towpath to a pretty waterside pub on the outskirts of Bath.

'But you haven't been to any of the really important classes yet, the ones about labour and breathing. How're you going to know what to do when it happens?'

'Oh, it can't be that difficult, and I'll still have midwives there to talk me through it all. I can always read up about it.'

'I'm not sure, Holly.' Alice frowned at me.

'No, really, it was so humiliating. I just can't face them again. They looked so disgusted with me.'

'I'm sure it wasn't that bad. If I knew one of my guests at a party was ill I'd feel really sorry for her. I mean, you can't help being sick, can you?'

'I know, but you're an understanding person,

these women were different. They were all just so sophisticated, I didn't fit in.'

Alice gave me a sympathetic smile. 'But you said yourself you didn't recognise half of them, it sounds as though they were mainly Philippa's snobby friends. The other women at the class would never know what happened.'

'But I would,' I insisted.

'You are going to have to work on your self-esteem, my friend. It's been suffering ever since you discovered you were pregnant.'

I cupped my chin in my hands and stared balefully at her. Usually Alice was the one that needed a confidence boost, but lately that had all changed. Ever since she had begun her relationship with Simon she had been happy and self-assured. It just goes to show, I thought, that the people you surround yourself with can make a huge difference to the way you feel about yourself.

'You're right,' I said to her, 'but I'm not going to boost my confidence by setting myself up for abject humiliation. The only thing I had in common with Philippa was the fact that we were having babies. There's no point me trying to pretend I'm like her to be accepted. Besides, it doesn't matter what the other women are like, I just can't face any of them again. I'd rather go it alone and just be me. Warts and all.'

'Fair enough,' Alice said. 'Just promise me you'll read up on breathing and all that stuff you need to know. You're not going to go into denial and pretend it'll just pop out in your sleep, are you?'

'Cross my heart.'

* * *

We returned our empty glasses to the bar and started our walk back to the city centre. I wasn't sure if it was the half of lager I had drunk, but I was feeling so drowsy, I hardly had the energy to stand up. When I walked along the canal path I was aware that I had adopted that classic pregnant waddle, with my hands resting on the top of my bump. I felt like a caricature; it was hard to believe that I was going through all this, when only last summer motherhood had felt like a lifetime away.

'Gosh, your bump is really looking huge now, Hol,' Alice said, staring at it in wonderment. 'Have you still managed to escape getting stretch marks?'

I nodded, stroking the steep curves of my body. 'I know, I've been really lucky there. You realise there's only seven and a half weeks to go 'til the big arrival. It's not far off now.' I felt a tingle of apprehension as I spoke.

'Shit, it really has flown by.'

'Everyone that comes in the café has been asking me when it's due, it's ridiculous, even people in shops, complete strangers. I must look ready to drop.' I spied an empty bench looking on to the water and flopped down on to it, breathing heavily.

'Poor thing, you look so tired,' Alice said, sitting down next to me. 'Perhaps we should call for a taxi.'

'Good idea,' I said eagerly. The heat of the sun was making me feel giddy and I needed to be sitting in my cool flat. Alice took her mobile out of her

317

handbag and dialled the number, asking them to pick us up from the pub we had just been in. We wandered back to the car park just as a taxi rounded the corner.

'The Owl and Pussycat on Church Street?' Alice asked, opening the passenger door.

'Yes, love, hop in,' the driver said, lighting a cigarette.

I fell gratefully into the cab. It appeared to have been upholstered throughout in shaggy fur; even the roof looked hairy. The windows were shut tight, and with all that insulation and cigarette smoke, the car was stifling. I could barely catch my breath.

'So, when's it due, darlin'?' he drawled, pulling away from the car park and out on to the little country road.

Alice and I exchanged amused looks and I turned back to the driver, looking puzzled.

'When's what due?' I asked innocently.

'Oh, er, y'know, the sprog?'

'What sprog?' I said, as Alice kicked me and tried not to laugh. The driver went quiet and appeared to be giving his cigarette a lot of attention.

After a minute or two, Alice broke the silence. 'So, how many pounds did you lose last week?' she asked, her hand clamped over her mouth to stifle a giggle.

I looked at her, wide-eyed, then said, 'Well, only two, but I did have that gâteau at the weekend so I'm not too disappointed.'

'That's brilliant. I have to say, Weight Watchers is an inspiration, isn't it?'

'Well, it worked wonders for you, didn't it?' I said, with mock admiration. Alice looked as though she was going to burst and had to look out of the window to distract herself.

The car pulled up outside the café and I reached across to pay the driver, who seemed unable to look me in the eye. We scrambled out of the car and watched the cab drive slowly down the street. The driver looked like he was swearing to himself and banged his head against the steering wheel. Alice and I fell about laughing.

'You're so cruel, that poor man looked mortified,' Alice said eventually.

'Well, it serves him right for practically suffocating us in that thing,' I said, still laughing, as I hunted in my bag for the door keys.

Another car pulled in to the narrow street and I recognised it immediately; it was Marcus's. The smile on my face vanished. 'Oh God,' I whispered.

Alice whirled around. 'What? Who is it?'

'It's Marcus. He said he'd come around if he'd heard from Tom.'

Alice looked back at me, worried. 'Oh babe, do you want me to stay?'

'It's okay,' I said. 'I'll probably be better on my own.'

Marcus parked his car along the pavement and waved at us.

'Listen, I'll make myself scarce and I'll call you later, okay?' Alice said, giving me a fleeting hug before she wandered off down the road.

I stood outside the café entrance, jangling my keys

nervously as Marcus approached me. He smiled easily and pecked me on the cheek.

'Hey, Holly, what's up?' he asked when he noticed the look on my face.

'Have you spoken to Tom?' I asked, cutting out the greetings.

'No, have you?' he answered confused.

I relaxed again, letting out a sigh of relief. 'No, sorry, I thought that was why you'd come and I got a bit nervous, that's all.'

'Sorry, Holly. He hasn't called. I phoned the consulate but they couldn't help. They suggested the British Council.'

I looked at him, puzzled. 'I don't know who they are.' I turned to unlock the café door and gestured for him to follow me inside.

'They apparently have administrators that look at applications from Indian students wanting to come to Britain. They have contacts in Bombay and know students that live locally that might also have contacts out there and be able to help.'

I led the way to the counter and grabbed two large tumblers and a couple of small bottles of lemonade from the chiller. Marcus sat down at a table by the window and I joined him, pouring out the drinks. 'I can't believe it's so complicated, I mean, what if somebody had died? There must be an easier way?' I sighed, watching the bubbles as they fizzed in my glass.

'I'm afraid it's notoriously difficult to find anybody in India, there's probably enough missing or displaced people there to fill a whole city.' Marcus took a large sip of his drink and rubbed his face with his hands. He looked tired.

'So, what can the council do?'

'Well, they're not permitted to give out the names of any of their Indian students, but they did say they would pinpoint any that looked likely to know people in Bombay and pass a message on to them. If someone thinks they can help they'll call me.'

'But if Bombay is so huge how could they help?' I said, overwhelmed by how hopeless the situation seemed.

'Well, I wasn't sure of that myself, but the woman I spoke to was quite reassuring; she said that for a student to get into Britain they'll almost certainly be well connected. They're bound to know somebody that could put an advert in a café window or ask around the youth hostels for me. She also said that for the size of Bombay, the places that backpackers go are pretty limited; they all hang out in the same districts, drink at the same bars, there aren't that many places he could be.'

'So, what happens now?' I asked.

'Well, I guess we wait for someone to call me. I don't know how likely it is that anyone will, though. They have no reason to want to help me out, do they?'

'Marcus, I'm really sorry,' I started. I felt so guilty for creating this situation.

'Look, Holly, you musn't keep apologising for this. Maybe if Tom had been in touch more often, or left contact details we wouldn't have this problem now. You must have been pretty shocked when you

321

found out you were pregnant. It's not surprising.' He smiled at me. 'Just try not to worry, we'll sort this for you.' He took another sip of lemonade. 'Now, how are you coping? Tamsin told me about your trip to hospital. You've got to take it a bit easier now, I don't want your blood pressure soaring again.'

'Oh no, that was an odd blip. I've been monitored closely by the midwife every week and my blood pressure hasn't risen since then, thankfully.'

'Glad to hear it. Actually, Holly, I was thinking,' he began warily. 'You realise, you feel more like a daughter to me. Well, maybe a daughter-in-law.' I grinned at him, touched. 'And, I guess I feel, well, Fiona and I feel like we want to help you, make things a bit easier. We were wondering if there was anything you needed?'

'Oh Marcus, that's really kind of you, but I think my mum's already bought everything I could possibly need. It's just a case of getting myself organised now, I guess.'

'Well, that was where I was thinking I could come in handy,' he said. 'You can say no if you want, I won't be at all offended, but I was thinking I could help prepare the nursery. Tamsin told me you were going to use your spare bedroom but that you hadn't made a start yet. I thought, as I've only got one other job on at the moment, I'd love to have a go at it for you.'

I felt tears of gratitude welling in my eyes. The nursery had been playing on my mind for weeks now, but my spare time had been taken up with wedding cake orders, and I was beginning to think

322

it would never get done. 'That would be wonderful,' I said hoarsely. 'If you're sure you don't mind?'

'Holly, it would be a great pleasure,' he said earnestly, then whipped out a tape measure and a small notebook from his pocket. 'Now, shall I take some measurements and we can knock some ideas about?'

The following Saturday I was making the most of a peaceful afternoon. It was another hot day so the café had been slow. I sat on a stool in the kitchen looking over the books whilst Maggie dealt with the waning number of customers.

'God, he so blatantly wants me it's embarrassing!' Maggie joked as she brought in a tray of dirty glasses for the dishwasher.

I looked up from my paperwork and shot her a concerned glance. 'I hope you haven't been flirting with the customers again, Mags, poor Noah is going to end up a nervous wreck.'

Maggie laughed so hard she made the glasses on her tray rattle. She put it down and started to stack them in the basket ready to be washed. 'Noah's got nothing to worry about, I think I've grown out of students. I like a real man, with a real disposable income,' she said wickedly.

I leaned back on my stool so I could see into the café and identify which one Maggie was talking about. There was a choice between an elderly man in a tweed jacket or Ajay, the student who was always offering to buy Maggie a coffee.

'Has Mr Fitzpatrick been trying to pull you again?'

323

I teased, 'I told him he's got to take stronger pills if he wants to impress your sort!'

Maggie flicked some of the suds out of the dishwasher at me and they landed in my hair. 'Cheeky cow!' she said, laughing and checked the café to make sure no one had heard.

Ajay looked up at the two of us giggling and raised his mug of coffee, winking at Maggie. As I watched him I remembered what Marcus had said a few days earlier. 'Hang on, I think I need a word with him, actually,' I said, putting down my pen and hopping off the stool.

'Holly, don't say anything, please . . . what are you doing?' Maggie said through gritted teeth, looking panicked.

'Don't worry, it's not about you,' I said and grabbed a pot of coffee and an extra mug and went over to join him.

'Hey, Ajay, mind if I join you?' I asked, hovering over his table. He put down his paperback and shook his head, gesturing for me to sit down.

I sat opposite him and poured us both out another coffee. He was looking at me with curious amusement, waiting for me to say something.

'You're Indian, right?' I blurted stupidly.

'Er, last time I looked,' he quipped, smiling quizzically.

'No, I'm sorry, I mean are you actually from India, or were you born in Britain?'

'I'm from Jaipur, in India. I've been here two years, doing engineering at the Uni. Why do you ask?'

324

I took a sip of coffee and started telling Ajay about my problem finding Tom, and he listened, nodding, and looked sympathetic. I finished by explaining how Marcus had been told that his best bet was to ask somebody who knew people in Bombay and get them to help.

'Right, I see. And you want me to help you?' he asked.

I smiled sheepishly. 'Could you?'

Ajay leaned back against his chair, his eyes briefly strayed to the kitchen where he could see Maggie cleaning the work tops. He smiled kindly at me, placing his hands behind his head and said confidently, 'Of course.'

Ajay explained that his cousin was an Anglo-Asian priest, who lived in the Catholic area of Bombay; he worked with the Salvation Army there and often helped to find missing people. 'I will call him tonight and get him to ask around. It might take some time, there are a lot of places where Tom could be and Peter has a lot of duties, he's a busy man, but I know he'd help you if I asked him.'

'Really, are you sure? It's a big favour to ask.' I was so grateful I didn't know how I could thank him.

Ajay looked at me seriously. 'Holly, in our culture helping your family is not considered to be a favour, it's an obligation, and an honour.'

I got up and kissed him on the cheek, thanking him for being so kind, then went to fetch a pen and paper so I could write down Tom's description and my contact number. When I walked into the kitchen

I saw Maggie staring at me, her eyebrows raised in surprise.

Just over a week later Marcus and Fiona had come around to put the finishing touches to the nursery.

We had spent the morning talking about the baby, joking about who it might look like, how well it would sleep, and wondering where Tom was now. Ajay had called to tell me that Peter was now looking for Tom, but so far had not had any luck. He had covered a lot of ground though and was convinced that it would only be a matter of days.

As we talked, Marcus finished painting the cupboard doors and Fiona made herself comfortable on my sofa where she was hemming a quilt she had made to match the curtains. I was cooking them a Sunday lunch in the flat to thank them for all their help and was scuttling back and forth from the kitchen to the nursery, checking to see if Marcus needed any help, and preparing various vegetables.

I stood in the doorway, admiring the transformation. 'It looks fantastic.' The walls were now a sunny yellow, and Marcus had painted a frieze of animals, running at waist height around the room. He had built a fitted wardrobe and cupboard into the far right corner of the room. The doors were painted in cheery primary colours. An owl and pussycat mobile hung over the cot, and the curtains were now hanging in swags at the window, matching the colours of the walls and wardrobe perfectly. Marcus had even made a set of shelves for one wall, and I had already put out all the teddies my friends had bought, alongside the delicate-smelling baby toiletries that had already given the room that unmistakable baby perfume.

Marcus stood up from where he had been crouched on the floor, painting the last patch of the cupboard door. 'I think we're just about done,' he said, nearly leaning to rest against the fresh paintwork, then thinking better of it. 'How's Fi getting on in the living room?' he asked, dipping his paintbrush into a jar of spirits.

'I think she's nearly finished too,' I said. 'Just in time because the lunch will be ready in about twenty minutes.'

'Excellent, it smells wonderful. Just enough time for me to wash up and put the tools away then.' He turned to where he had left a drill on the changing table, rested it on top of a box full of heavy equipment and stooped down to pick it up. As he stood back up he winced in pain, dropping the box down on the floor.

'Marcus, are you all right?' I asked, rushing over to him. He was bent double; his hand was on his chest and he was breathing hard.

'It's okay, love, I had it before, the other day. It's just a twinge. Probably just a spot of heartburn, from the Indian Simon cooked last night. It had more chillies in than chicken. I've never seen so much colour in Alice's cheeks,' he joked, but something in his face told me he wasn't so sure.

'Do you want me to get Fiona for you?'

327

'No, no, she'll only fuss over me. You know how she goes on about my workload. No, don't worry, it'll pass in a minute.'

He didn't move from his stooped position.

'Why don't you sit down?' I persisted. 'I can go and fetch you a glass of water, and I've got a bottle of indigestion remedy that'll help if it's heartburn.' I steered him over to a squashy beanbag chair and sat him down, then rushed off to the bathroom. I poured him a drink and fetched my catering-sized bottle of remedy. When I returned Marcus was still sitting hunched up on the beanbag. I crouched down in front of him and scrutinised his face. He was ashen grey and a film of sweat had formed on his forehead. My stomach turned over.

'Marcus, I think I'd better get Fiona, you really don't look too good,' I said gently, putting the bottle and the glass by his feet. I waited to see if he'd protest but instead he just nodded his head, still clutching his chest. He appeared to be in too much pain to talk. I didn't want to alarm Marcus by yelling for Fiona, I knew my voice would give away how frightened I was. Instead I raced off to fetch her.

Fiona looked up when I burst into the room and knew at once that something wasn't right.

'I think you'd better come and take a look at Marcus, he's not well,' I said, fighting to stay calm. She threw down her sewing and followed me back to the nursery.

When we entered the room we saw that Marcus

328

was now on his hands and knees on the floor. Fiona ran straight to him. 'Honey, what's wrong?'

'My chest, and my arm,' he whispered breathlessly, barely audible.

'Call an ambulance!' Fiona shouted at me.

I ran from the room to the telephone on the coffee table and dialled 999; my hands shaking so violently I could only just hold the phone to my ear.

After I had rung for an ambulance I ran straight back to the bedroom. Fiona was crouched over Marcus, who was moaning softly. She was stroking his back telling him to relax and he was going to be just fine.

I paced the room, wandering to and from the window impatiently, as though I was attached by a rubber band. I scrutinised the street below but it was empty.

Only about five or six minutes of pacing and scrutinising later, an ambulance drew up outside the café. I felt my heart sink that they had arrived so fast, as though they were confirming the seriousness of the situation by acting promptly.

I ran down to let them in. Two ambulance men greeted me at the door; one was carrying what looked like a black briefcase and the other, a fold-up chair. I beckoned them to follow me, explaining Marcus's symptoms as we climbed the stairs.

Fiona moved away from him, making way for the ambulance men as they knelt down beside him.

'Hi, Marcus, I'm Richard,' one of the men said, speaking quite loud and deliberately clear. 'I'm just going to take a look at you.' He unbuttoned Marcus's shirt and began to examine him.

I went over to where Fiona was standing, putting my arm around her shoulder. She looked on, helpless, and I felt her shivering. The second man was asking her questions about medical history, and Fiona explained that Marcus's father had died of a heart attack, aged only fifty-six. Her voice was small and fearful, it could almost have belonged to a little girl, and I heard her whisper, 'He will be okay though, won't he?'

Neither of the men heard her. 'What we are going to do is monitor your heart on an ECG we have set up in the ambulance,' one of them said.

Marcus struggled to stand up, but couldn't. The two men lifted him on to the canvas chair.

Marcus didn't say anything, he sat uncomfortably in the chair; his eyes were squeezed tight and beads of sweat trickled down his face.

After they had carried him down the stairs, Richard retrieved a walky-talky from a shoulder strap.

'Yes, suspected MI, ETA, eight minutes,' I caught him saying as he climbed into the back of the ambulance, lowering a ramp for Marcus's chair.

I stood watching; a sense of unreality numbing me as to what was going on. Marcus was pushed outside with Fiona never leaving his side. She was holding his hand and telling him over and over that he was not to worry, he would be all right. His colour was frighteningly pallid and his eyes were still shut tight in pain. He didn't look like Marcus, not tall, well-built, healthy and cheerful Marcus. Instead he looked vulnerable and old. A thick grey blanket was wrapped around his shoulders.

Fiona's face was taut from trying to stay in control. She climbed into the ambulance with the men and looked back for me.

'Can you call Simon and let him know what's happened?' she asked and I nodded, watching as they shut up the back doors with a loud clunk.

I caught the second ambulance man saying when Marcus was out of earshot, 'Don't put the siren on Rich, just the lights. Don't want to scare the shit out of him and make it worse.' He saw me looking up at them from the street and he winked. 'Don't worry, love, I'm sure he'll be fine.' Then his colleague climbed into the back of the ambulance and it pulled quickly away, its blue lights flashing and reflecting eerily in the windows of the shops as it turned a corner out of sight.

I stood alone on the pavement, shocked and cold. With the ambulance gone, I was suddenly aware of the silence in the street. I could hear myself gulping for breath, and realised I had been sobbing. A bleeping noise back in the flat broke my chain of thought and I recognised the sound of the oven timer telling me that the lunch I had cooked was ready.

CHAPTER TWENTY-FIVE

I tracked Simon down at Alice's flat. I explained what had happened over the phone, but it was hard to gauge how he had taken it as he went almost silent. He arranged to come straight over and pick me up then drive us all to the hospital.

I wandered through the flat as I waited for them to arrive. The lunch was still sitting in the oven, cold and congealed. The table was set with three places and I paused over Marcus's chair, playing with the cutlery I had set out for him, imagining us all sitting around the table, laughing and chatting as Marcus complimented my cooking. I fought the urge to slump down and cry; I wanted to be controlled and strong for Simon when he got here. I didn't want him to panic; it could all still be a false alarm after all.

I walked away from the table, intending to go to the bathroom and splash my face with water, but I passed the open door of the nursery and was drawn inside. The water and medicine bottle were both still sitting on the floor, untouched. The beanbag chair was indented where Marcus had sat. His tools were packed neatly in the large plastic container. I peered inside at the well-used contents. The drill was coated in a fine plaster dust and I caught sight of a fingerprint on its casing. My throat constricted and I looked quickly away. The nursery looked immaculate and I felt a sudden surge of guilt. I knew he had been overworked recently and the job in France had put him under considerable pressure. I shouldn't have let him work so hard on the nursery. I should have insisted he use the quiet time in his schedule to rest. What if he only offered to help out of a sense of duty, not really meaning it? The thought made me feel nauseous. Deep down I knew he wouldn't have done that, and he had seemed really happy whilst he had been here. But guilt still nagged at me. I turned my back on the room; the cheery colours seemed inappropriate now.

I fetched my jacket and keys and walked slowly down the stairs so I could wait for Simon and Alice in the street. I couldn't bear to be in the flat. The smell of the lunch made me feel sick.

I heard Simon's car before I saw it; the brakes squealed as it approached the bend in the road that led to my little street. He rounded the corner and sped towards the café; gravel sprayed up as he skidded beside me. I climbed in the back and Simon took off again, not speaking.

Alice turned and gave me a grim smile. 'Are you okay?' she asked, searching my face.

I nodded glumly, watching out of the window as we made our way out of the city centre. There were people sitting outside in the sunshine sipping drinks in café bars. Others were holding hands, walking to the park with children in bright-coloured buggies, not a care in the world. I stared at them, frowning.

We didn't speak again until we arrived at the hospital. Simon ran on ahead and I couldn't keep up with him. My bump was now so large it restricted me from doing anything too quickly.

Alice held back, waiting for me. 'Did it look serious?' she asked when Simon was out of earshot.

'I don't know, Al, it's hard to tell. He was conscious, but he looked terrible, pale and clammy. And the look on his face,' my voice began to tremble, and I swallowed hard. 'You could see he was in a lot of pain.'

Alice fell silent again and we followed Simon as he ran down a corridor, having just spoken to a receptionist.

We found Fiona standing in a waiting area. She saw Simon and hugged him hard; she wasn't crying yet she looked drained of any emotion or colour. She smiled kindly at Alice and me.

'It seems he was having a heart attack,' she said quietly. 'They are trying to stabilise him now.'

'Will he be okay?' Simon asked her.

'Well, he's still relatively young and healthy, that's got to count for something. I'm sure he'll be fine,' she said hollowly and patted his hand.

'Can I get you a drink?' Alice asked, keen to do something to take their minds off waiting.

'Thanks, Alice, I'll have a coffee,' Fiona answered. The calmness in her voice was infectious and I

334

found myself relaxing slightly; if Fiona thought he would be okay, I was happy to believe her. Simon, however, was growing more and more tense. He turned down a drink and Alice wandered off in search of a vending machine.

'What the hell are they doing in there?' he said moments later, looking around for someone who could tell him what was going on.

'Simon, try and stay calm, they're very busy. They promised to keep me informed if there was any change. I'm sure he will be fine. Why don't you have a walk, take your mind off things?'

'No, I'm not leaving 'til I know what's going on,' he insisted, slumping down on a plastic chair and rubbing at his face with his hands.

I left them to find Alice and helped her carry the drinks back to the chairs.

'I'm really sorry, I can't tell you anything. As soon as Doctor Rankin is available, he will come and find you straight away,' a nurse was explaining to Simon when we returned. She turned back to her desk and picked up a trilling phone.

Simon clenched his fists and began pacing again.

An hour and a half later we had still heard nothing. Fiona's coffee was sitting beside her untouched. I was still taking minute sips from mine, despite it being cold and barely drinkable. I needed something to do.

'Mrs Delanci?' a voice asked, catching everyone's attention.

'Yes.'

'I'm Doctor Rankin, I've been looking after your husband. I'm sorry you've had to wait so long. I'm afraid to tell you Mr Delanci has suffered a severe heart attack. We have managed to stabilise him, and although he is not out of the woods yet, he has been moved to the intensive care ward. You may see him.' He looked at the three of us as we stood protectively around Fiona. 'But I must stress that he can only have one visitor for now. He's had a major ordeal and needs to get plenty of rest.'

Alice and I nodded, but Simon looked upset.

'I'm sorry, you should be able to see him in the morning,' the doctor said to him, then turned back to Fiona, taking her arm and leading her to the intensive care ward. 'I'll explain your husband's condition on the way.'

We followed behind, unsure what to do next. At the ward we stopped at the reception desk.

Fiona turned back to Simon. 'Darling, I know it's hard, but I think it's better if you go. I don't think much else can be done now and I'll stay with him tonight. Why don't you go over to our house and call some people, let them know what's going on? I'll phone you later and you can see him first thing in the morning.'

Simon nodded reluctantly and they hugged each other again before she was led across the room to a bed that had been screened off with curtains.

'It's got to be here somewhere,' Simon moaned, riffling through piles of paperwork. We had spent the past half an hour looking for Fiona's address

336

book so that we could call some of her friends and relatives, but the house was so chaotic it would have been difficult to locate a room, let alone an object. It felt strange going through their personal things without them being around. I felt like I was trespassing, but it had to be done. We had tried to call Tamsin and let her know, but her housemate had informed us that she had taken the twins over to a friend's house and wouldn't be back until quite late tonight.

'Got it!' he called, waving the address book in the air triumphantly. 'It was in Mum's handbag.' He skimmed through it for a moment then looked up. His face was drawn and tired. 'Right, I guess I'd better start calling people,' he said, obviously not relishing the prospect.

Alice squeezed his hand supportively. 'Do you want us to leave you to it?' she asked.

'Why don't you go order a pizza, I'll pay,' he said. 'I don't think I've eaten all day, and by the sounds of it Holly hasn't either. I guess we ought to have something.'

Alice and I went off to the kitchen in search of a menu; I could remember seeing one on the notice-board.

'I'll get my mobile, I think I left it in the hall, you pick out what you fancy,' Alice said, leaving me alone in the kitchen. My stomach rumbled; I was starving, I hadn't eaten all day. I didn't care whether I ate or not, but I worried that the baby was beginning to suffer for it.

I hunted through the various menus, letters and

phone numbers that had been pinned on to the notice-board. Many of them scattered across the floor the moment I touched them. I bent down to retrieve them. A postcard that had fluttered under the kitchen table caught my eye. It was a picture of a tropical beach, a little Indian boy in the foreground holding an enormous swordfish over his head. My heart skipped a beat, suspecting it was a postcard from Tom. I glanced around guiltily then picked up the card, turning it over. I recognised the writing immediately and began to read his scrawly writing.

Mum and Dad,

I arrived at Bombay four days ago. It's a mad place, lots of terrible poverty. Bit depressing actually, but a real life-changing experience. Dad – you'd love the architecture! Met some excellent people in a youth hostel. Best of all, met the most beautiful woman I've ever seen, we've spent a lot of time together now and she's helped me see what's important. Mum would love her! Tell you all about it later. Had Bombay belly twice already, curries are top, though funny how no one in Bombay has heard of Bombay potatoes!

I'll try and call soon, but it's difficult here. Lots of love, Tom.

I sat on the kitchen floor reading and rereading the card. It felt as though I was being stabbed over and over again. My jaw had fallen open and tears

338

swelled in my eyes. He'd met someone else. Why hadn't they told me? Hope drained away from me and a painful thought crept in, in its place. Maybe that's why Marcus had offered to help me; out of pity.

I heard Alice coming back down the hall and I sprang up, pinning the card back where it had come from.

'Did you find the menu?' she asked when she came back into the kitchen.

I stared blindly at the notice-board, unable to take my eyes off the picture of the Indian boy on the beach.

'Look, here it is, right under your nose,' Alice said, picking off the leaflet and waving it in front of my face. She saw my expression and stopped smiling. 'Oh Holly, you poor thing. You've had an awful day, haven't you?' She enveloped me in her arms. 'Marcus will be fine, I'm sure. You heard Fiona, he's still young and fit.'

I nodded, trying to smile; ashamed that it wasn't Marcus I was upset about. I was so selfish and trivial. Marcus could have died today and there I was concerned with my love life, I thought angrily. I had to think about Simon and how I could help them. I tore myself away from the notice-board, joining Alice at the kitchen table and looked at the menu. But my stomach was clenched in a sickening knot; I didn't think I could manage to eat a thing.

As it happened, despite the delicious-looking fresh pizzas most of them lay untouched in their boxes.

Simon took small bites between phone calls, but he looked too tired to eat. Fiona called to say that Marcus was still stable. He hadn't spoken much as his painkillers had knocked him out. She asked Simon to bring some things in for her in the morning and rang off. Then Tamsin returned Simon's call when she got back from her friend's house. She took the news quite badly and insisted on driving straight over. I tried to talk her out of it but she hung up before I could say any more. I wasn't sure Simon was up to another dissection of the day's events.

To my relief Simon suggested that I stay over. The thought of returning to the empty flat and the remnants of the dinner and Marcus's things lying about was daunting. I didn't feel up to facing them tonight, lying alone with the memory of the expression on his face, weak and helpless. I wanted to be with friends.

Simon suggested I have Tom's old room and my heart flipped; being so close to his personal things, sleeping in his old bed and possibly sensing him, smelling him, would be a cruel torture. Like being starved to the point of desperation, then having a sandwich held tantalisingly close, yet just out of my reach.

'Oh, I'll be fine on the sofa, honestly,' I said, panicking.

'No really, Hol, Tom would insist I'm sure, and you can't sleep on the sofa when you're nearly eight months pregnant. You wouldn't fit!' he said, gesturing at the three-seater, which I had to admit did look uncomfortably narrow.

340

'Why don't I sleep in the guest bedroom?'

'Well, you could, but Tamsin will probably be sleeping there.'

'That's okay, I'll share with her,' I said resolutely, ignoring Simon's puzzled expression.

Tamsin hadn't minded at all; Simon had already gone to bed when she arrived, so we sat up for a couple of hours talking, then put the twins to sleep in Tom's old room and shared the double bed in the guest room. Lying awake in the pitch dark I could tell Tamsin was also awake, worrying about Marcus. I toyed with the idea of discussing the postcard with her, but it didn't seem right to bother her about it now. I remembered Marcus telling me that Tom had called him once from Bombay; that must have been after he had sent the postcard. I wondered what else he had said about the woman. I wondered what she looked like, what her name was. I had an image in my mind of a tanned, exotic woman, well travelled, that he could chat intimately with for hours at a time, sharing experiences and adventures. Maybe he needed someone more like him, with his yearning for travel, someone he could take off with on a whim. He could never have had that with me, I was too tied to the café, and now to our child. Again I remembered the time we had gone climbing together. He had been so keen to involve me that I must have been a real disappointment. Maybe I should have tried harder to get involved with his interests. Maybe he really had seen me as the 'scary business woman' he always joked about me being.

I started to wonder what would happen when he found out about his dad. Would he return home early with this woman in tow? It would be more than I could bear. I wanted to sleep, block out the thoughts of Tom and Marcus that were hurting so much, but my mind was racing, inventing a whole selection of worst-case scenarios to pick and choose from.

On Tuesday I managed to see Marcus. Visiting, at first, had been restricted to only the closest family members. Fiona had been almost permanently at his bedside and I had persuaded her to let me give her a break. The staff hadn't looked happy with me visiting at first, until Fiona explained that, to Marcus, I was as good as a daughter. I got Maggie to hold the fort back at the café and drove over at half past two that afternoon.

I went straight to the intensive care ward where we had left Fiona on Sunday night. She had told me he would be there today and moved to a recovery ward tomorrow. What she hadn't prepared me for was the shock of seeing him look so vulnerable. In some ways he looked even worse than he had done on Sunday. The head nurse at the main office on the ward pointed out his bed to me and I stood back for a moment, looking at him.

He was lying on top of the blankets in a pair of pyjamas. His top was unbuttoned halfway down, showing several adhesive pads attached to his chest; wires trailed off from them, leading to machinery by his side, monitoring his heart. His bedside cabinet was swamped in flowers and cards, but in stark contrast to the vivid colours of the blooms, his face was pale and lifeless. He was half-hidden by an oxygen mask that was sending out a fine hissing mist over his nose and mouth. There were half a dozen other patients in the ward, but I was chilled to see that Marcus must have been the youngest person in the room by a good twenty years. It seemed so unfair that he had to go through this at his age.

I approached the bed where he was listlessly leafing through the morning's paper, his eyes drooping, half-shut. He didn't see me until I was standing by his feet. When he looked up and recognised me he gave me a weak smile and took his mask off. I went to pull up a chair to sit down beside him, but he patted a space on the bed and moved his legs so I could sit opposite him instead. I passed over a get well card and looked around the ward to make sure there were no nurses in earshot, then I leaned in and whispered, 'I heard you emptied out the local florists, so I made you this instead.' I handed over a container full of fresh fruit salad I had made that morning.

Marcus smiled as I passed the box over and he peeled the lid off, examining the contents.

'I grated some stem ginger on the top,' I explained. 'It's supposed to be packed full of restorative ingredients, I've been getting through tons lately,' I added self-consciously.

His face brightened instantly into a weak but wicked smile, and I was cheered to see a flash of the old Marcus again.

'That looks delicious, Holly, and so thoughtful. Thank you,' he said putting the box on top of the cabinet.

'I wasn't sure if I was allowed to bring in food, have they put you on a low cholesterol diet?'

He rolled his eyes. 'Ugh, it's awful, and they boil the flavour out of the vegetables in this place. I've had tastier ice cubes. There's a dietician coming to see me tomorrow apparently. I spoke to a guy in the bed opposite yesterday. He said he's not allowed anything over ten per cent fat and only three eggs a week. My morning omelette has more than that. I'm having a culinary crisis. Thank goodness I knew I could rely on you to perk me up, I don't know how they expect me to get my energy up in here. What they give me wouldn't set a sparrow up for the day.' Marcus laughed a little then held his chest and winced.

My heart flipped. 'Are you okay? You want me to call the doctor?'

'Oh, God no, I've been prodded and tested and monitored until I feel like a lab animal, don't subject me to any more of that.' He took a sip of the iced water by the bed.

'How are you really? Are you still in much pain?' I asked him.

'Oh, it's not too bad now. Just a bit tender I suppose. I'm sorry I scared you, Holly, I really should have waited until I got home, shouldn't I?' He was talking much slower than normal, and stopped intermittently to catch his breath

'Don't be ridiculous!' I said, amazed that he was

344

apologising for getting ill. 'I'm the one who's sorry, I only wish I'd known. I never would have let you work so hard on the nursery.'

'Now you're being daft. No one could have known, and doing the nursery was practically a holiday for me. It was easy work compared to some of the contracts I'd taken on lately. You mustn't worry about that. I just wish I had at least waited until after lunch. If I'd known I was going to have to survive on prison food, I'd have fed myself up a bit first.'

I laughed, relieved that he seemed to have kept his dry, teasing humour.

'I don't suppose Tom has been in touch, has he?' he asked hopefully.

My heart started beating faster at the mere mention of his name. 'I'm afraid not. I called Ajay and explained what happened; he said he would chase up Peter and let me know as soon as he's heard anything. I called the consulate, I thought they might be more helpful now, what with you . . . y'know, but they still said there was nothing they could do. '

Marcus smiled and patted my hand. 'Thanks for trying, Holly. I just wish I knew where he was. I really think he needs to be here now, for your sake too,' he said seriously. 'If only he knew, I'm sure he'd be on the next flight back.' He shook his head and looked at me. 'I'm sorry, I've been feeling quite melancholy this morning. I've been thinking a lot about the business and the future. I guess I've had a warning about my appetite for hard work, and I

345

don't need to be told twice. I really want to talk to Tom about it. I'm sure he'd love to take over from me. He's got a real flair for design and he's always been really keen in the past. I know he's capable. But I don't want him making the same mistakes as me, taking it all on single-handed. The business needs more staff to delegate the workload to . . .' he trailed off, then, looking embarrassed, 'gosh, here's me kidding myself I can step back from the company, and yet here I am harping on about it again. Anyway, I don't want you to worry about Tom, I don't think he'll end up like his dad, he's got a much healthier balance between enjoying life and working hard. Actually I wish he'd tip the scales a *little* more in favour of working hard, but I'm sure he will when he returns. That was always the plan. But anyway, whatever happens between you two, I know he'll want to help with the baby as much as he can.'

I sat listening to Marcus, my heart sinking. His last comment said it all; he knew there was no future for us now.

We chatted a while longer about Fiona and my pregnancy. I was trying to stay upbeat and positive for his sake, but I was relieved when I saw he was tiring of talking. It took a lot of energy for him to speak, and so I took this as my cue to leave. I got off the bed and kissed him goodbye.

'You take care of my little grandchild, won't you?' he said, holding my hand tightly as I got ready to go, I squeezed it in reply and left him to rest. I turned around when I reached the office at the far end of the ward and, glancing back, I saw that Marcus had already nodded off.

That night, after a half-hour attempt to reassure Mum over the phone that the stress of Marcus being ill wasn't making my blood pressure rise again, and promising to put lavender oil in my bath, Alice saved me by coming over for a coffee.

'How's Simon bearing up?' I asked her as we slumped down together on the sofa.

'Well, I haven't seen him today. He's been staying over at Fiona and Marcus's house since Sunday, I think he feels he needs to be close to his mum. Especially with Tom not being there. He's taken this week off work to be around for her.' She nursed her drink, holding it against her chest. 'He's so thoughtful, isn't he? I remember when Oliver's mum got gastric flu, and he complained about her wheezing down the phone. No, Simon is so different, he's just, I know it sounds like something out of old romantic novels, but he's just such a gent. I didn't realise they still existed, but I don't care how unfashionable that is these days, it works for me every time.'

'You really like him, don't you?' I asked, smiling at her. It felt strange watching Alice's relationship with Simon grow. She was getting close to Fiona and Marcus now, slotting in as one of the family. I felt a pang of jealousy as I realised she was taking my place as an honorary daughter.

Alice grinned at me, biting her bottom lip. 'Do you know, I always thought you'd get it together

347

with Simon. You were always so close, and I know he used to have a thing for you.'

I forced a smile. 'Oh, he was never serious about me, and I was only close to him because he knows Tom better than anyone. Maybe it was the best way for me to find out what Tom was like, seeing as he was hardly ever around to talk to in person.'

'The next best thing, hey?' Alice said smiling. 'Well, it's a good job nothing ever happened between you, because I've never been happier in my life,' she confided sheepishly, looking at me from under her lashes. 'You know, obviously what has happened to Marcus is just awful for everyone. But in a funny way it's helped me to cement my feelings for Simon. I think I love him.'

By Wednesday night I was able to relax a bit. Marcus had moved into a recovery ward that afternoon and was off the monitors; he appeared to be out of danger and according to Fiona was looking more like his old self. Still, we were told that forty per cent of heart-attack victims died in the first few days, twenty-five per cent of those remaining died in the following year. They were chilling statistics that I tried not to dwell too much on. I knew things would never be the same again for them.

Maggie had been brilliant at subtly taking over the jobs in the café, leaving me enough time to relax and put my feet up, without feeling like I was being molly-coddled. So I had enjoyed a much slower paced day. That evening I decided on an early night and was just getting undressed when the phone rang.

'Hello?' I yawned into the phone.

'Holly, it's me.'

For a brief and heart-stopping moment I thought it was Tom, but I knew the voice didn't belong to him, despite its familiar tone. I paused, unsure.

'It's Ajay, did I get you out of bed?'

My hands started to shake and my knees went weak as I anticipated what he was going to say. 'No, no, don't worry. What's happened?' I asked, not wanting to delay any news with small talk.

'Peter just called,' he said. 'He knows where Tom has been staying.'

I sat down, clutching the phone tightly in my hand. 'Has he spoken to him? Does he know what's going on? Is he coming home?' I blurted.

'Whoa, hang on. Let me tell you what's happening,' he said calmly. 'Tom has been staying at a youth hostel near the Taj Palace. That's one of the biggest hotels in Bombay. He's been having breakfast in there most mornings apparently. One of the staff there recognised his name and told Peter where he was staying. He went to the hostel but he wasn't there. The couple who run it said that Tom has gone on a trek that could take anything between a week and a fortnight. They know he was heading to the Taj Mahal with a couple of friends, but don't know where they are planning to stay. The good news is he'll definitely return to the hostel as he left a couple of bags there with the owners.'

When Ajay had finished talking I managed to start breathing again. 'So he still doesn't know we're looking for him?' I said weakly.

349

'I'm afraid not,' Ajay said, 'but Peter did leave a message at the hostel saying that Tom should call home urgently, and in the meantime Peter will make some calls and try and trace him somewhere on the trek. Most people stay overnight at Agra so he can ring the hostels there. And there are a few other touristy places he could stop off at as well so he may well find Tom before he returns to Bombay.'

I was twisting the cord of the telephone around and around between my fingers, trying to digest what he was saying to me. After a long pause I managed to say, 'That's really good news, Ajay, I can't tell you how grateful I am that you've gone to all this trouble.'

'It's nothing, really. I'll let you know if anything else happens, okay?'

I said goodbye and then immediately called Fiona. All my anxieties about contacting Tom had left me. No matter what happened with us, the most important thing was that he knew what was happening. It sounded as though Tom had moved on to forming other relationships; I just had to accept that and carry on. But I'd worry about that later.

Fiona was over the moon when I told her what had happened. She wanted to try and call some bus and train companies in India herself, just so she felt as though she was doing something. She felt as though it might be easier to find him now she knew where he was headed. She hung up almost straight away so she could get some numbers from international directory enquiries.

Half an hour later she called back to say she hadn't had any luck. I told her not to worry, the longest we would have to wait was two weeks, and if Peter was lucky it would be much sooner than that. She thanked me for finding Tom, even though technically I hadn't, and made me promise to call her as soon as I heard any more.

I went to bed then, my mind churning furiously. Finally the waiting would be over and I'd see Tom again. I stared longingly at the photo of him that was propped up next to the bed. Until this evening, he had felt impossibly far away. Now, he felt only just out of reach.

The next day, I found concentrating on work almost impossible. The phone was livelier than ever and every time it rang I had an adrenalin surge, expecting it to be Ajay with news of Tom. My mind was only half on what I was doing and I made countless idiotic mistakes. I forgot to put yeast in the bread dough, I put milk in a vegan's coffee, and put so much cleaning solution in the dishwasher that bubbles oozed through the door and forced off the water pipe connected at the back. Water gushed out like an erupting geezer before Maggie and I fought past the torrent to switch it off and wrestle the pipe back on. The customers who could see what had happened applauded us as we surfaced from the kitchen, our soaked clothes clinging to us and our shoes squelching. After this Maggie could take no more and insisted I finish early and leave the rest to her.

I trudged up to the flat sulkily and threw off my sodden clothes. The baby seemed to have been woken up by all the chaos and was stretching and squirming in my tummy as though she was warming up for an aerobics class. I stood in front of the full-length mirror in a pair of white knickers, staring transfixed at my bump. It had grown so big, so quickly. As I watched, the whole of my bump began to move. At first it twitched, then as the baby shifted all its weight to the left-hand side of my body, my bump also moved across until it was completely off-centre. It was a weird thing to see; my whole body changing shape and contorting. A smaller lump appeared on one side, pushing against my skin, and I felt it, imagining it was the baby's hand or foot. When I pressed against it, it shot back in and the whole bump moved again over to my right this time. I gasped as a strong sensation of the baby stretching its arms out made my bump elongate into a warped sausage shape, and I thought I saw a hand pushing out against my skin. I touched it lightly with my fingertip, and it stayed there for a moment, protruding peculiarly, then I felt the baby squirm again and settle. I stroked my vast expanse of tummy, talking soothingly to it, calling it 'my little pumpkin'. I was so moved by what I'd seen; it was as though even in the womb, my baby was trying to reach out to me.

Before I had become pregnant, I had always imagined that the movements you felt your baby make were small and unnoticeable with the naked eye. I was amazed to see the undulating shape of my baby

352

just under the surface of my skin. I surveyed the bump from every conceivable angle, unable to take my eyes off it. When I looked underneath (which is quite tricky and involves a certain amount of leaning backwards until you nearly tip over, and tilting the mirror at an angle), I was taken aback by what I saw. Somebody must have snuck into my bedroom in the night and stencilled a comprehensive London street map on to the lower half of my abdomen in dark purple ink. I was startled at first and fingered the lines on my skin with confusion. Slowly it dawned on me that despite my preconception that I had unusually elastic, youthful skin, I had been sporting stretch marks all the time. They had simply been hiding where I wouldn't normally spot them without an angle-poise mirror.

I sighed, saddened that my chances of wearing a bikini and looking halfway attractive had diminished further. Not that I had had the bravado to wear a bikini in nearly four years now, but I had always entertained an image of me (especially on Saturday nights, before the lottery draw) clad in a two-piece, on a white sandy beach in the Caribbean like Carol Smillie, looking ravishing. I had always hoped a bikini body had only eluded me before as I simply hadn't the time or occasion to devote myself to it. Maybe I could learn to tie a sarong properly to make me look elegant and tropical, yet hide my unsightlies, a bit like a young Judith Chalmers. Still, at least my chest had gone up a whole size, making me nearly the size of the average British woman. My Wonderbras had eventually threatened to cut off my circulation some months ago and I had given in to shopping for maternity bras with Tamsin. Unfortunately, as women's breasts are supposed to get bigger during pregnancy, they seemed to assume that the average pregnant women was as well endowed as any page three girl, and also didn't feel the need for any extra uplift, padding or pretty lacy bits. I had a sneaking suspicion that maternity bras were a design throwback from the 1950s, as any that did fit me gave me an odd, angular and pointy profile, like an early Doris Day. Maternity knickers suffered a similar design flaw, having all the size and shape of a fitted sheet and sporting a gusset you could park a car on. I had finally given in and just bought bigger sized Marks and Spencer's. I admired my inflated chest, wondering saucily what Tom would think, then decided that he'd be horrified at my nipples that had also expanded and now reminded me of a pair of dinner plates.

I began to dress in a pair of comfy jogging bottoms and an Adidas sweatshirt. I liked wearing sports clothes as maternity wear as I figured anyone that saw my hugely bloated figure might assume that I had been really fit and athletic before I became pregnant and my figure might not be a thing of the past. The phone rang as I was searching for a pair of slouchy socks. It was Fiona.

'Hi, Fiona, how is Marcus?' I asked.

'He's perked up a lot today,' she replied, sounding happier than she had done in days. 'He was talking about when he's coming out and he's got a lot more energy. Poor thing's never been so stationary.

Anyway, he told me to thank you for helping find Tom, I think it's a load off his mind. He really didn't need the extra stress.'

'Fi, I think it's the least I could have done under the circumstances,' I insisted, sitting down on the bed.

Fiona mentioned that Marcus would be allowed to leave hospital a week on Sunday, exactly a fortnight after the attack and we chatted about the possibility of a surprise welcome home party that afternoon. Marcus had mentioned many times how he hated having visitors in hospital; they all acted nervous around him and couldn't relax in the clinical surroundings. Fiona had thought it would be nice for him to catch up with friends and family in a less alien environment. I was happy to be invited and we made a provisional agreement to make it for that Sunday at lunchtime.

'I guess there's an outside chance Tom might be back by then as well,' Fiona said hopefully.

CHAPTER TWENTY-SIX

A week on Thursday Fiona called me early in the morning, just as I was preparing to open up the café.

'He's just called,' was all she said when I answered the phone. I knew instantly who it was and what they were talking about.

'What did he say?' I whispered breathlessly.

'Well, the phone line was pretty bad, but from what I could gather he had received a message at a hotel he stayed at on the way back from his trip. It's a good job he got it because he was about to extend his journey to visit some temples. He called as soon as he could. I told him about Marcus and he was quite upset and worried. I tried to convince him that he was out of danger now, but I think he felt pretty bad about not being around when it happened. He told me he would try to get home as soon as he could. I said there was no rush now, but he said he'd never forgive himself if his dad had another attack, and besides, he wanted to come back and help with the business. I think he was worried that Marcus would be tempted to throw himself back into work.

It's going to take Tom several days to travel back to Bombay from where he is now, but he'll try to get a flight out as soon as he gets there.'

I smiled to myself, relieved to know he was on his way back, and proud of Tom for insisting on being there for his dad. I loved the way he was so close to his family.

'Did you mention me?' I asked, fiddling nervously with the phone cable again.

'Holly, I'm so sorry, I didn't know what to do about that. With him insisting on coming home, I couldn't decide if it was better to tell him then, or give you the chance to discuss it with him face to face. He was also quite blown away by the news about his dad. I thought it might be too much for him hearing more news as well. I was so undecided I thought I would discuss it with you. The chances are he'll call back anyway to tell us when his flight is, so one of us could speak to him then. Or now we have the number of the place he's going to in Bombay you could leave a message for him there. What do you think? Are you annoyed?' Fiona asked, concerned.

The truth was I didn't mind at all. For Tom to have heard it from anyone other than me would have seemed like I was hiding behind other people, and Fiona was right, he had endured enough shocking news. He'd be home any day now so I'd wait and tell him as soon as he returned. I wanted to see his face when I discussed it with him. I agreed with Fiona that that was the best thing to do.

'And are you still on for Sunday? I've arranged

to pick up Marcus from hospital just before lunch, so we'll still be set to arrive back at about half past twelve. It won't be a big do, just close friends and family. They'll be arriving throughout the morning with food and drink, so I thought you might like to come early and spend some time with Simon and Alice.'

'That'd be lovely,' I agreed. 'Are you sure it's safe to surprise Marcus in his condition?' I asked, entertaining an unpleasant image of us jumping out at him from behind the sofa and watching him collapse again.

'Don't worry, I'll drop a hint that there are some people there to say "Hi", and we'll avoid springing out on him, I think,' she said.

I told her to expect me at around eleven and rang off to call Ajay and thank him.

Sunday morning was sweltering from the moment I opened my eyes. When I drew back the curtains I saw that the sky had a misty hue that I could tell would be burned away in a couple of hours. I showered and dressed in a light floaty summer dress and tied my hair back into a high ponytail. I looked so wholesome it made me smile at the image I portrayed. I imagined myself with a pram, tending to a little baby and the image was no longer terrifying, it was cosy and exciting. I had been observing Tamsin closely throughout my pregnancy and she'd helped me to realise that being a single mum was also liberating and rewarding. I admired how she coped and she had become a role model for me.

I wrapped up Marcus's present whilst I ate my breakfast. I had bought him a set of watercolour paints and a hardbound sketchpad. I knew that when he was younger he had been a keen painter; there were pictures dotted throughout the house that he had done during his art degree. Now he was stepping down from the business Fiona had mentioned that Marcus had been talking about taking it up again. The perfect hobby for a man who needs to de-stress.

At eleven o'clock I set off to the Delancis' house. I rolled the windows down, letting the breeze cool my face. I had the radio on and sang loudly to an old U2 song, remembering that Tom had a copy of it he'd often played when I'd been to his house. When I pulled up at the drive I noticed there were already half a dozen cars there. Someone had tied pearlescent balloons to the fence post at the far end of the drive and also around the front door. The windows were all wide open and I could hear the sound of laughter coming from the back of the house. Rather than knock on the door I walked around the side passageway and out into the garden. I spotted Tamsin and the twins first, who were playing on a rug, under the shade of a tree. I walked over and joined them, making a space for myself on the rug. The twins both looked up at me, gurgling and smiling.

'Wouldn't you rather sit in a comfy chair? I can go and fetch one,' Tamsin said, standing up to fetch me one of the garden chairs that were spread out across the lawn.

'Oh no, I'm fine here,' I insisted, gesturing for her to sit down with me. I looked around the garden and spotted a few familiar faces. Fiona was buzzing around, laying food out on a bench in the shadow of a large parasol and hadn't seen me arrive. The others were either helping her or sitting in a group on the patio. Most were relatives I vaguely recognised from past parties. A couple of them had watched me cross the grass to Tamsin when I had arrived. It was obvious they had been looking quizzically at my bump. I wondered whether it was common knowledge that I was carrying Tom's child. I doubted it would be; Fiona was quite discreet. But as most of them would have recognised me as Tom's girlfriend they must have suspected. I felt self-conscious sitting there knowing they were wondering what was going on. I expected I'd be asked about the baby several times throughout the day, and I wasn't sure what I should tell them. It seemed disloyal for these virtual strangers to know that Tom would soon be a father when he didn't even know himself.

'Don't panic,' Tamsin whispered, giving me a conspiratorial smile. 'I'll protect you from the old duffers. That's why I positioned myself out here, thought you might appreciate not being barraged with questions as soon as you arrived.'

'You're an angel.' I grinned back at her, grateful that she understood. Alice came through the back door then with a large plate of sandwiches; she placed them on the bench then looked up and caught my eye. She waved happily and came over to join us.

'Hey, babe,' she greeted, kissing me on the top of my head. 'How are you feeling?'

'Oh, not too bad. Tired, but well. Where's Simon?'

'Having a shower.' She leaned in closer so an elderly couple touring the garden couldn't hear her. 'He was trying to talk me into joining him, but it felt a bit odd in his parents' house, you know. I'm so glad Marcus is home today, it means Simon can move back to his house tonight, and we can, er, relax a bit. Am I completely selfish?' she asked laughing naughtily.

I felt a jealous pang at how uncomplicated their relationship was. 'You, Alice will always be the total opposite of selfish,' I assured her.

'Hey, Tom's probably going to come back tomorrow,' Alice said. 'How are you coping? Are you nervous?'

'Terrified,' I said. 'I haven't any idea how he'll take the news.' I decided that now was as good a time as any to mention the postcard I had found, and filled them in on the details. Now Marcus was coming out of hospital, I didn't feel so bad about talking about my own worries.

Alice's eyes grew wide when I told her what it had said. 'I can't believe this. Why didn't you tell me earlier? Holly, you must be devastated,' she gushed, her eyes shining bright with tears of sympathy. I tried to shrug it off. I had been hoping Alice or Tamsin would have known something about it, but they both insisted they knew nothing. 'Honestly,

Hol, if Simon had known anything he definitely would have told me, if not gone straight to you. You know how much he cares about you. Are you sure you got it right? I mean surely if Marcus and Fiona knew Tom was seeing someone else they'd have warned you,' Alice said, looking at Tamsin to back her up.

'I'm sure Alice is right,' she agreed.

'I'm not so sure,' I said. 'The postcard was pretty recent. Maybe they were planning to tell me over the lunch I cooked before Marcus got ill. They've had a lot to deal with since then. Fiona makes a real effort not to get involved in our relationship, she probably thinks it's something that Tom and I should work out on our own. Besides, I think the postcard speaks for itself.'

Alice sighed, shaking her head. 'This is awful. I was so sure you could work it out. From what Fiona told me, she thought Tom was crazy about you. It always seemed like you'd get it together when his trip was over, and he just hadn't wanted to get too serious before then. I mean Tom's always been really into you, he's never really had any other relationships, has he?'

'Not that I knew of, but it wouldn't have been difficult to hide them from me, it wasn't as though he was ever around for more than four or five months at a time.'

'It was probably just a little indiscretion, nothing serious. You'll have to ask Marcus what's going on,' Tamsin said.

I grimaced. From what Tom had said in the card,

362

it was definitely serious. 'I don't think I want to talk to Marcus about it. He's got other things on his mind and I'd hate to admit I'd read his post, it's embarrassing. Besides, I'm not sure I could cope with the truth right now,' I whispered and looked away from them to the garden, indicating that the subject was closed.

Fiona came out a moment later to announce she was off to fetch Marcus; she waved at me gesturing to explain that she was in a rush and would chat when they returned, and then she hurried away.

I watched as Callum rolled over on to his front and attempted to crawl towards a bush. His legs pumped up and down as he tried to negotiate a hump in the grass. Tamsin hadn't noticed he was stuck so I scooped him up and sat him on my lap. His head bobbed happily as he spotted my necklace and swiped at it like a kitten after a ball of wool. He felt solid and warm in my arms and I was swelling with pride that he wasn't wailing at being in such a close proximity to me. He stared at me, taking in every detail of my face; he was mesmerised. Then he began to turn a deep plum colour and made a weird grunting noise.

'Is he all right? He's not choking, is he?' I blurted, looking fearfully at Tamsin to help me out.

'Number two,' she explained, amused. As if to prove her right, something felt as if it had exploded in Callum's nappy, lifting him ever so slightly into the air.

I plonked him back down on to the grass by his

sleeping brother, amazed at his complete lack of modesty as he strained and groaned.

'I'd better change him,' Tamsin said eventually. 'Unless you fancy it, for a bit of practice?'

I had a feeling that the contents of your own child's nappy were an awful lot easier to cope with than that of another parent's. I politely declined and excused myself to find some drinks for us.

I was relieved to find the kitchen empty and helped myself to three tall glasses from the drainer. As I poured out a drink I sneezed hard, and felt that tell-tale damp feeling you get when you're eight months pregnant and lose the ability to control your bladder under pressure. I cursed under my breath and looked around but I was still alone. I knew I'd have to change. I checked my pocket for my car keys. There was still time for me to nip back, change and be back in time for Marcus's return. I peeped out into the garden and saw Tamsin dressing Callum.

'Are you all right, Hol?' Alice said, wandering into the kitchen and making me jump. I spun around so my back was against the kitchen unit. 'I thought you might want some help carrying the glasses out.'

'Oh, right, excellent. Thanks,' I stuttered.

Alice looked at me suspiciously. 'Are you sure you're okay?'

'Of course. Er, actually, I just realised I've forgotten Marcus's present. I think I'll just nip back and fetch it.' The present was actually sitting on the passenger seat of my car. I willed Alice not to walk me to the car and spot it.

'Do you want me to go for you?' she offered.

364

'No, no, thanks. It won't take me long. I'll just go now, shall I?'

'Okay.' Alice stayed where she was, waiting for me to go. She gave me a confused smile, then took over pouring out the drinks. I edged out of the door, keeping my back to her, then scrambled through the house and out to the car.

When I got back to the flat I was beginning to feel strange. I was sweating profusely and the wet patch on my dress had grown considerably during the drive back. I felt a strong spasm spread across the lower part of my bump. I ran to the bathroom, stripping out of my dress as I went. When I took off my knickers I noticed a small spot of blood. I sat down on the loo, my head spinning. I felt a release of fluid as it splashed into the toilet and this time I was in no doubt. That definitely hadn't come from my bladder. My waters had broken. I stared around in horror. This wasn't meant to happen yet. I had a party to go to, and still had four weeks to go to prepare for this moment. I sat for a few minutes trying to clear my mind enough to come to a decision on what to do, but my brain refused to make sense of anything and I stared dumbly at the bathroom floor. I was racked with another wave of pain that stayed with me for a few seconds then eased off. This is it, I thought, numb with fear. I did my best to clean myself up and walked trance-like to the phone. Who could I call? I hadn't decided on a birthing partner, fancifully hoping Tom would be home and willing to hold my hand. I had briefly discussed it with Alice; I knew she'd be a very willing participant, but we'd never come to a concrete agreement and I found it hard to pick between Alice, Maggie and Tamsin, who I knew would all have been delighted to have been asked.

I checked my watch. Marcus would be arriving at the party any minute now. I couldn't ruin the party for them. I remembered Maggie saying she was staying in today and wouldn't be seeing Noah until the evening. I picked up the phone and dialled her number.

'Maggie, it's me, pick up the phone . . . Please hon, I need you . . .'

'Hello,' she croaked sounding as though she had just been raised from the dead. 'Holly, is that you? Why aren't you at the party?'

'I think it's started,' I almost shouted down the handset.

'Well, you'd better hurry up then, or you'll miss it, you daft bat!' she snapped, amused.

'No, not the party, the baby. My waters have broken and I'm having contractions.'

'Oh my God!' she said and slammed the phone down. I stood holding it to my ear listening to the silence in a state of shock, and then she picked it up again.

'Sorry, Holly, what's going on? What are you going to do?'

'I don't know,' I blubbed. Fear was beginning to take hold of me.

'Right!' Maggie said authoritatively, realising I

366

was losing my marbles and needed someone to take control of the situation.

'Is your bag packed?'

'Not really,' I muttered, feeling foolish for being so unprepared. Another contraction shot across the lower half of my body and I moaned softly stroking my bump to help ease the pain.

'Okay, I'm coming over. I'll be ten minutes. Holly, are you listening to me? I want you to call your midwife, tell her what's going on, throw some things in a bag and try and time your contractions. And don't panic.'

I nodded and breathed out slowly to calm myself down, then the phone went dead again. I checked my watch then sat on the edge of the bed waiting for another contraction. Six minutes later it came. I rummaged in my bedside cupboard and found my address book. In the front of it I'd written the number of the maternity ward and I dialled it with shaking fingers.

The midwife I spoke to advised me to run a warm bath whilst I was getting my things ready and then try to have a relaxing soak. She sounded calm and unperturbed so I felt my panic subside a little.

I raced around the house with my bag, throwing in pyjamas, my new nightie, socks, the new pack of knickers I had been saving, a change of clothes, my phone book, a bag of boiled sweets to keep my energy up, Tampax, my wallet, a towel, my photo of Tom (well at least he was there in some form), and my lucky paperweight. I grabbed another bag from the top of my wardrobe that I had already packed for

367

the baby with things like tiny baby grows, nappies etc. I stretched into the air to retrieve it and felt another contraction take hold. I froze, waiting until it passed, then carried on packing.

I put the bags and the baby car seat by the door ready for Maggie to arrive then I went to turn off the taps in the bath and climbed into the soothing water. I lay there wondering whether midwives routinely advised baths, not to benefit the woman in labour necessarily, but to make sure their patients arrived all fresh and hygienic, making their job a bit more pleasant, rather like a dentist advising you to brush your teeth before an appointment. I toyed with the idea of shaving my bikini line and having a trim when I heard Maggie burst into the flat.

'Holly, I'm here, where are you?' she yelled wildly.

'I'm in the bath,' I answered, surprised at how much calmer I sounded than her. She knocked on the door and I called her in.

'How're you doing?' she asked sitting opposite me on the loo.

'Not bad,' I answered truthfully. 'It all seems a bit unreal. Like it's happening to someone else.' I stopped talking, breathing through another contraction.

'Do you want me to call anyone before we go?'

I nodded. 'My mum. It's too soon to call the Delancis' house yet, they'll all be welcoming Marcus back. I'd rather wait until I know the party has settled down a bit. And besides, it could still be a false alarm.'

Maggie nodded, understanding. She hopped off the loo and went into the bedroom to call my mum.

'No answer,' she shouted a minute later. My heart sank with dismay. Of all people, my mum should really be holding a twenty-four hour vigil by the phone, waiting for the big event. I checked my watch again; my contractions were coming at alarmingly regular four-minute intervals. I wasn't really sure if this was quick as I had missed the antenatal classes on birth and hadn't read up about it, having taken to reading Harry Potter instead. But I was sure that on the telly women were always having contractions at ten or twenty minutes apart, so I felt it was time to get into the hospital. I struggled out of the bath and dressed in a fresh summer dress and slipped on my sandals. I didn't want to waste time drying my hair, which was now long enough to stretch down my back, so instead I tied it back into a ponytail, knowing it would dry quickly in the intense summer heat.

Maggie threw my bags into the boot of her car and we pulled off towards the hospital. I had to beg her to slow down as she drove hunched over the steering wheel and I watched as the rev-counter kept leaping sporadically. She beeped at the traffic lights and swore at a man in a BMW that cut us up. 'I've got a woman in labour here, you moron!' she yelled out the window, causing several pedestrians to turn around and stare at me. I hid my head in my hands, mortified.

'It's really not too bad, Maggie,' I reassured her.

369

'It's a bearable kind of pain.' I was hoping she'd calm down if she knew I was coping, but she just nodded as she took a corner on the wrong side of the road.

I tried to call Mum again from Maggie's mobile but still no one answered.

When we arrived at the maternity ward I was shown into a private room with a bed, a TV and an en-suite bathroom. I was pleasantly surprised at how cosy it looked.

Maggie plopped down on the bed surveying the room happily, then was shooed on to a chair by the midwife.

'Make yourself comfy, put on your nightie and I'll pop back in five minutes to examine you, okay?' she said, then disappeared.

'Why don't you put the television on,' I suggested, 'It might distract me.' Maggie flicked it on, but faced with the entertainment wasteland that is Sunday afternoon telly, we decided not to bother.

I dressed in my nightie and hunched over, leaning on the bed, as I was gripped with another contraction. Maggie looked at me fascinated, and winced when I groaned in pain.

'You're so brave,' she said.

I laughed hard at that. It seemed every decision I had made throughout my pregnancy had been cowardly; not telling Tom, avoiding his parents, skipping the antenatal classes, going into denial and pretending it was a vegetable plant, then going into denial and pretending that it was like having a virus and instead of going into labour I'd simply get better.

'You are,' she insisted. 'You've coped really well under the circumstances. I really admire that. I don't think I would have managed nearly as well as you.'

I smiled at her gratefully, and the midwife returned to the room. She looked suspiciously at Maggie. 'Are you Holly's birth partner?' she asked. Maggie looked at me, unsure what to say. I smiled at her, nodding that it was okay.

'Yes, that's right. The baby's father is out of the country,' she explained, obviously not wanting the midwife to get any odd ideas about us.

'Are you happy for her to be here whilst you're being examined?' the midwife asked me.

'That's fine,' I said. Hey, in for a penny, in for a pound and all that, I thought. It was going to get a lot more gruesome than this.

The midwife made me lie back on the bed and checked between my legs.

'You've done really well, Holly,' she said, obviously pleased with me, although I was sure I hadn't actually done anything yet. 'You're six centimetres dilated.'

How did she know that without a ruler?

She confirmed that my waters had broken then listened to the baby's heartbeat and felt my abdomen so firmly the baby kicked back at her, and I smiled, impressed that its spirit was still evident. That's the way, pumpkin, don't put up with that kind of crap, I thought resting my hands against her protectively.

'There's nothing to do for the moment other than

371

let nature takes its course. You've got Entonox there,' she offered, pointing out the gas and air canister rigged up by the bed. Another contraction came.

'Yes please,' I blurted, making a grab for the facemask. The midwife switched it on for me then and said she'd be back to check on me in half an hour and to buzz if I needed anything.

I nodded, breathing in the dry gas. I experienced a mild head rush, as though I had downed a glass of wine and I went with it, letting my head loll backwards. Maggie watched me curiously; I could tell she was dying to have a go.

An hour passed with me pacing the room, inhaling deeply from the mask which was now as attached to my face as my own nose. The pain was getting more intense but I was still coping okay. Maggie rubbed my back, held my hand and had the occasional puff of gas between my contractions. We seemed to find the whole situation amusing and laughed at the funny contraptions that were lying around. Maggie discovered metal stirrups attached to the end of the bed and slid them up and down, giggling like a school kid.

'They'd have to kill me first!' I said, horrified at the cold steely appearance of them, leather straps swinging from the top. It reminded me of the torture devices I'd seen in a war museum. Another contraction caused me to whimper in pain and suddenly it wasn't funny any more. Maggie massaged the base of my spine and soothed me as though I was a baby.

Two hours later the midwife returned. 'How are you, love?'

I nodded grimly.

'Sorry I haven't been in much, I'm delivering a baby in the next room as well. It's a busy day today.' I wasn't thrilled at the thought of having to share the midwife with another woman.

'Does it get any worse than this?' I asked pathetically as she examined me again.

'Well, I couldn't say for sure. All women are different and their experiences are so varied. Eight centimetres, that's excellent.'

I noticed she avoided eye contact as she said this and felt she had changed the subject for a reason. 'But usually would you say it got worse?' I pressed. I needed to know, I could only just handle the pain if it stayed at this intensity, but if it got worse I knew I'd need help.

The midwife pulled a face, 'Oh, I really couldn't say, Holly, some do find it worse. Others prefer it because they at least feel that if they're pushing, they're helping,' she trailed off inconclusively.

I heard a woman screaming in the room next door. It made my skin prickle with its blood-curdling pitch. I noticed Maggie had heard it too. Her eyes were bulging and she was looking anxiously at the midwife for an explanation.

'Is that normal?' I squeaked, hugging myself as I rocked on the edge of the bed.

'Oh yes, sounds a lot worse than it is. I wouldn't worry about that. I think some women find that yelling or screaming helps when they're pushing.

373

It's not really because she's in pain. It helps them focus their energy positively, a bit like when you hear weight-lifters grunting before a lift,' the midwife joked. I stared blankly at her, not amused. She excused herself to see to the screaming banshee next door and Maggie and I looked at each other, concerned.

'Do you want to try and call Mum and Fiona now?' I asked her, trying to distract myself again by thinking of something else. Maggie seemed glad of an excuse for a break and hurried out of the room. Sitting in the silence, breathing through another contraction, I heard the woman next door again. It was difficult to decipher but it sounded something like, 'Ahhh, oh God, ahhh. I can't. No, shit, shit, shit!' Funny, none of the contenders on the World's Strongest Man had ever yelled that as they tried to lift an Atlas ball. Despair washed over me and I felt myself beginning to cry, softly at first, then harder and with an edge of desperation. What the hell was I doing? I would never cope with this on my own. No one even knew I was here. Would Tom want to be here if he knew? I wasn't sure if I'd want him there. After months of seeing the most beautiful sights in the world, and quite possibly gazing into the eyes of his beautiful new girlfriend, the sight of me, sweaty, make-upless, panting and groaning with my legs akimbo, wouldn't exactly fill him with desire and yearning. He'd be out of the door so fast it would bring a whole new meaning to the phrase 'paternity leave'. I had lost him for good.

When Maggie returned I could tell from her face

374

something was wrong. Tears flowed harder than ever. I couldn't bear any more bad news at that moment.

'Wasn't there anyone there?' I asked, sobbing into a paper tissue.

'Still no answer at your mum's, I'm sorry.' Maggie shuffled her feet nervously.

I could tell there was something else. 'What? Did you manage to contact Fiona? What's happened?'

'Well, actually, I have spoken to Fiona. They had all been really worried about you disappearing like that. Apparently they tried to call your flat several times. They had thought you may have gone into labour and tried to call the ward, but they refused to give out information to anyone who wasn't immediate family. They wouldn't even say if you had been admitted.'

'Maggie, tell me,' I hissed, wishing she would stop beating around the bush. I was in no mood to be messed with.

'Well, it's Tom.'

Oh God. Those words were enough to reduce me to jelly.

'He's back home. Apparently the airline was able to get him straight on a flight back to Heathrow and he turned up at the party about an hour ago. He hadn't even had time to call and warn them until he was in England.' Maggie waited for me to say something, but I just stared back at her, the news not registering. A moment later I doubled over in agony, 'Oh shit!' I groaned.

375

'Do you want me to call the midwife back?' Maggie asked. I shook my head furiously, not wanting to think about what was happening to my body, I only wanted to know more about Tom.

'Was he alone?'

Maggie looked confused at this question. 'I think so, Fiona didn't mention him being with anyone else.'

'Does he know about the baby?'

'Yes. Fiona and Marcus took him aside when he arrived. He was pretty shocked apparently. The party finished soon after Tom had come back, and Alice and Simon have been talking to him as well. But Fiona didn't say a lot else. She said not to worry and that she's thinking of you. She asked if Tom wanted to see you, would he be able to visit the hospital. I told her I wasn't sure and he'd have to call the maternity ward and ask.'

'I don't want him here,' I cried, crouching on the floor and burying my head into the stiff sheets of the bed. I did want him here; I wanted him here desperately. I felt as though my knight in shining armour had charged back into town, just in time to save me from this despairing pain and isolation. I wanted more than anything for him to burst through those doors and take me in his arms and cradle me. He'd brush away the matted sweaty hair from my eyes and look at me, saying that he'd look after me now. I wouldn't have to be alone any longer. The girl in India meant nothing and only served to help him realise his feelings for me. But that wouldn't be how the scenario would really play out. In reality he would be shocked and hurt, possibly even furious with me. He wouldn't feel the strong bond of parenthood yet, with so little time to get used to the idea. He hadn't felt it grow inside him, seen its hands and feet as it had shuffled about, he hadn't felt it hiccup, or kick when I played it Fat Boy Slim. To him it would just be a huge shocking mistake, a grim realisation that life isn't just exploration and mindless fun; we would be an inconvenience.

I cried out in pain, but this time there was no contraction, the pain was even worse than that, far more lasting.

CHAPTER TWENTY-SEVEN

When I was about five months pregnant my mother had reassured me that labour was a beautiful experience, the actual pain being similar to period pain. When I was being driven to the hospital I had recalled this comment and I had been happy to agree with her. Now that I had endured the whole experience from start to finish, I can safely say that labour is as far removed from period pain as athlete's foot is from having your leg slowly removed with a blunt section of cheese wire.

I lay curled, foetal-like and sore on the bed in the middle of the night. Babies were crying intermittently and I listened to the sound of their mothers lulling them back to sleep, or cooing gently, encouraging them to latch on to a milky breast.

I was fascinated by the different cries the babies had. Before having my own I had thought all babies sounded the same. Now I realised that they are as different as fingerprints or snowflakes. I gazed watery-eyed at the crib where my baby lay sleeping. I had only heard it cry once, when it was being checked over after the birth. Since then it had been contented and sleepy, but I knew that if it should wake up and cry in the night, I would recognise the soft 'la' sound blindfolded. To me none of the other babies in the ward sounded nearly as lovely, they had high-pitched squawks like little birds. But mine sparked off an emotion in me I had never come across before. It was a mixture of unconditional love, pride and relief that it was okay and the pain had finally come to an end. But above all, I was consumed with a protective urge that I was sure could empower me with the strength of a superhero if it was ever required. I only had to see another woman looking curiously over in the direction of the cot and I had to restrain myself from pinning her to the floor and yelling 'leave us alone, bitch!' Although realistically I was so tender, I doubt I would have been able to uncurl myself from the ball I was lying in, even for a trip to the toilet.

I had finally given birth at ten o'clock that night. Most of the details were a horrible blur. I hadn't wanted to recall specifics. My memory was reduced to snapshot images I had seen when I occasionally opened my eyes. Mostly they remained firmly shut.

I remember yelling at the midwife, 'what do you mean too late?' when she had informed me I was too far ahead in the labour to be given any drugs. I was limited to the gas and air, which at that stage was having about as much effect as paracetomol might have if your head had exploded.

I remember burying my head into Maggie's arm and crying pathetically, begging her to 'make it all go away,' when they told me the baby was stuck in an awkward posterior position, and I would need an episiotomy and a ventouse. I had felt as though the pain was causing me to slip in and out of consciousness; nothing seemed real any longer.

I remember peering through slits in my eyes at the man who was called in to perform the task of cutting me open and extracting my child. I had gawped in shock as he had walked in, dressed head to foot in clear plastic. He wore a shower cap, an apron that stretched down to his ankles, and most shocking of all, clear, rubber wellington boots. It was an image straight out of a horror film on alien abduction and experimentation, or *Vets in Practice*. Either way, I couldn't imagine he'd have cause to be wading in anything and found the whole thing horribly surreal.

I remember my legs swinging from the stirrups Maggie had been laughing at earlier. They were shaking from sheer exhaustion, making the metal fittings rattle so loud the doctor instructed a midwife to hold my feet still.

But my most consuming memory, the one that I think will stay with me always, was the feeling of my baby being taken straight from me and placed gently on to my belly. I remember the warmth and the sheer weight as our skin touched. I had sobbed with relief, and I remember the midwife asking gently, 'Holly, can you tell what it is?' The gas I had just inhaled for the delivery of the afterbirth must have taken effect and mixed with the delirium I had lapsed into, for at that moment I burst out laughing. I laughed as though I hadn't heard a joke my whole life. I pictured Rolf Harris bending over the bed, asking me if I could 'tell what it is yet?' and I nodded, smiling sleepily at the bundle lying on my flabby belly, pink and shiny.

'It's a girl,' I said aloud, staring down at his genitals in wonderment.

'Holly, it's a boy,' Maggie had butted in then, shaking my shoulder to make sure I was still conscious and taking it in.

'Yes, a boy,' I corrected, realising that I had been wrong all along, but not caring, and not feeling the slightest disappointment.

I had hugged everyone then, the midwives, the doctor, the paediatrician, and most of all Maggie, whose face was red and puffy. She had been crying, and I was touched to think that someone so uninterested in children could be moved to tears by the whole experience.

After we had been left alone with the baby and I had been cleaned up she said, 'You were amazing, Holly. The whole thing was probably the scariest, most amazing thing I've ever seen. I can't thank you enough for letting me share that with you.' We hugged again for the longest time.

She hadn't wanted to leave me, but the midwife had wanted to move me to a regular ward for the rest of the night and Maggie wouldn't have been allowed to stay there. She had promised to call everyone and be waiting at the door for the ward to open in the morning so she could tell me what they'd all said.

I couldn't believe I was now expected to get some rest. The memories of labour, thoughts of Tom, the wonder of the baby lying next to me kept my mind churning and churning. Sleep was impossible.

I was relieved to see the ward was a hive of activity very early in the morning, almost as soon as the sun rose. Mothers hobbled up and down the corridor in front of me, fetching nappies, glasses of water, making phone calls. I hadn't moved all night and when I tried, I found myself stiff and sore. My stitches were tugging tightly and I dreaded using the toilet. I sat up in the hard bed and felt blood flow out of me. I looked down, realising with embarrassment that the sheets were stained crimson.

I called a nurse to explain, and she drew the curtains and sat on the bed, giving me such gentle motherly attention that I wanted to hug her with gratitude. She gave me a bed bath, and the warm soppy water soothed the stinging that had been nagging at me throughout the night. When I opened my bag to retrieve some clean underwear, she spied my white cottons and tampons and gave me a sorry smile. 'Poor love. You obviously didn't know what you were letting yourself in for, did you?' she cooed, reaching into her trolley and passing me some panty liners as thick as sleeping bags. I took them gratefully, realising how nice it would be for me to sit on as much padding as possible. I was ashamed at my naivety. Using tampons would have been like lobbing a matchstick into the Channel Tunnel and expecting it to stop traffic.

An hour or so later I called my mum from the pay phone at the far end of the ward, never taking my eyes off the crib that was still parked, just in view, next to my bed.

'Why didn't you tell me how awful labour really is?' I asked her accusingly.

'Darling, if I'd told you the truth, you would never have ended up giving me a beautiful grandchild, would you? Let's just say a few white lies were a worthwhile investment.'

We laughed then and I forgave her immediately; the pain, however excruciating, had after all been worth it.

We had an emotional, excited conversation and I had to describe my baby to her in every little detail. His black shock of hair, his full rosebud lips, the blister on his finger where he had been sucking in the womb.

She promised to come down as soon as she could, and after a short stilted conversation with my dad I rang off and limped over to get some breakfast. I had entertained the idea of calling Marcus and Fiona, but without knowing how Tom was feeling I was scared to call in case he answered. I also would have found it difficult to remain standing much longer. The amount of blood I had lost left me feeling light-headed and faint. I returned to my bed to eat my breakfast and stare some more at my son.

At nine o'clock we were allowed to receive visitors. I managed to have a wash, brush my knotted hair back into a neat ponytail, apply mascara and dress in my nicest baggy check pyjamas. No one would have been able to tell I had a humungous sanitary towel wedged between my legs. I needed a bath, but that would have to wait until I returned home. I had fed my baby earlier that morning, with much juggling around and instruction from the midwife, and after a nappy change (the first I had ever managed in my life) he had fallen straight back into a deep slumber. His eyelids occasionally flickered and his fists punched in small quick jabs. I sat back, enjoying a triumphant sense of accomplishment in mastering so many new skills so quickly. The midwife had warned me not to get too complacent as babies seemed programmed to sleep almost exclusively for the first forty-eight hours after birth. 'Nature's way of giving the mother a chance to rest', she explained. But to me it didn't matter what she said. I was sure I had the most mild-mannered, beautiful baby that had ever been created. I leaned across and stroked his face. It was just the two of us now, and I had a feeling we would be just fine.

I stared through the curtains at the clock that hung over the double doors where the visitors would arrive, until my eyes started to water. I was desperate to see Maggie and find out what Tom had said. When the hands clicked over to nine o'clock my heart skipped in anticipation. At exactly one minute past nine a man delivering an enormous bouquet of irises walked grandly through the doors. Please let them be for me, I thought selfishly. I had always loved irises. I looked around the room; none of the other women paid the man any attention. I fought a smug grin as he had a word with the midwife and she pointed me out. I pretended to busy myself, folding some Babygros so as not to appear too expectant. When I sensed his presence at the foot of the bed, I looked up, pretending to be startled. He lowered the bouquet away from his face and I realised then, that this wasn't a delivery man. It was Tom.

He must have lost at least a stone since I had last seen him at Halloween. His cheekbones and jaw line were more prominent now, but rather than looking gaunt, he looked chiselled. His body seemed thinner, but his muscles were still well defined in the creased Kangol T-shirt he was wearing. His hair was shorter and bleached by the sun. His skin was deeply tanned, making his green eyes stand out with startling clarity. I was flooded with memories of our last night together, of how tender and loving he had been with me. How close we had become. It felt as though my oldest friend had just got back from a few days away. I couldn't believe how long it had really been. I wanted so badly to hold him again, for him to kiss me like he had done at Halloween. To joke and tease him like I had been accustomed to doing for years now. He looked fantastic, but his clothes were dishevelled and his eyes gave away a tiredness and tension I had a feeling I was the cause of. Too much had happened.

He passed the flowers over to me wordlessly. 'They're beautiful,' I said, smelling them with my eyes closed, not daring to look at him.

'They're from mum and dad,' he said flatly, and his words hit me as though I had just been punched. I hung my head, not daring to speak in case I cried.

'I would have brought you something, but I didn't know what . . . I just wanted to come straight here.' Tom walked over to the crib where our baby was lying, blissfully unaware of us. He watched him for a long time without saying a word. 'Why didn't you tell me earlier?' he whispered, his voice wavering.

My throat hurt so much I could barely swallow. 'I'm sorry,' I said, barely audibly. 'Tom, I didn't know what to do, or how you'd react. I was scared.' I blinked and tears splashed on to the flowers I was still holding.

He sat down on the edge of the bed and looked at me. 'This is all a bit of a shock for me, y'know.'

I finally looked him in the eye and nodded. 'I know. Are you angry?'

He sighed hard and thought for a moment. 'I was, but I've done some thinking, and I understand. I just don't know what to think. It's going to take a lot of getting used to.'

'Yes.'

A nurse walked into my cubicle, holding a clipboard. She looked between Tom and me then held up her hand, pointing to her watch. 'I'll come back in quarter of an hour,' she whispered, then went out again, shutting the curtains behind her.

Tom was still looking at me. 'How are you?' he asked.

'Sore,' I replied, smiling with embarrassment.

386

'Was it awful?'

I thought about that for a while, fiddling nervously with the hospital bracelet on my wrist. 'It could have been worse I guess, but then it could have been a lot better,' I said, looking sadly at him.

Tom looked away and watched the baby again. 'Is he okay?'

'Really well, yes. Perfect in fact,' I said, smiling proudly at the baby, who twitched and smacked his lips as he slept.

'Have you thought of a name for him yet?'

I shook my head and whispered, 'I wanted to ask you first.' After a brief silence I added, 'Tom . . . Can you ever forgive me?'

'I should have called you more often,' he said, ignoring my question. He turned back to me and placed his hand briefly on my arm. 'Look, I'll be back soon, okay? I'll come back tonight.' Then he got up and left.

I sat staring open-mouthed at the gap in the curtains, watching as he hurried down the corridor. I couldn't believe he had just taken off like that. There was so much we hadn't said.

A small middle-aged lady in an apron poked her head through the curtains and said chirpily, 'I expect you fancy a brew, don't you, love?'

CHAPTER TWENTY-EIGHT

Visitors came and went throughout the day. Maggie first, then Mum and Dad, and that afternoon Alice and Simon arrived, holding a giant cuddly moose with a bow around its neck.

'We couldn't resist,' Alice said, sitting it on the armchair and then went straight to the cot for a better look. 'Wow, he's a beauty,' she cried. 'Nothing at all like his photo.'

I looked at her quizzically.

'You know, the scan picture.'

'Less skeletal, you mean,' I said sarcastically and shared an amused look with Simon.

'Please can I hold him, please, please?' Alice begged, looking at me with such a doey expression I couldn't say no, and was proud to show him off.

Whilst Alice held him I explained what had happened with Tom that morning. 'How did he seem to you?' I asked when I had finished.

'He was pretty blown away,' Simon said. 'He didn't seem angry with you, though.'

'No,' Alice agreed. 'More . . . shocked.'

'And concerned,' Simon added. 'I think he just needs time to think.'

'But what did he say this morning?' I asked him.

Alice and Simon shared a worried look that made me nervous. 'What?' I cried, looking from one to the other.

'Oh, it's nothing,' Alice said.

Simon waved his hand at me. 'Yeah, don't worry about it.' Then he turned his attention to the baby, saying, 'Say hello to your Uncle Simon!'

Alice frowned at him, then looked at me, sighing, and sat down on the bed. 'It's just that he didn't stay at his place last night, or Marcus and Fiona's. He took off after dinner and this morning his bed wasn't slept in. You're the only one who's seen him. We didn't tell Marcus because we didn't want to worry him,' she added.

I felt a sinking feeling in the pit of my stomach. 'So what are you saying? Where was he?'

Eventually Simon said, 'We don't know, we thought you might.'

After Alice and Simon left the paediatrician came to see us. She said we could go home after dinner if I really wanted to. I packed up my bag and managed to get dressed, then sat on the bed, unsure what to do. I had told Mum I'd give her a ring as soon as I was ready to go home and she'd pick me up, but I wanted to wait in case Tom turned up again.

I hardly touched the meal and just sipped a cup of iced water that a nurse had brought me earlier. I fed my baby, changed his nappy then began to dress him in his outdoor clothes. I was struggling to put his hat on when a voice said, 'Going somewhere?'

Tom was standing at the foot of my bed. He was still wearing the same clothes he had been in earlier, except he now wore a thick navy fleece that made his hair seem even lighter. I looked up, longing to snuggle into his chest and hide from everything that had happened between us. He seemed nervous, and I noticed his hands were jammed into the pockets of his jeans. He was momentarily distracted by the sight of the little boy lying on the bed between us, clad in the sweetest white all-in-one and topped with a pointy white hat with a star on the top that made him look like a tiny wizard.

Tom laughed at him squinting out from under the hat, and as though he'd read my mind, said, 'He looks like a baby Harry Potter,' and smiled at me. 'Holly,' he started, and a chill of anticipation ran through me. 'I . . . er . . . I spoke to the receptionist and she said you could be discharged as soon as you liked now.'

I nodded. 'I said I'd call Mum and get her to pick me up when I was ready. I think she was expecting me to have to stay in here until at least tomorrow morning, though. To be honest, I'm just desperate to go home and have a bath.'

He rocked back and forth on the heels of his walking boots and looked at me, unsure, then said, 'My, er . . . my car is outside. Can I take you home?'

'Sure, I'd like that,' I said, aware of how polite

we were being with each other. It felt awkward, unnatural.

I strapped our baby into the car seat, covering him with a blanket and Tom picked up the bags that were sitting ready on the bed.

'Christ, what have you got in here?' he groaned, stooping from the sheer weight of them.

'It's all for the baby,' I said with wide-eyed innocence, praying he wouldn't look inside and see how many different outfits I had taken that were still neatly folded and unworn.

Walking out to the car, we hardly said a word. Tom kept having to stop and wait so I could catch him up. It took all my effort to try and walk normally, and not like John Wayne after a riding accident. At the same time I was trying to hold my stomach in, which was about as pointless as trying to stop the tide from coming in.

When we were in the car I asked Tom how his dad was, hoping to ease the tension by sticking to a 'safe' subject.

'He's not bad, actually,' Tom said, steering the car out of the hospital car park. 'I thought he'd look a lot worse. But he seems to have recovered pretty well so far. It scared him though, I think he wants me to start taking on more responsibility with the business. He seems to have gone completely off the thought of work.'

'And are you ready for that?' I wondered aloud, hoping he had got the travel bug out of his system for now.

Tom nodded and looked briefly at me. 'Yeah, it

391

should be good actually. I reckon it's about time I started thinking about the future too.' He looked back to the road and my stomach flipped. 'Dad's been singing your praises,' he carried on. 'Says you've been a big help, and told me how you managed to find me in India.'

I blushed and looked out of the window, saying softly, 'I should have done something sooner.'

Tom went quiet after that and no more was said until we had parked and unloaded the car. Tom produced a set of keys, ready to let us in.

'Hang on,' I said, confused. 'Where did you get those from?'

He started walking towards the café, carrying the baby in one hand, my bags in the other and the keys between his teeth. 'From Maggie,' he muttered.

I followed him curiously. He opened the side door that led up a flight of stairs to my flat.

'Stay there,' he said, putting the baby's car seat down by the bottom step and positioning me next to it. He bounded up the stairs with the bags, letting himself into the kitchen, then he returned, picked up the car seat and took that up to the kitchen as well. When he came back again he took my elbow as though I was something very delicate and led me slowly up the stairs.

When I entered the kitchen the first things I noticed were the helium balloons that bobbed brightly in the room. They were blue, with 'CONGRATULATIONS' written on them in silver. Pale blue ribbons dangled beneath them. The flat was immaculate. The washing-up had been done and

392

the magazines and paperwork that had littered the living-room floor had vanished. There was a huge vase of flowers sitting proudly on my coffee table. I hesitated by the door, looking at the vision before me. For a brief moment I thought I was in the wrong flat. It had been years since I had seen so much of my floor at any one time.

Tom guided me further into the room, kicking the door shut behind him and dropping my keys on the gleaming kitchen counter. Walking through the kitchen and into the living room I spotted a pile of presents on the floor, wrapped in various shades of pastel paper.

'Some of these are from Mum and Dad,' he explained. 'Some are from Maggie and Noah, Simon and Alice. You even got one from Andy, you remember my cousin?' He looked at me slyly. 'You seem to have made quite an impression on him! And these are from me,' he finished, pointing out a separate little pile. 'I went out this morning after I saw you. I didn't feel right not getting you both something.'

'But . . . who did all this?' I asked, looking around the room.

'I saw Maggie when I got back from shopping. She said she'd just been to see you and that you looked really tired. We wanted to do something to help. Do you mind?' He looked at me with his deep green eyes and I melted.

'Of course I don't mind. This is amazing. Thank you.' I wanted so badly to kiss him, but there was still this painful distance between us.

I looked at our baby, who was still fast asleep.

'When do you think he'll wake up?' Tom asked.

I laughed, 'How long's a piece of string? He might go for another hour or so if I'm lucky though.' I checked my watch. 'I only fed him an hour ago.'

'Listen, I've got a suggestion. Say no if it bothers you . . . me being here, that is. But I was thinking you could have a bath and relax a bit. I'll hold the fort here, and if he wakes up I'll call you. Then if you're hungry I could order in some food and we could talk. If you feel up to it. Or I could see you tomorrow, maybe, if you don't . . .' he paused, running a hand nervously through his hair and gave up. He looked so uncomfortable I didn't know whether to laugh or cry.

'I'd love that,' I said.

Lying in the bath, I was so conscious of Tom being in the house and the fact that the baby could wake up at any moment that I only stayed in the water for ten minutes. The hot steamy water left me feeling giddy and tired, so I climbed out, wrapped a dressing gown around me and padded into the bedroom. I squeezed the water out of my hair with a towel and put on another pair of black knickers and a maternity pad. I sat down on the bed, feeling deeply unattractive. For Tom to come from exotic women to me must be such an anti-climax for him. I lay my head on the pillow, not wanting him to see me looking like this.

A knock on the door woke me up and I sat up with a start, straightening my dressing gown. My hair was still wet and I realised I'd dozed off. 'Yes?' I called out shakily.

Tom opened the door and peered around it. He saw me yawning on the bed and walked in, placing the car seat so it sat facing us by the door.

'Still not woken up then,' I said looking at the baby, relieved to see him still sleeping.

'No, your mum called, though. I said you'd call her back later on.' He walked over to the bed and sat down, picking up the hairdryer that I'd left on the floor. He turned it on to the slower setting and started to dry my hair. I stiffened, embarrassed at first, then soon relaxed as the warm air hit me and closed my eyes. Tom gently ran his fingers through my hair and I breathed in the clean, soapy smell of his hands. I peeked a look at him. He was concentrating on what he was doing, his expression serious. It felt strangely intimate.

'Tom, did you come home on your own?' I blurted.

He looked at me, taken aback, 'Of course I did, what do you mean?'

I sighed and looked away from him, ashamed at having to admit that I'd read his mail. 'I read your postcard. I know about the woman you met in India.'

His face registered recognition and he turned off the hairdryer, setting it back down on the floor. 'You mean Devi,' he said, reaching into his back pocket of his jeans and pulling out his wallet. He flicked it open and retrieved what looked like a Polaroid photograph.

Oh God, please don't show me what she looks like. It was bad enough when she was a figment of my imagination.

He passed the picture over to me and I took it, feeling sick to my stomach. I tried to make a face that said I was okay with this, that I could handle his relationship with someone else. My heart was breaking so badly I felt sure he could hear it shatter. I took the photo and looked at the woman in it. She was sitting on a beach, looking out to sea. It was hard to guess her age but she could have been in her early forties. Her face looked calm and she appeared to be deep in thought. In her arms was a girl who was grinning at Tom, her eyes adoring. They were both certainly beautiful, their hair falling in long messy waves against dark skin. Both were barefoot and dressed in dirty rags.

'They lived on the streets near where I was staying,' he explained. 'Meena, the little girl, used to beg there. Everywhere I went she'd follow me and hold my hand. She'd turn cartwheels in the middle of the street and try to teach me games. She told me that her parents died she was a baby. Devi is her grandmother. They both beg for money to survive. I couldn't believe how happy they were, always smiling and laughing. It made me think about a lot of things.'

I passed the photo back, feeling not just ashamed, more completely sordid at having jumped to the wrong conclusion.

Tom looked at the picture, smiling fondly, then tucked it back into his wallet.

396

'She looks lovely,' I said, my cheeks burning. But one thing still bothered me. 'But Tom, where did you go last night? Simon said your bed hadn't been slept in.'

He smiled shyly at me. 'I went to the barn. Remember the one I told you about ages ago? The one I found when Grandad died. I guess I had a lot of thinking to do and I just needed to be by myself. Holly, you've got to realise I never thought about anybody else the whole time I was away,' he said seriously, holding my gaze. 'I missed you so much I nearly called the whole thing off and came home anyway. I wanted to talk to you about it but it was hard with you being so far away. And now I know what happened,' he said looking over at our baby, 'I wish I'd never gone.'

I began to cry and he held me, wrapping me in his arms and kissing the top of my head. 'We'll get through this, Holly. If you want me around then I'm here for you. I'm not going anywhere.'

I answered him by tilting my head and kissing his lips, my heart pounding with happiness.

Tom had nearly finished drying my hair when our baby started to wake up and cry. Tom bent over the seat and plucked him out. 'Come on then, little Harry,' he said, pushing his hat back away from his eyes and holding him at arm's length, unsure how to hold him. The baby stopped crying for a moment and yawned and Tom laughed at his comical expression. 'He is magic, isn't he?' he said, passing him to me and watching him fondly.

I took the wriggling baby, putting my little finger

in his mouth to pacify him for a moment and looked at Tom, grinning. 'We could call him Harry, couldn't we? It does seem to suit him.' We shared a look, then Tom got up off the bed.

'Why don't you feed Harry and I'll order us a pizza, then you can come and open all your presents.'

I happily agreed and got up to make myself more comfortable on the bed, wincing as I slowly lowered myself back down.

'Are you all right?' Tom asked, and I nodded. He took some more cushions off the armchair by the bed and put them behind my back, positioning them until he was satisfied that I was comfortable. He kissed my forehead and said with mock regret, 'It's going to be ages before I get you in a climbing harness again, isn't it?'

I pretended to try and flick him with my towel and we laughed together. He ruffled my hair affectionately, just like he used to, then he walked out of the room, glancing back briefly to look at us both. The tension between us had left and I smiled at Harry, feeling excited about the future for the first time in a long while.

CHAPTER TWENTY NINE

Every year since I can remember, someone would always ask me on my birthday, 'Do you feel any older?' And to be honest the answer was always no. Of course I had many drunken conversations with friends about just how much things had changed for us; how kids seem much older than we did at their age, how music was at its peak during the New Romantic years and how we wished we had appreciated our pubescent figures rather than taking for granted that we would always be able to wear hot pants and look sexy. I also occasionally forget my age and actually have to work it out mathematically using my date of birth. But these unavoidable signs of ageing are a gradual metamorphosis. It never seemed to strike me more on the actual day of my birthday, not until today.

Today is my 28th birthday. My first birthday as a mother. It seems a huge turning point in my life that from now on these occasions would always be different. In the past we had celebrated with drunken get togethers and mad nights out. Not that I wouldn't have those again, I'm sure I will, maybe even tonight, and I'd probably appreciate these nights out more than ever before. But something subtle has changed in me. I don't think it is noticeable, and it hasn't changed the way I behave with my friends. It is more a shift in my perception of everything around me. My life has more richness and depth to it. I have something to focus on that for once in my life isn't just about me and my personal well-being. I am still going to go out with all my friends tonight, but that edge of recklessness and selfishness has gone. It has been put to rest, and in its place is a stronger more self-assured me. I have found what I was missing in my life, have tried it on and found it suits me down to the ground. And despite feeling more knackered, more in need of a holiday than ever before, and suffering occasional bouts of paranoia that my baby might not be normal and still breathing in and out, I am happier than I have ever been.

I tucked the soft fleecy blanket around Harry's plump little body. He was lying in the pram by the window of the nursery, his chest rising and falling at regular intervals, having just nodded off to sleep. I checked my watch; Mum would arrive soon to baby-sit for us. Tom, Alice, Simon, Maggie, Noah, Tamsin and Charlie were waiting in the living room for me to get ready and I could hear the sound of them laughing and joking, in high spirits.

Alice sneaked into the room and peeped over my shoulder to look at Harry.

'Ooh, I want one,' she whispered glassy-eyed, and passed me a large gin and tonic.

We tiptoed out of the room and into the bedroom where I could finish off applying my make-up. I checked my reflection in the full-length mirror. I had recently had my hair cut into a shoulder length layered style and I fingered the ends of it, feeling sophisticated in my scoop neck, tight black dress. It was the first time I had worn anything so clingy since before I was pregnant and I enjoyed feeling sexy again. My tummy had nearly vanished, leaving behind only the stretch marks and bump that reminded me of a hot water bottle with just a small amount of water in it. But overall I was glad to be back in my old jeans and saucy little knickers once more.

'You're a knock-out,' Alice said, admiring my reflection.

'You can talk,' I countered, checking out her gorgeous new camisole and linen trousers. 'Love suits you,' I teased.

Alice sat herself down on the bed. 'Holly, can I tell you something? Something BIG. I'll burst if I hold it in any longer.'

I span around, ears pricked with interest; I could tell by the tone in her voice that this was serious girl news. I sat with her, urging her to continue.

'Well,' she started, glancing bashfully at her hands, then she held them up for me to inspect, grinning broadly. I didn't understand for a moment, then the light twinkled on her jewellery and I caught sight of a stunning diamond solitaire, set in white gold. An engagement ring. I drew a deep breath and nearly squealed with excitement, but Alice clamped her hand to my mouth and gestured for me to keep quiet.

'We're going to announce it tonight in the restaurant, but it didn't feel right not telling you first.'

I turned her hand through all angles admiring the ring, and brimming with excitement. 'I'm so happy for you, Al. You really deserve this. And Simon is perfect for you.' I wanted to barrage her with questions: When? How? Where? I wanted to know every soppy detail, but we didn't have much time and I knew I'd have to wait until we were properly alone. We chinked our glasses together and hugged.

'Isn't it amazing,' Alice said wistfully. 'You're a mum, I'm getting married, Maggie's in her longest relationship ever. Things were so different this time last year; you weren't even pregnant. Now you and Tom are practically a married couple yourselves.'

Alice was right; things had changed dramatically in such a short time. Tom had moved into the flat last month. It had seemed an inevitable progression in our relationship as he had been spending so much time over here anyway. I wasn't sure if we would ever get married, but the thought wasn't an unpleasant or scary one. For now, though, we were both happy as we were, still finding out about each other, enjoying the thrill of discovery and growing closer all the time. I was in no doubt that I loved Tom; I had only to watch him playing with Harry and my heart swelled with pride. He told me often how he felt about me, and we were comfortable to let it take its natural course.

We often talked about the past. Tom swore he

had begun falling in love with me a long time ago and was curious as to where along the line things changed for us. He often quizzed me about how I felt about him leaving, if I had been upset, or if I had been tempted to ask him to stay. He swore blind that if I had asked him, he would have cancelled his flight there and then. I never confessed following him to the airport. Instead I teased him mercilessly, enjoying the attention and pretending I had been blasé about the whole thing. This topic of conversation would usually deteriorate into a mammoth tickling session, which resulted in me pleading a weak, post-labour bladder and threatening to wee on his lap.

I finished off my drink, enjoying the heady sensation it left me with. I was anticipating an exciting night ahead and looked forward to Alice and Simon's announcement so I could discuss it at length. We were going to have a brilliant night. 'Come on, Al, we'd better go and see what they're up to,' I said, getting up off the bed and grabbing my handbag.

In the living room, everyone was huddled together finishing off the last of a bottle of wine. The television was on quietly in the background and the *EastEnders* credits were rolling. Noah executed the perfect impression of Frank Butcher, making Maggie howl with laughter, and Charlie joined in then, attempting a Bianca, which sounded more like Bruce Forsyth.

'At last,' Tom said, watching me walk in. His eyes scanned my body and I saw a saucy smile flicker on his lips, I knew what he had in mind for later and I gave him a coquettish look as I carried on into the kitchen to fetch another bottle of Chardonnay from the fridge.

I wandered around the kitchen, checking the bottles of milk were all ready in the fridge for Mum, although I doubted Harry would wake up. I poured myself some wine from the half-empty bottle, listening to the sounds of my friends enjoying themselves in the other room. Something was happening. Maggie and Alice were squealing loudly and the lads sounded so excited I thought for a moment they must be watching football. Tom yelled for me to come quickly and so I grabbed the wine and poked my head around the wall curiously.

'Turn it up, quick!' Maggie yelled and Tom dived across the floor to fetch the remote control and sent the volume climbing.

'What's going on?' I asked perching on the sofa.

'Shhh!' Simon hushed urgently as the others laughed, looking transfixed at the television.

'You're on the telly,' Tom whispered, not taking his eyes off the screen, but yanking me down next to him. I concentrated on what they were watching, trying to understand. It appeared to be one of those docusoaps, talking to real people about their everyday lives. I recognised the commentator's voice. I thought it was the guy from *Bergerac*. Jim or John Nettles.

The scene was a busy airport; a security guard was talking to the camera. 'Oh yeah, you see everything 'ere, life's never dull in this game,' he was

404

boasting. The camera then panned back to show a frantic scene unfolding as crowds of people were being evacuated from a building. The commentator continued in his smooth, dry voice, 'Ken had to get the crowds of people out of the building fast, and an evacuation began to take place.' Ken was shown efficiently ushering people towards the main exit, saying, 'Quick as you can please, try not to panic.'

The scene was sickeningly familiar. I knew exactly what was happening.

'There you are,' shouted Charlie pointing to the screen, but everyone had seen me. It was immediately apparent where I was, as it appeared that I was at the centre of the mayhem. The camera focused on a couple of security guards marching me off; I looked badly dishevelled and struggled to break away yelling, 'Tom!'

Alice and Maggie clamped their hands to their faces and cried out in disbelief. The commentator explained how their camera crew had subsequently been evacuated as well whilst the confusion was sorted out. There was an interview with the Russian man whose bag's contents had been mistaken for a bomb, and the old lady who had started the panic off, explaining how suspicious she thought I looked, all red in the face and panicked. How she was sure I had shouted 'bomb', and it was an easy mistake to make. The commentator amusingly explained how the panic had amounted to no more than a lovesick young woman trying to reach her boyfriend before he flew off to America. They showed more footage of Ken showing everyone back in and explaining to the camera how, with Heathrow being such a high security risk for terrorists, they have to take these situations very seriously. He went on, in what I found to be a rather patronising tone, about how their job would be a lot easier if people didn't leave unidentified packages lying around, and were aware that running about and yelling could quickly give rise to a panic situation. The programme switched scenes then and showed Jeremy Spake arguing with a foreign businessman who had turned up drunk for a flight.

My face was hidden in my hands and I could feel the heat of my cheeks making my palms sweaty.

When it was over everyone applauded and I felt myself being patted several times on the back. They were all laughing, amazed at my dramatic fifteen minutes of fame (it was probably only two, but had felt like a lifetime).

'Ahh, Holly, don't look so embarrassed,' Alice encouraged. 'We're your friends.'

'I can't believe you never told us about that. You're such a dark horse,' Maggie was saying in disbelief.

I just wanted to disappear, to be reduced to a speck and bury myself in the carpet.

'Oh poor you, you've gone so red,' Simon said sympathetically, but his concern only made my cheeks grow hotter.

I peeped through the cracks in my fingers and stole a glance at Tom. He was looking at me intently, his smile gentle. 'I can't believe you came to the airport,' he whispered to me, as if there was no one else in the room; then he wrapped his arms around my shoulders enabling me to hide my face in the folds of his jumper. He stroked the back of my hair affectionately. 'You're so sweet,' he said, kissing the back of my neck and chuckling to himself.

We were pelted with cushions then, as the others tired of our private moment.

I raised my eyes and gazed at Tom as our friends laughed, continuing to bash us with pillows, trying to provoke us into fighting back, but we ignored them, caught up in our own secret world. 'Love you,' he mouthed and I beamed back at him, squeezing his hand tight, then we looked at each other knowingly, grabbed the cushions we had been sitting on and bombarded our friends with heavy blows, laughing as they tried to fend us off.